THE
STAGE
KISS

THE
STAGE
KISS

A Novel

AMELIA JONES

alcove
press

Published in the United States by Alcove Press, an imprint of The Quick Brown Fox & Company LLC.

Alcove Press and its logo are trademarks of The Quick Brown Fox & Company LLC.

Library of Congress Catalog-in-Publication data available upon request.

ISBN (paperback): 978-1-63910-584-7
ISBN (ebook): 978-1-63910-585-4

Cover illustration by Ana Hard

Printed in the United States.

www.alcovepress.com

Alcove Press
34 West 27th St., 10th Floor
New York, NY 10001

First Edition: December 2023

10 9 8 7 6 5 4 3 2 1

For Rompire.
You must allow me to (remind) you how ardently
I admire and love you.

The Kennedy Center

Eisenhower Theater | July 17–August 6

The John F. Kennedy Center for the Performing Arts

Broadway Center Stage
presents

Based on Jane Austen's *Pride and Prejudice*

BOOK BY
JULIA MILLER

MUSIC AND LYRICS BY
**JULIA MILLER, ANNA E. COLLINS,
& EM SHOTWELL**

Elizabeth Bennet..VERONICA WEST
Fitzwilliam Darcy..BRENNON THORNE
Jane Bennet..GABRIELLE NATHAN
Mrs. Bennet..IRIS KLEIN
Mr. Bennet..DAVID CLARKE
Charles Bingley..JONATHAN MARCH
Mr. Collins..ADAM EISNER
George Wickham..LAWRENCE BAXTER
Lydia Bennet..LILIANA SANCHEZ
Miss Bingley..JESSA BROWN
Lady Catherine de Bourgh..CARLA BRODERICK
Mr. Gardiner..MATTHEW GLYNN
Mrs. Gardiner..KELLY JANSEN
Charlotte Lucas..BRIDGETTE VAUGHAN
Georgiana Darcy..EMILY BAKER
Mary Bennet..KRISTI THOMAS
Caroline Bennet..ALEXANDRA TATE
Ensemble................MADDOX HOWELL, HEDY INGRAM, MARY JAMISON, BOB SLOAN, CHUCK TOBIAS

At this performance:

The role of

ELIZABETH BENNET

will be played by

EDEN BLAKE

CHAPTER ONE

If there was such a thing as Broadway royalty, Brennon Thorne was the king, and tonight his majesty would make his long-awaited first appearance. The members of the cast and crew who had never met him were abuzz with rumors, gossip, and musings of what he would be like in person. Those who had performed with him in the past all said the same thing: "He's a dream to work with."

Of course, everyone knew that when a Tony Award–winning actor had signed a contract to headline a tour for two months, he must be looking to attract a wider audience—especially if his leg of the tour included Los Angeles—but if Eden Blake got lucky, once or twice during the next eight weeks, she'd find out for herself what it was like to work with a dream.

"That's him. Tall, dark suit—over at the bar. Do you see him?"

There were too many people packed into the South Carolina bar for Eden to follow her taller friend Maddox's gaze.

"He's with Adam," Maddox added.

Eden fought the urge to roll her eyes. Knowing Thorne was with Maddox's crush Adam didn't improve her ability to see beyond the crowd. The entire cast and crew had jumped at the chance to attend this party. At the theater a few doors down, the company had just nailed their Greenville closing night performance of *Liz and Darcy: The Musical*. While the company managers hadn't splurged on an open bar or rented out a separate room, they had sprung for unlimited free appetizers at the large brewery.

Thorne's arrival was certainly cause for celebration, but tonight, they were also saying goodbye to Donovan Yates, who'd been playing Mr. Darcy on the tour since their opening in Houston five months ago. No one was super sad to see Donovan go—he was definitely *not* a dream to work with, a bit of a pill in fact—but there were no hard feelings. He was moving on to bigger and better things. The New York directors had tapped Donovan to take over the lead on Broadway now that he'd proven he could charm as Darcy on the road.

It was exactly the kind of big break Eden was looking for, too.

"Do we drink first or stay sober to introduce ourselves?" The question came from Liliana. Of the people Eden had met since rehearsals began in Manhattan, Maddox and Liliana had become her two closest friends on the tour. Early on, the three of them had agreed to pool their per diems and share accommodations on the road. Treating each new city like its own vacation, they rented an Airbnb at each tour stop. They'd had a blast and saved tons of money on hotel costs. If an actor was willing to give up Manhattan for a while, and stayed smart about living on the road, they could return to the city a lot more financially secure.

"Drink first. No question." Eden's skin tingled with nervous excitement over the prospect of meeting someone like Brennon Thorne. His rock-solid reputation was intimidating, especially compared to her own fledgling career, but she was the standby for Elizabeth Bennet, which meant there was a chance she'd get to perform with him at least once on the tour's next stop in Washington DC. She wanted to make a good first impression.

Thorne was known for his consistently show-stopping performances, and the breakout hit *Rooftop Lullaby* two years ago had earned him his first Tony: Best Performance by a Leading Actor in a Musical.

Eden had been lucky enough to see it once, but during that particular matinee, the role had been played by Thorne's standby.

These next two months, Eden would be able to see the award-winning actor onstage any time she wanted, and if Veronica West's behavior got any more unpredictable, Eden could be thrust into the lead at a moment's notice. The thought sent another thrill through her as she, Maddox, and Liliana hugged and air-kissed their way through the raucous room, complimenting the night's performances and bemoaning the loss of Donovan.

As much as their outgoing leading man could be a pain in the ass—consistently late, occasionally handsy with the ladies—he'd been on tour with them for the last five months, and change was weird. Breaking in a new cast member could take a hot minute in a medium-sized ensemble like theirs. *Liz & Darcy* had twenty-four songs and six large dance numbers. The Darcy character alone had seven costume changes. Assuming he'd arrived well-rehearsed, Thorne would nail it, but no one could predict whether he'd click with the cast, especially since he was such a big name.

The way Maddox told it, when a name dropped in, things could go either way.

Unlike Eden, this was not Mad's first tour. The stories he told . . . God, she could listen to them all night. Being a part of this world—even though she was only a standby for the lead and rarely performed—was a complete dream.

Landing against the huge bar, Liliana easily caught the attention of a nearby bartender. With thick, raven black hair and ample cleavage always on display, getting noticed had never been Liliana's problem. She played Elizabeth Bennet's troublesome younger sister Lydia in the musical, and this role was her big break, too—she'd understudied the role of Nina on the tour of *In the Heights* for a few months before this, but she'd only gotten to go on in the role once. Now, she got to perform eight shows a week while Eden waited in the shadows for her rare chances to step into the spotlight.

Eden ordered a Patrón to shoot and a beer to sip. Liliana and Maddox followed suit. He raised his glass. "To the union."

"To the revolution," Liliana and Eden chorused as they clinked their shot glasses and got their party started.

"Adam adores him," Maddox offered, regarding Thorne. Adam played the show's obsequious clergyman Mr. Collins. He and Thorne had previously worked together on *Sunday in the Park with George*. "Says he's a dream to work with."

He must be, as it seemed impossible for anyone to describe him any other way. Eden glanced down the bar, having to lean to catch a glimpse of the man of the hour. She could only see the back of his head. He had hair almost long enough to pull back, but not long enough to look like he'd stepped straight out of nineties Seattle. His height set him apart. "Six four and striking" was practically Thorne's brand.

"Didn't Adam go to Juilliard with him?" Liliana asked Maddox.

Maddox made a noncommittal sound. "How would I know? Juilliard wouldn't have me."

"Oh, stop." Liliana nudged him with her shoulder. "The admissions committee probably cries their eyes out every night with regret."

"I'm still waiting on my formal apology." Maddox raised his stout to his lips and gave Eden a faux-smoldering look over his glass. Dark-eyed and dead-sexy in his own right, Maddox only had eyes for Adam. The two had been circling each other from day one in rehearsals, but had yet to turn themselves into an item. Maddox claimed he was taking things slow on purpose, trying to send and perceive "vibes" or whatever, but as far as Eden could tell, the feelings were super mutual, and they should hook up already. The pining and puppy-dog stares were getting exhausting. "Should we make our way over?" he asked, all too eager for more noncommittal flirting.

Eden held up a finger as she took several long gulps of her beer. "Two Patróns would be too much, wouldn't it?"

"Yes," he said firmly, giving her a scowl that said *Behave*.

Oh, as if she'd do anything but. Eden set down her glass with finality and glanced Thorne's way again. This time, the famous actor was turning toward the bar. She caught a glimpse of his bearded profile, the straight line of a perfect nose—and then his dark gaze met hers with a suddenness that jolted her like a jump scare. She found herself momentarily breathless as his stare sucked all the oxygen from the room, like it was made of fire. No doubt he could command the Winter Garden stage—any stage—he could probably rule the world with a presence like that.

Just as quickly, he glanced away.

"Holy shit, he's hot," she babbled the moment she caught her breath.

"This is news?" Maddox asked.

She wished she hadn't listened to him about that second tequila shot. "I only mean pictures don't really do him justice."

Mad tipped his glass toward hers. "Heard he's single again."

"Wasn't his girlfriend supposed to take over Lizzie for the summer, too?" Liliana asked. "What happened with that?"

Eden didn't know much about the casting change-up. As the standby for Lizzie Bennet, her own contract was set. All she knew was Veronica had planned to return to New York for two months while Broadway's Chloe Rhodes stepped into the lead to play opposite Thorne, but for some reason the plan changed back in April, and Veronica had agreed to stay on. Since whatever had happened didn't affect Eden at all, she'd thought little of it.

"According to Adam," Maddox said, "Thorne planned to back out when Chloe did. Guess he changed his mind."

"I can't blame him for not wanting to spend the summer in the city," Eden said, reminded of her own sweltering apartment.

Liliana turned to glance down the bar at the actor. "Makes me wonder if he has his sights set on Veronica."

Everyone knew Thorne only dated leading ladies. Broadway was practically littered with superbly talented, broken-hearted women who'd briefly starred as the love interest in the actor's life. Chloe Rhodes had only been his latest casualty.

Still, the man was attractive, and the appeal was obvious.

Eden and Liliana bared all their teeth at each other to check for food or lipstick smears. Once they declared each other good, Eden ran a hand through her sideswept bangs and arranged the rest of her thick, shoulder-length hair before doing an outfit check. The V-neck of her red dress wasn't gaping, and it had been recently dry-cleaned. Everyone else may have seen her in it six times already over the last several months, but according to her mother, a well-fitted red dress always garnered compliments and made an impression. Eden hated to admit Terry Blake had been right again.

Liliana echoed her next thought almost exactly. "We need new clothes."

"For real," Eden agreed.

"Eden! Did you see me tonight? Wasn't I incredible?" Veronica West barreled toward them much too fast, arms open, red wine in hand, and Eden had no time to react.

Despite Maddox's attempt to slow the drunken actress's momentum, Veronica's glass tipped slightly, and a single drop of wine landed on Eden's left boob, exactly to the right of where a nipple would be. The stain darkened the area enough to create some anatomic confusion as to the shape and placement of Eden's breasts.

Eden shut her eyes and took a long-suffering breath. "Awesome. Thanks V."

"Oh, dear. My apologies." Veronica's other hand reached out to brush the drop away, but this time Eden managed to sidestep her.

She reached behind the bar, having to crawl across the bar top a bit to accomplish it, and grabbed a dry cocktail napkin. She attempted to blot the wine stain. Even though it was red on red, the spot stood out.

Eden shared an annoyed glance with Liliana. Veronica was a lot when she was sober, but drunk Veronica was especially extra. However, according to Eden's agent, Veronica was the reason Eden had gotten this job. Never one to pull punches, her agent had told her the standby casting had come down to looks—"You could be Veronica West's sister, you look so much alike." And that's the way it sometimes went on Broadway. Right look, right time.

Eden didn't think she and Veronica looked *that* much alike. Other than having brown hair, brown eyes, and similar builds, there weren't many similarities. At five six, Eden was average across the board. She sported a C-cup, could wear a size six or eight depending on the day, and in general could pass for any number of other actresses looking for their big breaks. However, Eden's face was rounder than Veronica's. Her lips, eyes, and nose were fuller, larger—like someone had drawn her with a marker, while Veronica's face had been precisely rendered with a sharpened pencil. A slash of a mouth, narrower eyes. They were both beautiful in their own ways, but they hardly looked related.

However, if the Broadway directors hadn't seen a problem, Eden wasn't about to point one out. The most important similarity was that their vocal ranges lined up. Both sopranos, their respective Lizzies complemented the Darcy baritone. Though, Eden had heard Brennon Thorne's vocal range was wider than what was required for Darcy. He was touted as a performer who could sing anything.

"Have you met Brennon yet?" Veronica persisted.

"We were just headed in that direction," Maddox told her.

"I'll introduce you. He and I went to Juilliard together."

Maddox flinched, triggered all over again. Meanwhile, Veronica had taken hold of Eden's hand and was dragging her across the crowded room. Liliana and Maddox trailed behind them.

"Brennon! Brennon!" With Veronica's years of vocal training and theater experience she was more than capable of projecting over noisy crowds. With the scene the actress was making, Eden's face would be as red as her dress by the time she met the show's new leading man.

Both Thorne's and Adam's heads turned their way as they approached. Next to them, moving steadily closer to Brennon Thorne's side, was Gabi, who played the show's lovely and reserved Jane Bennet.

Rather than the vague grin of cautious curiosity the lanky blonde usually gave Eden and her two friends, tonight Gabi's icy blue gaze had a slight edge to it. Like she was marking her territory.

If the rumors were true, Gabi's bed would be mighty cold without Donovan in it these next few months. It appeared she'd already selected his replacement.

Adam, in contrast, had a warm smile for Maddox, which Mad returned shyly as a flush crept up his neck.

Brennon Thorne's dark eyes swept straight past the others to land on Eden, and he scowled.

Like, actually scowled at her.

Intimidated all over again, Eden gave herself a quick pep talk. So what if he'd made a name for himself? So what if he had the kind of career she'd grown up both craving and envying? He was only a man. Luckier than some perhaps, better looking than most, maybe, but still—human with flaws and everything. Right? Surely he had flaws.

"Brennon." Veronica's voice maintained its diva air of authority even as she wobbled on her high heels. She bumped into Eden again, and the motion made Eden do a balance check.

She forced a smile as Veronica righted herself, aiming it first at Adam, and then turning it on high for Brennon Thorne, who did not return it.

Instead, he locked eyes with her, and his scowl deepened like a villain plotting his next move. With his long legs and broad shoulders, he cut a dramatic figure in his dark suit. His burgundy dress shirt was open at the collar, revealing the barest hint of olive skin. Six four. Striking. Both were true. She could do without the *scowling* though.

Anxiety stiffened Eden's smile at the edges, but it stayed in place.

"Brennon, this is my standby, Eden," Veronica said. "And this is Liliana, she plays Lydia, and Maddox—he's one of the swings—"

"And *my* friend," Adam said, almost possessively.

Eden could practically feel Maddox turn into a puddle at the introduction. He'd be a mess of hypotheses later, keeping Eden up half the night with an in-depth analysis of this interaction. She should be paying more attention to their dynamic, but Brennon Thorne's intense scrutiny had made her brain go all melty. Mercifully, his scowl relaxed, and he took a long sip of his beer. After sharing a quick glance with Adam, Thorne turned his attention to Veronica. "Please sit, V." Indicating the barstool next to him, he reached a hand out to help her onto it. "You're safer here."

The deep resonance of his voice sent a wave of chills up Eden's bare arms.

"Welcome. Pleasure to finally meet you." Maddox offered his hand.

Thorne shook it and glanced again at Eden. "With all the noise I didn't catch your name."

Fighting a sudden urge to lower her gaze and curtsy, Eden stuck out her hand. "Eden Blake."

"Have we met?"

As his large, cool hand surrounded hers, her heart pounded against her ribcage. "No."

His hand lingered for an extra-long moment as his gaze narrowed with scrutiny. "You're familiar. Where have I seen you?"

"She's my standby, hon," Veronica reminded him.

He spared Veronica a glance before releasing Eden's hand and asking her, "What have you been in?"

Eden hadn't been in anything of note—nothing he would have seen, certainly. Off-off Broadway productions, new plays at experimental venues. He definitely didn't frequent any of the restaurants where she waited tables and occasionally broke into song; she would have noticed him. So she pulled out her most impressive credit to date. "*A Doll's House*? At the Arden Theatre Company in Philly last year?"

The scowl was back. "I detest Ibsen."

Eden's flailing grin went gritty. She particularly enjoyed Ibsen. In a tight voice, she replied, "Maybe I just have one of those faces."

Something dawned on him, a spark of realization. "No . . ." He tucked his chin, smiling to himself. "Husband couldn't get it up. Right?"

A combination of horror and total exposure wiped Eden's face clean of expression.

It had been two years, but the commercial still played. No one had ever, *ever* recognized her. This was the worst sort of blindside.

Her mortified expression gave her away, and Thorne roared with laughter.

Adam watched him, a baffled look on his kind face. "Eden's not married." He turned to her, puzzled. "Are you?"

Before she could answer, Thorne got his laughter under control and explained to his friend. "The Citaltfor commercial. You've seen it, right? Older guy, young wife—" He gestured at Eden. "He can't get it up, she's concerned, they go to the doctor together, it's all very serious and alarming until the doctor hands over the prescription. Cut to the next scene and cue side effects, and there's the happy couple, sex life restored, dancing the tango and having the time of their lives at a Sandals in Jamaica."

And then, as if suddenly struck by the realization that he'd seen her half-naked in a black bikini, he glanced at Eden's chest, eyes zeroing in on the poorly placed wine stain.

She had to say something. Had to do something. Had to somehow rise above this expanding hole of humiliation. But she had nothing. No comeback, no smart remark, nothing except to say, "It was actually filmed in Florida."

Thorne threw his head back and laughed again. Adam backhanded him across the chest. "Brennon, Jesus." He shot an apologetic look at both Eden and Maddox. "My friend here really shouldn't drink. What are you having, Eden?"

Brennon Thorne's hearty chuckle finally died down, and he took another long swallow of his beer, staring at Eden now with an amused twinkle in his eyes.

A dream to work with, my ass. She regarded him, his elbows braced on the bar, his long legs crossed at the ankle. He looked every bit the rich, spoiled, Tony Award winner no one dared piss off.

"It was an amazing performance," he said. "I never would have guessed you were only *playing* a woman with a disappointing middle-aged husband. Let me buy you a drink—it's not every day I meet a real celebrity." He waved the bartender over.

Did he think he was funny? Charming? *Really?*

"I'll buy my own drinks, thank you." Her voice was hard enough to cut glass.

Brennon either didn't notice, or didn't care. He smirked and gave her a condescending wink. "Big Pharma pays well, does it?"

If she hadn't set her drink down to come over here, the remains of it would be splashed on Brennon Thorne's smug, superior face. He really did lead a charmed life.

Gabi was practically a puddle of giggles, and even Veronica, who had always seemed to be on Eden's side, was now chuckling at the way Thorne continued to mock her.

Eden's wit felt like it had been surgically removed. Honest work—and *erectile dysfunction*, for that matter—weren't meant to be objects of ridicule. "It was two years ago."

Somehow that only made everyone laugh more. Even Liliana's mouth turned up in an amused grin before she caught a glimpse of Eden's flushed face. Her friend's expression went blank in a split-second show of solidarity. At least Adam had her back, taking his cues from Maddox, whose dark eyes narrowed in on Thorne with displeasure.

The "legend" was undeterred. He raised his glass in a fake toast. "After that tour de force it's amazing you haven't managed to land a television series by now. That tango should have more than earned you a spot on *Dancing with the Stars*."

Maddox lifted a hand to Eden's shoulder and gave it a warning squeeze.

Veronica's smile dimmed as she glanced between Eden and Thorne. Even Gabi's giggles quieted. They were catching on. Brennon Thorne was a drunken ass.

With the tide turning in her direction, Eden rallied. "Always so wonderful to meet a fan who's made such a study of my earlier work. Do you subscribe to my newsletter?"

The corners of Thorne's eyes crinkled in what looked to be an almost genuine smile. She might have swooned had she never met him. "Is there a link in your Instagram bio?" he asked. "What's your handle?"

Fuck this guy.

She pasted on a saccharine smile. "Try searching 'limp dick.'"

He blinked, his teasing grin fading.

"Look at the time! We should get going," Maddox said. "We're on the early flight, remember?"

"Yeah, and I haven't packed a thing yet," Liliana added.

"Catch up with you later, Adam?" Maddox asked, a note of hope in his voice.

"We're on the later flight," Adam said. "But let me know where you guys are staying when you get there. Maybe we can all grab dinner."

"We'll see," he replied smoothly, still playing it cool. "Eden, shall we?" Maddox and Liliana flanked her as they walked away from the bar. She held herself straight and steady, refusing to shrink a single inch.

Brennon Thorne's blatant ridicule meant nothing. He'd only be around for two months, and if, God forbid, they ever had to appear on stage together, she hoped he'd act like a professional and treat her with some fucking respect.

It was abundantly clear now that "appearing onstage opposite Brennon Thorne" would look much better on her résumé than her miles-long list of embarrassing commercials.

"How much *does* Big Pharma pay anyway?" Liliana asked as the three of them stepped out onto the street.

Eden grimaced. "Not nearly enough."

CHAPTER TWO

Adam snatched the beer from Brennon's hand and set it on the bar top with a clatter and splash. "Wow."

Brennon quickly retrieved the bottle and took a swallow. "What?"

"That was Maddox, by the way. The one I told you about."

"I gathered that." Brennon scanned the room again. No sign of his Juilliard nemesis yet, but he was ready, if a little on edge, for a confrontation if it came to it. Every beer helped.

"Did you have to be such a dick to his friend?"

Brennan balked at the unexpected remark from his best friend. "*I* was a dick?"

"A *colossal* dick. And not in the good way."

Brennon chuckled, finishing his drink. "But have you seen that commercial? That tango—"

"Everyone's seen that commercial. You must have been paying pretty close attention, though. I've been working with her for months and never would have recognized her from that."

"It's on all the time."

"And yet . . ."

Brennon offered his ginger-haired friend a smug, one-shouldered shrug. "I'm good with faces."

"And terrible with actual people."

Terrible? Brennan had been going for relatable. They were all in the same business, were they not? It was a party, was it not? He offered up a solid defense on his own behalf. "It was funny. I wasn't the only one laughing."

Adam glared at him. "Eden wasn't."

"Fine. Point taken, but she got a jab in at the end. You're probably overreacting." To Brennon's left, Veronica also eyed him judgmentally. "You thought it was funny, didn't you?" he asked her as some doubt managed to creep in.

She gave him a slow blink and a slight shake of her head. In a flat voice, she said, "You're hilarious, Bren."

Brennon stiffened. "If you two didn't want me here, you shouldn't have begged me to come."

"Beg" may have been an overstatement, but Adam and Veronica had both heavily advocated for him not to back out of the tour once Chloe unceremoniously dumped both him and their summer plans. While Brennon was glad to be out of New York where there were reminders of his ex everywhere he turned, the musical was a different sort of reminder. Their plan to guest star as the leads this summer had been in the works since last December. Unfortunately, since then, Chloe had developed other interests—namely, her best friend Rachel.

"We're both very happy to have you," Adam said, clearly ready to smooth things over. "I'm glad Veronica finally managed to talk you into it."

"Someone needs to keep you two out of trouble," he mumbled, grateful for the subject change. From what Brennon had witnessed so far, particularly the way that swing Maddox had undressed Adam with his eyes, the potential for offstage distractions among cast members was high. Unnecessary entanglements led to unnecessary drama.

"Good luck with that," Veronica said.

She was his case in point. "One of these days you'll start listening to me," he told her.

"Maybe one day I will." She stood. "I'll catch up with you two in the morning. I want to leave while I can still walk home."

"We'll walk you." Brennon signaled for the tab.

Veronica placed a warm hand on his cheek and gave him a smile. "I'm a big girl. I can take care of myself. Enjoy your drink and try not to make everyone hate you on your first night."

Brennon blinked in surprise. "Was I that terrible?"

Veronica gave his cheek a light tap and walked away.

Adam picked up where she'd left off. "All I wanted was for you to meet Mad, and you spent the whole time making fun of a Citaltfor commercial."

"I met him." He'd sized up his friend's latest crush in an instant. The two men had practically had sex with their eyes while Brennon had been trying to place the red-lipped brunette at Maddox's side.

Adam was at the point in life where he wanted to settle down and have a family, but his career was in a place where he still had to pay his dues with tours and too much travel. The people he met on the road were unlikely to want anything more than a casual screw from time to time, but Brennon's friend was a romantic. The way Maddox had stared at Adam had been too hungry, or thirsty, or whatever it was they were calling it these days, and in no way had he appeared interested in shopping for the pedigreed French Bulldog of Adam's dreams.

"*And?*" Adam nudged.

Maddox had definitely made an impression, but at the moment all Brennon could conjure in his mind's eye was a red dress, red lips . . . "I was unimpressed."

Adam's shoulders dropped in defeat. "I get this isn't your usual crowd, but while you mingle with the peasants, try to remember not many people have had your kind of luck."

Brennon bristled at the comment he'd heard dozens of times through the years. Initially it had been easier to reject, but the truth was—luck ran out. Was Adam one of the many waiting for him to finally fail? He shook off the uncomfortable thought. "I've made good decisions. I'd hardly call my success luck."

Adam let out a short laugh, his usually affable pale green gaze tightening with cynicism. "Okay."

Emboldened by the two local IPAs he'd drunk too fast, Brennon rose to his friend's challenge. He would not be so easily led away from his point. "One decision I consistently make is to keep my pants on around other actors during a run."

"Yes, I know." Adam's expression soured.

Brennon noticed, but if he was to be any help to either of his friends these next two months, he couldn't keep quiet. "You've been working years for a chance like this."

"I get it—"

"Did you come here to have some messy showmance with some random stranger, or are you here to finally get your break?"

"He's not some random—"

Brennon cut him off. "In a year you won't even remember these people."

Adam responded with earnest disbelief. "We're like a family."

"Every show feels like that. Then closing night comes and everyone moves on. It's the nature of it. It's like graduating from high school. Are you still friends with those people?"

Adam snorted. "No, but I wasn't friends with them then, either."

"That's my point. How do you want people to remember you? As a professional? Or as *that guy*?"

"Cerise and Daniel met on *Phantom*."

Brennon set his empty glass on the bar. "They're an exception."

"Or they're proof of *my* point."

"Name me another couple who came out of a show together, and I'll name you ten actors who directors refuse to work with because they caused too much unnecessary drama." He was already ticking off unhireable actors in his head when Adam slammed him with:

"Jonathan still gets hired."

Brennon grimaced at the unpleasant reminder of Jonathan March's presence on the tour. He played Bingley in the production, which meant it would be impossible for Brennon to avoid him. Jonathan still considered Brennon his nemesis, and Brennon was all too happy to play the part. March was a waste of a Juilliard degree. "Jon hasn't ever landed a lead."

"Because he sleeps with actresses? You do it all the time."

"Hardly. I've never once begun a relationship in the middle of a run. Jonathan treats his conquests like dirt and disrupts the company dynamic. Do not compare us."

"Fine. You're nothing like him. Neither am I. Neither is Mad."

"You barely know this person," Brennon insisted.

"I know he's not an asshole." Adam glared at the next drink Brennon picked up. "Last one, promise?"

"Sure." Brennon got to work on it. The craft brew had gone down bitter earlier, but it tasted much smoother now. "How do you know he's not an asshole? It wouldn't be the first time you were taken in by a pretty face and left . . ."

"Left what?"

Hurt. Brennon wanted to say hurt, but the conversation was taking a turn he hadn't intended. He needed this tour to be a vacation. A break from his own increasingly miserable existence in New York. A chance not to feel so alone. Thinking of home and his own most recent relationship failure was a heavy weight on his heart. He shut his eyes and savored the humid South Carolina air drifting past him as more patrons came and went through the nearby door.

Adam reached up to ruffle Brennon's hair, an obnoxiously loving gesture Brennon would allow from no one else on the planet. "Be nice to me," Adam said. "You know I break easy."

That he did, and it was Brennon's point. "I'm always nice to you," Brennon said.

"I'm one of the lucky ones, then. And I'm glad you're here." Adam's smile was warm, but his tone held some resignation in it, too.

"I wish I'd been ready two weeks ago. I would have liked to perform here." Brennon gestured to the room, to South Carolina in general.

"We've had a blast. The crowds treated us like rock stars."

Before Brennon began rehearsals for *Liz and Darcy,* he'd done a two-month guest run in London, playing Jean Valjean in the West End production of *Les Misérables.* The audiences in London were different than American crowds. Not better or worse, but Broadway had a particular energy—a madness he'd grown accustomed to. He'd missed home, but not enough to go back.

Two weeks of rehearsals in New York had him itching to be on the road again. His apartment held memories of Chloe everywhere. Having coffee with her two days ago to tie up some relationship loose ends had been brutal.

So many accusations and apologies, so few fucks to give.

Learning she'd been harboring feelings for her best friend for months had been one thing—finding out their entire circle of friends had known about it and not mentioned anything to him was entirely another. Adam and Veronica were the only ones exempt from Brennon's resentment. They'd been on tour when everything blew up.

Finished with their drinks, Brennon closed out the tab and met Adam at the door. They stepped into the muggy Southern night air, inhaling the fragrance of honeysuckle and the earthy scents of the nearby river.

"Adam—wait up!" Gabi stubbed out her cigarette on the curb and hurried to catch up with them, her long legs making fast work of it. "Oh, hey, Brennon Thorne." She grinned, showing off a mouthful of teeth so white they glowed. He'd recognized her when Adam introduced them. She'd been in the ensemble of *Sweeney Todd* a few years back when he'd played the title role. She'd come on strong then, too.

He gave her a nod. "Gabi."

"I never asked what you thought of the show."

She didn't mean the show, of course. She meant her own performance in the show. As Jane Bennet, her woeful solo had been mildly wrenching. She was talented. "You were very good."

She gave a little bow even as she managed to walk backward in front of them both. "Thank you, sir. Looking forward to working with you."

"Gabi understudies for Lizzie," Adam explained.

How many understudies and standbys did the main character have? "How would that work? Your part isn't insubstantial."

"It's a touring ensemble," she explained. "Both female swings know my part, and I think the rest of us all know at least two roles, right, Adam?"

"True," Adam said. "But Darcy and Lizzie are the only ones with paid standbys."

"It'd basically take an act of God for me to step into the lead," Gabi said. "But I'm always ready."

Brennon understood the desire to rise to the top, but he often had the sense that the understudies and standbys who occasionally went on opposite him were trying to climb over him to do it. It was a constant struggle to get them to tone themselves down—play the actual role rather than show off every skill in their set.

He'd had mixed experiences. Paid standbys with nothing to do but wait around for the actor they covered to lose his voice or break an actual leg during a performance tended to be both ingratiating and exhausting. The only real draw to this production was the opportunity to work closely with Veronica again. He planned to coordinate their call-outs to avoid playing opposite the standby, especially now that he'd met her.

As Adam, Gabi, and Brennon turned off the main drag, the bars and restaurants gave way to a neighborhood of older, bungalow-style homes. "This one's us." Adam pointed at the third house on the right.

"Are you staying with us tonight too, Brennon?" Gabi asked.

Brennon hadn't bothered getting a hotel room for one night in Greenville. Adam had insisted there was space in his king-sized bed for them both, so Brennon had saved himself the hassle of making another reservation. The three of them, along with Veronica, would all have separate rooms in the house in DC. On a tour like this, being around the same people day in and day out could get old quick. Sharing a house was one thing, but no one on a tour would ever share a room if they didn't have to. "I thought I might save a few bucks."

"See how the other half lives?" Gabi joked.

Brennon grimaced. "Something like that."

Once inside, they all said good night, and Gabi headed to her room.

Veronica's bedroom door was closed when he and Adam passed it in the hallway. "How is she doing, really?" Brennon asked.

Adam gestured to his own room and Brennon walked in first. "Moody as usual, but no red flags."

"Good. And she and Jonathan . . .?" Brennon left the question unfinished, as the thought of the two of them at Julliard still made his stomach churn.

Adam sighed. "It's been touch and go."

Brennon chose not to pry any further. There was only so much he actually wanted to know. He'd see for himself soon enough.

Adam's bedroom was in perfect order. Bed made, suitcase packed. His clothes for the next day along with his overnight kit were laid out neatly on the dresser. Brennon was glad to see that his own bags had been delivered and were positioned next to Adam's, ready to go, next to the door.

Stepping out of his shoes, Brennon stretched his toes inside his socks and nodded toward an open door. "Bathroom?"

"Go ahead," Adam said.

Once he'd washed up, Brennon caught a glimpse of himself in the mirror. The cheap fluorescent lighting revealed more flaws than he was used to seeing at home.

Jesus. Had he aged ten years in the last three months? He hadn't been sleeping well for a while, but the dark circles beneath his eyes would take more than a little stage makeup to remedy. He was pale, too. A result of a cloudy spring in London and too much time spent in dark theaters.

He needed to get out more. Sleep. Drink less. Exercise.

"I'm turning over a new leaf," he announced as he emerged from the bathroom to his audience of one.

"Excellent," Adam said. "When can we schedule your haircut?"

Brennon chuckled. "No one's touching my hair."

His friend mocked disappointment. "A shave then? Something?"

"I'll shave Tuesday before the show."

"Thank God." Adam smirked. "What new leaf are we turning?"

"First I plan to get a good night's sleep, and then it's time to get my beach body back." He patted his belly.

"I hadn't planned to mention it."

"I'm glad you didn't."

"What did they feed you in London anyway?" Adam asked, eyeing Brennon's midsection.

"There was a great deal of potatoes."

"Can you still count your abs?"

"Only up to four."

Adam laughed. "I think I'll take a shower."

Brennon organized himself for the morning and lay down for the night.

Once he was done in the bathroom, Adam tucked himself in on the opposite side of the bed. "Not to beat a dead horse, but I'm afraid you didn't make the best first impression on Maddox . . . or his friends."

Brennon closed his eyes. He was sobering up and didn't want to remember it. The Citaltfor joke hadn't aged well. "You wouldn't force me to apologize, would you?"

"I mean—it wasn't *not* funny."

"You have to admit—there's a large gap between peddling hard-ons and taking the stage at the Shubert."

Adam snort-laughed. "Eden's sweet."

"Sweet won't cut it in this business. She should know that by now."

"She made it this far," Adam said. "I imagine she's doing something right."

Eden was beautiful and likely in her mid-twenties—she had that working in her favor, but she wasn't getting any younger. Making it on Broadway was especially hard for women. There were only so many roles, and so many talented women coming into the city daily to claim them. The ones who made it had to have the grit, the look, the luck, and a huge skill set. "She any good?" Brennon asked.

"Of course. Everybody here's great."

"Hope I don't embarrass you Tuesday night."

Adam laughed again. "Good night, my King of Broadway."

"Sleep tight, young prince."

His friend hummed a satisfied sound. "Sweet talker."

"So, I did some digging." Gabi plopped into the seat next to Brennon's in the airport terminal where he waited to board the afternoon flight for DC. She held out her phone, a YouTube video paused on the screen.

Brennon eyed it skeptically. "Digging?"

She grinned, a naughty glint in her bright blue eyes. "I figured an actress couldn't land a Citaltfor commercial with no résumé, so I Googled Eden. You'll die. Trust me." She thrust the phone between his face and the book resting on his lap.

"If it's porn, I'm not interested."

"It's better than porn." She shook her phone. "Watch it."

Gabi wasn't giving up. He gave her a dark look, hoping she'd get the message that her methods didn't impress him. "Fine."

She flashed him a triumphant smile and pushed the play button with her thumb.

A young woman jogging down a suburban street took over the screen. There was Eden, a huge grin on her face, full breasts bouncing in an unsupportive sports bra, dark hair flying high in a ponytail. In the next scene she bent over to pick up the mail on her front porch, and in doing so apparently threw out her back. She rose in dramatic and excruciating pain, her face twisting with agony. She was laid up on the sofa in the next scene, and the actor playing her husband handed her a hot and cold patch.

She applied it to her bare lower back, and the relief was instantaneous.

She was cured.

It was some of the most over-the-top acting he'd ever seen.

He couldn't suppress his laughter.

"Wait." Gabi giggled. "There's more."

Time flew in the terminal as they watched Eden's long commercial career unfold on YouTube. She'd been at it a while—since she was a teenager in braces.

"How did you find all this?" Brennon asked.

"Cyber-stalking is my superpower."

"Remind me never to get on your bad side."

"Oh, please, it's funny. It's not like I'm arranging a showing for the cast. Just thought you might get a kick out of it."

He had, but even he could acknowledge that everyone had to start somewhere. Clearly Eden was trying to make a career transition, although from the looks of it, she had a long way to go. Brennon handed Gabi back her phone. "What do you know about this Maddox person?" he asked.

"Mad? He and Eden are besties. Are you asking if they fuck?"

Brennon's lip curled in distaste at her crudeness. So far, Gabi had failed to impress. Why hadn't Adam and Veronica found a less obnoxious cast member to split accommodations with? "No," he said, not bothering to disguise his annoyance. "I wanted to know whether you knew what sort of person he was. Adam talks about him."

"Tell me about it." She sat back in her chair, arms folded, and chin tilted in thought. "I don't care for him. There've been rumors."

"What rumors?" Brennon asked.

"About some back-and-forth blow jobs between him and Nate."

"Which one is Nate?"

"Oh, he played Wickham before. Smaller part, no solos. He left the tour about a month ago to do *Moulin Rouge* in Chicago."

"I see." Tours were known to be hotbeds of promiscuity between young cast members. "And so?"

"I think Nate ended up feeling a little used."

Brennon scowled. "How's that?"

"Well, Maddox had only just come out as bi, you know, and Nate was apparently his first guy or whatever. Anyway, there were some dramatic backstage goings-on one night in San Antonio. Mad called out the next night, and then Nate was off to Chicago. That's all I know."

"Who was being dramatic?" Brennon pressed, because from the coy purse of her lips and swift glance away, it was obvious she knew more.

"Both. Nate told Donovan that Mad was under the impression if he did Nate a few 'favors,' he'd get to perform Wickham a few nights."

Ah. The very essence of why understudies and swings could become a problem. The information annoyed Brennon, but it was no shock. He looked up as Adam returned from Starbucks with his and Brennon's coffees in hand.

Brennon glanced past him. He was alone. "Where's Veronica?"

"Restroom," Adam said. "What are you frowning about?"

"Nothing," Brennon said.

Gabi gave Adam a nonchalant shrug. "Just catching Brennon up on our little traveling circus."

The flight crew announced their first boarding call, and Brennon took his coffee from Adam before standing to gather his carry-ons. He'd used his miles to upgrade himself, Adam, and Veronica to first class.

"See you at the capital, boys," Gabi said.

"What was that about?" Adam asked as the two men made their way to the ramp.

"She was reminding me how bad career decisions can follow a person around forever." His words were pointed. For everyone's sake, he hoped Adam would steer clear of men like Maddox and Nate.

Adam shot him a wounded look. "Why don't you trust me not to be an idiot?"

"It was only a general observation."

"I'm guessing you think asking Mad to have dinner at our place tonight would be a bad idea."

"I do. We're here to work, and I have to be up early tomorrow." He and Veronica were scheduled to be at two local TV news stations for interviews starting at six thirty AM. "I'll need to shave."

"Oh my God, yes. Can I watch?"

Brennon chuckled as he held up his phone for the flight attendant to scan his boarding pass. "Are you always this clingy?"

Adam nudged Brennon's shoulder with his own and gave him a sly wink. "Only after I've slept with someone."

CHAPTER THREE

With the entire morning off, Eden woke up early with Maddox to hate-watch Brennon Thorne and Veronica West's interview on WUSA. Turned out he was every bit as pompous on screen as off, even without the beard. Afterward, Mad left for a run, and Eden returned to her bed, planning to sleep in as long as possible.

The entire cast and crew had a two PM call time for their orientation to the Kennedy Center's Eisenhower Theater. No one, not even standbys, were exempt.

At ten AM her mother started calling.

Eden sent the first two calls to voice mail, but her mother was nothing if not persistent.

"You're not up yet?" she asked in response to Eden's groggy hello.

"I am now."

"I've been sitting here patiently waiting for you to tell me everything there is to know about where you're staying, how Veronica's health seems today, and what Brennon Thorne is *really* like."

That last question stuck in Eden's craw, but her answer addressed another. "Veronica is the picture of vitality."

"That's too bad. Have you arranged anything with her for a chance to perform? You know I can get tickets just like that." The snap of her mother's fingers traveled the cell towers from Indiana to DC.

Eden cringed. Not at the idea of her mother traveling to one of her shows, but the expense. Last-minute flights didn't come cheap, and her mother's credit card bills were a constant source of stress headaches. Another one was already brewing at her temples. "You'll be the first to know."

"How's the house?"

"It's nice." Eden glanced around her small bedroom. Bigger cities meant tighter accommodations, but the townhouse in Georgetown was clean and well-kept. The neighboring house obstructed the view from her window, but the hardwood floors caught the morning sunlight filtering through the wood shutters just right.

"Any excursions planned?"

"The only one I know about so far is the botanic garden next Monday."

David Clarke, the actor playing Lizzie's beleaguered father Mr. Bennet, was big on organizing cast field trips. Attendance was optional, but Eden managed to go on most of them. The group rate David always got made sightseeing both fun and affordable. Plus, he was a good time—a delightful character actor, whose résumé put everyone else's to shame. David had been making a living on Broadway since his twenties. Now in his sixties, he was single, ready to mingle, and lived to plan company outings. So far Eden had seen Graceland, Alcatraz, the Alamo, and more. They'd even zip-lined in Georgia, which had *not* been Eden's favorite.

"With three weeks you should be able to see everything in DC," her mother said.

"I imagine so."

"Did you get a chance to introduce yourself to Brennon?"

Brennon. Like her mother was on a first-name basis with him. "Yep. Met him, had a laugh, moved on with my night."

"And what's he like?"

"I found him somewhat disagreeable."

Her mother laughed. "Listen to you. My own little Lizzie Bennet."

"Men in real life don't redeem as well as Darcy did."

"Preaching to the choir, sweetie."

Eden was well-aware. Her mom had firsthand experience with a man who only thought of himself—Eden's father. Her parents' marriage ended when Eden was two, but to hear her mom tell it, things had soured long before that. Her dad had been gone a lot, a workaholic who thought Terry should spend more time homemaking than managing her toddler's career. It was only one of many disagreements they'd had before they both realized their goals would never align, but Eden's mom never voiced a single regret. As her only child, Eden often felt the burden of being her mother's first choice. Fortunately, they were usually on the same page as far as Eden's career was concerned. Usually.

"He'll be great for the tour, though," Eden admitted. "Which I guess is awesome for me, long-run."

"I don't know how you do it, dealing with all these uppity Broadway people."

"They're just people, Mom. We're all out here working hard. Chasing dreams, et cetera."

"Speaking of which, I've been looking at TV agents to be on the lookout for when you get to LA."

Eden sighed, long-suffering and loud. "Can I please get through this tour first?"

"You could, or you could take advantage of every opportunity while you're on the road. Get your face in front of some people who could make a real difference for you instead of moping around in the wings waiting for a chance to shine onstage."

"Wow, Mom."

"You know what I mean."

Born with the cheeks of a Gerber baby, Eden had inspired Terry Blake's talent manager tendencies from her first month of life. Modeling as an infant parlayed itself into acting the instant Eden learned how to string words together. That's when her mother began carting her to one audition after another. By the time she'd gotten to high school Eden had a full reel and a résumé three pages long.

It hadn't gotten her any friends, that was for sure, but it impressed her theater teacher, and Eden ate up the attention. It gave her a stellar work ethic and dreams so big she could barely contain them. In South Bend, résumés like Eden's stood out. Never mind if she was actually talented or not—she was a local celebrity.

Her mom thought Eden was spinning her wheels trying to make it on Broadway, wasting her youth and beauty on a career she hadn't been groomed for. If Terry Blake had her way, Eden would land a five-year contract with *General Hospital*. Now, *that* was what her résumé had prepared her for. But the truth was, she *did* have talent and a great voice. Even her modest success thus far in New York proved it. Her mother had strenuously objected when Eden decided to move to the city two years ago, but Eden was determined to make it on her own.

If it hadn't been for all those damn tap classes and singing lessons, Eden might never have caught the Broadway bug. Served her mom right for scheduling her to within an inch of her life during her formative years. Working two jobs and auditioning five days a week was a breeze compared to the day-in, day-out beating of building an impeccable skill set.

Now that Eden had a legit agent, however, her mom's finances had taken a hit. Eden helped when she could, but this tour was her first substantial, steady paycheck ever. Empowered by her new ability to both pay her rent in New York and start making a dent in a few of her mother's debts, her constant guilt had eased. Since most of the charges her mother incurred over the years had been on Eden's behalf, she felt obligated to lessen the financial strain. If her standby role here gave her a leg-up in her New York auditions next year, maybe neither of them would ever have to worry about money again. Making it on Broadway paid big. Imagining what a relief it would be caused determination to stir in her blood.

"Send me lots of pictures," her mother said, wrapping up the call.

"You got it."

"And let me know if anything happens with Veronica—"

"You can put away your voodoo doll. What's meant to be will be."

Her mother tsked. "That attitude won't get you anywhere."

Eden laughed. Her mom was a lot, but as a one-woman fan club, she was unwavering.

Eden, Maddox, and Liliana walked to the Kennedy Center from their townhouse, and it turned out they weren't the only cast members who'd managed to snag a place so close to the venue. By the time they arrived, they were walking in a group of eight people, ready for their tour of the famous performance space, including the Eisenhower Theater where they'd be performing for the next three weeks. The afternoon was warm, but not as humid as South Carolina. Eden was pleased to note her hair had held up fairly well on the walk.

Shayna, the stage manager, along with the company manager's two assistants, stood outside the main entrance, checking her watch. Everyone gathered around, waiting for the stragglers.

Brennon Thorne, Adam, Veronica, and Gabi were among the last to arrive.

Shayna—a woman so tough and grizzled Eden was positive no man alive could beat her in an arm-wrestling match—squealed when she saw the group of them, her intricately woven braids bouncing as she raced down the steps and leapt at Thorne, engulfing him in a hug. Clearly they'd worked together before.

Brennon stumbled off balance and let out a self-conscious laugh. It was almost charming, but mostly it left Eden feeling a little sorry for Shayna.

"We're so lucky to have you," the stage manager gushed.

"Happy to be here," Brennon said as he coolly scanned the crowd.

He wasted not one lingering glance on Eden as his eyes swept over the faces in attendance, but then his gaze stilled, and his spine stiffened further, if that was possible. She turned to see who'd snagged his attention.

Jonathan March, who played Darcy's best friend Mr. Bingley, glared back at Thorne.

Eden looked up at Maddox to see if he was watching the micro-drama unfold, but he and Adam were already locked in a longing gaze-fest. Figured.

Now that the entire company had shown up, they filed inside. Eden dutifully listened to the local theater manager's speech about the history of the Kennedy Center and all the legends who'd come before them to perform there. Entering the Eisenhower Theater the way an audience member would, the cast walked down the aisle and met onstage to look out at the large house. Theaters were never as magical with all the house lights on, but Eden didn't love them any less. The smell of wood polish, the well-worn carpets, the familiar sights of scuffs on the stage, which now featured their own set, lovingly and hastily crafted by a crew that had probably worked all day yesterday to put it back together, made their brand-new venue feel like home.

Before the performers went to get mic'd and lit to make sure everything was working right, their guide led them out of the theater and showed them to the backstage door.

On a long hallway, there were two principal dressing rooms and two larger ensemble dressing rooms—boys and girls. Shayna pointed Brennon to his (the larger of the two principals), and showed Veronica to hers.

"Oh!" the actress said when she saw it. "Carpet. Nice!"

Though it was cozier than Brennon's, Veronica's dressing room had a lovely vanity and a velvety love seat set on a clean, plush rug. The walls were painted a rosy shade of peach, and when Veronica stepped in to have a look around, she glowed, looking twice as beautiful as usual. Nothing like good lighting.

After the theater tour, Eden took up her usual post next to Kenneth in the audience seats while the crew walked the cast through their sound check. Kenneth was the standby for Mr. Darcy, and though he and Eden didn't talk much, they shared space well. Kenneth had a killer résumé and was a consummate professional—Eden had actually once seen him perform on Broadway in *Hamilton*, during the week he was covering George Washington. He had a wife and two kids back in the city, so he wasn't as involved with the ensemble as Eden. Any time off they got, he was visiting his family, either out here on the road or on quick trips back to Manhattan.

"He seems like a dream to work with," Kenneth said when Thorne exited the stage at the end of a scene.

Eden rolled her eyes and kept her mouth shut.

She checked the time on her phone. It was almost four o'clock. Act Two was just getting started after some issues with the lights during "Nothing To Say," Veronica's dancing duet with Thorne.

The two of them sang the first verse and chorus full-out, and Eden had to pretend she wasn't a ball of absolute goo after finally watching Brennon sing live. Unfortunately, hearing him at his best did nothing to drown out the memory of the way he'd laughed at her Sunday night.

Scrolling her Instagram next to Kenneth, who snored lightly, Eden yawned, snapped a selfie, and added a Kennedy Center hashtag along with about fifteen others to mark her spot this day in social media history. As she considered catching her own catnap, the lights came up once again on the stage.

Gabi stood alone, left of center, with her hands up in a "so, now what?" gesture. She wasn't supposed to be alone.

Where was Veronica?

"Veronica!" Shayna shouted. "V! Get your ass out here, we don't have all day."

Kenneth shot to attention beside Eden. "I'll help track her down." He sped down the aisle like he'd been sent to rescue a child from a house fire. If there was a job to do, Kenneth would find it. Eden had a feeling his apartment was spotless, and he ran all the errands. Being a standby must be torture for someone always so eager to get to work.

Liliana poked her head onstage from behind one of the curtains. "She's not in her dressing room."

"Did she go for a smoke?" Shayna asked, baffled.

Veronica didn't smoke.

Shayna turned her attention suddenly to her Apple Watch and made a face Eden could only describe as contained rage. It was a cartoon face. Bulging eyes, steam coming out of the ears, etcetera.

Sharply, Shayna turned to the house seats. "Eden. Onstage. Now."

Brennon watched in horror from the left wing as Eden took the stage. This was not good. Not good at all. Memories of her standoffish reaction to him at the bar Sunday evening put a low buzz in his ears. The words "limp dick" resurfaced and caused an unpleasant pang south of his waistline. He turned to the company manager's assistant standing nearby, a small worm of a man everyone referred to as Peck. "Is someone looking for Veronica?" Mild panic crept into his voice.

"We'll track her down," Peck said. "It's just tech."

Yes, but tech rehearsal was mandatory. An actor couldn't simply walk out on it because it was boring. It was part of the job, and Veronica had shown no signs of strain so far today. Genuinely concerned for his friend, Brennon performed a thorough search backstage, with plenty of time to spare before he was next expected out front. He and Kenneth teamed up to look for Veronica in every place they could find. No luck. An assistant waved him back toward the stage for the scene where Lizzie comes to Pemberley. It involved a grand staircase, a subtle but powerful entrance, layered emotions—

It's just tech. He didn't need to be perfect. A deep breath quieted Brennon's sudden, unfamiliar uncertainty, and he rushed up the stairs.

"Stop there," Shayna shouted at him. "The light's not hitting him right. Jesus, it's like we don't go through this every time."

Brennon waited at the top of the staircase for the crew to adjust the lights until his face was in shadow. He'd be stepping into the spotlight as he made his way down the stairs, then his spotlight would meet Veronica's spotlight—

Eden stared up at him as the light moved out of his eyes.

She had a wry smile on that lush, red mouth of hers, and his recently collected thoughts abruptly snagged. Though she wore a simple, sleeveless sundress decorated with flowers in every color of the rainbow, in his head, without meaning to at all, he pictured her in the sports bra and leggings from the hot-and-cold patch commercial. The bouncing breasts, the bundle of mail that must have weighed two hundred pounds, the overblown look of agony on her face as she pretended to injure herself.

With no hope of schooling his runaway thoughts, he laughed.

Mostly to himself.

Somewhat out loud.

Eden's eyes narrowed into a glare.

Although he was able to quiet his chuckle, a smile remained. It hardly seemed worth it to attempt to repair her impression of him for half a tech rehearsal. Veronica would turn up. He might as well have some fun.

"All right, Brennon, go ahead."

The light now in place, Brennon took his time coming down the stairs.

"Eden—" Shayna barked. "Test your mic. Sing the song. Let's go."

Eden cleared her throat.

Rookie mistake.

Shayna groaned as a tiny whine of feedback echoed through the house.

"Sorry," Eden whispered, and then she cleared her throat again.

Brennon couldn't keep the growing smirk off his face. "Better just to belt it out," he advised her.

Without another blink, she squared off with him and let her clear soprano ring out. Eight perfect notes sent chills racing up his back to blow his mind.

"Turn her down one tick, and let's move on," Shayna said into a walkie-talkie. "Lights up for the Inn."

Eden turned on her heel and strode to stage right, which was her mark for the scene at the Inn. The set changed flawlessly, and the lights followed suit. And still, the sound of her singing voice echoed in Brennon's head. He needed to hear her sing again. Veronica was good, great even, but Eden's voice was as clear and flawless as a diamond. It had sliced straight through his guard, and he wanted her to cut him with it again.

But Shayna didn't make her sing for the rest of tech.

Not even when they stood once again in the spotlight together, six inches apart, for the kiss at the end.

No one kissed during a tech rehearsal, of course. It was all about lighting and sound. Though their bodies were a hair's-width apart, Eden stared over his shoulder at a spot in the distance. Her warm breath blew in regular gusts across the side of his neck. As his awareness centered in on the spot, Brennon gazed over her head at Shayna while she made what appeared to be extensive notes in her binder.

Eden lifted her hand to scratch the end of her nose. Her fingertips grazed his chest, and he sucked in a shocked breath at the contact, drawing his torso out of accidental touching range.

She gave him a flat look. "Oh, pardon me."

It was only tech. They would locate Veronica, and he'd likely never have to stand onstage with Eden again. No woman had ever put him so instantly on edge. She should come with a warning label. "Best not to speak," he said, determined to engage no further.

She glared up at him. "Noted."

"Places for the wedding," Shayna barked.

Eden and Brennon immediately stepped apart while the rest of the cast gathered onstage. After they walked through the last scene and their curtain call, the company formed a circle for their final talk about who'd be in the audience that night, and how important it was to make a great impression for the national press.

"Eden, Brennon, hang back a minute," Shayna said as she dismissed the rest of the cast and crew.

Brennon and Eden shared a wary glance. He tightened his jaw. Shayna's defeated tone sparked something very near to dread inside him.

She approached the two of them with a grim set to her mouth. "Veronica's sick, as I'm sure you both gathered. Let's run your songs, your blocking. I need to make sure tonight's not going to be a complete disaster."

"No pressure," Eden mumbled.

"Think again, young lady."

"I was kidding."

"Don't talk," Shayna snapped. "It's time to earn your paycheck."

CHAPTER FOUR

Earn her paycheck? The words smarted like a slap. So uncalled for. It wasn't like Eden sat around eating bonbons and reading magazines all day while everyone else performed eight shows a week. As if. There were understudy rehearsals at least once a week, put-in rehearsals, and she'd even performed the role eight times already. Shayna knew she could do it.

Brennon Thorne, though, peering down his nose at her with his arms folded and brow arched, looked skeptical—a direct shot at her ego.

And also a shot of adrenaline. Fine. She'd show them both.

Right off the bat, this was way different than working with Donovan.

She'd known it would be, for a variety of reasons.

First, Brennon Thorne was better looking. Donovan was a great-looking guy, of course, but Thorne was next level. He moved better. He commanded more space. His voice was deeper, his eyes were darker, he was, all in all, *more*. Donovan was VHS. Brennon Thorne was high-definition.

"That's not the step."

Second, Brennon Thorne apparently knew *everything*.

Eden closed her eyes and inhaled deeply. For being the new kid in town, the man had an awful lot of notes. "That's how Veronica does it."

"Actually, Veronica does it correctly," he said.

"Remind me, then," Eden said through gritted teeth.

They were working on the ballroom dance. The blocking had been set in stone long ago on Broadway. It wasn't possible she'd done it wrong. But maybe it was just too hard for him to see her feet from all the way up there. Nevertheless, he corrected her.

The song "Nothing To Say" was an ensemble piece, but also a duet of asides between Elizabeth and Mr. Darcy while they danced and continued to misunderstand each other.

"If I had one piece of advice . . ." he began at the end of the dance.

Eden swiveled her head to glare up at him.

"It's only that you're rushing the choruses. Your voice is—it's nice. No need to rush it."

Her eyes narrowed. *Nice?*

Her voice was *nice?*

For their second duet—"What's Happening?"—she took his snobby note, and she began to understand what he'd meant by *nice*.

His singing voice was sublime. It hurt her to listen to it. The ache in it, the passion, all the feelings he layered in every word, each intonation. She could masturbate to it.

When the song ended, Shayna said, "Eden, you missed three movements."

Thorne said, "Actually, I counted four."

And she was over it.

By the time they approached the end, and Lizzie was accepting Darcy's offer of marriage, Eden wanted to shove Brennon Thorne into the front row.

But first, they had to kiss. This was no longer merely a tech run-through—this was their only rehearsal before their very real press performance tonight.

Her stomach flipped. Her voice shook as she forced herself to gaze adoringly up at him.

Per the choreography, his right hand would go to her waist. She'd then touch his chest with her right hand. Next, he was to caress her cheek and press his forehead to hers. He would sigh, and sing a line.

She would respond with her line and lift her hand to his neck. They'd sing a line together, then she'd rise to her tiptoes and press her lips to his.

Once their mouths connected, he would pull her to him and stage-kiss the daylights out of her while the lights went dark. There would be no tongue. Tongue was too much for a musical.

"The music plays . . ." Shayna cued them.

Thorne's right hand went to Eden's waist as he sang his part. She placed her hand on his chest, over his long-sleeved gray Henley. His heart pounded against her palm. His knuckles brushed her cheekbone.

Wait. That wasn't how Donovan did it. Donovan had more of a caress/cupping move. Should she mention that? Or was that not how they did it on *Broadway*?

Thorne leaned in, and Eden got all buzzy for a second. She blamed his voice. He was singing, and the vibrations of his baritone resonated in his chest and also on her mouth, and it was . . . confusing. It was one thing to appreciate his talent on an intellectual level, but the way her body heated at his intense nearness was purely physical. Despite their height difference, their bodies fit together alarmingly well.

He did the sigh, the one where Darcy's tight shoulders relaxed because he'd finally gotten the answer he was looking for—one he'd fought hard for—one he'd changed his mind for.

Eden licked her lips, her mouth suddenly dry. He sang his line.

She managed to choke hers out. She moved her hand up his well-defined chest, over his broad shoulder, and slid it around his neck, lifting onto her tiptoes and raising her chin to angle her lips.

"Try to remember you're in Regency England on an estate, not a commercial set in Florida."

She blinked and stepped away from him. "Excuse me?"

"That was contemporary. That movement. What you did there."

"What I did where?"

"The hand, Eden," Shayna said.

She snapped her attention to Shayna. She'd forgotten anyone else was there. "I'm sorry?"

Shayna waved her pages of notes at them. "He's right—lift the hand, don't slide the hand."

Eden's cheeks flamed with embarrassment. "Of course."

"Do it again. I need to see the kiss so we can work on that if it needs it. The chemistry here is . . ." Shayna frowned. "Concerning."

Eden bit her lip to keep from arguing. She had to channel Lizzie. Who was Lizzie in this scene? Lizzie was relieved. She was in love. She was humbled.

Eden toned herself down.

She softened her singing voice. She got the movements right. He still did the knuckle thing, which she wanted to discuss with someone important later because it created sensations inside her she'd prefer not to feel in front of a live audience, but she was a professional. She'd manage. *Lifting* her hand off his pounding heart, she placed it on the back of his neck while she rose to her toes and adjusted her mouth to meet his.

He gathered her body close, and his ever-so-slightly parted lips pressed into hers. Warm. The bristle of his five o'clock shadow abraded her chin. A wholly unprofessional sensation stiffened her body against his, even as, per the Broadway choreography, her body bent backward in his embrace.

Eden's mouth was plush, redolent of honey. The kiss was meant to be Regency. A long lingering meeting of barely parted lips, some tender movement, but restrained. Proper.

The pulse pounding upward through Brennon's groin was anything but proper.

Her nose was velvet warmth against his cheek, her hand on his neck feather-light, and fuck him, but her last line, the softened way she delivered the final notes, had nearly brought him to his knees with regret for being hard on her. She was . . . So. Fucking. Good. Raw, yes, and grossly inexperienced, obviously, but the talent—he wanted to reach into her with his tongue and taste the fundamental essence of it.

"Good enough," Shayna said. "A little less stiff tonight, Eden, okay? I get this is last minute. Go get some dinner, you two, and we'll see you back here at seven-thirty. Actually, Eden, make it seven, in case we need to make any last-minute alterations on your costumes."

Eden practically ripped herself from Brennon's arms and wiped her mouth with the back of her hand as she glared at him.

Charming. He glared back.

"Any other notes?" Eden asked Shayna.

"I think we covered everything."

Brennon spoke up, "Actually—"

"I wasn't asking you." Her hardened eyes eviscerated him.

He shut his mouth. She had a point. He was only going to say how much he'd liked her choice with the last few lines of the song, but he could save it for another time.

He left the stage more worked up than usual. It was unthinkable that someone who'd been in an infomercial for Shake Weights could perform with as much subtlety as she had this afternoon. While her endless Shake Weight demonstration had made a certain sort of impression on him when he'd watched it with Gabi at the airport, Eden was clearly meant for the stage. In a few years, with another role or two like this under her belt, he'd be running into her in his own circles back home, maybe even starring with her in *The Sound of Music* or *Guys and Dolls*, if either of those rumored revivals panned out.

She was, in a word, extraordinary.

Performing with Veronica when she got over whatever had taken her out of the theater today would be easier—she was by far the more seasoned actress and extremely talented in her own right, but the last hour he'd spent with Eden, discovering her as he had, had been one of the most exciting hours he'd spent on a stage since his Broadway debut.

Brennon requested an Uber to take him back to the townhome he was sharing in Georgetown with Adam, Veronica, and Gabi, rather than walk twenty minutes. The drive took just as long because it was rush hour, but he needed to conserve his energy. He and Eden were on a tight turnaround due to the extended rehearsal.

Back at the rental house, Adam was setting out dinner. Chicken fettuccine and La Croix on ice. "How'd it go with Eden?"

Gabi, already seated at the kitchen island, snickered.

"She's very good," Brennon said, unable to keep the note of surprise from his voice.

"I might have mentioned that the other night," Adam said.

"You might have."

Adam served Brennon a plate of pasta and cracked open another can of coconut sparkling water. Brennon thanked him and had a seat. Ray LaMontagne played in the background. At least fifty percent of Brennon's muscles relaxed.

"So . . . V's not here," Adam said.

Brennon's concern for his long-ago ex and now dear friend tightened his chest. He glanced up at Adam. "Her things?"

Adam gave his head a slow shake. "Maybe she decided to go with a hotel?"

"And not tell us?" Brennon wound some noodles around his fork and speared a chunk of chicken. "Shayna only said she was sick."

"More like she vaporized," Adam said around a mouthful.

"Have you tried calling?"

Adam gestured at the kitchen. "I was making dinner."

Brennon looked down at the dish he was enjoying. "It's very good. Thank you."

42

"Do you think Maddox would like it?"

Brennon held in a sigh. "I don't know. Does Maddox have any issues with dairy? Is he gluten-free? All things to consider."

"He eats cheeseburgers."

"Then I don't see why he wouldn't."

Gabi's phone buzzed beside Brennon's elbow. "It's Veronica," she said.

"Is she all right?" Brennon asked.

"I'll let you know. I'm gonna take this upstairs." Gabi gathered her plate, drink, and phone and left the kitchen.

Knowing Veronica was at least alive, Brennon allowed himself to relax and refocus on Adam. "Where were we?"

"I guess what I'm asking is do you think Maddox would like if I cooked a meal for him. Like this. Is that a thing a guy likes?"

"You're a guy. You've dated men. Exclusively, as I understand it."

"Sure. I have, but Mad just came out as bi a few months ago. I don't want to overwhelm him."

Brennon swallowed his food and worked on rounding up another bite. "Has *he* dated men before?"

"How are we defining dating?"

Brennon gestured at his food. "This feels like a date."

"He has some experience. As far as a relationship . . . we haven't really delved that deep."

"How deep *have* you delved?"

"Not as deep as I'd like to." Adam laughed, catching Brennon's upward glance. "Sorry—couldn't resist. I know I sound like a mess, but I haven't been this boy crazy since I saw *The Perks of Being a Wallflower* in high school."

"What makes you think this person is interested in a relationship?" Brennon asked, because from what he'd heard it didn't seem to be the case.

"There was some drama in Texas," Adam confided. "I gave him some advice. We ended up talking for several hours. We'd both had a few drinks."

Brennon scowled. He didn't understand this story, or how it in any way addressed the question he'd asked.

"Evidently, he'd never been with a man before. Nate—the guy he hooked up with—used to play Wickham—"

Brennon cut him off. "I've heard about Nate."

"Anyway, Nate was his first guy he ever kissed and . . . whatever. Like I said, he more or less came out on this tour."

"And you're what? Mentoring him?"

"Please, Brennon. Try not to talk about things you can't understand."

Brennon waved a hand in surrender. "I'm only asking . . ."

"What I'm trying to explain is we had a very open, honest conversation, and I felt a connection."

Ah. Exactly as he'd feared. "You supposed this feeling was mutual?"

"Connections usually are."

"No." Brennon shook his head firmly. "No. We just got to town. Tonight's the press opening, and we open to the public tomorrow. It's time for you to focus." His friend was due for his big break. A role in this touring production put Adam a single step away from the Broadway stages—*if* he played his cards right and didn't throw it all away on a swing trying to get ahead. "Whatever's going on between you two can wait."

"I don't feel like you're taking this as seriously as I want you to."

Brennon set his fork down and folded his hands over his plate. "I don't understand why you're spending so much mental energy on what essentially would amount to a hookup."

"Are you listening to me? If a hookup was all I was after, I would have done it by now."

"What are you after, then?"

"I really like him, Brennon."

"Based on what?" All he'd seen so far was the two of them eye-fucking each other across various distances. What he'd heard, from both Gabi and now Adam, didn't sway his opinion on Maddox in the least.

"I have a feeling about him."

Brennon scoffed. "That's called an erection."

Adam narrowed his eyes. "It's more than that."

"What makes you think he isn't angling for something else from you?" Brennon asked.

Adam shook his head, not getting the implication. "Like what?"

"Like your part. LA is just around the corner. An opportunity to go on in your place would get him much more exposure than dancing in the background."

Adam sighed heavily. "You've been listening to rumors. Do me a favor, especially if Gabi's the one filling your ear. Don't."

Brennon picked his silverware back up. "No one wants to be a swing forever."

"Why not? He gets paid more than I do."

"Not as much as they pay in Hollywood. Or for a principal part."

Adam cleared his plate from the counter. "You're so cynical."

"And you're distracted."

Adam, as though he knew he'd be getting nowhere convincing Brennon that his obsession with Maddox was anything other than a waste of time, changed the subject. "I told Peck I'd go to the wine and cheese thing tomorrow. I think most of us are going since we're here three weeks."

"I'll be there," Brennon assured him, provided they were able to track down Veronica. No way would he be guiding a standby along on his arm in front of the press and DC donors.

"Maybe you'll get a chance to talk to Mad more."

Brennon sighed. "Jesus."

Eden could barely swallow her food at dinner. She drank her water, wishing it were wine. Her mother called again, shooting her anxiety up another three notches, and Eden put her phone on Do Not Disturb. Maddox rose from the table, taking the water from her hand and removing it to the kitchen.

"You don't want to have to pee the whole time," he said.

"Thorne was treating me like I've never done this before," Eden reminded him.

"Who cares? You know you have. I know you have. We all know you've got this, so stop doubting yourself."

"I can't believe he brought up that commercial again."

"Agreed. That was low." Maddox ran some water over the growing pile of dishes in the sink.

It had been more than the mention of the commercial, though. Thorne and Shayna had both treated her like she didn't belong. That she was a poor substitute for the real thing. A chore.

She managed to choke down a single soft taco before heading to the shower, imagining the collective groan from the audience of press and VIPs when they learned Veronica West was out for the night. Sure, stuff like this happened all the time, but it meant she'd have to win them over. Make them forget they were missing something. Make them give her a chance, and all without making it look like she was trying too hard, which of course she would be because this job meant everything.

Proving she could hold her own opposite someone like Brennon Thorne would be a huge achievement.

Drying her hair, she drank her honey tea, heavy on the honey, to coat and soothe her throat, preparing it for the workout it would get onstage. She kept catching herself holding her breath and had to remind herself to breathe as she applied her contouring foundation. Since her call time was earlier than anyone else's, she requested a rideshare and waited in the living room with her makeup case in hand.

Maddox and Liliana came to the door to wish her well, giving her tight hugs and telling her to break a leg.

"It's gonna be a great show," Liliana assured her.

Eden gave them both a confident nod.

While Darcy had always been the draw, and Brennon Thorne was quite the get for a tour, Lizzie was onstage nearly the entire show, featuring in almost every scene. The majority of her costume changes would take place in the wings, but upon her arrival to Veronica's dressing room, all eight Regency frocks were hung on a rack, and two costume handlers were there to fit her.

Aside from the need to bind her more ample chest to squeeze into the garments, the fitting went as smoothly as it could have. She and Veronica were approximately the same height and width. Same shoe size even. But Eden still felt like she was playing dress-up.

The last time she'd performed onstage in Nashville hadn't been anything like this. It had been a Wednesday night during the second week of the run. There had been a pre-scheduled put-in rehearsal the day before, where she'd performed opposite Donovan and most of the principals, and she'd been ready to go. Confident. But tonight was a press opening. Critics would be there; reviews would be written. A fine tremble ran through her entire body, and she prayed her nerves wouldn't cause her to make mistakes—make a fool of herself.

"You look beautiful," Maddox said when he poked his head into the dressing room a few minutes before curtain.

In full makeup, Eden turned to give him her best version of a smile.

He grinned. "Try not to show Thorne up too much during your duets."

Already in costume and groomed as an 1800s-era gentleman, Maddox was dashing. Swings were nothing if not intelligent, confident, and calm under pressure. At a moment's notice, Mad could be asked to play the part of Wickham, Collins, or Bingley. He and the other three swings spent twice as many hours in rehearsals as any of the principal cast and knew the script better than anyone. Mad's good looks, combined with his immense versatility, had made him highly sought after in recent years, and on top of that, he was rapidly becoming one of Eden's favorite people.

"Bennet family—places, please!" One of the stagehands called from the hallway outside the dressing rooms. "Five minutes until curtain. Eden?"

She stood. After what happened that afternoon, with Veronica disappearing, it wasn't surprising they'd singled her out to make sure she was still there and ready to go.

"Love you, boo," Mad said and gave her a wink as he cleared the way for her to exit.

"Good show," she said to him.

"Good show."

Shayna spotted her in the hallway and personally escorted her to her mark onstage. "You'll be great, Eden."

After the rehearsal earlier, Eden hadn't expected a show of support so much as a warning about what would happen if she blew this. Shayna's kind words helped settle her down. "Thank you."

The audience's chatter fell to a hush as the house lights went down. Shayna left the stage, and the actors froze in their places for the opening tableau. Anticipation nearly caused Eden's lungs to burst. She closed her eyes, exhaled, and mouthed the words *You've got this.*

The curtain lifted.

Iris Klein, the charismatic older woman playing Mrs. Bennet, rushed in from offstage and exclaimed, "Netherfield Park is let at last!"

In the pit, the conductor lifted her baton, and the musical began.

The entire performance passed in a blur. Eden had no time to worry about whether she deserved to be there—there was too much work to be done. Singing, dancing, emoting, dressing, and undressing. She cursed herself for not doing enough to maintain her fitness on the regular. She should have eaten both tacos. She should *not* have let Mad steal her water from her.

She even turned into a bit of a diva backstage in the second act, demanding her honey tea and nearly biting her dresser's head off about it. But all was well when Bree had it ready before the next scene. Eden apologized as profusely as she could before she had to rush back into the spotlight.

The kissing part went off without a hitch or a single "contemporary" move from Eden, and the kiss itself blinked in and out of her mind like it had barely happened. Despite the limited VIP audience, the applause was simply too loud for her to even notice Brennon Thorne's warm lips, or the way he still smelled like fresh towels and mint after two and a half hours onstage.

The cast could always tell when a show was going well from the beginning, and it would almost always get better from there. With each scene the energy swelled as everyone fed off each other's performances. The audience played an essential role. Once they'd bought in, their support carried the cast on higher and higher clouds with each and every number. That night, by the end of the show, Eden was soaring.

At the standing ovation, she was breathless. Spent. Beaming.

If this was the last time she ever got to perform the role, she'd take her seat backstage for the rest of the run, happy and proud of what she'd been able to accomplish in a mere 150 minutes.

"Do I have some news for you," a voice said from her dressing room doorway after the curtain call. "Great show, by the way."

Eden's head snapped around to look over one bare shoulder.

This was a surprise.

Jonathan March, broad-chested and built, blocked the light from the backstage hall. Handsome in that frat boy way that had probably gotten him typecast as a Disney hero more than once, he gave her his winning grin as his eyes skimmed her half-bare upper body. "Should I come back in a few minutes?"

Eden shrugged the outer dress of her costume back onto her shoulders as she turned to face him. "It's okay. What's up?"

"Veronica went back to New York. No one knows when or if she'll be back."

At first, Eden's heart sank, worried for the star of their show. "What happened?"

Jonathan shook his head like the answer to the question didn't concern him at all. "Who knows with her? Did you hear what I said?"

Eden considered the words. The implications. "Do you think they'll recast her?"

"After tonight? Fat chance they'll want to hire someone else. You were fantastic."

"Oh." She smiled. "Thank you. I thought it went well."

"You thought it went well?" He entered the dressing room, mostly closing the door behind him. "Eden, you were brilliant."

Her cheeks heated. She wasn't sure whether it was due to the compliment or Jonathan's attention. Both were unexpected and overwhelming. "Thank you. Again," she stammered.

"We should grab a drink. How long will it take you to change?"

"Only a few—but I should get home. I'm exhausted."

"Fair enough. Listen—you'll have to be at the wine and cheese thing tomorrow now."

She supposed she would, if everything he said was true. After the public opening night, it was customary for some of the cast to attend an afterparty for the donors and other VIPs who supported the theater. The company manager would draft a few people to attend no matter what, but they were all invited to volunteer. Hey, free wine and cheese, right?

Maddox always went, so she and Liliana usually did, too. Lately though, Mad had been using it as another excuse to flirt with Adam, which left Eden trailing around behind Liliana while she received kudos on her performance as Lydia. "Is this official?" Eden asked.

Jonathan jerked his head in the direction of the door. "Peck's been out in the hall pacing for ten minutes. I assume that's what he's here to tell you."

Eden inwardly groaned. The news of her good fortune coming from Peck made it feel so much less glamorous.

But nothing had happened yet. Jonathan could be wrong. It wasn't like no one ever started rumors here.

She moved past Jonathan's Gastonian bulk and peeked into the hall.

Sure enough, Peck stood outside. He was shorter than Eden, but he had a way of puffing out his chest to try and make himself seem larger.

It didn't work.

"There you are," he said.

"Did you knock?" she asked.

"I spoke with Shayna and Judith."

Eden's eyes widened. Judith was the company manager. Good news or bad, this was real.

"We were happy with your performance tonight. With Veronica out indefinitely, we'll be having you take over her role for the time being. How about that?"

Well, when he put it that way. "Thank you," she gushed. Impulsively, she hugged the smaller man, and a little gasp came out of him. His hand moved down her back, getting perilously close to her ass.

Squirming away, she caught a glint of interest in his eyes she hadn't wanted to see.

"I hope Veronica's all right," Eden said.

Jonathan stepped in, slinging an arm around Eden's shoulder and moving her a step away from Peck. "V always lands on her feet. Great choice, Peck," he boomed. "We should leave Eden to get changed. I had a question for you about my paycheck anyway."

Peck's slimy gaze crept all over Eden, but he allowed Jonathan to usher him out of the dressing room.

Her dressing room. Her pulse leapt in her throat.

Holy shit.

She'd landed the lead.

CHAPTER FIVE

After finally getting a hold of Veronica, and having a very pointed conversation with Shayna, Brennon had come to terms with the fact that Eden would be his new leading lady.

Veronica assured him everything was fine—she only needed some time to "think about things." Knowing she was home safe in New York did little to make him less annoyed with the fact that she'd practically abandoned him in the middle of a tech rehearsal when he'd only decided to go through with the tour because of *her* eleventh-hour request.

Shayna assured him that if Eden didn't meet company standards, the New York directors would recast, but she urged him to give her a chance. "You looked good together yesterday."

Shayna was nothing if not a good judge of talent.

Turned out she was right. Eden performed even better on their public opening night, and Brennon found himself running out of reasons to be pissed. He got lost in the lyrics of her songs, hearing the words in a way he never had before. Her choices brought out a depth and a nuance he'd only witnessed a few times on a musical stage. She was brilliant, and she was beautiful, and he, like the character he played, found himself taken in by her, and despising himself for it.

Brennon knew better than most that a magical presence onstage spoke of nothing beyond it. People were talented or they weren't, but offstage, people were only people. Some good, some not. Jonathan, as he proved once again that night in all three of his duets with Brennon, was a highly capable performer, but he was a complete ass in real life, and nothing Brennon had seen so far from Eden told him she'd be any less disappointing on a personal level.

But performing with her was like meeting his match. A soulmate of a leading lady. It made him never want to do a show without her in it again. It astonished him that she hadn't truly been discovered yet. That no one had seen what she could do and snatched her up.

It was easy to let her shine, to stand aside and give her the spotlight she deserved. Her raw talent fascinated him. Granted, she hadn't been trained by the best as he had, and her résumé was a joke, but after a few more weeks working with him, she'd be capable of headlining on Broadway, winning awards, making herself a name. Maybe she'd send him a note of thanks one day for his support.

He should make an effort to get on speaking terms with her, he supposed. During Act Two, Brennon made a decision to stop by her dressing room after the show and give her his compliments. But first, they had to make it through another kiss.

As he drew her close in their final duet, anticipating the honey-eyed scent of her mouth, his wonder and appreciation of her evolved. Beyond admiration, her proximity stirred more specific sensations. As her lower back arched beneath his hand, and she looked up at him adoringly, her warm fingertips on his neck sent a shock down his spine and tingles across his scalp. Acutely aware of every place their bodies touched, he felt himself stiffen. Everywhere.

Suddenly flushed, his gaze fell to the thin line of cloth binding her breasts, barely visible above the bustline of her dress, because, yes— Veronica did have smaller tits, and of course they'd have to bind Eden's to make the costumes work. Eden's breasts were fuller and rounder— likely soft to the touch . . .

A stinging pinch on the nape of his neck was a harsh reminder for him to lift his wandering eyes and sing his next damn line. For half a startling second, he had to backtrack to remember how far into the song they were, and what came next, but the music and his training took over, and he choked it out somehow.

Eden's mouth lifted as they sang the final line to each other. For his pride's sake, he arranged his hips away from her as their lips touched.

The scent of honey filled what remained of the air between them, but tonight her lipstick was sticky with it. As he fought to catch his breath, her kiss pressed in slightly, like his inhale had created a vacuum. For a heartbeat, both their mouths fully connected. His tongue, which he always kept neatly tucked away during stage kisses, began to move.

The lights went down. Eden retreated, turning her back on him, and rushing off for her costume change.

There was a great deal of muscle memory involved in a kiss. Excuses could be made for not following the blocking to the letter. The mouth wants what the mouth wants.

At that moment, his mouth had wanted her mouth. All over him. All up on him. In close proximity to some part of him for as long as was reasonable.

Mercifully, he did not have to remove his trousers for his final costume change. No one had to see the evidence of what his wandering mind had conjured onstage.

After the show, it was easy to talk himself out of what he'd been thinking during the kiss. With appropriate distance and no orchestral accompaniment, it was only a matter of enough minutes passing to get back to the reality of their situation. Despite his unanticipated physical reaction to her, there were certain truths at play.

He was Brennon Thorne, Tony Award winner, Juilliard graduate. A Broadway name. She was a standby with a golden opportunity, her biggest claim to fame a Citaltfor commercial. Ridiculously talented, perhaps, but also equally ridiculous. If Brennon was expected to work with her for the foreseeable future, he had several questions for her. He needed to get his hands on a Playbill and examine her bio, but perhaps he could address some of his questions that evening at the donor party.

Where had she gone to school? What kind of formal training had she had? What did her theater résumé look like aside from the dozen commercials she'd done? Would she be able to graciously answer the question he knew she'd be asked repeatedly that night over wine and cheese?

"What's it like to work with Brennon Thorne?"

The grand chandeliers in the lobby made Eden's champagne glass sparkle like it had been dipped in glitter. The low hum of conversation from groups gathered nearby was not loud enough for Brennon's new costar to pretend she hadn't heard the well-meaning theater donor's question.

Brennon glanced from the older woman to his effervescent leading lady, eagerly awaiting the latest rendition of her pat answer.

Eden's smile faded slightly on this, only the third time of being asked, as they made their first circuit through the reception.

The brightness in her tone gave nothing away. "I'm really learning so much. He's a real dream to work with."

"You're too kind, Eden." Brennon gave his new costar a slight nod and turned his attention back to the couple who'd introduced themselves seconds ago to compliment their performances.

"Where did you train, dear?" the woman asked.

Brennon looked to Eden again, curiosity spiking. He'd been hoping someone else would be the first to ask so he wouldn't have to. Since they'd joined up to make their rounds, she'd been reluctant to speak to him without prompting. He'd missed her in her dressing room, and he still hadn't found a moment to tell her what a nice job she'd done tonight.

"Oh, here and there, you know, back home. My mom had a whole team of people working on me since I was in diapers."

The older couple seemed to think this was an adequate answer, and a charming one, too. They both chuckled fondly.

"If you'll excuse me, I'm being beckoned." Eden stepped out of their small circle and headed across the foyer. Brennon followed her retreat with his gaze, unable to help but notice the way her tight black dress hugged every luscious curve of her.

His bile rose as she approached Jonathan, the huge bear of a man he'd once called a friend.

If she knew what was good for her, she wouldn't be grinning up at the prick like that. But judging by her career, or lack thereof, it was obvious Eden had struggled in the past with making smart choices.

Not his problem. His mouth twisted grimly as he picked up a full glass of wine to replace his empty one.

Adam stood with Gabi near the exit, and Brennon wondered if it wasn't time for all of them to head home. He made his way over to them but was stopped too often by people wanting to meet him, ask him why he'd decided on a tour, whether he was thinking of making the leap to film, what his last project had been, what his plans for the future were.

He'd had weeks to consider the questions, and he purposely left his answers vague and open-ended. He spoke about the sights he was eager to visit in DC. His delight with this particular role. The break from New York.

Eden's sparkling laugh kept pulling his attention.

As he neared Adam and Gabi, Eden dissolved into giggles a hundred feet away. Brennon turned to look at her, nearly bent in half at something Jonathan, who still hovered over her, had said. The fool was red-faced and full of himself, all too proud of his own ability to charm her.

Brennon's blood simmered with hate.

"Having fun yet?" Gabi asked as Brennon finally reached them.

"Time to go?" he asked.

"Can't," Adam said. "I promised Mad I'd have some cheese with him, but he's been talking to those three little old ladies over there for fifteen minutes."

Frustrated, Brennon glared at his lovesick friend.

"Babe." Gabi rested a hand on Brennon's arm, and he fought the rude urge to pull away. Physical touch was not his love language—at least, according to his ex. After she'd forced him to read the eponymous book, he'd been inclined to agree. He didn't appreciate it as a rule, but especially not from someone pretending to know him better than she did. "It's only been twenty minutes. Peck would gut us all if we left now."

"I haven't even seen Peck," Brennon grumbled.

"That's because he's been sniffing after Eden," Gabi said. "Following her around like a lost puppy."

Brennon scanned the room, and sure enough, as Jonathan shifted his weight, a sliver of Peck appeared six feet behind him, eyeing Eden like she was a juicy ribeye.

Brennon scowled. "Has he been doing that the entire tour?"

"Not with Eden, but I think Veronica was considering a restraining order." Gabi laughed. "He must have a thing for leading ladies."

Adam laughed. "You should send him your playbook, Bren."

Brennon turned his unhappy expression on his friend. "Meaning what, exactly?"

Adam kept a straight face. "You have some experience seducing successful actresses. Maybe Peck could learn something from you."

Brennon's mouth twisted as he waved a hand around the room. "Who else am I supposed to meet? What would you have me do to widen my pool of options? Tinder?"

Adam was no longer listening. He straightened, his body in full alert mode. "I think I see my opening. Don't wait up."

"Adam—"

"I can't hear you, Brennon."

His friend hurried away, heading straight for Maddox, who, for the moment, stood alone. Adam was too quick to fill the void, and Brennon sighed.

"You're still worried about him?" Gabi asked.

"Yes. We all should be. Once you start screwing your way through the cast, it's a short walk to Brooklyn community theater from there. Reputation is everything."

"So, *you* would never . . ."

Brennon grunted, taking a long drink from his wine. "On a tour? Absolutely not."

"Ah, but on Broadway, it's okay?"

"Of course not. But this is worse. You all live together on the road, eat together, go to all the same events. There's almost no escape. Say, things go bad—"

"I'm not disagreeing with you, Brennon, but we have needs." Gabi lowered her voice. "All of us."

"Then I would suggest a kind stranger."

She narrowed her eyes. "Is that what you do?"

Never. Brennon was not loose with his affections, and his hand performed quite nicely when called upon. "I'm on a break from strangers and other unnecessary entanglements," he said.

"Hmm . . ." Gabi pursed her lips thoughtfully. "Seems you haven't really gotten into the spirit of things."

"Spirit of what things?"

"Life on the road. It's easy enough to separate the job from your free time. So long as everyone is on the same page, there's no reason we can't enjoy ourselves every now and then."

He glared down at her. "How often do you make arrangements like that?"

"Donovan and I had a rather lovely one, in fact."

"Ah."

She smiled mildly. "And I'm starting to miss him . . ."

"Let me stop you right there."

"Boo." She pouted, then batted her eyelashes up at him. "Will you noodle on it at least?"

"Yes, Gabi. I'll let you know if I have some sort of hookup emergency," he deadpanned.

"Ha!" She burst into a grin. "You're really something, you know?"

"I've been told I'm an absolute dream . . ."

She raised an eyebrow. "Have you also been told not to believe your own press?"

At that, he grinned. Another scan of the room revealed Eden stranded with Peck, but no sign of Adam or Maddox.

"They've disappeared," he mumbled.

"I'm not surprised," Gabi said.

Thoughts of Adam's career meltdown faded as Peck stepped ever closer to Eden.

Jonathan, to no one's surprise, had abandoned her, and now the little man was practically backing her into a corner. While pissing off the company manager's assistant wouldn't end anyone's career, it could make life on the tour uncomfortable. Peck could reassign her dressing room, "accidentally" short her on her paychecks, deny her vacation requests. Middle management required a delicate touch. "Maybe I should—"

"Brennon Thorne, there you are!" Another group of rich older women swooped in to praise his performance, and thoughts of rescuing Eden went immediately to the back burner, where frankly, they needed to stay.

"My hotel room has a view . . ." Peck paused dramatically. "Of the Potomac."

His breath smelled of cheese and wine. Not in a good way. He was standing much too close, and with every word he crept closer. Eden dreaded the moment his tiny erection would bump her thigh. "Oh."

"Beautiful at night—with the moon."

"I'm sure."

"I have some vouchers for a river cruise in my room, was planning to give them out to a few people, I don't know if you'd be interested . . .?"

She guzzled the last bit of her wine and gave him a tight grin. "Maybe?"

"Why don't we head back there, once this winds down. Take a look and see . . . what appeals to you."

Dear God.

"I'm actually super-exhausted," she feigned. "This role is so demanding."

"Enjoying it?"

"Oh, definitely." Eden found herself walking a very thin line between enthusiasm and *get-the-fuck-away-from-me*.

"The producers and directors offered to recast, you know."

Eden's stomach soured at the reference. Peck had no say in what the directors did—did he? "Whatever's best for the show," Eden said as he inched ever closer, his head leaning in slightly like he wanted to whisper something in her ear.

She coughed suddenly. "Sorry. Wrong pipe."

He maintained his modest distance. "I absolutely *love* you in the role." He said the word *love* in an exaggerated way, letting his tongue linger a moment too long against his top teeth. "I'd like to get to know more about you. We haven't really had a chance . . .'"

"Peck, are you hogging our leading lady?"

Jonathan stepped up next to Eden like a knight in shining armor, even going so far as to slide an arm around her waist. He cleared his throat. Normally she wouldn't have noticed the common noise, but after yesterday's tech rehearsal she felt the need to bond with someone over controversial vocal habits. "I found even more people who want to meet you, Eden."

"I guess that's what we're here for." She gave Peck a smile she hoped came off as sincere, and let Jonathan lead her away.

He was laughing, and she should, too, but fight or flight had kicked in, and she was dealing with the remnants of her adrenaline rush. "You've made an impression on the little Pecker, I see."

Okay, well, that made her laugh.

"Let's get another drink in you and schmooze some donors," he said.

"Sounds like a plan."

Two drinks later, Eden had done all the schmoozing she cared to do. Her cheeks ached from smiling, and her throat was scratchy from talking. She needed to rest her voice, drink some tea, and go to bed.

Maddox was nowhere to be found, and Liliana was teaching a group of women some ridiculous TikTok dance move. People were finally starting to filter out, though, and fewer and fewer of the cast remained. All the good cheese was gone, and Brennon Thorne had long since left the building.

While Jonathan was content to let a spunky old lady feel his bicep, Eden was ready to go. "I think I'll request a ride and head to the house."

"Up for a walk?"

"Sure!" She was glad to be asked. It was only a mile, and the night was mild and breezy. She enjoyed walking, but would never do it past midnight in a strange city alone, especially with Peck lurking. "I should let Liliana know."

Jonathan smiled amiably as she left to catch up with her housemate.

Liliana glanced over Eden's shoulder at him. "He offered to walk you home? Get it, girl."

"Oh—no . . ."

She rested a hand on Eden's bare arm. "He has a bit of a reputation, you know?"

"I'm aware. That's kinda the thing about reputations."

"I've heard it's a well-earned one, if you know what I'm saying . . ." She chuckled.

"Look." Eden angled in to murmur closer to Liliana's ear. "I'm not saying it's not gonna happen. I'm horny as shit. I haven't gotten laid since the last night we were in New York. But he's not really my type, and this job is harder than it looks. So, I don't know."

"No harm entertaining the thought." Liliana shrugged, and they stepped away from each other. "I'll collect Mad, and we'll head home in a few, so—keep that in mind."

"I'll do my best to keep my legs closed one more night."

"No one would blame you if you lost the battle."

Leaving the Kennedy Center with Jonathan at her side, Eden let out a satisfied sigh filled with both exhaustion and a heady sense of owning the night. "I can't believe I'm here."

"We're lucky to have you." Jonathan offered his arm as they approached the steps. Eden grabbed on and leaned in, letting her head rest on his enormous deltoid.

"If only you could carry me the rest of the way."

His responding laugh was warm. "What question did you get asked the most tonight? I bet it was the same as mine."

"You think? Was yours what's it like to kiss Brennon Thorne?"

"More or less."

"And what did you say?" she asked.

"Same thing everybody says—he's a dream to work with." From Jonathan's lips the words sounded particularly bitter.

Eden glanced up at him, surprised. Everyone else always expressed the sentiment with the utmost reverence and respect. Rapture, even. "Don't tell me you're not a member of his fan club? I thought I was the only one."

It was a few steps before Jonathan spoke again. Finally, he dragged in a ragged breath and said, "Brennon and I go back, actually."

"Juilliard?"

"Yeah. Juilliard," he replied with a harsh note of resentment.

Hmm . . . maybe there was more to this handsome brute than met the eye. "Was Juilliard not all it was cracked up to be? Tell me more. I've spent too long being jealous."

"Juilliard was fine. Constantly living in Brennon's shadow, however . . ." He scowled, giving his head a firm shake. "Now *I* sound jealous."

"Are you?"

"Sure. Look at his life. His parents are richer than the Rockefellers, he's tall, good-looking, great voice—he always gets the girl, and he *always* got the lead. From day one. Teachers loved him, directors love him, everybody loves him. Even . . . God . . . why am I talking about all this? Sorry." He cleared his throat. "Tell me more about you. Anything besides what it's like to kiss Brennon Thorne."

"Wait—no—hold up." This was a conversation worth pursuing. "Did something happen between you two?"

"It's not worth mentioning," he demurred.

"Oh, I disagree," she said.

"No, you have to work with him every day—"

"So do you."

"Don't remind me," he said.

As Darcy's longtime best friend Mr. Bingley, Jonathan had two duets with Thorne. It was the only two times Eden wasn't onstage. Her breaks.

"How's it been?" she asked.

"It's tough," he said. "I won't lie and say I was thrilled he joined us like everyone else was. I mean, it's good for the show, I realize that, I just—couldn't it have been *anyone* else?"

Something in his tone spoke of genuine hurt. Eden squeezed his massive arm. "You don't have to tell me what happened, but I'm a good listener. According to my roommates, anyway."

"I can't believe I'm still so pissed about it. It was such a long time ago. I'm over it. Really."

They slowed their pace, and he finally spilled.

"We used to be close, me and him, until there was this one role—at Juilliard."

"What role?" Eden asked, thrilled to be getting her tea a few minutes early.

"Hamlet."

"Whoa."

"Exactly. I wanted it so bad, I could taste it, you know?"

"Sure."

Jonathan blew out a shaky breath. "Anyway, I was dating this girl back then. I really cared for her—the big feelings, you know? But I *needed* to be Hamlet. I needed to prove to my parents and everyone that I hadn't ridden into Juilliard based on my looks and my scholarship."

Eden nodded. "I totally get it." She'd been trying to get away from her past for years.

"So maybe I wasn't paying enough attention to her. Maybe I put her on the back burner for a second, but in the end it was fucking worth it, because I got it. I got the role."

Ah, so Brennon hadn't always gotten the lead, apparently. "That's amazing. But what? Did something happen with the girl?"

Jonathan sighed, then cleared his throat again. "Well, everybody thought Brennon would be a shoo-in for Hamlet. He was rich. Perfect. A teacher's pet. But instead of being happy for me—instead of finally letting me have my damn moment—he slept with my girlfriend. She was lonely. She was having a hard time. She needed the attention, and he was more than happy to step into *that* role, to screw with me."

"Oh. My. God."

Jonathan waved his hand like he could brush the whole mess off. "It's in the past. A long time ago. She and I are still in touch, but it was hard on her. She ended up taking a break from school for a while because she was basically wearing a red A on her chest."

"How awful. For both of you."

"It was bad. But so that's it. That's the story. My big beef with Brennon Thorne. He's an opportunist and an asshole. No, you're not the only one to see it. You just saw it quicker than most. So, I'm impressed."

Eden had so many questions. "I don't get why she left, though. Was he horrible to her after the fact?"

Jonathan cleared his throat. Again. Eden was beginning to suspect he had a vocal tic. "Well, I mean, I couldn't go on with her at the time. I was too hurt. But she went to a pretty dark place when we broke up."

"Oh." Though Eden had been in one serious-ish relationship, she had yet to meet a man she could love enough to be hurt like that, but her roommates back in Manhattan were constantly getting their hearts broken by men who didn't return their feelings.

"And of course Brennon dropped both of us like we were the anchors holding him back, and maybe he was right, 'cause look at him now."

She nudged Jonathan with her elbow. "Hey, you haven't done so bad yourself."

"I'm still pretty fucking far from a penthouse on the Upper East Side."

"Give yourself a minute. Not everyone is an overnight success. Luck runs out anyway."

"I keep waiting for his to."

"Maybe he's unlucky in other ways." Eden did her best to be generous about it, but not one word out of Jonathan's mouth shocked her. Brennon Thorne's true colors had shone through only seconds after they'd met. And again the day after, with all the rehearsal notes he'd given her when it wasn't his place to direct her at all. The fact that he'd destroyed relationships and disregarded the struggle of others to get where he'd gotten came as no surprise from someone who'd been born into wealth and entitlement. She could hardly fault him for prioritizing his career, but betraying a friend like that . . .

"I'll steer clear," Eden said.

"I wasn't trying to talk shit," Jonathan said. "Sorry if it sounded like it."

"You can talk all the shit you want with me about Brennon Thorne."

"What'd he ever do to you?" Jonathan chuckled.

It was only a matter of time before everyone knew about the Citaltfor commercial, so she told Jonathan what happened at the party on their last night in Greenville.

Jonathan hummed in understanding. "Back when we were still friends, he beat me out for Cyrano. He could tell I was upset about it back in our room—and, wanna know what he said? 'Scholarship kids don't get leads at Juilliard.'"

Eden stopped walking. "Are you joking?"

He held up a hand like he was being sworn in for testimony. "Swear to god."

"Has he said anything to you since he's been here?" Eden asked.

"I don't speak to him offstage. Learned my lesson a long time ago."

Eden could barely catch her breath. This was all so much worse than just a spoiled star showing off all his tricks. "Thanks for sharing all that with me. If you ever need to vent, I'm your girl."

"Speaking of which . . ." He reached out with both hands and took hers. After giving his throat another good solid *ahem*, he said, "Maybe we could grab a drink one night this week, after we're all settled in?"

There, beneath a streetlight, with the Colonial townhouses behind him, Jonathan didn't look so much like the all-American captain of the football team anymore. He looked more like Thor after a rough day trying to save the world, and the appeal wasn't lost on Eden.

However, the cardinal rule of hooking up was not to get too personal. She feared she knew Jonathan a little *too* well now, and they still had months to go on the tour. "We'll see."

He slumped. "You're killing me. I told you all my secrets, and I walked all this way." He delivered the last line with a teasing smile.

Eden cast her gaze away and said softly, "Ask me again another time."

"Mm . . ."

His sexy, rumbling sound stirred something inside her, but she'd made it five months without a hookup, and now she had everything in the world to lose if it went wrong. Eden gave Jonathan's hands a final squeeze and said good night.

CHAPTER SIX

The greenroom at WRB-TV had two teal sofas and a glass coffee table topped with a spread of pastries. Brennon Thorne had a sweet tooth and a lifelong struggle with ignoring his baser urges. He considered the sugar-crusted, strawberry-filled croissant for a long moment, but ultimately opened his phone to distract himself.

One of the first ads he came across on Instagram was an equally attractive array of Danishes available for online ordering. According to the description, they arrived frozen and only needed twenty minutes in the oven. His stomach growled. He reached for the ice water.

The door whooshed open behind him. At the feminine sigh, he straightened and turned. The sight of Eden Blake disrupted every single one of his vital signs.

Her plump lips thinned with a grimace. "Peck didn't mention you'd be here."

"He failed to mention your attendance to me as well," Brennon informed her, not bothered by her unexpected arrival. On the contrary—she looked far better than the pastries. A short-sleeved sundress the color of a marigold paired with her dark hair and topped with those red lips made her look like a treat to taste and savor. Not for him, of course. He'd sworn off both sugar *and* actresses.

Her nose wrinkled in distaste. "Do you always talk like that?"

He closed his phone screen. "Like what?"

"Like a spoiled duke at the beginning of every single historical romance novel ever written."

He lifted a brow. "Is that what I sound like?"

She made her way across the room to the opposite couch and took a seat. "Most of the time."

"I'll just rest my voice, then."

"Fine by me." She took out her phone and started scrolling.

Occasionally her eyes lit with interest, but more often they narrowed. She appeared to be squinting at her screen. "Do you normally wear glasses?" Brennon finally asked.

She glanced up at him. "Pardon?"

"You seem like you're having a hard time seeing your phone."

"I have a headache."

"Maybe you should put it away, then," he suggested.

Glaring now, she snapped, "Maybe you should mind your own business and stop staring at me."

Heat filled his chest, creating a flush that would turn his neck red in a few seconds if he didn't get himself under control. "Touché."

She smirked and squinted back down at her screen. After a moment she seemed to heed his advice and turned it face down on her lap. "I've actually never done one of these."

"One of whats?"

"Press days."

"Ah. They're nothing. Quick Q&A and you're on to the next one." He gestured to the tray of pastries. "They usually feed you, too."

Her gaze drifted to the same strawberry croissant he'd been contemplating. "Did you have one?"

He patted what was left of his London potato belly. "Pants are just starting to fit right again."

Her brow lifted, and her lips pursed prettily. It was a *tell me more* look, but the two of them weren't friendly, so he opted to leave it at that.

Obnoxiously, she bent forward, the front of her dress falling victim to gravity and revealing a nude bra and the upper swells of her breasts. He tapped a finger against his stomach and bit the inside of his cheek as she picked up the strawberry croissant and brought it to her perfect lips.

She stared blatantly at him as she opened her mouth and stuffed a portion of the pastry inside. A large portion—a mouthful. She worked it past her lips while uttering a soft moan of pleasure at the taste.

Her dramatic demonstration proved irrationally erotic. Brennon knew what was coming and yet had no defense against it. His cock throbbed, and an erection took shape. "How is it?" he asked while she chewed.

Her eyes widened, and she nodded, giving him a thumbs up with her free hand. "You should try one. Live a little, Thorne." Spoken with a mouthful of food, the words came out garbled, far less sexy, but the ship had sailed.

"Just Brennon," he said.

She swallowed her bite. "Try one, Brennon."

The sound of her calling him by his name helped his problem not at all. He grew frustrated with himself and his body's absurd reaction to her. "I'd rather not. I wouldn't be able to stop wondering if there was something in my teeth on camera."

She scowled, chewing her next bite much more thoroughly.

He grinned, smug at the rise that got out of her. She set the unfinished croissant on a napkin and got out her phone to check her teeth with the selfie camera.

Unfortunately, he was then subjected to the sight of Eden Blake touching up her lipstick.

Forever.

It was an absolutely eternal process that generated within him a complete film reel of NSFW images and a full hard-on. Artfully draping an arm across his lap and lifting his ankle to rest on his knee, the fabric of his pants disguised the problem but did nothing to relieve the strain of it.

One of the producers poked his head in to let them know they'd be back for them in five minutes. "Could you point me in the direction of the ladies' room?" Eden asked the man.

"Right this way," he said. "You look lovely, by the way."

"Wow. Thank you. My leading man here didn't mention it, so I was stressing a little. I probably don't even really need to pee, I'm just nervous. It's my first time doing one of these."

"Allison is great," the producer told her while Brennon internally cursed himself for failing to compliment her again. Actresses, as a rule, were sensitive about their appearance. No wonder she'd been disappointed by his presence. He literally never had a kind word. But then again, neither did she.

The producer showed Eden to the bathroom across the hall. "It'll be just like chatting with a friend."

"Thank you so much. Everyone's been great so far." The greenroom door finally closed behind them, and Brennon adjusted his erection, which was deflating by the second.

Eden never came back. The next time he saw her was on the set, where she sat with perfect posture a chair apart from the hostess of the morning show. The chair closest to Allison Hardwell was for him. He took it, and Eden fluffed out her hair.

Wafts of sweet magnolia blossoms and lemon tickled his nose, hitting a specific pleasure center in his brain. He'd never smelled the combination before, but he was instantly enamored of it. Shortly, he and Eden were mic'd and the cameras were rolling.

"We're back with the two newest stars of the Broadway hit *Liz and Darcy: The Musical*, which just opened at the Eisenhower Theater on Wednesday. Eden Blake has recently taken over the role of Elizabeth Bennet, and Broadway's own favorite leading man Brennon Thorne just premiered for a two-month run as the notorious Mr. Darcy."

Allison shifted her attention from the camera to Eden and Brennon. "Eden—what's it been like, working with Brennon?"

Brennon tried to school his features into a bland but pleasant expression while cringing inwardly at the piece of shit question Eden had been asked a hundred times already. It had nothing to do with her role, or her talent, or her at all. "He's an absolute dream of a leading man. We're all so lucky to have him."

The false and forced way she said it—Brennon could hardly bear the sound. For the first time in his life, the words embarrassed him.

Their second interview was nearly identical to the first. In an effort to steer the conversation away from himself, he'd brought up Eden's commercial work, thinking it would give her something more to talk about than what a legend he was, but she'd only paled and shut her mouth. Her demeanor toward him had deteriorated from there.

Leaving the studio not with Eden, but within eyeshot of her, Brennon was inclined to mention he'd noticed that she hadn't been given much of a chance by either reporter, and not to take it too personally. But on the sidewalk ahead of him, Eden was busy with her phone. Whatever she was trying to do on it was delayed multiple times from its constant buzzing. She huffed with frustration and walked faster.

"Do you want to share a ride back to Georgetown?" he asked when he caught up to her. It was the right thing to do, though part of him dreaded a "yes" like he'd dread an asteroid headed straight for earth.

"No."

Thank god.

"How will you be getting back?" he asked.

She glared at her phone, punched the screen again. "I'm trying to request an Uber."

He assumed her phone wasn't cooperating. He'd have to renew his offer, despite his better judgment. "I have one on the way," he told her.

"Good for you."

Strike two. If she refused again, he'd strand her without another thought. "It would be better for the planet if we split it."

She looked up from her phone, flipping the hair out of her eyes, and giving him the full brunt of her brown-eyed glare. "I'm surprised you'd even want to be seen with me."

The accusation took him aback. "Pardon?"

"I'm clearly not operating at your level. I'd hate to drag your famous name down by association."

What?

"I'm sure I have no idea—"

"Save it, *Brennon*. I'll get my own ride."

Had she slapped him? It sure as hell felt like she had.

"Look—I realize we might have gotten off on the wrong foot—"

She declined another call, a frustrated growl rumbling in her throat.

"Who keeps calling you?"

"None of your business." She gave a dramatic stamp of her foot and turned sharply away.

Actresses . . .

Every woman he'd ever dated had been an actress, and he had a higher tolerance for their antics than most, but Eden needed to remember who she was dealing with. He was her coworker, not her whipping boy. He girded his loins.

"Let's get something straight—"

Her hateful over-the-shoulder glare made him lose his train of thought, and some of his composure along with it. "Ridiculous," he muttered, loud enough for her to hear. "Absolutely not worth it." He spun away from her and headed for the street. His car should arrive any second.

"I don't need your fucking approval!" she called out as she walked away.

Lucky for her, it wouldn't be forthcoming.

The lyrics in the first half of "Detestable Man" felt more meaningful to Eden that night. Tapping into her alto to really volley the musical phrases around, her voice made her own hair stand on end.

Sadly, the song switched in the middle when Darcy/Thorne strode onstage to interrupt her, and her character had to start regretting her vehemence.

Brennon definitely had a touch more wariness in his eyes as he crossed to meet her at center stage to present her with Darcy's letter.

The tempo of the song slowed as she pretended to read the fake scrawl on the page. The song continued, but Lizzie's tune changed, all second-guessing herself and shit.

Whatever. *Eden* was still pissed.

But it also felt like she'd gotten a power-up.

Unfortunately, so had Brennon.

Their songs sizzled, gazes lingered, and the atmosphere charged between them as they met at center stage for their final duet. The audience was already cheering and applauding before they'd even opened their mouths to sing a note.

He was on fire, passion burned in his eyes, and Eden felt wild and unleashed. When his upstage hand moved to rest on her waist as it was supposed to—*the way they did it on Broadway*—he clutched her hip instead.

She bit back her gasp of surprise and dug very deep to find the necessary tone of sweetness and humility to sing her next line as she went to rest a hand on his chest. Making a new choice, she took hold of his lapel and gave it a slight tug in her direction. See how he dealt with that.

Thorne didn't miss a beat. They were both *in this*.

When he bent to press his forehead to hers, a deep breath made her chest swell, causing her corseted breasts to graze his coat. Obeying the pressure of his hand against her lower back, her hips met his hips, which meant they'd skipped ahead. She didn't mind, provided he could handle a little improvisation.

Rather than lift her hand and place it all lady-like on his neck, she fingered his lapel, running her knuckles up and down the length of his torso as she angled her head to meet his mouth. They sang their final line. His arm wrapped around her waist to clutch her close.

Eden went completely off book. She slid her hand through his hair as his barely parted lips met hers. The audience roared with applause, the lights began to fade, and she sent her tongue out to lick him.

She meant it as a joke. Like a Wet Willie. She wanted to annoy him. Make him squirm. Throw the smug jerk off his game.

He didn't laugh, though. Nor did he squirm. In a move she never would have predicted, he pressed in, capitalizing on the openness of her mouth to steal a full two-second Frencher.

Not only that, but her own tongue met his stroke for stroke, because—*fuck*—he was so minty. And sweet. Was that strawberry? *Yes.* He felt good. Very, *very* good . . . so warm, her knees softened.

What the hell were they doing?

Both hands on his chest, she shoved him away. A rush of air from the theater instantly cooled her wet lips as she gaped at him in shock. Anything she said could get picked up by her mic, so the rant she wanted to unleash on him would have to wait. And she had a wedding dress to get into. Racing away, she met Bree backstage.

"What the hell was that?" Bree mumbled.

Shit, had she seen that? Who else had?

They couldn't have. The lights were down. Nobody backstage watched them anyway. "I shouldn't have changed so much, I know. I think we just felt the moment a little differently tonight."

"I'll say. I think I had an orgasm."

Overwrought, Eden laughed so hard she snorted, but by the time she had to hold hands and fake-marry the asshole one minute later, her sense of humor had left the building. A standing ovation slightly restored Eden's faith in the universe, but she planned to have a very strongly worded conversation with her leading man backstage.

Unfortunately, by the time she arrived at their side-by-side dressing rooms, Brennon Thorne was nowhere to be found.

"Eden!" She turned to see Jonathan approaching, his hair mussed and his cravat all undone. "Great show." His eyes did a sweep of her entire body. "How 'bout that drink?"

Still wound up from the unexpected nature of the onstage kiss, Eden said yes to the drink.

She would consider what to do with the rest of Jonathan's implied offer afterward.

Two drinks in, Eden was giggling like a school kid out with her crush. Jonathan had a million and one stories about auditioning and landing roles both big and small, both on and off Broadway. He'd been in everything from *Wicked* to *The Lion King*. He had, in fact, played Gaston in *Beauty and the Beast,* which pleased Eden to no end.

He claimed his dream role was Jean Valjean, but he wanted to play Hagrid just as much.

"Mine's Sally Bowles."

Jonathan leaned back in his chair and gave her a nod of approval. "Fishnets would look good on you."

That's what guys always said when she told them that. "It's about the music for me."

He clearly realized she wanted to keep things friendly and changed the subject. "How did your interviews go this morning?"

"Ugh." She drained what was left of her second drink. At first, she thought she'd handled the intimidating situation of being in public with Brennon Thorne well, but after two interviews where she'd been treated by both him and the journalists like a slight step above arm candy, she'd been less cautious with her words than she would have liked. And Thorne's gentlemanly veneer had fallen away in a hurry.

He'd called her ridiculous. Not worth it.

Though her temper had been partly to blame, his words had stung. Eden was sick of talking about him. Plus, giving him any space in her mind meant she would have to revisit what they'd done onstage that night.

A great performance was its own adrenaline rush, and both of them had been phenomenal. Maybe in all the madness he'd missed his mark slightly by clutching her hip, and she'd gone overboard from there. Of course, she could have gotten them both back on track by returning to the original choreography, but she hadn't. She'd wanted to tease him. Punish him. Insist he treat her as an equal.

But somehow, with that brief but overpowering kiss, he'd managed to wrestle the upper hand back. He'd kissed her as if to say, *Don't fuck with me.*

Which, of course, only made her want to fuck with him more, but she was going to have to think of a less sexy way to do it. His attention was confusing. That morning in the greenroom at the TV station, he'd barely taken his eyes off her, staring the way a man would if he were interested or attracted. But the way he spoke to her—*about* her—left her wondering if he only viewed her as a curiosity, something he couldn't quite make sense of.

The kiss, though? If he had meant it as payback, it probably shouldn't have turned her on so much. She still got sweaty thinking about it. But if she took him at his word from earlier, he'd be totally slumming it by getting involved with the likes of her—so, whatever drove those brooding stares, he probably hated himself for it as much as she did.

Though, she couldn't say she hadn't entertained her own thoughts about him since their first minty stage kiss. While Jonathan failed to spark her curiosity, she could not say the same thing about Brennon Thorne, despite everything she'd been told. Physically, he checked all the boxes Eden found irresistible in a man. Height, hair, handsomeness. Brennon Thorne nailed the trifecta, and while she wanted to ruin his life after that kiss tonight, she also wanted to rip open her bodice to get closer to him.

It was a real conundrum. One she'd have to think about late into the night and experiment with . . .

"Another round?" Jonathan asked.

"Mm . . ." Eden looked at her watch. It was only eleven. She had all day tomorrow to rest. "One more."

He went to the bar, and Eden checked her phone. Her mother had been relentless today after watching Eden's interviews. Eden had hoped a quick phone call with her that afternoon would be enough to tide her over until the weekend, but the woman had taken to wanting constant updates on Eden's performances, and despite Eden's pleas that voice rest was an important thing she should be doing, her mother insisted.

Eden refused to engage this evening. Next week, when her mother came to the show, she could decide for herself how Eden was performing the role. For tonight, Eden needed to decide what she was going to do about Jonathan.

The two dirty martinis she'd enjoyed lubricated some of her more complicated thoughts, letting them slide past each other more easily. She allowed herself to imagine what it would feel like to have a man's hands on her bare skin after five long months. Large hands, in fact. Great big paws of hands.

Sadly, the thought of Jonathan's hands didn't really do much for her.

The door of the bar swung open, and Eden turned her attention to the trio coming in.

Adam appeared first, in all his ginger glory, then Gabi. Brennon Thorne brought up the rear, pointing to a recently vacated booth near the door. Brennon sat next to Adam while Gabi spread out on the other side.

It wasn't a big shocker they were there. The cast tended to scope out one or two places in each town to hang out. For whatever reason, they liked running into each other offstage. Eden enjoyed it because it gave her a sense of home in whatever town they occupied, like they created their own little neighborhood wherever they went.

Running into Brennon Thorne, however, was the exception. She needed a break from him.

While she pretended not to pay any attention to their party, she happened to notice him noticing Jonathan coming back to the table with their fresh drinks. The men shared a long, hostile stare before Jonathan broke eye contact and set Eden's drink down in front of her. A final look at the booth revealed Brennon openly staring at her once again, but this time, the look on his face was unmasked disdain.

Her immediate urge was to lean across the table and plant a big, sloppy kiss on Jonathan's mouth in front of everyone, but the truth was she had no desire to kiss Jon. Maybe a switch would flip, and she'd suddenly become more into him, but tonight, with Brennon sucking all the air out of the room, her brain couldn't make the leap, not even for her poor, horny body's sake.

Jonathan's face was grim as he settled into his seat.

"After this one, maybe we call it a night?" she suggested.

"I can't keep letting him get to me like this. Let's enjoy our drinks and conversation. Pretend he doesn't exist."

Good plan. Unable to execute.

While Brennon, Gabi, and Adam were clearly engaged in a serious and animated discussion, Eden was keenly aware of Brennon watching her as closely as she watched him. His magnetism, which had probably served him well in his career, was both drawing Eden in and giving her a stomach ulcer.

She made up her mind to speak with him before she left. Air needed to be cleared, and boundaries needed to be put back into place.

After she finished her drink.

CHAPTER SEVEN

Adam had been a jerk since Brennon woke that morning. He'd called out for the performance, failed to do a single one of his chores at the house, and gotten into a shouting match with his agent on FaceTime. By the time Gabi and Brennon got home from the show, he'd calmed down and suggested drinks. At that point, his eyes were swollen like he'd had a good, long cry.

Gabi was finally the one who got him to talk. She reached across the table, took hold of his hand, and gave him as sincere of a look as Brennon figured she was capable. "Did something happen with Maddox?"

Adam's jaw tensed, and his hand curled into a fist. Brennon braced himself for his friend's rage, but instead, Adam sniffed, wiping his nose on his sleeve. He responded in a thick voice. "Yes, and I'd rather not talk about it."

It didn't take a relationship expert to understand that Adam hadn't followed Brennon's advice about steering clear of romantic entanglements while performing in a show together. Brennon had met a hundred Maddox Howells since he'd left Rhode Island to attend Juilliard. To get ahead, some people would stop at nothing, damn the consequences. Brennon was no stranger to their strong come-ons.

The night he'd met Maddox in Greenville, it had taken Brennon exactly two seconds to size him up. The way he'd practically undressed Adam with his eyes right in front of everyone. It had been blatant and in poor taste. It added up, after all. Maddox was only recently out as bi, so he was clearly in an experimental phase, not at all ready for the type of relationship Adam desperately craved. And after what Gabi had shared with him at the airport, about Maddox hooking up with a former cast member to get a few performances as Wickham, Brennon knew all he needed to know. Maddox was not a man anyone should consider taking home to their mother, especially his soft-hearted friend, who had a history of trusting the wrong people far too easily.

As Adam's closest friend, Brennon considered it his duty to ensure this "relationship" didn't continue. It would help to know how far things had gone, but he didn't want to pry. Especially not within earshot of Gabi.

"Would you excuse us a moment?" he asked her pointedly.

Gabi pointed at her chest in shock. "Me?"

Adam glanced up at her with watering eyes. "Please, Gabi."

"Fine," she huffed. "I'll just be at the bar, I guess."

In a cloud of perfume and indignance, Gabi swept her clutch off the table and left them alone.

"What happened?" Brennon asked, straight to the point.

Adam couldn't seem to bring himself to make eye contact. "We hooked up. At the wine and cheese thing."

"And . . .?"

"You were right."

Obviously. "He was only interested in sex?" Brennon asked to confirm.

"Apparently."

Brennon's nostrils flared with the next breath he took. "And how far did it go?"

"He sucked my cock, Brennon. Is that what you want to hear?"

Brennon winced. No. He had not wanted to hear that. Blow job would have sufficed. "Did you return the, uh . . ."

Adam blew out a breath of total exasperation. "Oh, for God's sake. No. I gave him a fucking compliment, and apparently that was too much for him, and he bolted. I haven't heard from him since. It was humiliating."

Brennon put a hand on his friend's shoulder and squeezed. "I'm sorry."

"Yeah?" Adam sighed. "Me, too."

"Maybe you should take a break," Brennon suggested.

Adam looked up. "From Mad?"

Brennon leveled a cold stare at his friend. "From the show. Go home, see your friends, walk on the beach for a day . . . audition for something better than this." Brennon gestured at the bar.

"You want me to leave the show?" Adam asked with heartbroken eyes and a cracking voice.

"I want you to take some vacation days. Think about what *you* need. What did your agent want, anyway?"

"Gavin Knight's leaving *Liz and Darcy* at the end of the summer."

Brennon's head jerked slightly in surprise. Gavin played Bingley on Broadway. It was a role Adam could grab for himself in a heartbeat. He'd be better at it than Jonathan Fucking March any day, but as Jonathan played the role here on tour, the directors would be looking at him for it—unless Adam got to them first. "They're auditioning?" Brennon asked, careful to keep his tone measured.

Adam sucked on his cheeks and nodded down at his drink.

"When?"

"Soon."

Brennon lowered his voice and got serious. "Adam."

Their eyes met.

Adam hadn't been focused for weeks, mooning and going on about a man who couldn't care less about him, nor see how exposed Adam's heart was, how easily he could be hurt with a single word. He was still in therapy from his last break-up with a man who'd been a gaslighting cheater, and Brennon would not abide the mistreatment of his best friend, not if he could cut it off at the pass.

Brennon's own relationship history had taught him more than he'd ever wanted to know about all the lies people tell themselves to excuse another person's lack of interest. He should have seen it coming with Chloe, the way all their other friends had. He'd ignored his instincts, wanted so much for her to be the one who gave him a fighting chance.

He should have known she'd given up. That she'd reached the same conclusion all his other lovers came to about him: that he was too ambitious. A waste of time, energy, and love. That he would never have the capacity to be everything for anyone. Slivering himself into pieces for different roles for so many years and pouring his heart into his work left nothing to give a lover, but it was still there—still beating in his chest begging someone to help stitch it back together again. But Chloe had always been a woman who had little control over her own impulses. And now Adam had found Chloe's equivalent in Maddox. His friend needed to get his priorities straight. Focus. And forget.

Adam rested his head on Brennon's shoulder. Brennon wrapped an arm around him, giving him another squeeze. "I am thinking about it. I just thought . . ." He had to pause to gather his composure. "I thought there was more to me and Mad."

Without either of them having noticed, Gabi had stealthily slid back into the booth, having likely caught the tail end of their conversation. "I don't know if this will make it better or worse," she said, "but I kind of made a pass at him when we were in Nashville."

Adam startled, lifting his head to stare at her in shock. "You what? You knew I was interested . . ."

She shrugged off the accusation. "I was drunk, and nothing happened, calm down. He turned me down flat. Said all he was interested in seeing on the tour was dick. *All the dick*, was I think how he put it."

Adam froze. Brennon took back his arm of support as they let Gabi's words sink in.

But Adam didn't keep quiet long. "That's not what it seemed like."

"How did it seem?" Brennon dared to ask.

"Like he wanted *my* dick. Very specifically."

Brennon sighed. This was taking a turn.

"Maybe he wasn't as into it as he thought he would be?" Gabi ventured.

Adam's jaw locked as he stared across the table at the sharp-eyed blonde. "Pretty sure that's not how it works, Gab."

Something she said must have struck home, though, because Adam's hands shook. He glanced at Brennon. "Maybe we should take this to the bar."

"Aw, come on," Gabi complained at being excluded a second time.

But Brennon whole-heartedly approved of this idea. He stood and waited for Adam to slide out of the booth before they set off across the room. As they passed Eden and Jonathan's table, he glanced down at her. Her red lips practically screamed for his attention.

She laughed, clearly and loudly, almost pointedly at something Jonathan had said.

Brennon fought a powerful urge to pull up his own chair and explain a few things about the man sitting across from her, but he had bigger problems. Eden would have to fend for herself. Jonathan's true colors never managed to stay hidden long. He did have a few choice words for her friend Maddox though, if he dared show his face tonight.

Seats were hard to come by at the crowded bar, so Brennon and Adam stood a few feet away to see if anyone cleared out. "You need to be smart now, Adam."

Adam glared at Brennon, at the unspoken implication that he'd been an idiot. But he did take the point. "I have some vacation time. I'll take a few days. Call my agent. Set something up."

Brennon had no desire to be stuck on the road without either one of the friends he'd come to spend time with, but this version of Adam wasn't what he'd been looking for either. If some time at home could get his friend's head on straight, Brennon was willing to make the sacrifice. "Take two weeks."

"You don't think he was ever interested in me, do you?" Adam asked him.

"Interested in playing your role? Maybe," Brennon answered truthfully. "If he thought you weren't going to offer him a few days here or in LA, especially after he got down on his knees, he probably lost interest." Showmances were predictable and doomed as a rule.

"I would have let him if he'd asked . . ." Adam's eyes lost focus as his gaze drifted past Brennon.

"Then you do need a break. Trading favors with a swing isn't in anyone's best interest."

Adam gaped a moment, but then his mouth turned down in resignation. "Excuse me. I need a minute." He left for the men's room, and Brennon inched closer to the bar, still shaking his head at this unfortunate turn of events.

"Pardon me, sir. A word?"

Brennon turned to find Eden standing beside him. His entire body clenched in one long, painful cramp. His gaze went straight for her mouth—no lipstick. What had happened to the lipstick? He glanced at Jonathan to see if his face held any traces, but Jon's head was turned away.

Brennon's blood simmered beneath his skin, heat building. He didn't trust himself to speak, so he answered her with an expectant raise of his eyebrows.

"That was totally inappropriate," she said.

He stared at the route to the restroom Adam had just taken, wondering how she'd caught on to any of what they'd been discussing. "It's none of your business," he said, to use one of her phrases from their disastrous morning at the TV stations.

"When you go off book and shove your tongue down my throat, I believe that is my business."

His heart rate spiked. This wasn't about Maddox then. "You licked me."

"You grabbed my hip! The lick was just a joke—"

"That was as good as a fucking permission slip," he said.

Her jaw dropped.

"And since when have you and I joked?" he added. "Ever?"

"Oh, I can remember a few hearty laughs you've had at my expense."

His mouth twisted at the reminder. "You're saying you felt violated?"

Her mouth opened to respond, but she snapped it closed, a tiny frown forming two creases between the drowning pools of her eyes. "I don't like to be surprised onstage."

He growled his response. "Neither do I."

She hollowed her cheeks like she was chewing on them in thought, her eyes still narrowed and fixed on his. "So, we both screwed up. We agree to agree."

"Agree to what?" He was seething, tense. Any moment he would detonate like a grenade. Her proximity did the most outrageous things to his body chemistry.

"To stick to the script," she said.

"Of course," he snapped. "I'm a professional."

Her head whipped back. "Are you saying I'm not?"

"Tonight, I was forced to wonder."

She made a noise of pure frustration, then softened her tone. "Look, you're right. What I did was stupid."

Brennon gave a long, slow blink, attempting to hide his shock. "Is that an apology?"

She responded with a contrite, if not curt, nod.

"Well, then," he said, unsure how to handle her like this, but relieved they'd found an accord.

Her narrow glare, however, hadn't budged. Somehow, she was still unhappy with him. Her head twitched like she was waiting for him to go on.

Brennon found himself squinting at her, as though taking a closer look could help him figure out what the hell she wanted now.

Then it clicked. The calmness of certainty relaxed his tense shoulders. He couldn't remember any woman in his past or present demanding exactly what she needed from him on the spot. There was a part of him that deeply appreciated it. "I apologize for letting it get to me." More like he'd lost control when her tongue had entered his mouth, but there was no way he could admit to that. "It won't happen again."

"Fine, then."

"Good," he said.

She gave him the briefest of all smiles. "I'll see you tomorrow night."

"Enjoy your evening," he said without meaning it at all.

She glanced back at him like she'd heard the lie and smirked, which somehow hit harder with no lipstick on her mouth.

After finally purchasing another round of drinks for his table and opening a tab, Brennon made his way back to the booth where Adam had returned, ready to change the subject. The conversations that followed dragged on for hours as they managed to run up his bill and close down the bar. Liquor flowed, hangovers loomed. Brennon would have left long ago, but he stayed to keep an eye on Jonathan—make sure he didn't try anything with Eden. Not that she was any of his business, but Jonathan had a reputation for disrupting company dynamics with the way he toyed with actresses. It wouldn't surprise Brennon at all if Veronica's absence had something to do with him. The man had been stringing her along since Juilliard . . .

One extra drink tipped the balance between drunk and hammered. The room wobbled in Brennon's vision, and chunks of the night blurred together.

More drinks appeared on the table. More people joined them. Other actors from the tour. Strangers. *"Shots!"*

Gabi laughed . . . Someone stroked Brennon's arm . . .

"Do you mind? No touching . . ." He'd lost track of who was where.

"You still awake, Thorne? Are we boring you?"

He switched to water. Cool and not wet enough for his dry mouth.

Jonathan cleared his throat nearby. Nails on a chalkboard. The man was probably riddled with polyps.

Where was Eden? Where was her lipstick?

Images of the people surrounding him swam in his vision. A loud laugh from the group filled his ears.

Fuuuuck . . .

Reality wavered.

He needed to get home. He gave his head a firm shake and drained the last of his water.

"Where'd your little friend go, Jon?"

Gabi had asked the question. Brennon struggled to pay attention to Jonathan's answer. He didn't catch it. There was too much noise. But apparently he felt he had something to add. He heard himself speak, though it was like hearing it from across the room, "Steer clear of Eden, March. She doesn't need the distraction."

"Everybody needs a distraction. Eleven months is a long time." The asshole chuckled.

Gabi's laugh cackled. She eyed them both with interest, as she brushed her thumb across the screen of her phone.

Someone gave the back of Brennon's neck a squeeze. Brennon turned a glare on the offender, but it was only Adam. "Let it go," his friend said.

"Or were you looking to score with another leading lady?" Jonathan scoffed.

"Please," Brennon said. The comparison insulted him on every possible level. "She's not a leading lady yet."

Gabi stared at her phone with a growing smirk. "This is getting interesting. Who would she choose, I wonder?"

"Three nights in LA says it'd be me, Thorne."

"She's spending three nights with you in LA?" Brennon arched a brow, an earnest, if not futile effort to disguise his growing irritation.

Gabi leaned in. "I think what your old friend is saying here is that if he bags Eden first, you'll step aside as Darcy for three nights in LA."

Rage flickered in Brennon's core, but the alcohol quickly doused it. "Animal," he mumbled.

"What was that, Thorne? Do we have a bet?"

"You're disgusting."

"Let's go, Bren," Adam mumbled beside him. "He's always brought out the worst in you."

Adam wasn't wrong. Brennon stood, knocking his knees against the table. Drinks wobbled, beer splashed. Jon grinned stupidly as he held out his hand to seal the deal.

Brennon knocked it away. "If she'll have you, take her."

"Don't think you've got a chance against me?" Jonathan taunted.

"If I wanted Eden," Brennon drawled, the alcohol revving his temper, "I'd shine a spotlight on my bed, and she'd come running."

A sharp thwack on the back of his head snapped Brennon's mouth shut. "Let's. Go," Adam growled. "Now. Before you make an even bigger ass of yourself."

Adam took hold of Brennon by the arm and shoved him away from the booth. "God help you if you remember any of this tomorrow," he muttered.

"What?" Brennon asked, struggling to remember it already.

"You've got yourself a bet, then, Thorne," Jonathan called after them.

Brennon shouted back, "Take your best shot, you son of a bitch."

Brennon woke up with the worst hangover of his lifetime.

Gabi lay sprawled in bed next to him wearing only a bra and panties. She looked a little worse for wear with a streak of mascara on her cheek, and eyeliner darkening her under-eyes.

Wait.

He checked himself. Still zipped and dressed except for his shoes. He hated to think he'd been that far gone last night. Crisis averted.

He sat slowly. The base of his skull dragged and throbbed, like an anvil was attached to it.

They were in Adam's room.

Where was Adam?

He felt his pocket for his phone. With three percent of its battery left he was able to determine he hadn't missed any calls or texts, but he sent Adam a message anyway. "Checking in. You okay?"

"Babe . . ." Gabi whined as he moved to stand. "Snuggle with me."

He avoided her outstretched arm. "Go back to sleep, Gabi."

They both reeked of alcohol. A few of the later moments of their evening trickled in as blurry memories. Adam packing. Gabi's cackling laugh. Jonathan's compulsive throat-clearing. Eden . . . she hadn't been at the table with them. Surely, he would have remembered. So, she'd left then? Before closing time? Brennon rubbed his face with both hands, trying to jog a more coherent timeline loose. He rarely drank himself into a blackout, but he couldn't remember anything after people started buying rounds of shots. He should have learned his lesson during his *Phantom* run when, during a very drunken all-nighter, he'd agreed to provide sperm for two of his friends to make a baby with. Another friend who'd witnessed the conversation had mentioned it to him later. He'd felt horrible about taking the offer back. Fortunately, the couple had understood.

An unnamable tension brewed in him as he attempted again to put the pieces of last night together.

His phone buzzed in his pocket as he headed to his own room. Adam returning his text.

Took your advice. Rented a car and I'm at the beach. Already talked to Peck. Have a call with my agent this afternoon. Take some aspirin and thx for being my friend.

Brennon started to text back to ask which beach, and if there was anything he needed to know about last night, but his phone died. This sucked. He plugged the phone into his charger and took off his clothes, tucking himself into his own bed. Not only was he alone on a tour he should have backed out of when Chloe had, he'd failed to protect either of his friends from themselves. What good was he if he couldn't even manage that?

He'd been too distracted.

Working with Eden was getting to him, but he had a reputation to uphold. He needed to follow his own advice: keep his head down and focus on his performance. With Adam and Veronica gone, there wasn't any other fucking thing to do. Except wonder if Eden wound up in Jonathan's bed last night.

Groaning, Brennon curled onto his side, and something clicked. *I'd shine a spotlight on my bed, and she'd come running.*

You've got yourself a bet, then, Thorne.

Liquor shots and testosterone were a terrible combination. Brennon covered his face with his hands.

This was bad.

Unnecessary drama. Hurtful if it got out. Toxic to an ensemble. He should never drink in public. Adam was right—Jonathan always brought out the worst in him.

He needed to set things right with Eden before Jonathan had a chance to put his own twisted spin on what happened last night. Jon wouldn't hesitate to use his words against him if he thought it would win him favor with Eden. Brennon's only hope was to get to her first, explain, and apologize.

He might be done dating actresses, but he still had to work with them.

CHAPTER EIGHT

Eden washed two ibuprofen down with some water and refilled the glass from the tap.

"What time did you get home last night?"

She startled at Maddox's voice and whirled to face him. He was fresh-faced and well-rested, but his tight-mouthed expression was either grim or annoyed. She couldn't tell which. "Late. I went to a bar with Jonathan after the show."

"Oh?" He picked up the empty coffee pot and brought it over to the sink. "And how was that?"

Eden remained unimpressed. Jon was nice enough, but the chemistry failed to ignite. Maybe she was too used to dating musicians, guys in bands her mother would never approve of. The fact that Jonathan matched every criteria on her mother's ideal mate checklist was a turnoff. "What you see is what you get with him," she said. "Good body, good for a couple laughs, otherwise . . . meh."

"Did you see Shayna's email?" Maddox asked, likely as bored by the topic of Jonathan as Eden was.

"What'd it say?"

"I'm playing Mr. Collins tonight. Again."

Eden squinted up at him. "What's wrong with Adam? He hardly ever misses shows."

Mad shrugged as he shoveled grounds into a coffee filter.

"You think he's sick?" she asked.

"Eden if he were sick, I'd be sick."

"Oh." She considered alternative ailments. "What if it's food poisoning?" She noticed then, the dark circles beneath Mad's eyes. "You think it's something else?"

He pushed the button to brew. Leaning against the counter, he folded his arms over his chest and averted his eyes.

"Something happen at the wine and cheese thing?"

"We . . ." He took a second and swallowed hard. The words came out like he could barely stand to put voice to them. "Hooked up."

Eden's adrenaline spiked. But this should be great! Why did he look so pitiful? "And . . .?"

"Ends up he's not at where I'm at. It's fine. My mistake."

He did not sound fine.

Eden remained optimistic. "He's been after you for weeks! Surely it wasn't as hopeless as you're making it sound."

"I think you and I both read too much into that."

"You're saying he was only interested in *one* hookup?" she asked.

Maddox nodded.

There was just no way. They'd been acting like they wanted to have each other's babies for over a month now. "Are you sure?"

"I mean, I was there. He barely let me get five words out—he put his cock in my mouth, then after I blew his mind, he *laughed*. Maddox rubbed at his brows, eyes closed, then sighed heavily. "And he said something like 'Wow, swings really can do anything.'"

Eden's jaw dropped. "What?"

"Those exact words."

"But the blow job . . .?"

Maddox rubbed his face before hanging his head. "Technically, I started that."

93

"So the five words you got out were . . .?" Not that she couldn't guess.

He squeezed his eyes shut and said in a small voice, "Please let me suck you."

Eden bit back her totally inappropriate grin. "I see. And then what?"

"After he . . . finished, he said what he said, and I left. He got what he came for, I guess."

"Oh, Mad." She put her hand on her chest, like her own heart was the broken one. "I'm sorry."

His jaw twitched. "It's fine. I just assumed it'd be different with him."

"Me too. He's always been so sweet to you."

If anything, her words only seemed to rip his guts out more. "I mean, it's possible he was only teasing . . . The more I thought about it, I figured . . . Maybe I overreacted . . ." His thought trailed off, and then he gave his head a firm shake. "But now he's gone, without a word. So, either way, it obviously didn't mean anything."

She rushed toward her friend and wrapped him in the tightest hug she could manage.

Not all show friendships lasted, and even fewer of the romances did, but she had a feeling she and Mad would be doing this life together for the long haul. She wanted him to find the person who made him happy, kept him centered, and broke through his stoic shell. If she'd been able to find his warm and gooey center, she was sure he'd find another person who would, too.

Maddox got the official phone call from Shayna early that afternoon informing him he'd be filling in as Mr. Collins for the next two weeks. Another swing would arrive from New York the following morning to begin rehearsing Maddox's place in the ensemble.

The first company outing in Washington DC was at the United States Botanic Garden on their first golden day of the sit-down. It was their second Monday in town, and no one had anywhere to be or anything to do. The show had adjusted to Adam's sudden absence. The new swing was unbelievably adaptable and talented, and despite all the recent upheaval, they'd closed out the week so strong that Judith, their company manager, had granted them a full day off. No put-in rehearsals, no understudy rehearsals, no tech—nothing. Peck took credit of course.

Most of the cast usually participated in these scheduled field trips—but since this was a golden day, a number of people had taken the chance to meet up with friends in town or get back to the city, maybe catch a few meals with their families. Some were resolute loners who wanted to take the day to rest or sightsee on their own terms. Today, it was the usual suspects. Eden counted nine other actors at the entrance to the garden and was surprised to see the great Brennon Thorne out and about among the flowers and exotic plants. He didn't seem like the type to mingle with commoners.

He acknowledged her and her housemates' arrival with a nod, but since he was wearing sunglasses, it was impossible to say whether he was nodding at *her*. She nodded back, just in case. No harm, no foul.

David made sure everyone had a brochure, a map, and sunscreen. Eden wore a wide-brimmed hat, but she took a few drops from him to protect her shoulders. Maddox brooded beside her, but Liliana was living large off the two mimosas she'd had with brunch, chatting delightedly with other cast members.

Jonathan strolled up with Shayna and gave Eden's hand a squeeze in greeting. "You look very nice today."

She raised a freckled shoulder coquettishly and grinned.

"Oh! There you are! I found you!" The voice was shrill. Loud. Bone-gratingly familiar. "Thank goodness. I thought I'd be late. The cab driver absolutely would not listen to my directions!"

Every hair on Eden's body stood at attention as she turned to see her mother charging toward the group of them, arms waving like she was trying to flag down a helicopter.

"Eden!" she squealed. "My baby girl. Surprise!"

"Mom!" *What the fuck?* "Hi! Oh my god!"

Oh my god.

While her mom pulled her into a bear hug, Eden shared a horrified stare with Liliana, the first person she made eye contact with.

Her mother drew away, a few frosted strands of hair coming loose from her ponytail. Her run must have been intense, because beads of sweat were gathering on her upper lip. "Introduce me!" she stage-whispered.

Eden had a pretty solid shield up most of the time, a thick skin that had saved her from the sting of multiple rejections over the years. But with her mother standing there, in the company of her biggest accomplishment, Eden felt like she was wearing nothing but fig leaves that were two sizes too small—utterly exposed for who she really was. Coughing through her suddenly clogged throat, she struggled to put names with faces. A flush heated her cheeks and chest.

Maddox moved in protectively beside her, but the rest of the cast also began their approach. *Just get it out of the way, Eden. Maybe she has other plans. Maybe she'll go away . . .*

Still uncertain of her voice, she made an introductory gesture and forced some words out. "Let's start with Maddox and Liliana, I've mentioned them."

"Of course. Maddox. Eden said you'd moved up to play Mr. Collins, yes? Huh. I don't see it, you're almost embarrassingly handsome, aren't you?" She gave Eden an over-the-top wink. Shaking his hand, she said, "I'm Terry. I'm Eden's mom."

No shit.

After greeting Liliana, her mother took over her own introduction process. Having acted as Eden's career manager for her entire life, her mom was no stranger to schmoozing. But impressing car dealership owners in Indianapolis was a little different than charming Broadway up-and-comers—much less the elite.

"Ah, the man himself. Mr. Thorne, I'm Terry Blake. So wonderful to make your acquaintance."

Eden gave Brennon Thorne a hostile stare as he lifted his hand to greet her mother. He'd better be nice.

"Lovely to meet you," he said. "It's just Brennon."

"*Just* Brennon. Ha. Well, *Brennon*, tell me—what's it been like working with my daughter? Quite the little star, isn't she?"

Gabi nearly lost it. She attempted to cover her bursting laugh as a cough, but Eden sent a truly murderous glare her way, before returning her attention to Brennon. God only knew what he was about to say.

"She's an absolute dream of a leading lady," he said with a deferential nod Eden's way.

Asshole.

"Anyway, Mom, we were about to head into the garden, soooo . . ."

"Not to worry." Terry whipped out a folded sheet of paper from her Louis Vuitton Neverfull. "I printed out my map of the gardens, and I know exactly where the best views are."

Maddox gave his hands a little clap. "Wonderful." He presented an arm for her. "Shall we, Terry?"

"Oh! With pleasure." They walked ahead through the gate with Liliana, and Eden turned to see if Jonathan was anywhere nearby to offer her cover.

Instead, Brennon stepped up to walk beside her. "Fun twist," he said with zero smirk or any expression whatsoever.

She held in a groan. "Shut up."

"You know, I've been waiting more than a week to get asked that."

Eden shot him a suspicious glance. "Get asked what?"

"What it's been like to work with you. But you get all the good questions."

So smug. "Clever answer. Where've I heard that one before?"

"It wasn't a lie."

"Gosh, thanks, I'm flattered." She shoved her hands into the pockets of her Kelly green sundress and tried to walk more quickly. His legs were long, though; he had no trouble keeping up.

"It's true. You have good timing, a great voice—"

"I thought my voice was just nice."

"A *great* voice, a lot of spunk, and a real sense of adventure. I never know what I'm in for when I come out onstage with you."

"That doesn't seem like a good thing." She was shrinking by the second. Predictability was important in a show—trusting your costars not to go rogue.

He gave her shoulder a casual nudge with his upper arm. Or maybe he accidentally drifted too close as they continued to stroll side by side. "There *is* a sense of riding a little close to the edge of a cliff about your performances."

She stopped walking and turned to look at him. "Seriously?"

He shrugged. "I enjoy it."

"You're old, though."

His brow furrowed. "Pardon?"

"What if I was onstage with someone who has their shit less together? Do you think I'm a problem?"

"Old?" he asked.

"You know what I mean."

The corner of his mouth twitched in amusement. She wished she could see his eyes. He was hard enough to read on a normal day, and she was sort of desperate for any advantage on this humiliating morning.

"You said *old*."

"I meant *experienced*," she tried to explain, growing more paranoid by the second.

He grinned, clearly enjoying her suffering. "But the word you used was—"

"Old. Okay. God. I know what I said."

A full smile broke out on his face, and Eden's mind went completely blank. *Wow.* The gleaming white teeth, pink lips, dark stubble combo did something to her insides Eden wasn't sure she approved of at this early hour.

"All I was trying to say is I've enjoyed working with you," he said.

Had someone put him up to this? Why was he being so nice? "That's not what if feels like."

"You'll have to take my word for it then."

Eden wasn't sure how good his word was, but she had to admit, this was the least condescending he'd ever been. Then again, the man was known for his acting talent. She glanced a few yards ahead on the path, where Maddox had her mother under complete control.

"Have you heard from Adam?" she asked.

Brennon brushed at a small leaf on his sleeve. "Hmm?"

"Adam. Your friend who took a two-week vacay with no notice? Have you heard how he's doing?"

"I'm sure he's fine."

"You don't talk to him?"

"No, I have."

He seemed content to leave it at that, but for Maddox's sake, Eden couldn't. "Will he be back?"

"Up to him."

She scowled. "Why are you being weird?"

"I'm sorry—were you and Adam forming a strong bond I didn't notice? How is it any of your concern how he's doing or whether he'll be back?"

She huffed. "You're impossible."

The furrow in his brow deepened. "Great. Now I'll have that damn song stuck in my head the rest of the day."

The song "Impossible" was a bit of an earworm from the musical. Once it got in, it took days to find its way out. It was her and Maddox's number now, and they'd been singing it on and offstage far too often lately for Liliana's taste. It had already been in Eden's head for months. No wonder she'd said it out loud. She smirked. "You're welcome."

"I noticed—" he began, but cut himself short.

"What was that?"

He glanced down at the path beneath their feet, brushing away a speck of dirt with one of his stylish sneakers. When he finally spoke, his voice sounded slightly off. Like his cocksure certainty about all aspects of life had taken a coffee break. "I was only going to say I noticed you have a lot of sundresses."

She pressed her lips together in an effort not to smile. He didn't deserve it. "You noticed that, did you?"

"But this is the first time I've seen you in a hat."

"Besides all six of my bonnets you mean?"

"I—hmm . . . I suppose you have a point." He shoved his hands in his pockets and kept his gaze on the pathway.

Since their conversation of nonstarters was going nowhere, Eden finally started to notice the flowers. It was a rhododendron explosion all around them. "Eyes up, Thorne, you'll miss all the pretty things."

He glanced back up at her and stood still. "Eden . . ."

She couldn't handle it anymore. She reached up and took his sunglasses off.

Her mistake. His dark gaze pierced straight through her.

Her chest felt suddenly tight, and without any bindings or corsets whatsoever. Everyone always said he was so captivating onstage. They were missing out. His direct attention was positively drugging.

"About the other night at the bar—" he began.

"Honey, why are you dragging your feet?" Her mother made yet another graceless crash landing into the otherwise peaceful meadow of her life. Jonathan was with her, his big muscles bulging from a T-shirt half a size too small. It was like being descended upon by locusts, and yet, somehow their timing worked. Eden let out the breath she'd been holding for so long her lips were likely blue. "Roses are just up ahead," Terry exclaimed. "They're your favorite!"

Jonathan took her hand, shouldering right past Brennon as her mother chirped with excited sounds, calling out the names of all the flowers she recognized. "Daisies! Roses! Eden! Look! Hydrangeas, oh!"

Jonathan bent down to murmur in her ear. "Saved you."

"Right." Eden cast a final glance over her shoulder at Brennon, his dark eyes locked on their retreating forms. A flutter unsettled her stomach. She turned back to the path quickly and lengthened her stride. "Thanks for the rescue."

"She's not that bad," Liliana said as she and Eden brought their wine onto the patio Monday afternoon. They had two hours before Terry would be treating the group from today's outing to a steak dinner. "Why the hell are you crying? Calm down."

Beyond the fact that her mother could not afford a steak dinner for two, much less ten, Eden's embarrassment from Terry's sudden and outrageous appearance at the gardens had built and built until it finally overtook her. She'd been crying on and off since they got back to the townhouse. "Did you not hear her telling the entire cast about how I didn't get to play Sandy in my community college's production of *Grease* because of my chin acne?"

"That's not how she said it."

"But it's what happened. And they all know now. That I couldn't even get a lead in *community college*."

"Oh, Eden, nobody cares about stuff like that."

"Easy for you to say. You went to *Yale*."

Liliana sighed, but Eden found no satisfaction in her roommate's inability to argue the fact that she had, indeed, gone to Yale. On a full scholarship. For *acting*. "You have way more TV work than any of us, though."

Eden gaped as even more tears streamed down her cheeks. "Infomercials and 'TV work' aren't the same thing."

"Well, look at us now. Who's the leading lady and who's the obnoxious little sister?"

"I'm just the standby."

Liliana rolled her eyes. "And now you're starring with Brennon Thorne. Who gives a shit how you got here? You're here. Enjoy it, or I'll break your leg and take over the part."

She was right, dammit. Eden wiped her tears. "You couldn't. You're too short for the costumes."

Lili snorted a laugh, but Eden sensed her friend's patience was thinning. "I should enjoy it while it lasts, right?"

Liliana gave Eden's arm a sharp but playful slap. "Who says it won't last?"

"It feels too good to be true," Eden admitted.

"Well, don't jinx it. Jeez. Come on. We should start getting ready for dinner."

At the reminder of their dinner plans, Eden wanted to cry again, but for Lili's sake, she kept the tears inside.

An hour and a half later, she and her two housemates met downstairs and headed for the steak house. Nearly everyone who'd been on the outing today within earshot of her mother's shouted invitation had shown.

A rare night off. Free food. Who could refuse? But Eden couldn't think about the credit card bill tonight. Brennon Thorne was gracing them with his presence, and she needed to keep her wits about her.

Jonathan was the only person missing, but Terry was thrilled with the turnout, acting like the absolute belle of the ball and telling the most excruciating stories about Eden's successes and failures to anyone who would listen.

Eden loved her mom. Most people, in fact, loved her mom. Vivacious and bubbly, she'd never met a person she couldn't strike up a conversation with, but that was the problem—she never *stopped* talking. And Eden was her only child, her pride and joy. She'd fight anyone who got in her daughter's way, which was why Eden had finally dropped out of community college and moved to New York.

She'd needed to know she could make it on her own, but after listening to her mother's constant recitation of her lengthy résumé,

Eden wondered all over again if she could build the kind of success for herself that her mother had managed to piece together for her.

Gabi and Brennon sat together, across from Eden and Maddox. Her mother was at the head of their long table on Eden's right. Eden caught Gabi laughing and whispering things to Brennon, who would grin and nod and occasionally whisper something back, to which Gabi would burst into peals of bell-like laughter and make Eden want to throw a spoon at her.

"Eden, Brennon—sing us a song," Terry called when the salad course was cleared.

"Mother!"

Brennon glanced at Eden with shocked eyes, scandalized by the mere suggestion, causing Eden's mortification to reach *next level* status. Gabi elbowed Brennon in the side, but he only turned to her and scowled.

"Oh, Eden—I can't wait for tomorrow night," her mother said. She brought her hands together in a commanding clap. "Sing for your supper, young lady."

Eden gave her a wide-eyed look of *shut the fuck up please.* "Absolutely not."

"Come on, Eden," Gabi laughed. "Don't be shy, I'm sure you'll sound fine without the orchestra."

Gabi needed to shut her face.

"Let's do *our* song, Eden," Maddox said as he threw his napkin onto his plate.

"Spare us!" Liliana said.

Everyone else also groaned in agreement.

Her mother brought her fistful of fork down on the tabletop. "Somebody sing me a song!"

Every ounce of blood left Eden's face in a heart-dropping rush.

Brennon instantly pushed his chair back and stood. He offered a hand across the table. Eden looked at his hand first, then up at him in terror. His dark eyes wreaked havoc on her senses. "You don't have to do this," she said.

"It's my pleasure. May I have this dance?"

Oh, Jesus. He'd already started the song.

With no other choice now but to roll with it, Eden took his hand and glanced at Gabi, who was usually right by her side in this moment onstage, but Gabi aimed a pout at Brennon, who kept his gaze on Eden. Turning to Maddox instead, she sang, "Well isn't this quaint, he's lost his restraint when faced with intolerable me . . ."

Her mother squealed and clapped. Brennon's hand gave hers a warm, reassuring squeeze. She hated how much she appreciated the gesture. She rose on a wave of humiliation and shot a look at her mom to shut the hell up and let them get this over with.

It was impossible to know who made the decision, as she and Brennon had done this same dance several times now, but the two of them danced the full length of the banquet table, moving behind the other cast members, who remained seated. They came together with touches across the tabletop and brief glances, as though the number had been choreographed to be performed at a steak house all along.

There were plenty of people in attendance who had parts during the dance, and Eden kept hoping they'd get up one by one and form a sort of Broadway tour flash mob around her and Brennon, but no. They chewed their buttered rolls and watched the embarrassment unfold, looks of delight on their faces.

Brennon's singing voice was ridiculous.

He was disgustingly charming. And adorable. And so hot, God . . .

Why was he doing this to her, in front of her mother and everybody?

By the time they sang the final notes a cappella, and everyone burst into uproarious laughter and applause, Eden had decided she hated everyone. Except maybe, weirdly, Brennon Thorne.

Wait, no. She hated him most of all.

CHAPTER NINE

On Broadway, it normally took Brennon several minutes to get into a theater and twice as long to leave. Inevitably, fans crowded the stage door, he'd sign their Playbills, pose for selfies, and give his thanks for their support. Out here, in the rest of America, he wasn't known like he was in New York. His comings and goings at the theater were simpler affairs. In the nearly two weeks since they'd begun their run at the Eisenhower, he'd been asked to pose for only a handful of selfies outside his scheduled public appearances.

Friday night before the show, however, a modest crowd of seven women waited for him at the stage door. He checked his watch and gave the ladies a smile. Over the next several minutes of signing and picture-taking, he learned they were a theater club from New Jersey. They saw plays and discussed them once a month the way some people did with books. Buzzed from pre-show cocktails, they swarmed him in a cloud of laughter and perfume, spinning tales of the shows they'd seen him in over the last three years. *Rooftop Lullaby* was a favorite.

"You a hundred percent deserved the Tony for that," one of them said as she crowded close to him for their selfie.

"It was a wonderful role," he replied through his smile.

"Oh, look, Eden! Have you two gotten a selfie yet?"

"Mom!"

Brennon's gaze snapped to Eden and Terry Blake as they approached the steps leading to the backstage door. His forced smile faded as he realized what a ridiculous spectacle he was making of himself with these fans so far from Broadway.

"Go on—get up there—I'll take your picture," Terry insisted, giving her daughter a small nudge in his direction.

"Mom, I have to get ready for the show." Eden's cheeks were starkly red. She kept her eyes trained on the ground as she grabbed the stair rail.

"Suit yourself. Don't mind if I do, then. Here." Terry thrust her phone into her daughter's hand and hurried toward him. "Brennon. Fancy meeting you here. Excuse me, ladies, if I could just cut in, my daughter needs to get ready for her performance. I'll only be a quick sec."

Eden was clearly mortified, so Brennon made a quick decision not to drag this out any longer than was necessary. He closed the distance between himself and Eden's mother, slung an arm around her shoulders, and bent until their faces were somewhat level.

Eden bared her teeth at both of them in a grimace of a smile Brennon was afraid he could never unsee. "Say cheese!"

"Cheese!" Terry echoed.

Eden snapped the photo and nearly threw the phone back at her mother. "Let's go. Sorry about that, everyone. Enjoy the show." She hurried past his fans and rushed inside.

Terry tossed them a toothy, apologetic grin. "I better follow her, I don't want anyone to kick me out. Thank you, Brennon. Have a good show."

"Of course," he said as the two of them disappeared into the building. He turned back to the ladies, determined to get this over with. "Now where were we?"

After the last Playbill was signed, and the women left to find their seats, Brennon finally made it inside the theater. Backstage was bustling as stagehands and dressers went from room to room, repair-ing hems, fetching props. On the way to his dressing room, he passed Eden's.

Her door stood half-open, and though chatter from the ensemble dressing rooms filled the hallway, Brennon could easily overhear the conversation between Eden and her mother.

"Of course I'm glad you're here, but I'm not twelve anymore, Mom. I don't need you talking for me or trying to make friends for me. This was a job I got all by myself."

"I know that, sweetie, and I only want to enjoy it with you. I couldn't be prouder."

"You're making me feel like a joke!"

"Then maybe we should work on your sense of humor."

"Mother—God. Just zip me and stop talking."

"You've worked as hard as any of these people here. You're no joke. Just because you didn't go to some fancy school and people aren't clamoring for your autograph doesn't mean you have anything to be ashamed of, and neither do I. Listen."

Brennon paused with his hand on his own door latch. He should go inside, give them their privacy, but he found himself hanging on every word, wanting to hear what Eden's mother had to say next—what would justify the way she kept embarrassing her daughter in front of her coworkers.

"Your star is so bright. I saw it inside you from day one. Forgive me if I get excited about it from time to time. I've worked hard for this, too."

Eden's response was muffled, but Terry's voice carried as well as any Broadway actress's.

"Now, you get out there and show them who you are. The toast of any town lucky enough to have you."

Eden's answering sniff was loud enough for Brennon to hear. Uncomfortable with how long he'd lingered in the hall, he entered his dressing room and closed the door. Terry Blake was absolutely correct.

Eden was exactly where she was meant to be, peaking at the perfect time. Her shame and insecurity weren't necessary. She'd all but made it, and would continue to do well.

Although Brennon had never been accused of having a particularly soft heart, he'd never been so alarmingly disarmed by another person's discomfort. Instead of wanting to knock on Eden's door and tell her to stiffen up and take the stage like the pro she was, he battled a very strong urge to offer her a warm hug and assure her everything was going to be all right. Terry was outrageous, but her daughter was a gift. She deserved to be noticed, deserved the center stage and the tricky solos. Brennon resolved to do his best that night to stay out of her way and let her shine like the star she was meant to be.

Eden was off from the start. Brennon watched from the wings, waiting to enter for his duet with Jonathan as she garbled a word and missed a mark. Brennon's heart seized with anxiety. She was tense, her timing was off, and her voice unsteady.

As the musical wore on, Eden's performance continued to lack luster, which was incredibly unlike her. Usually the pulse of energy that moved the play forward, tonight she was an anchor weighing it down. She'd gotten in her head, second-guessing, and she couldn't seem to move on. Brennon often likened this kind of night to an Olympic figure-skating performance. If a skater fell on the first jump, there was really no recovering.

But Eden needed to figure something out. The New York directors would arrive Monday to give their notes. Eden had to know her career depended on her ability to be consistent.

She faltered in her first dance with him. The performance they'd given at the steak house on Monday had been ten times better than the one onstage at the Eisenhower that night. Eden was slow on the pick-ups, then over-sang to compensate. It was beyond obvious that her mother's weeklong visit was wearing on her.

In her duet with Gabi, she cleared her throat, causing a whine of feedback to pierce the house. Maddox was with Brennon backstage during the throat-clearing debacle, tightening the strings on his breeches, and he looked out at the stage in shock.

"What is she doing?" he whispered.

"She's falling apart," Brennon replied.

Maddox glared at him and went back to adjusting his costume.

Brennon could barely bring himself to watch the next number. It was a complicated ensemble piece and, while Maddox's character was the featuring player, Eden's inability to keep up stood out.

So much for staying out of her way. Brennon took the stage determined to salvage the night.

The next piece was a duet of theirs with supporting characters' dialogue interspersed. He entered upstage of her, and she looked up at him from where she sat on a settee with a cup of tea in one hand and a saucer in the other. Everything about her, her questioning eyes, the carriage of her shoulders, spelled shame.

He gave her the warmest look in his arsenal, character appropriate, and also straight from the depths of his increasingly besotted heart.

He recited his line. "Join me."

"What's happening?" she sang as she set her tea on the saucer and stood. The cup rattled as her hand shook.

She wasn't perfect in the song, far from it, her spark had gone out in the first scene, but she made it through the rest of the show error-free.

The kiss at the end though, that felt different.

Her song did, too. He heard the lines differently.

I will walk by your side.

I will be your bride.

The words for the first time lifted him, the way they must have lifted his character. A feeling emerged in Brennon's chest—one of warmth, caring, relief. The lyrics felt almost—aspirational.

She raised her hand and placed it on his neck, angling her chin to position her mouth appropriately.

He had to think. He had to really, intensely focus on what exactly was the job he was being paid to do, because her mouth, her parted lips . . . He wanted to push his entire soul into them. Give her some of his confidence, his certainty—help her understand she was exactly where she belonged. On a stage with him, in his arms.

He lowered his mouth to meet hers. Against his neck, a gesture so small no one would be able to see, but Brennon felt to the core of his being, her fingertips gave the gentlest press. His entire body responded to her touch and kiss with a flush of heat.

Her tongue tasted like honey.

And then it was gone. As the stage went dark, their mouths closed to each other immediately.

"Thank you," she whispered quietly enough that the mic wouldn't pick it up. While there was no raucous round of applause as there had been during some of their other performances, the audience did clap. A smattering instead of a roar, despite the fact that the kiss had been the most honest, the most heartfelt—the most real.

She'd kissed him.

Her body began its usual retreat from his embrace, but for the first time he struggled to let her go. There was so much he wanted to say to her. Ultimately, she placed her hands on his arms and pushed them down, escaping to her dresser for the final costume change.

The double wedding scene and the curtain call went without further incident, and as they left the stage, the cast seemed to breathe a collective sigh of relief.

To be fair, Eden's off night was no worse than dozens he'd witnessed in the past by stage actors far more experienced than she, but the way she'd let it affect her, her inability to bounce back, needed to be addressed. She needed to take the stage Saturday afternoon strong and confident. Consistency was the hallmark of professionalism on Broadway.

Though the taste of her mouth still lingered on his tongue, Brennon was determined to confront the issue of her performance head on. The sooner they dealt with it, the better.

"Come in," Eden called from her dressing room in response to his knock.

Brennon opened the door a crack, unsure what might happen to him either physically or emotionally if he saw her in any state of undress. The kiss at the end had left him off balance. "Eden, may I have a word?"

"If you've come to give me notes on the performance, you can skip it. I already know how bad I sucked."

In a Taylor Swift sweatshirt and cutoff denim shorts, Eden sat at her dressing table, staring at her own glum expression, and removing pins from her hair one by one. Dark locks loosened and fell, and Brennon had to reorder his thoughts, fill his lungs, and gather his composure. His advice to Adam had been timely and correct, but he found himself leaning toward following a different set of rules.

No. He hadn't come in here to start some sordid affair. He'd come with a different sort of proposal. "You didn't suck."

Her lips curled in a wry grin, and her chest moved with a short burst of what might have been a dismissive laugh if she'd allowed it. "Then what are you doing here?"

She removed a pin from near her right temple, and her bangs fell in a slanting swoop across her forehead. It had the effect of loosening his thighs' connections to his knees. "I don't want you to take this the wrong way. To think I'm patronizing or condescending—"

"Spit it out, Brennon."

"Do you have plans tomorrow?"

She turned to him, her eyes wide and her brow scrunched. "Why?"

"I thought perhaps—I mean—I wondered if you'd like a chance to go through some of the scenes without an audience—with me—"

She tilted her head, regarding him with a baffled expression.

"What I mean is, I want you to put tonight out of your mind and start fresh."

She didn't look any less confused.

He searched for the right words. "It would be like a workshop."

"A workshop."

Terrible word choice, but here they were. "Yes."

"Why would I want to do that?"

It was the one question he hoped she wouldn't ask because he'd done nothing to recommend himself to her as an ally. "I don't want you to get in your head about tonight's performance. It could negatively impact—"

"Make you look bad, you mean?"

He gave her a harsh glance. "No. That's not what I mean."

"What exactly are you offering?"

"My time, and my advice," he said.

"Wow." She shook her head and turned back to the mirror. She took two more pins from the back of her head, releasing the remainder of her thick hair. It brushed her shoulders in one sweeping whoosh. "I guess I'd be a fool to turn down the great Brennon Thorne."

He bit down on the inside of his lower lip. He'd known the offer wouldn't be received well, but he refused to take it back. He'd done this with other costars before, however it was usually at *their* request. He understood why she found the offer insulting, but that didn't make it any less necessary. He—*shit.*

He shut his eyes as the truth of the matter surfaced. He cared about her.

"Only if you think it could help," he said.

She regarded him with a titled head and softened expression, the frown gone. "I guess you don't get too concerned about things like directors' performances anymore."

"I guess I don't." Brennon's reputation was solid. Even if one performance was weaker than another because he had a headache or his voice was strained, his work ethic and consistency were two of his greatest assets. He viewed directors' performances as opportunities to improve, reminders of things he'd let slip in the day-to-day grind of playing the same role over and over. But Eden had to prove she was capable of carrying the role for the foreseeable future. With no standby of her own, the directors could easily decide to recast, rehearse a name in New York for a few weeks, and put Eden back in the job she'd been hired for—a backup. He hoped he didn't have to say all of that out loud. That she was smart enough about her own career to know what was at stake.

She seemed to be contemplating those very thoughts as she scrutinized him. "What would this look like? Would we meet here?"

"I thought—something more casual . . ."

One of her eyebrows arched in question.

"Our townhouse has a large backyard—"

"No offense, but I'd sooner drown in the Potomac than hear Gabi's opinion on everything I'm doing wrong."

Encouraged by the lack of a flat-out refusal, Brennon rushed to reassure her. "Gabi sleeps until one every day. I'd insist she leave us alone."

Eden grinned. "You'd insist, huh? I wish you could hear yourself talk sometimes, you sound like a—"

"A spoiled duke. I remember."

"Ha. I was going to say a Harvard professor."

"Ah."

"So, I guess I'd have to get there early," she said.

A warm burst of excitement began in his stomach and spread through his chest. His shipment of frozen pastry had arrived that morning. He could have it ready for her arrival, along with fresh coffee, or juice—*both*. He checked his watch to see if he had time to run to the grocery store. At this hour, it would probably have to be a convenience store. He had no idea how she took her coffee, and asking felt like too much.

"Eight?" he asked instead. Although nine would be better. He'd need to pick up everything. Sugar cubes, half-and-half, artificial sweeteners . . . no . . . None of that sounded right . . . "Nine," he amended.

"Should I be nervous?"

He had that question covered. "I've been told I'm somewhat of a dream to work with."

Her smile was genuine and breathtaking. "I'll be the judge of that."

While Thorne had claimed he had no notes on her performance and only wanted to help erase the memory of her dismal night onstage, Eden's mother was a different story. Because she was leaving town on an early flight the following day, Terry wanted Eden to spend the night with her at her hotel. Mad had cooked them all dinner at the townhouse, then Eden packed an overnight bag and brought it with her to the theater, but after the shitty show, the only place she wanted to be was alone in her bed. Between performances and her mother's need to see every sight in DC this week, Eden was fundamentally exhausted.

"Are you remembering to exercise? Your energy seemed a little low."

Eden sipped her tea on the couch in her mother's suite and stared at the small notebook on the cushion between them. ENERGY was capitalized and underlined, with three trailing exclamation points. She'd been a bit off all week, but tonight she'd totally fallen apart.

"Probably not as much as I should be," Eden said quietly.

"Maybe we shouldn't have had such a large meal."

Eden had only had a salad at dinner, but whatever.

"The chemistry was all there, though. I was happy to see that. Tell me, has your agent been down to see the show yet?"

"That's not really how it works, Mom."

Terry gave a lift of her eyebrows that signaled she was insulted. "I'm all ears. Would you like to explain to me how a New York theater agent does their job?"

"They get actors auditions. Negotiate contracts."

"And that's that? They don't offer ideas on how to improve?"

One of Terry Blake's biggest dreams was to become the parent of a household name. Although Brennon Thorne was uber-famous on Broadway, there were very few people in South Bend who'd ever heard of him. Reese Witherspoon, however—well, one would be hard-pressed to find anyone in the world who couldn't immediately picture her and say what they'd loved her most in.

Her mother saw Eden's love of Broadway as a detour, or maybe even a rebellion. She tolerated it, the same way she'd tolerated Eden's endless string of hot musician boyfriends, but she'd never stopped trying to steer her daughter back onto the path of TV and film, as though stage and screen were anything alike, and one could simply replace the other.

Eden stopped trying to explain it a long time ago, and she certainly didn't want to reopen that can of worms tonight. Her own doubts were too big, and the upcoming directors' performance felt like an axe hanging over her head.

"I know what I need to do, Mom," Eden said.

"What's the plan, then?"

"Exercise, vocal rest, more protein . . ." *Some alone time . . .*

Her mother sighed and closed the notebook. "You have to keep your eyes on getting to perform in LA."

Los Angeles was a golden opportunity for touring actors. Film and television executives would attend over the four weeks they performed there. If an actor wanted a screen career instead of a stage career, LA shows could mark the beginning of their transition. But Eden couldn't think about that. She had to focus on holding on to the opportunity she'd been given here. She wouldn't make it to LA if the directors decided to recast the role.

Her phone buzzed, preventing her from having to respond to her mother's comment.

There were two texts—one from Brennon, with the address of his Airbnb, and another from Jonathan, inviting her, Mad, and Lili to lunch the following afternoon. Along with it, he sent a link to a restaurant review. Eden clicked on it and was excited to see it was a new restaurant run by a chef she'd seen on a competitive reality show. She responded quickly: *Count us in!*

Surely Brennon would be done "workshopping" her by lunchtime. She responded to Thorne's text with a thumbs up.

"I should shower and get to bed," she told her mother. "We both have to be up early."

"You weren't at your best tonight, Eden, but you were still wonderful. I hope you know how proud I am of you."

Eden smiled at her mom. Her biggest fan from way back. Terry might not be perfect, may even be an embarrassment sometimes, but Eden appreciated her support more than words could say. "Thanks. But if you ever make me sing for my supper again, I'll disown you forever."

Her mother laughed, gathering Eden in for a warm hug that felt like home. "Brennon Thorne couldn't take his eyes off you that day, you know?"

Immediately Eden backed out of the embrace. "What day?"

"Your golden day. At the gardens. At the steakhouse. You didn't notice?"

"No! I—he barely tolerates me on a good day."

Her mother's lips pressed together thoughtfully. "That wasn't what I saw."

"You're delusional."

"You don't find him attractive?"

"Everybody finds him attractive—"

"The feeling appeared to be mutual."

"Mom!"

Her mother smoothed Eden's stiff, hair sprayed bangs off her forehead and cupped her cheek. "You could do worse."

"Have you heard him talk? There's a rod stuck so far up his ass I'm surprised he can even sit down."

"Oh, that poor man. He has no idea what he's in for with you."

Eden covered her heating cheeks with both hands and shook all thoughts of being in anything other than a musical with Brennon Thorne out of her head. "I'm gonna need you to stop. There is no room in my life for even entertaining this ridiculous conversation." She stood and set her tea down on the end table. "He's one of the best actors in New York. Of course he looked like he was in love with me—that's the role."

"The role is he sits across a table from you for an hour and memorizes the way you chew your food?"

"Ew. Mom!"

Her mother laughed. "Oh, go take your shower. But be kind to him the next time you see him. You never know what can happen."

Lost for words, Eden waved both her hands in the air to shut this nonsense down and stormed into the bathroom. Her mother was out of her mind.

Although . . .

The memory of the kiss onstage that night overtook her in a rush, sending an intense flutter of desire to her belly.

The brief taste of his tongue had happened so quickly she'd almost thought she'd imagined it. Or had she started it? And his grip on her had been tighter, hadn't it? She'd had to remove herself from it with some force.

No, he'd been compensating for her performance. Adding more passion to distract from her lack of energy.

That's all it had been. Acting.

She could not allow herself to confuse his performance with his personality, even if the thought of exploring the man himself sent a throb through every cell in her body.

CHAPTER TEN

Eden's touring wardrobe wasn't exactly stacked. She had enough clothes to make laundry an imperative about every ten days. Therefore, she wore the same yellow dress she'd worn on their press day over to Brennon's house. Since he'd commented on her dresses, she assumed something had stood out. Good or bad, she had no way of knowing, but she never felt more confident than when she was in the yellow dress, and lord knew she needed all the confidence she could muster Saturday morning.

On first impression, Brennon's digs, though only a few blocks away from hers, were both bigger and more expensive than her own crew's Georgetown rental. The landscaping out front, complete with overflowing window boxes and gas lanterns, must have cost a fortune to rent. She'd walked, counting it as her daily exercise.

Brennon opened the door when she knocked lightly. She desperately didn't want Gabi to wake up early from the noise and witness her housemate's random act of charity.

Through it had been a struggle to get moving this morning, the sight of him perked Eden right up. He looked absolutely unreal.

Though he kept his face clean-shaven for the musical, Thorne's signature look was bearded. He'd originally been known for his antiheroes—his dark, brooding looks were partly the reason. Sweeney Todd, Jean Valjean, the fucking Phantom of the Opera . . . This morning, he was unshaven and alarmingly handsome in black joggers and a fitted black tee. He smiled, and it about knocked her over. "Good morning."

The sweet smell of baked goods combined with a hint of fresh-brewed coffee drew Eden forward. "I wasn't told there'd be breakfast."

He stepped aside to let her in, gesturing across the length of the space. The open concept enabled her to see all the way past the living and dining areas to the large kitchen, which included French doors leading to the backyard. Yep. Way nicer than their place.

"Would you like some coffee? Or I have tea, or—juice?"

"Do you have any honey? It's how I take my tea."

He nodded once. "I already put the kettle on."

Their place hadn't come with a tea kettle. Fortunately, Eden traveled with an electric one.

They stared at each other a moment. Eden didn't want to go barging into the kitchen and start opening cabinets, but he didn't seem inclined to invite her any further in yet. He remained somewhat frozen. So much charisma onstage, but here in his living room, he was as awkward about having people over as any run-of-the-mill introvert.

Maybe, per her mother's advice, she could give him a small break. "It's a beautiful day."

"Thank you," he said.

A laugh threatened, but Eden managed to keep it to a cheerful smile. "You're welcome."

He shut his eyes and took a breath, like he was trying desperately to recall his next line, the one that would move them both past the wrong one he'd just uttered.

"I assume you haven't had your coffee yet," she teased.

"Perhaps I've had one too many."

She glanced at the kitchen. "Sounds like I have some catching up to do."

He gave her a strained smile. "Let's go find that honey."

Brennon headed toward the kitchen. She followed, looking around to try and discern anything about him from a place where he didn't live.

The living room was pristine. Not a treasure out of place.

The honey he'd mentioned needing to rustle up sat in the center of the quartz kitchen island in a fancy jar with a wooden honey dipper artfully positioned alongside it.

"Ah. There it is." She pointed.

If Eden wasn't mistaken, a hint of pink crept up his cheeks behind his morning stubble, but he turned his back to her before she had a chance to confirm or snap a quick photo.

"I've been up awhile. I might add some whiskey to my next coffee," he muttered.

The kettle on the stove whistled softly, and he shut off the flame. At the same time, the oven timer went off.

"What are you making? It smells good."

"I saw an ad on Instagram," he said.

Eden sat on one of the island's stools and waited to see what came out of the oven since his answer hadn't been much help. He moved smoothly through the space, finding her a mug, arranging hot pastries on an oval platter, and pouring water from the kettle over a tea ball infuser into her cup. Eden was mesmerized. She was glad she'd worn a dress. It was beginning to feel like a special occasion.

"Do you host a lot?" she asked.

His attention on her mug, he glanced up at her without raising his head. It made his eyes look way more heated and gorgeous than he probably intended. Her pulse jumped in her neck.

"No," he said. "Is it that obvious?"

He might have been joking, but instead of the wry, sarcastic smile one would expect after someone made a funny remark, he returned his gaze to the tea and laid a hand across his stomach. It was a gesture she'd seen him use both onstage and off when he seemed to be thinking particularly hard about something. Her own eyes were drawn to the flat plane of his abs. Often he'd—oh, there it went—the slight tap of his index finger. She wondered what was on his mind.

"You didn't have to go to all this trouble," she said.

"Then let's pretend I didn't." His face was definitely pinker than when she'd arrived.

Her hands were cool, though. If she pressed them against his cheeks, maybe they could balance each other out. Blinking away the intrusive thought, Eden picked up the honey dipper. Dangling from the end was a handwritten price tag. She bit her lip and smiled. Turning her attention back to Brennon and his darkening cheeks, her thoughts spun as the human behind the legend slowly emerged. Her body warmed from head to toe. Never had she been more attracted to any man in her life as she was in that moment.

Don't let your guard down, Eden.

She returned the utensil to its spot next to the honey jar and cleared her throat. The second she did, he glanced up at her, the familiar annoyed pinch back on his brow. "That's a terrible habit," he said. "Hard on your vocal cords."

Brennon Thorne had returned. Thank God. She'd been a heartbeat away from pushing him against the counter and having her way with him. "Is that scientifically proven, or . . .?"

"It can aggravate polyps."

"I don't have any polyps that I'm aware of."

"Yet," he corrected.

"I don't know how I've survived all this time without you."

"I imagine your mother would caution you against it as well."

Eden schooled her expression, folding her hands and crossing her legs. She kept her mouth shut.

With the tea properly steeped, he set the infuser aside and reached for the honey. She swiped the jar away. "I got it," she said.

"Apple turnover?" he asked.

"Maybe in a minute."

Eden liked a lot of honey in her tea. Three dipper-fulls, it turned out, though she'd never used one. The honey in the jar was a rich golden amber. It clung to the wooden utensil and drizzled thick ribbons into her mug. When she looked up at Brennon as the third dipper slowly poured, she found his eyes fixed on the flowing honey. He swallowed like he was parched. While it annoyed her to admit her mother was right about anything, Eden could see how Brennon's intense gaze might seem a little . . . thirsty. "Should I make you one?" she asked.

"Looks very . . ." He ran a hand over his mouth. "Sweet."

"Well, I'll be singing a lot today . . ."

"I've always used mint candy," he said.

"I'm aware."

Their eyes met. His lips parted as if to say something, but whatever it might have been must have gotten stuck on the way out. They'd shared a dozen or so kisses so far onstage. His lips were never sticky, but they were always sweet. Last night, when their tongues met, she'd tasted spearmint. It had been absolutely wrong of her to seek more from a choreographed kiss, but his willingness to be in that moment with her, to give her the type of reassurance she needed and not criticize her for it, made her question some of her more uncharitable assumptions about him. And now she was curious.

She sipped the tea, but the syrupy warm liquid did nothing to settle her nerves or get her thoughts out of the gutter. She needed air. Nodding toward the back door, she asked, "Shall we?"

"Go ahead. I'll just be a minute."

Eden stood, taking her tea to the back patio.

Brennon spread his arms, grabbed hold of the countertop's edge with both hands, and hung his head. Either he'd have to run to his room to put his cock out its misery or find a way to control himself right then and there.

Eden. Pastry. Honey. The pleasure center of his brain had short-circuited when his mind began exploring the possibilities. He'd imagined drizzling the sweet liquid over her breasts with the dipper, sucking it away, stroking her tongue with his to taste the sugar.

The better part of valor here was probably to give in to the urge to jerk off, otherwise this would be happening all morning. Better to declare defeat.

Instead, he picked up an apple turnover and shoved half of it into his mouth, counting on his nervous system to make the changeover to resting and digesting.

He chewed thoroughly. Taking his own advice from earlier, he added a healthy splash of whiskey to his coffee along with some cream. He took a long sip, then finished his turnover. By the time he plated one for Eden, his lesser urges were more or less under control.

He found her outside on the deck, coating her throat with tea and honey. The dark waves of hair falling across her shoulders shone in the morning sunlight, set off by the marigold color of her fitted dress. The way it nipped in at the waist accentuated her rear end in the most irresistible way. He had no idea how he was going to get through this morning without throwing her to the ground and begging her to put him out of his misery. He took another, longer sip of his coffee.

"What's the plan?" she asked without turning to look at him.

Right. She was there to work. "The plan is to have some fun with it. Shake last night off," he said.

"So you don't have any pearls of wisdom? Tips from a legend? You just brought me here to sing and dance in the backyard? I mean—it's a very nice backyard." She nodded at the thick turf of St. Augustine, bordered on all sides with lush and well-planned landscaping. Japanese maples shaded mature hostas and elephant ears. Hydrangeas bloomed all around. Roses blossomed in yellow and pink.

Brennon had spent all his early morning hours here on the deck, enjoying the outdoor space. It had been the best part of being on the tour so far.

Perhaps the second best. "Unless you have a better idea," he said to Eden.

"Do you really think this'll help me?"

He took a few steps closer to her but stopped about three feet shy of his own reach. "Every performance is its own opportunity. Every scene. Every song. One missed mark doesn't ruin a show. Or one wrong note. We're human. We make mistakes."

She faced him, her eyes suspicious. "When was your last mistake?"

"No one's perfect, Eden."

"You don't have an example, do you?"

He did, unfortunately. Any number of them. The most recent was his entire relationship with Chloe, but he had a feeling that wasn't the kind of mistake Eden was referring to, and he certainly didn't want to wade through his list of romantic failures on a morning like this. "*Les Mis*, West End. April 13th. It was a Friday. I sang the lyrics to the finale instead of 'Come With Me' in the first act."

She giggled. "Were you ill?"

"I was exhausted. I hadn't slept the night before."

"Plus it was Friday the Thirteenth," she added.

He grinned, pleased they were on the same page. "That's what I told myself."

Her smile lingered. "Okay. Since it happened to you that one time, I guess you can at least pretend to relate."

The whiskey kicked in all at once. The muscles in his chest relaxed, and his breath flowed freely in and out.

"How was the rest of the show that night?" she asked.

"It wasn't our best night, but everyone still cried at the end."

Dropping her gaze, she sank her teeth into her plush lower lip as her mouth remained perfectly curved in that dazzling smile.

His thoughts drifted again, but he pulled them back. "It's natural that mistakes get to you. The trick is to learn to come at it again fresh."

Her smile faltered, and when she spoke again her voice was quieter. "Do you think they'll let me keep the part?"

Was that what concerned her? Brennon would be extremely disappointed if they didn't. "You don't need to prove anything to them. You're here for a reason. You only need to stop clearing your throat and take them along with you on your ride."

She glanced up at him, her eyes full of concern. "Do you think I'm any good?"

"You know you're good."

"Do *you* think I'm good?"

"You're a dream," he said honestly.

They stared at each other for a moment—long enough to make his heart pound, and then she rolled her eyes. Her words came at him in a rush. "All right, where do you want to start then? I'm meeting up with some people for lunch at one."

The mention of her plans sent a hollow pang through him, easily recognizable for what it was. Loneliness. "Who are you meeting?"

"Jonathan got a reservation at Hayden Burr's new restaurant."

Brennon's left fist clenched. He downed the rest of his coffee. He had yet to let her know what drunken asses they'd both been last week at the bar. He hated to ruin such a promising morning, though. Still . . . "About Jonathan—"

She held up a hand. "I get you two have history. I don't want to be involved."

It was enough to make him second-guess. He shook off his regrets for the moment. Perhaps there was a better time and place. She'd only just begun to let him into her life, and he was finding, more and more, it was a place he liked to be. "Fair enough. Let's start with our first dance."

"I'll do everything in my power not to clear my throat."

He had three hours with her and intended to make the most of every second. With any luck, she'd want to skip lunch and have another apple turnover with him instead.

"Do you have a favorite duet?" Brennon asked after they'd run through their own first song together.

Eden glanced up at him, now having to shade her eyes from the sun as it rose above the line of trees along the fence. "Like, from the show?"

"From any show. From anything."

Taylor Swift had some great duets, but Eden doubted Brennon Thorne knew any of them. "'Sixteen Going on Seventeen,'" she suggested.

Something like delight sparked in his eyes. "I played the Captain at Juilliard."

"Naturally." She nodded.

"But never Rolf," he added.

"Looks like now might be your chance? I mean—if that's what this was leading up to."

His soft laugh sounded almost shy as he ran both hands through his thick hair. The humidity of the morning made it wavier than usual. Eden blinked rapidly, looking away as her attraction spiked again. His face all exposed like that, all its contours and angles, its perfect proportions . . .

"If only we had a gazebo," he said.

"We have the deck."

He followed her sweeping gesture and stroked his beard thoughtfully. "This could work."

Brennon's Rolf was utterly disarming. It was the most flirtatious Eden had ever seen him, as the Darcy character he played was rather stoic and smoldering. The essence of this song, of course, was an older and wiser young man offering to lead the innocent young rose through a dark world of cads, dandies, and drinkers of brandies. Eden's Liesl reflected the irony. They danced, circling each other on the deck, and finished with a tandem flying leap into the yard. Neither of them stuck the landing in the plush grass, and they wound up on the ground, laughing, faces to the sky, Eden's last note still ringing in her ears.

"Are you all right?" he asked, rolling to face her.

She propped herself up on an elbow and glimpsed several blades of grass in his hair.

Simultaneously they each reached out to brush lawn debris off one another. Their hands crashed in the middle, and the brush of his skin, coupled with the nearness of his long body stirred a very particular desire between Eden's thighs. Swallowing hard, she guided her hand past his and proceeded to run her fingertips over his hair even as his own hand dropped, and his eyes closed briefly, letting her finish.

The memory of her failures from last night were distant and unimportant. Somehow Brennon had managed to replace them all with sunshine, roses, and his own warm regard. She felt confident again. Grateful.

"Guess we should get back to work," she said, once he was restored to his usual polished self. She took care of her own hair. Somehow, she didn't think she could manage to have him touch her the same way without squirming and moaning inappropriately. They had two shows to get through today—a matinee and an evening performance. It wouldn't do to be panting after him the entire time, although, after the last five minutes, she wasn't sure how that could be helped.

They pushed themselves to standing. Eden brushed the remaining grass from her dress and shook out her hair.

"Back to the musical?" he asked.

That was probably the safer bet.

She nodded. "Any song of mine that could use some work?"

"Nothing leaps to mind."

"Let's do 'Within These Walls' then," she suggested. He nodded once, and she began the song. With so many long, sustained notes, she'd love any tips for better places to breathe during it.

But when she was done, instead of offering suggestions, or even picking up with his own song after her solo, as he would in the show, he stood from where he was sitting on the deck steps and applauded her.

"Oh, stop. You'll give me a massive ego trip," she said.

"You get robbed of applause for that song every night because I start singing right on top of you. That scene could have been written better, to give the audience a chance to appreciate you alone."

"You only have a few lines before they start clapping," she said. "I still assume they're clapping for me."

Brennon's grin was absolutely heart-stopping as he approached, but when he glanced down at his watch, she remembered to check the time as well. She needed to get going if she didn't want to be late for lunch. Although she cared far less about it now than she had when she'd accepted the invitation.

"How do you feel?" He'd stopped too far away for her to touch him. She hadn't been considering a full-frontal hug or anything, but maybe a stroke of his arm, a casual sort of gesture that would show she appreciated not only his time, but his effort. And also perhaps hint at her strong desire to stroke his arm.

"Excited," she answered honestly.

His dark eyes explored her face, drifted to her neckline, and snagged briefly on her mouth before meeting her gaze again. "I think you're very good," he said, in answer to the question she'd asked before they'd begun. "They'd be wrong to recast you. You're doing everything right."

Eden stared up at him in wonder, too flattered to speak. She'd love to deflect some of the rapidly intensifying smolder coming off him with some quick-witted remark, but she had nothing, only a deepening desire to fall into his arms and be ravished.

Her need to get laid was now alarmingly specific as to whom she wanted doing the deed. Although after this morning, it was becoming harder and harder to discern whether it was because he was Brennon Thorne, six four and striking, or because he was this charming sweetheart who'd taken the time to buy her a honey dipper and roll around in the grass with her. Was she lusting? Or was she actually swooning?

"Thank you. That means so much," she said with a slow blink up at him, testing the waters.

Every night they parted with a kiss. It was a regular thing, an expected occurrence, the kiss at the end . . .

He glanced at her lips again, like he was thinking the exact same thing.

Her mouth watered. Wicked thoughts were the first to appear, convincing her that the primary driver here was lust, which felt altogether wiser and infinitely simpler to navigate. Thank God he was so hot and out of her league. Otherwise, this could have gotten complicated.

"I should head out," she said.

He swallowed, Adam's apple bobbing as he gave a quick nod. "Right. You have lunch plans. You should get going."

Neither of them made a move.

She came out and said it. "So, this is where we kiss, get married, and live happily ever after."

He dropped his gaze and cracked a smile. "You always nail that part," he said, because it was the one song they hadn't rehearsed today.

She kicked at a blade of grass with the toe of her red flat. "About last night . . ."

"Hmm?"

They both stared at the ground between them. Her attention shifted to his shoes, the lower halves of his legs. "I went a little off book again," she said.

"Every performance can't be exactly the same. There's no fun in that."

Her breath quickened as her gaze steadily rose to his thighs, his hips, the hand on his stomach, finger tapping. A muscle in his wrist pulsed with the repetitive motion. He had lovely skin, olive-toned and tanned. Fingers long enough to play any instrument he chose, long enough to . . .

She blushed at the thought. "It's always felt a little rushed for me."

"The ending?"

She nodded. "All that build-up for a few quick lines and a peck."

"Try slowing it down then," he said.

"But the music—"

"Not much anyone can do about the music."

"There isn't much opportunity to experiment with that part, I guess."

"I'll think on it," he said.

Needing to better understand what he meant, she glanced at his face.

Their gazes met and held across the generous space he'd left between them. "I'm sure we can come up with something," she said.

His lips parted, and his chest rose with a breath. Briefly, she was jealous of the air that traveled through his mouth, into his lungs, and the oxygen that made it all the way into his cells—to his heart.

In a few hours she'd get to put her hands on him, hear his rush of breath, feel his heartbeat. She was ready to skip to the end. "Thank you for this. And for breakfast."

"I hope you still have room for lunch." His mouth twisted grimly at the words.

"Would you like to come?"

He scowled, like either she'd overstepped or lost her mind. His answer was a scoff. "No."

Spine stiffening, she took her cue to leave. She refused to give into the rush of embarrassment that came with such a swift rejection. She was an actress. She'd been rejected a thousand times in her twenty-six years on this earth. "Okay. Anyway . . ." She drew the word out as she stepped past him and hurried toward the deck. "Guess I'll see you later."

"Eden, I didn't mean—"

"It's cool. Shouldn't have even offered. Jonathan's not your biggest fan, you know."

"Maybe I should explain—"

Nope. She didn't want to hear it. She wanted to leave on a high note. "No explanation required. I'll see you at the show."

She didn't turn around to check his expression or offer him a better goodbye. Also, if she looked at him again, she was afraid she'd never want to leave. Letting herself entertain the idea, even if it had only been for a split second, of spending the rest of the day with him had been foolish. Attraction aside, their lives were far too different.

She entered the kitchen through the French doors and found Gabi sitting at the island, her fingers tracing the floral design on Eden's bag. "You two kids have fun playing in the yard?"

Eden snatched her bag away and slung the strap over her shoulder. "We did, but I have to get going now."

"He never makes *me* breakfast." Gabi swept out an arm to gesture at the tray of turnovers.

Eden gave her a sympathetic smile. "Perks of being the lead, I guess."

Gabi's eyes narrowed. "Enjoy it. Things can change fast on tour. One day you're in . . . the next . . ."

Spoken like a true understudy. Eden kept her tone bright. "See you at the show. Fingers crossed I don't get hit by a car."

"Fingers crossed." Gabi's smile was smug.

Eden left it at that. It was a long walk to the front door, but she made it in one piece.

Lunch was delicious. Eden savored an incredible salad with fried goat cheese medallions, grilled marinated salmon, and a honey-lemon vinaigrette. It was like the chef had known her deepest culinary desires and designed a salad she could eat every day for the rest of her life and always be satisfied.

The conversation, however, was so-so. Jonathan, a self-proclaimed foodie, was determined to tell them everything he knew about each ingredient on their plates. He said he had the type of palate that could have made him a master sommelier, but he'd fallen in love with acting instead. He enjoyed the term "fun fact," and Eden made a mental note to count how many times he said it the next time they grabbed lunch at a nice place.

Maddox had the majority of her attention, though. Despite ordering what was arguably the most delicious-looking plate of food their server delivered, he did more rearranging of it than eating. Eden stared at the pepper-crusted filet on a bed of rich, cheesy polenta. "Did you have a big breakfast or something?"

"Not much of an appetite today," he mumbled. "Maybe I'll save this for dinner."

Liliana then made the mistake of asking Jonathan a question about truffle oil, and the man's face lit up like he'd been given the teaching opportunity of a lifetime.

With the two of them occupied, Eden pointed at Maddox's plate with her fork. "Do you mind if I try a bite?"

He shoved the plate at her and sighed heavily.

"Should I ask?" she wondered aloud.

"No," he said.

Despite getting to play the substantial supporting role of Mr. Collins each night, Maddox hadn't been himself since Adam left. While she'd known her friend's interest in the other man hadn't been a passing one, she now suspected Mad's feelings for Adam were stronger than he'd let on. He was more than disappointed—he was hurt.

Eden put an arm around her friend and leaned her head against his. "I'm here if you ever decide to talk."

He returned her one-armed side hug, then changed the subject the way he always did. "Take a look at them."

Across the table, Jonathan and Liliana were flirting. Lili moved her raven hair from one shoulder to the other, like she was considering throwing her no-sex-on-tour rule out the window, which was fine by Eden. At least one of them should get to have some fun.

She released Maddox from the hug and moved his plate back in front of him after stealing a bite. "Two performances today. You need to eat."

Sighing again, Mad lifted his fork and speared a slice of filet. "You sound just like your mother."

Eden poked him in his deltoid with her fork. "Don't make me put her on speaker."

CHAPTER ELEVEN

Eden dazzled in the first act, and Brennon wasn't the only one who noticed. By the time their angry duet rolled around, the matinee audience was eating out of her hand. Brennon even got a few boos, which didn't happen often, but it got Eden to give him a wink onstage, which sent his heart into palpitations. When the time came for him to interrupt her solo, the audience was back on Darcy's side, and an elderly woman in the front row mouthed the words of "Dare to Hope" along with him, tears streaming down her face as she clutched a tissue to her chest.

He and Eden shared the breathless stare that had been written into the scene, but she did something new—she touched her mouth, letting her index finger drag the surface of her lower lip. The surprisingly subtle gesture foreshadowed the kiss Elizabeth and Darcy had yet to have, but there was something distinctly *Eden* about it. Brennon wished he'd kissed her that morning, when they were alone, and not in character, while the sun, not a spotlight, had shone upon them both.

Would he be reading too much into it to think the kiss they would share in a matter of minutes would be different, too? Offstage he let himself imagine the moment—what he could do during those precious few seconds to let her know it was him, Brennon, kissing Eden, not Elizabeth. If he'd done what he'd wanted to do and kissed her that morning, it would have involved hands in hair and twining tongues, a passionate press of his chest to hers.

He would have run a hand along her jawline and brought his lips to her throat. She'd have arched her neck, and he'd have been in heaven. He got hard thinking about it.

Christ, he needed to control himself.

Fortunately, he had enough time offstage during the last act to do his final costume change in his dressing room. It was only a coat and cravat exchange that he could manage himself—the dressers had larger problems with all the women moving on and off the stage in the final numbers. Brennon took the time alone to get himself together and mitigate some of his excitement.

To masturbate, or not to masturbate, that was the question. It kept coming down to this.

Eden had gotten to him fast. Typically, he'd spend weeks contemplating the wisdom of a kiss, a fling, a relationship, but Eden tested the limits of his control like no one else ever had. He'd been drawn to her physically from the first, but in the past, his desire had been an easy enough beast to tame. He couldn't remember a time when he'd wanted to possess a woman's body as completely as he wanted hers. He ached to feel the softness of her inner thighs, to learn the shade of her nipples, to encircle her ankle with his hand.

He gave himself an experimental stroke through his breeches, and throbbed.

His body knew exactly what it wanted.

The time had come to make a decision. If he got started now, he'd have time to rub a quick one out, but then he'd get relaxed—maybe too relaxed. Maybe part of what made the lady in the front row cry was this unbearable tension. His intense craving for Eden had to be coming through in his performance, making people experience the torture the way he was experiencing it.

But not giving in to his needy cock meant he'd be walking onstage with an erection. One only he would be aware of thanks to the generous cut of the cloth of his pants, but one Eden would feel when their bodies came together for the kiss.

Did he want that?

Was it too much?

Of *course* it was too much. He was out of control.

Dear God, no one ever told him touring would be this exhausting.

There was a reason he'd told Adam to check himself over Maddox—because when one gave in to what one wanted, there were always consequences and confusion and cocks that refused to stay put.

Sinking onto the sofa, he slung an arm over his eyes. He was pathetic. When had he turned into this person?

Ultimately, he did not masturbate, but he did visualize masturbating, which was strange, yet it evolved rather organically in his mind as he gripped his own thigh and pictured gripping something a great deal firmer.

He was grateful when one of the stagehands stopped by to round him up. Walking, however, with a raging erection, was terribly uncomfortable. The breeches chafed.

Jonathan stood in the wings waiting for their cue to take the stage for their last duet of the afternoon. "How'd 'rehearsal' with Eden go this morning?"

Brennon cast a hard glare in his enemy's direction and didn't answer.

"I have to admit I didn't expect you to take me up on my offer," Jonathan said. "There's not much in it for you at the end of the day. Don't you already have a film agent in LA?"

Brennon had an agent for everything. He also had a manager, two attorneys, and a personal assistant named Edward who wrote science fiction and had created his own YouTube series based on the job Brennon paid him to do. "Stay away from her."

"Shine that spotlight on your mattress yet? Did it work?"

Brennon's stomach soured. It had been too much to hope that those words would be forgotten by a man who'd been determined to see him fail since the day they'd met. Brennon kept quiet, his eyes on Eden, now alone at the center of the stage as she sang the last few lines to end the scene. The reminder of his own horrible behavior that night at the bar killed Brennon's erection but fired up his rage. Jonathan's determination to drag Eden into their years-long feud hit too close to the bone. At Juilliard, this had all started over a girl.

The soundtrack played the cheerful first notes of Bingley and Darcy's second duet. Brennon threw back his shoulders, put a twinkle in his eye, a laugh in his voice, and shoved Jonathan onto the stage.

It was his second favorite part of every performance, and one of these days, he'd get the shove just right.

There was a note of something mischievous in Eden's eyes during their last song. Like she knew a secret she wasn't telling. Coy wasn't the best way to describe it, nor would it have been appropriate for the scene, but the way she played Lizzie in their final duet was less wistful and more *I can't wait to get to the wedding night!*

It was perfect for a matinee with as responsive of an audience as they had. Her excitement with her own performance was contagious, as her energy tended to be. The same could be said for all the biggest names on Broadway, along with the most notable up-and-comers.

Eden was as promising as they came, and he'd enjoyed nearly every minute of being onstage with her. But he wondered if this next minute would make the rest pale in comparison.

They approached each other as they sang "Laying Down My Pride," circling a moment before meeting at center stage. In the usual manner, her vocals put chills on his skin, but a new, raw desire stirred in his chest. His right hand went to her waist.

The choice she made next changed very little overall, but reflected her more excitable version of Lizzie. She stepped in closer to him and took hold of his cravat. Her spontaneous choice put her closer to him than she was technically supposed to be. The follow-spot operator quickly adjusted the angle of her light. Eden was utterly radiant, and her move thrilled him because it worked—both for the song, and for him personally, as a man who wanted her so much closer.

From that point forward, they were forced to wing it and choreograph the rest of the kiss themselves. With any luck, Shayna would be busy doing something else and wouldn't notice.

He sang the line that normally would have brought his knuckles to her cheek, but he touched her mouth instead, lightly, letting his finger slide from her top lip to her fuller, redder, bottom one. He was dying to taste it. She blinked her large brown eyes up at him and, instead of lifting a hand to his neck, yanked the cravat until their foreheads met, because in touching her lips he'd completely forgotten to do that bit of blocking, and it was her turn to save *his* ass.

Would this song never end so they could kiss?

One line to go. Together, she'd sing "I will be your bride," and he'd sing "You will be my bride," and that would be it. Their lips would finally meet.

The line lasted a lifetime, her wish not to rush the song granted by the way time itself slowed. Meanwhile, his hands moved from her waist to her back, and he was already pressing her body to his. She'd slid her arms up, and now both her hands were on his shoulders, leaving nothing between them but her bound chest and his erection.

Yes, it was back.

Anyone could have predicted it.

"Be . . ."

She rose onto her tiptoes, which she did every night, but this time she tilted her hips more than usual, which had the effect of grinding into an arousal that needed no further encouragement.

"My . . ." "Your . . ."

He applied enough pressure to her lower back to keep the full force of her pubic bone against the entire length of him. The side of her mouth that was upstage, hidden from the audience's view, pulled up at the edge, an indication that even though there were yards of fabric between them, she felt him.

And didn't hate it.

"Bride . . ."

As the impossibly long note wound itself down, and the music swelled for the kiss, Eden did something purely wicked.

She gave an adorable squeal and a bounce of her toes. The unexpected friction sent a powerful surge of desire to his already strained cock. It pulsed against her as their mouths finally met.

Open.

With tongue.

Suddenly consumed with the flavor of lemon and honey, Brennon sank in, her open mouth all the permission he required.

Eden's tongue found his in a long, luscious slide, and he nearly detonated at the heat of it.

The lights went down, and the cheering, which had begun the second their lips touched, doubled in volume. Their kiss didn't stop, but deepened. Sweet and wet, Brennon couldn't get enough. He was on the verge of losing himself in it, when someone walked past and flicked him on the back of the head.

Tempted to take Eden's lower lip with him, he disengaged from her mouth with one final tug on his favorite part. It was never completely dark onstage, so he caught the smile she gave him just before she turned to rush off for her final costume change.

Everyone but the stage manager and Peck thought it was their best performance yet.

"He kissed the *shit* out of me." Eden had elected to have this conversation with Liliana, since she wasn't sure Mad could handle any talk of sexy times without contributing to his ongoing existential crisis.

"I knew I should have been watching!"

"Watch tonight—God only knows what's gonna happen."

"Was it good?"

"If by good you mean requiring a cold shower immediately afterward, then I'd say it was better than that."

"Did you see him backstage?"

Eden hadn't, but not for lack of wanting to. Jonathan had come into her dressing room, droning on and on about restaurants they needed to try, and this chef or that one, and maybe they could go on their own next time, tomorrow night maybe? Finally, Eden faked a menstrual cramp and escaped the room to find Maddox and Liliana waiting for her to take their planned walk back to their townhouse together. Eden had managed to keep quiet about Brennon until now. She and Liliana sat on the patio, where they drank from a pitcher of Lili's fresh-made lemonade.

Eden was eating honey by the spoonful. If it was good enough for marathon runners . . .

"So, should we have the 'what does this mean' conversation?" Liliana asked.

"What this means is, I may very soon have the opportunity to hook up with Brennon Thorne, and I need to figure out what page he's on so I know where to shelve my expectations."

Lili put a lemon wedge between her lips and sucked. "I have mixed feelings about this."

Eden tapped her fingers against her mouth as she stared at the townhouse next door. She also had mixed feelings about this.

Brennon was notorious for having a penchant for leading ladies. The ones Eden knew about were all prominent names. Skye Forester, Gemma McClain, Chloe Rhodes, the list went on. Eden was a nobody compared to them. However, if he were only looking for a fun fling with a cute standby, then the elaborate breakfast spread he'd put out that morning would have been utter overkill. If he was genuinely try-ing to woo her . . . No. She tried to shake some sense into herself. It was impossible.

That erection, though.

Such an unexpected thrill to have that popping up in the middle of a stellar performance. Not for him, she was guessing, but she'd been absolutely delighted to stumble across that buried treasure.

She'd since become desperate to get her hands on it. All she had to do first was make sure it was available, and if there were any strings she should know about, or time limits to consider.

She needed to know *all the things*.

"I should go gargle," Eden murmured, still considering.

"And catch that cold shower?"

"Something." Eden took the jar of honey to her room and had one more spoonful before screwing the top back on. Her throat felt fine, but two performances in one day was straining, and she didn't want her notes going gravelly at the end right before she got to kiss Brennon again.

She ran a bath for herself and stripped. While the water heated, she allowed her gaze to drift toward the bedside table.

Why not?

She locked her bedroom door, made herself comfortable on the bed, and went to fire up her magic bullet.

Nothing happened.

She pushed the power button again, but the small device sat still in her hand. Useless.

"Damn it."

Using her hand, she made a go of it, but at the rate she was going, she'd be there all day and flood the bathroom. She'd let herself get too used to the efficient little vibrator, which now lay powerless on the bed beside her.

In the bathtub, she tried again, pinching her nipple and stroking her clit, which felt fantastic, but ultimately an orgasm was going to require more energy and focus than she had that afternoon. The water was making her sleepy.

It was a paradox, but the more she thought about Brennon, the more excited she got, and the further she got from release. Had the matinee been a fluke? Had she gone too far, as usual? Would they have a chance to discuss it?

Would he want to?

Too many thinky thoughts and not enough feely ones to get her there today.

Meanwhile, she closed her eyes and relived the kiss.

Eden avoided Peck with all her might once their trio straggled back to the theater. According to Shayna, by whom she'd already had the misfortune of being cornered, Peck was pretty pissed about Eden and Brennon's improv onstage, and Shayna hadn't loved it either. "Look, I know it's boring doing everything the same way every time, and I understand you performer types like to add your 'flavor' to things, but keep it to the acting. Not the blocking."

"Right." Eden nodded.

"That being said, I didn't mind the open-mouth kiss. Whatever works for you two."

Eden blinked, unsure how to take the note.

Shayna gave her an over-the-top wink and an elbow poke. "Gotta keep things interesting, am I right?"

"Totally."

"Good show, tonight. Break a leg."

"Uh . . . Thanks."

Eden assumed the open-mouth part had been exactly what had Peck's panties in a twist.

There was rarely a chance to run into Brennon backstage, but soon enough, they arrived at the Netherfield ball, and it was only a matter of a few verses before they'd be holding hands.

"May I have this dance?"

He looked formidable as Darcy tonight, gaze shuttered and dark, tension pulling his lips taut.

Eden turned to face Gabi, whose expression matched her own baffled one, per the characters, and sang to her as she placed her hand in Brennon's. "Well isn't this quaint/ He's lost his restraint/ When faced with intolerable me." Turning to Brennon, she nodded and curtsied. "Your dignity's secure/ I assure you, dear sir/ You don't have to be silent, you see."

He bowed, tightening his hand around hers and brushing the skin on the back of it with a firm sweep of his thumb. They began the dance, in and out of each other's faces, until they wound up at the foot of the stage, breathless and staring into each other's eyes. Whose turn was it to sing?

She'd lost her place.

Lost inside his eyes—

Yes, that was where this was headed. "That reply will do for now/ Let us dance the night away/Getting lost inside his eyes/Clearly we have nothing to say."

While the audience was less vocal and enthusiastic than the afternoon crowd, and the players were all digging deep to power through to the end of the night, they turned out a solid performance of the first act, and rallied until intermission.

Eden's pits were unusually sweaty, and she blamed it on Thorne, whose heartbreaking recitation of Darcy's letter just before the curtain fell touched every nerve she had. They left the stage in opposite directions, as usual, but met in the backstage hallway. The silent, no-touching walk back to their respective dressing rooms, where they each glanced at the other before opening their doors and disappearing inside, got Eden all heated up. Something was brewing, something was different, and she could hardly stand waiting to find out what.

A few of her questions were answered in their final duet.

The orchestra director lifted the baton, and the violins came in right on cue.

Brennon's right hand went to her waist. Eden placed her palm against his chest, and a rush of excitement filled her when their eyes met.

His dark gaze was a storm she got caught in. It was an interesting departure from the way they'd played it in the matinee. Eden's afternoon Lizzie had been sort of horny and virginal. That wouldn't work tonight with Brennon's choices. He was going full Christian Grey on her right now, and what the heck would Lizzie do if she found out Darcy had a red room at Pemberley?

Eden knew what *she* would do, but Lizzie was a different sort of person. She caught his hand against her waist as he was about to lift it to stroke her cheek. Instead of touching his neck, she took the cheek caress for herself, using her thumb to sweep a path over his cheekbone in a very comforting, very *settle down, dear* manner befitting the future wife of a husband who kinda scared her a little. She sang to him, and gave him her most generous, accepting smile.

He took hold of her hand, and she rose onto her toes, meeting his open mouth with hers.

Immediately, he gathered her close. Her arms wrapped around his neck, and she sank her tongue into his mouth. Lust, wild and wicked, took the kiss to a new level.

With one hand on her upper back and one pressed to the small of it, he held her to his body tightly, so tight she felt the throb of his erection against her belly, which said a lot both about his strength, *and* his erection, given all the clothes they had on.

She had like two seconds to kiss him before she needed to strip off her dress, and she made the most of it, doing her best to lick the minty, strawberry candy-coating off his tongue. A vibration in his chest acted as a sort of warning, but then his hand tightening on the back of her neck told her for sure she needed to wrap this up. They were about to start making sounds, and Peck would *absolutely* not be okay with that.

Parting, they hurried in opposite directions.

During the double wedding, where the entire ensemble sang, nothing memorable in the least had ever happened. All she and Brennon had to do was hold hands, smile at each other, and sing from time to time.

Tonight was another story. When everyone's attention was on Jane and Bingley, Brennon unclasped her hand, ran a finger down the center of her palm and then touched all four spaces between her fingers at the same time with a maddeningly erotic brush of his fingertips. She grabbed hold of his hand urgently and sang something to him that made no sense in her head anymore. Thank God her auto-Lizzie kicked in.

He brought her hand to his mouth and kissed it, which was also something he'd never done before, and she pretty much swooned onstage.

He didn't stop there either. Abandoning the hand holding entirely, he wrapped his arm around her waist, forcing her to respond in kind by encircling his. They waved, blew kisses, and sang merrily as they exited the stage together, covered in fake rose petals.

He tugged her hand. She looked up at him, ready to go wherever he wanted to take her—so long as he *took her*. In the dark, she could barely make out his face, and he didn't say a word. But he walked faster.

That's when she saw a whole new side of Brennon Thorne.

In the narrow space between the velvet curtain and the wall separating them from the audience, barely out of eyeshot from the crowd, he hesitated an inch from her mouth.

"Eden," he whispered.

They had maybe thirty seconds to get this party started and shut it down, so he really needed to skip to the good stuff. She took hold of

145

his face and ended the discussion, her mouth opening against his with the full knowledge that she could do it however she wanted and get in zero trouble at all. He groaned when their tongues met and grabbed her by the ass to grind against him. The poor man made erections like some people made snacks. One right after the other.

"My dressing room or yours?" she asked between kisses.

"Either. Both. I don't care." He sighed, taking her mouth again.

The full force of his sweet mint kiss made her thoughts go all soft and fuzzy. Her thighs ached. Her sex throbbed—demanding. She wanted to tug at his cravat, his breeches, mess up his hair in the worst way, but they had a curtain call to make. Bows to take.

Grasping at a thin thread of reason, Eden forced their mouths apart. She took his face in both hands to examine him. She did her best to put his hair back in order. In turn, he made sure her dress hadn't gotten bunched and a breast hadn't popped out.

"Good?" he asked.

She nodded and gestured at herself. "Good?"

"Better."

She frowned.

"Better than good—"

There was no time to tease him, he needed to take his curtain call. She followed close behind. They joined hands at the foot of the stage, bowed, and waved their thanks.

Meanwhile, her loins were on literal fire.

She couldn't get back to her dressing room fast enough. Or his, or—

Both.

CHAPTER TWELVE

This time, for the sake of his sanity and dignity, and his poor, throbbing cock, Brennon did masturbate in his dressing room.

With the door locked, and Eden on the other side of the wall, he indulged in the fantasy of everything he wouldn't get to do with her tonight because it was too soon, and he had to get this right.

Within moments, he'd reached a state of inner calm, and determined he was ready to face her.

He found her in her dressing room alone, sitting in front of her makeup mirror, wearing a yellow and pink silk robe. Her legs were crossed, and the fabric hung to the sides, revealing every inch of her legs.

"Do you wear that every night?"

"Depends." She flashed her gorgeous smile and gave him a clear-eyed look that was both innocent and diabolical.

"I should visit after the show more often."

"Let's see how this goes first."

He shut the door, threw the lock, and leaned against it. Glancing around the room, he noted, "The couch in my room is bigger."

"I would have stopped by eventually. Someone got impatient." She leaned toward the mirror to run a fingertip beneath her lower lip, perfecting her lipstick.

Only minutes before, he'd pictured his own dick smeared with the stuff. He swallowed and reined in some of his filthier thoughts.

The only thing that needed to happen tonight was to lay a foundation. Brennon had never traded in passing obsessions, and his growing affection for Eden would not stop with one kiss or one hundred. He knew himself, and he was neither a flirt, nor a player. Did he trust his feelings for her? No. He'd been fooled in the past by women who wanted to be seen with him, known in the context of their relationship to him, but Eden had wanted nothing to do with him since the beginning. That the door was open now was a privilege he'd earned, and he wouldn't take it for granted, even if it meant breaking every rule he'd demanded Adam live by.

This was more than a hookup.

Eden went to unpin her hair. Brennon stepped away from the door. "May I?"

She sat up straighter. "Thanks."

Moving into place behind her, he took the first of two dozen pins from her wavy brown hair.

They stared at each other through the mirror. He could barely keep himself from ogling her mouth, dying to press his against it again. There was no tried-and-true choreography to rely on in this room, and yet he still found himself waiting for his cue.

Layer by layer, her hair fell in dark chocolate waves. He ran his fingers through it, combing out the tangles as he went, lightly scratching her upper back. Her spine wiggled as she squirmed beneath his touch. The same soft scent of magnolia and lemon intoxicated him once again.

She lifted her mug of honeyed tea and brought it to her lips to sip. When she set it down, he noticed her lipstick hadn't made a mark. Fascinating.

"May I see something?" With two fingers on her chin, he turned her head to face him. He ran his thumb along that lower lip of hers, and it also came away clean.

"It's new," she said softly. Intimately. "I have to use a special make-up remover to take it off."

He stroked her lip again, and she sighed, her eyes drifting shut.

"Your hands are very . . ." Her words trailed off.

"Very . . .?"

"Expressive," she said.

"Should have been an artist," he said.

"Or a mime."

He laughed. Her eyes opened, and she smiled up at him. "You don't do that much, you know? Laugh. When you're not onstage."

"I do," he said, ready to correct every misunderstanding, put to rest all of her concerns, whatever she'd heard or felt in the past that could keep them apart a moment longer.

"Not around me, then. I mean, except for the night we met."

Ah. The Citaltfor commercial. He'd said worse things since, but he was determined to squeeze every ounce of pleasure from this moment. "Ironically," he said, returning to the task of taking down her hair, "I have not gone a single day around you without getting an erection."

It was her turn to laugh, but hers was high-pitched and surprised. Her hand flew up to cover her mouth.

"Joke's on me, right?" He smiled. It was a relief to laugh about it—his disastrous first impression.

"You're funny!" she exclaimed in disbelief.

"Hardly."

She hummed contentedly. "It's working for me."

"Try to manage your expectations," he said. Brennon knew himself to be many things, but the life of the party was not one of them. He took three more pins from her hair, allowing the majority of it to hang free. The only pin remaining was at her right temple,

149

holding back her bangs. As he ran his fingers through her dark locks to smooth them, she reached up and covered his hand with hers. Their eyes met again in the mirror. Her beauty took his breath away, as did his sudden awareness that nothing was binding her breasts beneath her robe.

With his throat suddenly dry, he forced a swallow. She stood then. After clearing a space for herself on her dressing table, she turned to face him.

Sliding her rear end onto the surface, she parted her legs.

Brennon fought to control his breath. Could this be the moment? His cue? His cock was certainly responding to the sight of her like that, desperate beast that it was, but Brennon hesitated, his desire matched equally with his need not to fuck this up. He feigned at least a modicum of confidence.

"May I?" He gestured to the space between her thighs.

"Please." The uptilted angle of her face caught the light differently, landing shadows in new places.

He moved the chair out of the way and stepped in front of her. "Anything I should know?" Lines not to cross, ticklish spots, biggest turn-on . . .?

"I'm not a virgin, and condoms aren't negotiable."

He attempted to school his expression. Jesus.

She went on. "It's also been a hot second since I hooked up with anyone, sooo . . ."

The words brought him selfish relief. He may never know where the hell her lipstick went that night she spent at the bar with Jonathan, but at least they hadn't left together. He placed his hands on the table, on either side of her, insatiable in his appetite to know everything there was to know about her. "No one here interest you?"

Her gaze swept his upper body and returned to his face. A flirtatious smile curved her plush lips. "What do you think?"

He leaned in closer, bringing his face near enough to smell the honey on her breath. "That I must've finally done something right."

"Just so you know, Thorne, ever since I got the lead I've become a bit of a hot commodity."

"Hmm . . ."

"Peck invited me to his hotel, Jonathan keeps texting me restaurant reviews . . ." She ran a finger down Brennon's throat, stopping at the space between his collarbones. "You bought me a honey dipper."

"It came with the house."

"Liar," she whispered.

Finally, their mouths brushed, but a knock at the door startled them both apart.

"Eden!" Maddox shouted from the other side. "You coming?"

She cleared her throat, and Brennon cringed at the sound. She gave him a look of pure exasperation. "Not tonight," she called out. "You guys go ahead. I made other plans."

"Later," Maddox said, as Eden slapped Brennon's arm.

"I don't have polyps."

"Famous last words," he murmured.

She grabbed him by the waistband and pulled him back to where he'd been before the knock. Her fingers lingered a moment longer against his lower abdomen before she removed her hand from his jeans. "Where's that guy who dragged me offstage and couldn't wait to put his hand up my dress?"

"Waiting for his cue, but you keep talking."

A shy smile formed. "I do have a few more questions."

He nodded for her to go ahead.

"What are we doing?"

"Oh."

She placed her hands on top of his and stroked the skin over his wrists. Sparks flew up his arms. "Is this like . . . a one-time thing? A secret thing? Is it—what is this?"

None of the above, he wanted to tell her. "I don't need it to be a secret."

"I might want it to be a secret," she said. "People could think . . ."

"Yes. They could." Whatever she'd been about to say wouldn't be wrong. People could think all kinds of things. It made no difference to him. He was Brennon Thorne. He didn't have a thing to lose anymore—except this chance with her.

Eden didn't live with any reassurances that the world would treat her fairly or give her the benefit of a doubt. All Brennon had to offer was the shield of his own reputation, and that would only work if she were his.

Given his history with women, the odds weren't in his favor, but his heart was throwing caution to the wind.

"So, we won't tell . . . about this *one time*, or . . .?" She left the blank for him to fill in.

"This *first* time," he supplied.

She mulled his statement over as she studied his face. "So there's no pressure for this particular performance?"

"No pressure," he assured her. "Of any kind."

She ran her hands up his arms, not stopping until her wrists rested on top of his shoulders. "Thank you for talking to me. I like to know what I'm signing on for."

"As do I." He loved her frankness, the vulnerability and the honesty in it. The intimacy nearly overwhelmed him.

"What's your availability like?" she asked.

He quirked a brow. "I imagine it's similar to yours."

"I didn't know if you have other hobbies . . . other *ladies* . . ."

Her final add-on surprised him. "I *also* have gone a hot minute without anyone else's company."

"So . . . you and Gabi . . ."

That was her concern? It was both disturbing and intensely flattering. "Never in a million years."

Eden visibly relaxed. "She acts a little possessive, so I wondered."

"Never. In. A. Million. Years," he repeated with special emphasis on each word.

Eden tilted her face, angling it perfectly for a kiss he'd never wanted to give anyone so much. "I don't have any more questions," she whispered.

"I have one," he said.

She grinned. "Fire away."

"May I have some honey? My throat's a bit dry."

Her hands cupped the back of his neck, and his brain dissolved as she drew him in for a long, delicious taste of the sweetest honey he'd ever licked. Her mouth moved forcefully against his, her tongue spreading the taste around. He savored every second. This was the perfect answer—exactly what he'd meant by the question.

"So good, right?" she whispered against his cheek.

He brought his hips to the edge of the table. Taking hold of her by the waist, he kissed her deeply, for once able to take his time and memorize the feel of her lush lips on his. He sank into the sweet heat of her mouth.

Her fingers tangled in his hair as her back arched. He kissed his way across her cheek, to her ear, and down her neck, every inch of skin as sweet and luscious as her mouth. She gasped at the flick of his tongue against her earlobe and again when his mouth met her bare shoulder. The robe slipped down her arm.

He wanted to taste every part of her but didn't know whether he had the green light to move past her neck. They should have covered all this in the question-and-answer portion, but her mouth was more than enough. Coming back to it, he pulled her lower lip between his, before covering her with a deep kiss. Her hips rocked up, greeting his friendly downstairs neighbor who was always up for anything.

Over his jeans, the palm of her hand moved in a firm rub down the entire length of his erection and gave his balls a squeeze.

"Shit," he muttered against her mouth.

"Told you it's been a while. And my vibrator's dead."

Pressing his forehead to hers, he huffed a laugh and let her feel his cock again. If she kept up much longer, he'd either come, or die desperate to.

Her nose brushed his as she gave him another long stroke. "You really are a legend, aren't you?"

He was so hard. So often men kept their hearts locked up and guarded, but their desire always showed, and Eden loved the feel of it. "You can touch me any way you want," she whispered.

She was ready for more. Not that she didn't appreciate his kiss; it was only that so many other parts of her demanded his attention.

Immediately his hand was inside her robe, on her breast, pressing and squeezing and rubbing. His thumb found her nipple and pinched it as though he knew exactly what she liked, like he'd had his eyes on her in the bathtub that afternoon while she'd lazily touched herself and thought about where she'd be six hours later. And here they were, with him picking up her slack the same way he had the night of her disastrous performance.

He'd been there for her then, and he was here for her now. *So here for her.* Emotion threatened, tangling with her desire and tightening her grip on him. She needed him closer.

Leaning back to give him better access, her shoulder blades and head touched the mirror. When he bent to lick her nipple, she could barely focus her vision anymore. Her hand released his cock to grip the side of the dressing table, hanging on for dear life as he devoured her breast. She watched him until she was so turned on she could no longer bear it. She was drowning in want. The achy throb built between her legs, her girl parts ready for the challenge of taking on the biggest name on Broadway, and one of the hottest men she'd ever met.

She hooked her calves around his thighs and drew his lower body closer.

She wasn't ready to face the fact that the logistics of getting fucked on the narrow dressing table were problematic. He was too tall, and the table was a weird height, and there were lights around the mirror, and her teacup sat only a few inches away. Breaking things wasn't on the agenda.

She gripped his hair and pressed her breast deeper into his mouth. "Couch?"

His head shook beneath her hand as his mouth traveled further down.

This was happening. Brennon Thorne was happening to her. On his knees, tall enough to make the dressing table seem like this was the event it had been built for, Brennon's mouth discovered what her own body was unable to hide. Eden inhaled sharply at the hot slide of his tongue up her slick seam. Her thighs shook, and she worried about her precarious balance, afraid she'd melt off the edge of the table. He ran his hands up her legs and took hold of her by the hips. She braced herself with a foot on his shoulder, her legs falling open wide for him. Keeping one hand in his hair and the other on the table, her position stabilized in time for her to weather the shocking sensation of having her clit sucked by a man who made a living with his mouth.

"Oh, God," she whispered in wonder. "That's really good."

Their eyes met. His were all dark, smoldering embers. *Fuck.* She'd never be able to look at him again without getting wet. She licked her lips and bit down as her chin trembled with a repressed moan. His gaze narrowed as his tongue parted her again.

Yes, please . . .

She threw her head back, and her chest heaved with a deep breath. It came out in a gasp as his tongue entered her barely, and then more, thicker and harder. Grasping her hips, he moved in a rhythm, kissing and licking and sucking. Sensation shot through her, moving in all directions, making her intensely aware of all her exposed parts. Her breasts were achy, wanting, heavy. She let go of his head to touch herself, squeeze her breast, pinch her nipple. His lips closed over her clit and tugged it gently. A connection between her breast and his mouth pulled taut. Another kind of duet manifested—one where they played off each other, building toward a chorus that required them to be in perfect harmony.

She rapidly lost the ability to remain still or quiet. Her hips moved to meet his mouth. Her breath came in long, broken moans and gasps. She rubbed her palm over her erect nipple while he worked her thoroughly with his lips and tongue. He bit her inner thigh, and a new gush of desire slickened her even more. For the first time, she felt something more than his mouth—fingertips and pressure, a stroke through the crease where her thigh met her hip, a knuckle brushing her outer lips. Teasing. Entreating.

"Yes, Brennon." Maybe he needed a reminder. "Touch me any way you want—*please*."

He let out a low growl and entered her. Two long fingers slipped easily inside as his lips continued to nip at the tight throbbing ball of nerve endings just above her entrance.

Her own hand grasped her breast as her back bowed, and she cried out—a high-pitched, staccato sigh. Items fell from the table to the floor as her body responded far too eagerly to this next level of debauchery. Her teacup was a goner, and so was she.

"Please—*oh God*—" She was unable to temper her reaction to him. In the play, Lydia's character was ruined when she ran off with Wickham out of wedlock, and Eden finally understood where the word must have come from—*ruin*.

She was coming apart, breaking down, falling to pieces. A chaos of sensations organized in her center, a heat and pressure swirling low and deep, focusing around his fingers as they pumped and twisted inside her.

Clenching, her body grasped at them.

"My Eden," he whispered, his breath hot on her clit before he sucked it into his mouth again.

Her body shook around him, tension swelled and shrank, col-lapsed and then burst—exploding outward as her hips came off the table. She reached for the wall behind her, shattering with a shocked, breathless cry. *Ruined.*

Slowly, his mouth moved over her belly, traveling up, tending to the poor breast she'd worked into an inflamed state. His tongue soothed her stinging nipple, and the light pressure of his softer touch was a balm to the scratch marks she'd left.

Her breath deepened and slowed as her awareness of him sharp-ened. Lifting a hand, she stroked his cheek, needing to see his eyes again, discover how she could move him as much as he'd moved her. Find a way to ruin him back.

He pressed a kiss into her palm, meeting her eyes as he stood. "You weren't wearing any underwear," he said.

Slowly coming back to her senses, a smile stretched her mouth.

Pulling the chair back to the center of the table, he sat down in front of her, lifting her feet to rest on his spread thighs.

Her robe was open. She was completely naked beneath it, knees bent, spread wide open still . . . And he'd taken a seat.

Cocking her head to the side, she pursed her lips and studied him. "Should we give the couch a go? I mean, if we could make *this* work . . ." She gestured at the table beneath her.

He wrapped his hands around her ankles, running his grip up and down her calves. Eden couldn't help but notice the bulge in his dark jeans. "Not satisfied?" he asked with a grin, because he had to know she was more than satisfied.

She placed a foot on top of his crotch, gently putting pressure on the length of him. "*I'm* good . . ."

He stared up at her with heated eyes. "If I give you all your pres-ents today, what would there be to look forward to?"

She giggled.

Wait, he couldn't be serious.

Her mouth hung open as his meaning registered. "We're not . . .? Brennon." He needed to see reason. She curled her toes around the tip of his hard cock. He suffered the overture with a low groan and then put her foot firmly back on top of his thigh, holding it there. "How very Victorian," she complained.

"Regency," he reminded her.

"Oh, what's the difference?"

"Shall I explain?"

"No, you shall not." She sighed and sat up straight, doing her best to refasten her robe, but the tie had slipped out of the loops at some point, and she didn't care enough to start crawling under the table to look for it. Besides, apparently she needed to get dressed.

Getting her feet back, she dangled them and slid herself off the table to land on the floor.

Right away he grabbed her and pulled her sideways across his lap. She turned to face him. He slid his hand inside her robe again, stroking her breast as he stared at her mouth.

"This can't be comfortable." She had to be crushing him.

"It feels good. You feel good."

Well, if they were just gonna stare at each other, she could stare with the best of them. He didn't have a breast she could fondle, though, so she traced the outline of his mouth before running her fingers through his hair. Their movements grew hypnotic—his gentle massage of her breast and the light tracks she made on his scalp. Their eyes closed, and their faces drifted closer. Lazily their lips met, and she lost herself in his slow, endless kiss.

CHAPTER THIRTEEN

The strawberry tarts came out perfect. Brennon snapped a picture with his phone and sent it to Adam.

His friend responded quickly with a text: *I'm assuming you'll add an extra half hour of cardio.*

Brennon planned to, but he had needs. At least Adam sounded like he was in decent spirits.

"Someone's in a good mood," Gabi said.

Brennon glanced up from the strawberries he'd been chopping to see her slink into the kitchen in her vintage slip nightgown.

"How can you tell?" he asked.

"You were humming something. I heard you when I was coming down the stairs."

He hadn't noticed.

She stretched and swept all her hair over her right shoulder before heading to the coffee pot. "So, what's up?"

"Hm? Nothing."

Gabi picked up the coffee carafe and took a long look at him. "You won the bet, didn't you?"

He glared at her. "There was no bet."

"I mean . . . you more or less agreed to it. I was sitting right there."

"I didn't agree to anything. Jonathan's a pig." Brennon picked up his tart and coffee, prepared to leave the room, but the wise ass look on Gabi's face touched a deep nerve. "There was no bet, and I didn't *win* anything."

"You seem awfully relaxed."

"Okay." He started for the stairs.

She tucked a lock of hair behind her ear and casually lifted her shoulder. "Also, I saw you backstage last night before the curtain call. A few of us did."

"Ah . . . Well . . . Hope you enjoyed the show."

"Eden could do a lot worse than the great Brennon Thorne, but where would that get her, right?"

"Fuck you," he muttered beneath his breath as he stomped up the steps to his room. She'd hit a soft spot like she'd known exactly where to find it. It smarted like a kick to the gut. Out of breath when he reached the top of the stairs, he slammed his door.

The sweet, flaky tart had a moderating effect on his temper. As he ate, he was able to shake off Gabi's words and at least some of her implications.

Eden was young and hungry, yes. She'd been given an incredible opportunity, both to perform as the lead on a successful tour, and to perform opposite him. Brennon might struggle with his sense of worth in personal relationships, but he knew exactly how much he was worth on Broadway, and it was a position few could claim. His name would wind up on her résumé and get directors' attention. At the end of all this, the possibility remained that he may only be a feather in her cap. A notch on her bedpost.

Although, he hadn't made it to the bedpost yet.

The possibility of it happening soon shook him. His desire stirred as memories of last night awakened all the places on his body she'd touched. His wrists, his shoulders, his lips. Jesus, her foot on his dick . . . He wanted more.

He wanted her tonight.

It felt too soon to call her, though.

He'd see her that afternoon for the Sunday matinee. He could stop by her dressing room before the show, or leave a note in it during . . .

His stomach was upset. Lust and excitement didn't mix well with the tart.

They needed a place to go. Not a dressing room, not this house with Gabi, who traded in gossip and innuendo, and not Eden's place with her roommates. Would reserving a hotel room be too presumptuous? Over the top? *Extra?* Adam would deem him the worst kind of hypocrite. He couldn't deny it. Adam had already had months to work out the kinks with Maddox and would get more still if he chose to return, but Brennon's time on the tour was short, and he needed to be alone with Eden. Alone, comfortable, able to really take their time and explore without the threat of injury or property damage.

He exhaled, trying not to get ahead of himself. The first step was to determine if she was interested in meeting again.

He'd walked her home last night, held her hand. Kissed her as they approached her house, and she'd been smiling, laughing with him, at him. Her kisses had been long and addicting, difficult to put an end to. His strategy of keeping himself in his pants paid off— always leave them wanting more, they say . . .

He didn't want to play games with her, though. She deserved better. Deserved to know he wasn't only interested in her for her pouty red lips or her soft, sensitive breasts—he wanted it all. He wanted to know how she spent her free time, how she decided what to have for dinner, where she dreamed of traveling. He wanted to be *involved* with her. Part of him was already invested.

He'd thought, after Chloe left him, he'd want to take his time with the next woman who interested him, hedge his bets. He'd also thought he'd never date another actress again. But from the moment Eden stepped into the spotlight and began to sing during their first rehearsal, something in her spoke to something in him. She surprised him, challenged him, entertained him, and if given the chance he would return the favor.

Unable to stop himself, he texted her. *I'd love to see you tonight.*

Eden bit her lip at the sight of Brennon's text. She smiled, the sun shining on her face through the open window. A warm breeze carried the smell of oak and the river blocks away. She stretched, the sheets sliding across her naked body and reminding her of Brennon's mouth.

"Yes, Thorne," she whispered. "Ruin me again."

Before she could respond to the text, however, her mother called, and her morning-after buzz died a swift and anticlimactic death.

"Hey, Mom."

"How was your week?"

Eden closed her eyes and settled in for the call, which lasted seventeen minutes and ended with Eden's promise to take a long, brisk walk in the sunshine for the vitamin D and cardio benefit. Having a cup of tea on the porch while she relived last night with Brennon in her dressing room over and over again for an hour would likely have the same effect on her heart rate, but fantasizing wasn't a weight-bearing exercise.

She swung her legs out of bed and pulled on her Lulu leggings and a sports bra. Throwing a hoodie on top, she went downstairs.

Maddox was on the couch with all the shutters closed, glued to his PlayStation. Eden sighed. It looked like someone else could use some Vitamin D. "Hey."

"Just a sec."

She waited a solid minute for him to arrive at the next checkpoint in his game. He turned to her with dark circles under his naturally deep-set eyes, which made him look even more hollowed out and broken. Scruff climbed his cheeks, and there was a coffee stain on the chest of his white T-shirt.

"Wow."

He glared at her. "Thanks."

She went through the room, opening shutters as she passed each window. "My mom wants us to go for a walk."

"I don't want to."

"Neither do I, but she's my manager, and we do what she says."

"She's not *my* manager."

Eden walked behind the sofa and put her hands on Mad's shoulders, giving them a squeeze. "It's a gorgeous day, babe. The sun is shining, birds are chirping, the world is turning, and we're going to go on a long, brisk walk through the nation's capital. Let's go find a cool monument or something. I hear this place is lousy with them."

He took one of her hands and held it, leaning to rest his bristly cheek against it. "You're a gem, Eden. But no." He dropped her hand and picked up his controller. "You're on your own."

"Where's Liliana?"

"Didn't come home with me last night," he said.

Eden scowled. "Has she checked in?"

"Relax. She left the theater with Jonathan."

"Jonathan? Seriously?"

"And what were you up to last night?" he asked. "Is everyone getting laid except me?"

"Nope. My balls are as blue as yours. Promise." Liar, liar, pants on absolute fire . . .

He chuckled.

Shit. Speaking of blue balls . . .

Eden raced back up the stairs and grabbed her phone, opening it to the screen with Brennon's text. Dying to hear his voice, she pushed the call icon.

"This is very nineties of you," he answered.

"I'm an old-fashioned girl."

"I could get used to this. Talking to you first thing in the morning."

Her eyes flew wide open, and she was glad she hadn't put through a video call. Her face was one big tell. That was not something a man usually said after a simple hookup. And she didn't hate it.

"Good morning." She put a little purr in the words for him. "I'd love to see you tonight, too."

"To clarify, I meant after the show."

"I gathered that, since it's a matinee."

"I was thinking . . ." he began.

"I'm listening."

"Dinner?"

Eden grinned. "Dinner. Sure, yes. What else do you have in mind?"

"What else do I have in mind? Well . . ." He cleared his throat.

Brennon Thorne cleared his throat. "Brennon!" she squealed.

He cursed.

"Your polyps!"

"I don't have polyps."

"Yet! Oh, God, but now it's only a matter of time." She laughed, snuggling into her pillow with the phone tucked against her ear, the sound of his chuckle vibrating her hand.

"What I was trying to say . . ."

"Yes?" She was tingling everywhere in anticipation of what she hoped he was about to ask.

"I'm not alone in my house . . ."

"Same . . ."

"If you wanted to spend more time together after dinner—"

She shoved her hand between her legs to quell the building excitement there. "Do *you* want to spend more time together?"

"To put it bluntly, I was considering a hotel room."

She closed her eyes. *Yes.* She loved it when he put things bluntly. Maybe he preferred her to be blunt as well. She pitched her voice lower. "Brennon?"

"Mm?"

"Make sure it has a big tub . . ."

All she heard was the slight clicking sound of his swallow.

"Hello?"

"I'm here," he said.

"I'll be a good girl this afternoon and stick to the original blocking, but I think tonight we should try some improv together . . ." God, she was *that* girl. The one that made corny theater jokes and giggled on the phone with her leading man crush.

"I'm sure I can think up some fun prompts," he said, because it turned out, underneath all the Broadway glitz, he was *that guy*, too.

She beamed. "See you at the show."

Eden set off on her prescribed walk at a fast clip, headed in the direction of the Potomac. The rush of her phone call with Brennon warmed her up, and she was already well into riding her second wind. Pulling up an upbeat exercise playlist on her phone, she connected to her wireless headphones and pushed play. It was mid-morning, and the temperature was in the high seventies but humidity thickened the air. She was already sweating when she turned left at the end of the block.

Maybe it was in the direction of Brennon's place, but that was only a coincidence. The houses on his street were nicer. She should have invited him on the walk with her. Then she could have swung by, picked him up, and they'd be making out on a street corner in minutes.

The thought got her even hotter. Of course she wouldn't have done that. Hadn't she been the one last night who'd wanted to keep this whole thing on the DL? And there were a million reasons for it. People would assume things—she was sleeping with him to get ahead, keep the lead, find an in with the bigger Broadway directors. She doubted whether he had the ability to produce any of those outcomes, but an actress sleeping with a more famous and *slightly* older man could never have anything to do with the fact that she actually liked him.

Wait . . . she didn't. Did she? Or was she so wildly attracted to him she could barely think straight? Probably the latter. She knew better than to read too much into a showmance.

She had no idea what was in it for him and didn't want to think about it too much. All she wanted to think about on her walk were ways to make him smile, things that might make him laugh, and anything she could come up with to make him groan. Tonight she'd want to be hearing much, *much* more of the groaning.

"Hey! *Hey! Eden!*"

Eden pulled out her earbuds and whirled around. Gabi jogged up in red spandex capris and a matching bandeau-style sports bra. She had the kind of slight, narrow build Eden once wanted in the worst way, until she'd discovered it was impossible to diet off her boobs or her ass. She'd come to terms with them both, but still sometimes wished spandex could look half that sleek on her. "Hey!"

"Where you headed?"

Eden pointed the opposite direction. "I don't know. Around."

"Mind if I join?"

"Sure, but if you're planning to jog, I'll catch up with you at the Kennedy Center around two."

Gabi laughed. "I don't mind walking."

They fell into step and continued in the direction Eden had been going. She deliberately took a turn away from Brennon and Gabi's house, though.

After a few steps, Gabi turned to Eden with a thoughtful frown. "I wanted to ask how Mad's doing? He hasn't seemed himself lately."

Eden didn't see any harm in the truth. It wasn't like everyone didn't know about Mad's crush on Adam. "Honestly," Eden said, "I think he misses Adam. He'll be back after the break, right?"

Gabi lifted a hand like it could go either way. "Who knows?"

"He's okay though, right? Do you talk to him?"

"He really only talks to Brennon."

"I hope he's doing all right," Eden said.

"Oh, he'll be fine."

Eden reined in her annoyance. Either Adam and Gabi were close, or they weren't. Eden never knew what she was going to get when she talked to Gabi. Lately it had been a lot of snark, so this friendly chitchat raised a few red flags. "Have you all known each other long?"

"I only met Adam in New York during rehearsals. I've been in a show with Brennon before—ensemble, you know? But, I mean—I've heard things from people in their New York circle."

Eden wasn't going to ask.

Definitely wasn't.

Oh, fuck it. "What kind of things?"

"You know, all that stuff about Veronica back when they were at Juilliard together."

Veronica? "Veronica West?"

"I mean, you saw how fast she took off the second Brennon showed up."

Eden had a bad feeling about this. Tension tightened her stomach, and her pace slowed. "Do you know the story?"

"Only what Jonathan told me. They dated at Juilliard, she cheated on him with Brennon, and afterward Brennon wouldn't give her the time of day, then she ended up having some kind of breakdown or something."

"That was Veronica?" It was almost too much to reconcile. Veronica was so self-assured. So confident.

"Yeah."

"Was he that big of an asshole? Maybe it just didn't work out?" God, listen to her defending him. Someone she barely knew. You'd think she actually *liked* him or something. Shit. She did, didn't she?

"If you were the lead on a tour, and your old crush showed up, would that be enough to make you give up your part?"

Of course it wouldn't have been. Eden was reassured.

Then Gabi went on. "My guess? It had to have been pretty brutal. Like, I think he probably slept with her and started rumors about her afterward. Something more on that level. I'm wondering if it happened again that first night in DC."

Eden had to slow down more. She was out of breath. Was there more to the story than even Jonathan knew? It was such a long time ago, though . . . Unless Gabi was right, and Brennon had rejected Veronica again after he joined the tour . . .

Did it matter? It's not like things between Eden and Brennon were serious. They'd barely even made out. Okay, well, more than made out, but still.

"He's a big deal, Eden. And he's known he would be since Juilliard. I mean, look at his career. Nothing's ever stood in his way. You have to be pretty ruthless to achieve that kind of success from the beginning. You and I both know that, right?"

Brennon's career wasn't only remarkable, it was also practically impossible. One in a million.

Gabi stopped, turned to face Eden, and put a hand on her arm. "Trust me—the man's reputation is the only thing that matters to him. Well, that and Adam's reputation." She lowered her voice and stepped in closer. "Look. If you want to know why Adam left—that was Brennon. He didn't want Adam getting involved with people like Maddox."

People like . . .? Eden needed to catch up, and she needed to do it quick. "Why?"

"He's really not a fan of your friend." She made a face like *Eek, shouldna said that.*

The day remained warm, but Eden's blood turned to ice. "What's wrong with Maddox?"

"He's kind of a—I mean, you know. All that business with Nate back in San Antonio . . ."

"Nate?" Eden gaped. "The asshole who outed Maddox at a bar in front of the entire company?"

Though he'd left the tour, the horribly awkward incident was still fresh in the company memory. "That was months ago. How would Brennon know about that?"

Gabi gave a thoughtless shrug. "It came up, and besides, a lot of people were talking that night at the bar. Remember, you were there with Jonathan? Maybe you'd already left."

"I remember the night." But she *had* left, and Jonathan hadn't. What had she missed?

Gabi tipped her head closer to Eden's ear, like she was telling a secret. "You have to know Mad hasn't exactly made a secret of wanting 'all the dick' on this tour."

Eden's head reared back. "Where did you hear that?"

"He told me himself."

"And you go around telling people that?" Eden asked, disgusted.

Gabi did not appear the least bit fazed. "I mean—it was relevant."

"You don't even know him!"

Gabi frowned at Eden like she was an idiot. "I know enough."

"Wow. So this is what you guys do together? Sit around and talk shit about how no one else is good enough to be around you?"

Gabi put a hand to her chest, pretending all shock and innocence. "It's not me! I didn't encourage him to leave. Look—I'm trying to protect *you* here. Some of us saw you sneak off with Brennon in the wings last night, and I thought before you got all starry-eyed over him you should know a few things. Sue me."

"That's it, then? That's all you've got? Everyone misled Brennon about my friend, and he felt like he needed to send Adam away? And a story from fifteen years ago that I've already heard?"

Gabi blinked rapidly, mouth moving like she couldn't even believe Eden wasn't buying the bullshit she was selling.

Eden turned to walk away.

"I didn't want to have to show you this."

Eden stopped short. "Show me what?"

Gabi appeared beside her again, holding out her phone with a video on the screen ready to play. "We have to stick together, or they tear us down one by one. Mad included. Watch it."

The video was dark, and the camera got jostled a lot, but it was easy enough to make out the bar from the night she'd gone out with Jonathan. It was simple to discern Brennon's distinctly beautiful face and Jonathan's gigantic leather watch on his muscled arm waving in and out of frame. Much of it was muffled, but Eden heard Jonathan ask Brennon if he was looking to score with "another leading lady."

Brennon's answer hit her like a gut punch: "She's not a leading lady yet." The arrogant sneer on his face indicated he was offended at the very idea that Eden had the opportunity to perform with him at all.

"Okay, fine." Eden attempted to hand the phone back to Gabi. "Thanks for the heads up."

Gabi made no move to take the phone back. "Keep watching."

Eden braced herself, though she didn't see how it could get much worse.

It only escalated as the men continued to take their drunken jabs at each other.

And then came the bet. Three nights as Darcy in LA if Jonathan managed to sleep with her first.

Brennon refused. She almost sagged with relief until he said, "If she'll have you, take her." Offering Eden up like a piece of meat.

Ouch.

Okay . . . Good to know where she stood with the guys . . .

And then: "If I wanted Eden, I'd shine a spotlight on my bed and she'd come running."

Eden clicked out of the video. "Fuck you, Gabi." She slammed the phone against the actress's bare stomach and let it drop before Gabi had a chance to catch it. The phone fell to the ground as Eden took off quickly in the opposite direction.

Over the course of the next two blocks, Brennon's words went to work on her, slashing through all her bravado, her false sense of accomplishment, and twisting the meaning of everything that had ever passed between them, each sweet word, each kiss—tainted with the truth of what he really thought about *people like* her.

CHAPTER FOURTEEN

Before the show, Eden called Jonathan. She couldn't bear the thought of speaking with Brennon yet. She was far too angry. The words on the video from both men had been out of line, but she hadn't expected much from Jonathan. Brennon's low opinion of her, however, landed so brutally against her chest it was amazing she could still draw breath.

Jon's answering voice was annoyingly smug. "Look who's calling. What can I do for you today, gorgeous?"

Had he always sounded so smarmy? It didn't matter. No more second-guessing. "Hey. Got a few questions for you."

He chuckled. "Okay, shoot."

Eden paced the living room behind the couch where Maddox still sat playing his game, but the sound was off. He was paying attention to her call. "About Veronica."

"Uh-huh."

"Have you heard from her at all?"

"Nope. But don't worry," he said dismissively. "I'm sure she won't be back anytime soon."

"Why are you so sure of that?"

"Who knows?" He sounded like he couldn't have cared less. "I guess from whatever Peck said."

"Don't you guys go way back? Don't you know her from Juilliard?"

Jonathan hesitated a beat. "Is this about her and Thorne?"

"Why didn't you say you were talking about her?" Eden asked sharply.

"She's an old friend," he said. "I guess not everyone minds sharing other people's business, but it's not really my thing."

Eden rolled her eyes and said for the benefit of Maddox listening, "So you didn't want to spill Veronica's business, but telling everybody what a bad guy Brennon is was okay?"

"Look . . ."

Eden was done being manipulated. "No, you look. You should have told me what was said after I left the bar that night. I know you tried to make a bet about me, and I think it's disgusting."

He cleared his throat. The sound grated so much, Eden held the phone away from her ear until he spoke again. "Eden, I was drunk. He and I get into it when we run into each other. It's inevitable. I was wrong to do that. I was being a jerk that night—the guy doesn't exactly bring out the best in me after what happened with Veronica. If you want to know why she left the tour, my guess is she didn't want to go up onstage with him every night for the next two months and pretend to fall in love. He treated her like she was nothing."

Nothing.

"He screwed with her and broke her heart. She was never the same after that."

Eden sucked in a breath. Tears stung her eyes again. "Why would you put me in the middle of that bet? What'd I ever do to you?"

"It was macho bullshit on my part. He mentioned me staying away from you, and I thought, hey—maybe I've got something with you he can't have, and yeah, I was an asshole about it. Like I said, I was drunk, and he got to me. I'm sorry."

The apology helped, but not enough. "So, what he said about me—"

Sharply, he cut her off. "Who'd you talk to, Eden?"

Typical. He would want to know how much information she had so he didn't incriminate himself. She didn't mind telling. If all the cards were on the table, it was harder to explain away the truth. "Gabi took a video of you guys that night."

"So you heard what *he* said, right?" His tone rang out more urgently. Jonathan clearly felt like he had an edge here. He wasn't wrong. "Tell me you heard everything. Tell me you understand what an elitist piece of shit he is."

Oh, she did. From the tips of her toes to the crown of her head, she understood exactly who Brennon Thorne was. He'd used a honey dipper and a promise of a workshop instead of a spotlight, but she'd certainly come running. He'd seen something his longtime enemy wanted, and he couldn't stop himself from taking it away. He'd fooled her into thinking he saw her as a leading lady, as someone who had a chance with him. The truth was on the tape. He only saw her as a standby. She'd been an idiot to believe someone like him could ever have any interest in someone like her.

His acting game was spot on though. Both onstage and off.

He didn't give a shit about her.

If you want her, take her.

She was nothing to him. To either of these men.

She was nobody.

"I heard you both," Eden said.

Maddox had stopped his video game. He reached out a hand for her. She took it and stopped pacing.

"Eden, look—don't go to Peck or Shayna about any of this, okay? It was just a joke. We were just messing around. Nobody was gonna get hurt."

Nobody was her. And maybe she would do exactly that. Go to Shayna and complain of a hostile work environment—toxic masculinity—but right now, she needed to think. More importantly, she needed to talk to Brennon. Face-to-face. Because he'd been the worse offender here by far. Jonathan may have thrown her out as a scrap to fight over, but Brennon did the damage. He needed to understand she was not some toy for him to play with out here on the road because he was bored or had something to prove. "We'll see." She clicked out of the call.

Maddox tugged her hand. She leaned her hip against the back of the couch, and he looked up at her. "Okay?" he asked.

She bit her lip to keep the tears from falling, but it was no use.

"Did he say he was sorry, at least?"

Eden managed a quick nod. Maddox had been the first one she came to with all this when she got back from her walk. He hadn't stopped his game, but he'd been listening when she spilled all the sordid details.

"They just don't see us, Eden. We're like scenery to them."

She nodded again.

"It does hurt, though," Mad admitted, a tiny ray of vulnerability peeking through his thick armor.

She squeezed his hand, angry all over again that Brennon's shadow of influence had engulfed them both and spit them right back out. "It does."

He blinked, and when he opened his eyes again, they were guarded and dark. "So, what's your plan?"

Eden did need a plan.

She'd gotten herself into this mess, after all. She'd bought into her own hype. After she'd scored the lead, of course the men had shown more interest in her—she'd finally been lifted high enough to be within their notice. Standing ovations, rave reviews, exclusive invitations.

But the truth hadn't changed. She was just a cute standby with a shit résumé, and dreams so big they blinded her. She wasn't brokenhearted, but she was ashamed. Embarrassed, furious, and disappointed in herself. She knew better. Biting her lip, she closed her eyes and inhaled.

Brennon had told her what he'd thought about her the first time they met. The fact that he still thought it? Big shocker, right? Men don't change. They just get horny and have the ability to put their values on hold when they think they might be able to get a piece.

Either way, Eden still had a performance to get through with him before she'd have a chance to confront him. She would not let him ruin her matinee.

She was fine. She was a professional. This wasn't the first time a person had tried to take advantage of her, and it wouldn't be the last. Today, he was only another actor in the musical, and she was the star for as long as she could hang on to it. *Know better, do better,* she told herself as she let Maddox's hand go and headed for the stairs. *This was not your fault.*

"I'll let you know," she said, and went to prepare for the Sunday matinee.

Eden lit up the stage again with her cherry-lipped smile and perfect soprano. By intermission, Brennon ached for her, searching every opportunity to find a moment he could steal with her, share a kiss, cop a feel—tonight he prayed he would discover what it was to be inside her.

Frankly, he didn't know whether he could tolerate it. Emotionally, he'd already found his breaking point. The sweetness of her on the phone that morning had been the most wonderful surprise. She'd all but told him outright she wanted him, and he'd wanted to go to her then, storm through her townhouse to find her, take her, ravish her.

Intermission went by too fast. He'd glimpsed her in the larger dressing room with Maddox and Liliana. She was already in costume for the beginning of the second half, and she sipped her tea, coating her tongue with the honey he wouldn't have a taste of for another hour.

He'd attempted to catch her eye, but she'd been listening to something Liliana was saying. His anticipation continued to build.

True to her word, she performed her part for their final duet as the Broadway directors intended. Sweet, demure. Proper. Her eyes sparkled, her lyrics were heartfelt. Her lips were soft and barely parted, but the charge that went through him when they brushed his was no less electric, even though her mouth remained choreographed and restrained.

He struggled to let her go, his body already under the impression she was his.

Turning to the right, she slipped out of his grip and hurried off the stage to her dresser to become Darcy's bride.

In the final scene, she kept a firm, tight hold on his hand, but he still managed to stroke the edge of her index finger with his thumb. Her hand stayed in character, and he made the conscious decision to stop trying to elicit an intimate reaction from her onstage. The time for that had passed. His job was to support her and allow her to shine in the role.

The rest of it could wait until tonight. Until he had her alone, finally, with hours together, and no chance of being interrupted. Perhaps by the time they arrived in Los Angeles they'd be renting a condo together, able to enjoy each other every hour of the day, both onstage and off. By then, he hoped she was so confident in what they could build together, she wouldn't care who knew where she slept at night. That she would claim him.

These were the kinds of thoughts he'd tried to quell throughout the day, but fantasies had a mind of their own, weaving themselves into tapestries of possibility and allowing him to indulge in his deepest desires—her—all to himself—all the time.

While it was far too much to hope after one night of pleasure, it was where his mind led him. Last night, it had been more than physical—there'd been laughter, teasing, inside jokes. Though she'd been the naked one, he'd been laid bare by her.

He knocked on her dressing room door before he left the theater, but she'd already left. He needed to leave, too. He wanted to shower, check into the hotel, get the room ready, make sure they'd both have everything they needed to enjoy a long night together without ever having to leave the place.

The suite at the Four Seasons was perfect. It had the large tub Eden had requested, a plush, king-sized bed he couldn't wait to sink into with her, and plenty of other surfaces they could work with.

Once he checked in, he scanned the room, envisioning the possibilities of her on the linen sofa, the woven rug, bent over that desk . . .

He ran a hand over his mouth in an attempt to get a grip on himself.

A text buzzed his watch.

Eden: *Forget dinner.*

His heart stopped. What?

A second text: *Let's meet at the hotel.*

Relief flooded him, followed quickly with a restart of his heart. Nearly dropping the phone in his rush to respond, he sent her a link to the hotel's directions and added some text. *Room 515.*

She answered immediately with a thumbs-up.

A mist of sweat broke out on him, forcing him to consider whether he should take another shower—a cold one. Instead, he opted to open a bottle of wine and have a glass. Brennon considered giving Adam a call to distract himself from the anticipation of Eden's arrival, but he thought better of it. He stood no chance of being able to keep the excitement out of his voice, or from going on and on about Eden.

Perhaps he'd been unfair with his friend about Maddox. If Adam had felt for Maddox a shadow of what Brennon was feeling, he shouldn't have discouraged him from pursuing it. He could have been more supportive. Instead of telling him to leave town for a while, he could have encouraged him to have a conversation to clear up whatever misunderstanding had soured the other man on his friend. It wasn't unbelievable that Adam, in his enthusiasm, had misspoken. His friend was nothing if not impulsive. The byproduct of such an open heart.

Brennon understood better now. His heart was also wide open, and it was terrifying. But there was a thrill in it, too. Letting his guard drop with Eden last night had both scared and excited him. His heart had beaten too fast, all day. He couldn't wait for what came next.

It wasn't as if he'd suddenly decided showmances were a great idea. They did have the potential to tarnish a good reputation and make a director hesitate to recommend or hire someone who caused unnecessary drama, but they didn't have to be doomed. Plenty succeeded. How else were they to meet new people, after all? Especially people who had similar interests and skin in the game.

The sit-down in DC would come to an end next weekend. After that, the cast and crew had a week off to go home and rest before flying out to Los Angeles. Brennon would catch up with Adam in New York, talk things through, and encourage him to get back to the tour if he hadn't heard back from his audition.

But a new possibility for his week off came to life in his mind as well. Eden in New York with him. Eden in his apartment. Eden in his bed. On his sofa. In his kitchen.

A knock on the door had Brennon bolting upright from his seat on the sofa. He ran a hand down the front of his black button-down shirt. He'd been dressed for dinner, but now the clothes felt like overkill. He should have stripped down to his T-shirt, but it was too late to change.

He walked to the door and opened it.

CHAPTER FIFTEEN

Brennon Thorne stood tall, all dressed in black. From his hair to his polished shoes, he cut a sleek figure in the doorway of his Four Seasons suite. On brand: six four and striking. Eden could forgive herself for having wanted him. She was only human.

"You look beautiful."

Did she? In jeans and an old white sweater, Eden had dressed down. She hadn't come to make a fashion statement. She came to draw a line.

Without waiting for an invitation, she walked into the hotel room and noted the open bottle of wine, the half-finished glass on the coffee table. She also caught the flicker of candlelight coming from the bedroom. She refused to glance that direction. The idea of it—as much as she'd longed for it this morning—constricted her throat.

The door clicked shut behind her, and she turned to face Brennon. All she could make out in his gaze was adoration. Want. The same worshipful sense of wonder she'd heard in his voice and felt from his lips last night. She tried to swallow, but it wasn't easy. Words got stuck in her throat.

"Wine?" He gestured toward the bottle.

Should she?

"No."

He bowed his head a moment, pretending to be awkward, at a loss. This whole show he put on about letting her lead the way.

She opened her mouth to speak—

"I have something to confess," he said.

Her lips pressed together, eyebrows lifted. Hope threatened. Maybe he would clear all this up.

"I didn't want to have to tell you this tonight. I thought I'd be able to be smoother, but seeing you now, I know I won't be. I'll say something or do something in a moment, and I don't want you to be surprised. If I'm going to make a fool of myself, I'd rather do it now— so you have the opportunity to walk away without it being too weird."

It was already weird. She had no idea where he was going with this, but she wanted to skip to the end. She couldn't stand the suspense.

"Eden . . ." He stepped closer to her. Took her hand. She fought the urge to snatch it back, the heat of it burning her, her body yearning to lean in to his touch, his warmth.

She wouldn't let herself.

"You—" He chuckled, almost shyly, but there was a hint of patronizing as well. "Are not the type of woman I typically find myself drawn to, but despite my better judgment, my past, the lessons I've tried to learn—I find myself falling for you. Whether I like it or not."

Every word grated her already raw nerves. Was she supposed to thank him?

As though he could tell she wasn't exactly swooning, he went on. "Shit. What I mean to say is—you're incredible. Talented. Beautiful. You make me laugh. You're smart, and you're exciting, and I find I don't care how embarrassing your mother is or how many infomercials you made in Indiana." He smiled like the thoughts amused him, still. "You deserve to be exactly where you are right now, starring in a show where you can show off how hard you had to work to build a dream out of nothing. It's like watching a rose bloom right before my eyes every time you're onstage. So, no—to answer your question from last night again with more clarity, I never wanted just one night with you. I want to spend every spare moment I have with you."

Apparently, Brennon Thorne currently had an opening for the role of Leading Lady Number Nine. Was he proposing a relationship? A fling? More?

No.

Eden smirked. She knew exactly what he was offering her—a spotlight, to which she'd supposedly come running.

She slipped her hand out of his and took a step back.

"That was too much," he admonished himself.

"It wasn't too much, Brennon. It was too far."

His forehead tightened in question.

She took hold of the sleeves of her sweater, balling her fists around the frayed hems. "I know exactly what you think of me. Of people like me."

He shook his head, playing the part of "confused man" like the consummate professional he was. "If something I said made you question—"

"Everything you said made it clear, actually. Maddox was only good for Adam to hook up with. You only invited me here for the same. There's no need to pretty it up with compliments or remind me how hard this must be for you to put all your reservations aside, and accommodate some standby who happened to get lucky for a few weeks."

His lips parted, dark eyebrows drawing together over widening eyes. A perfect portrayal of "panic." "Eden, you have to know by now that isn't how I see you—and as far as Adam goes, he made a mistake."

"Slumming it with my friend?"

"Yes—I—no! What?"

"I mean, you do realize not everyone gets their entire Juilliard education handed to them on a silver platter. Some of us have to start with nothing and make *infomercials in Indiana* and have our *embarrassing* mothers manage our careers. It can take us years to get taken seriously, because we've had to work for every break we ever got. I'm sure it *is* fun for someone like you to discover we actually have some talent—some *worth*," she spat. "But I am not yours to discover, do you understand?"

He tugged at his collar, pulling open the top button. "Why don't we have a seat—there's obviously been a misunderstanding, I'm not the best at talking to people." He gestured toward the sofa.

"I'm not planning to stay."

"Eden—" The pleading edge in his voice almost got to her. Almost.

"If you want to cut down on energy costs, you can go ahead and turn the spotlight off."

He glanced at her, his face wrecked with confusion. "Pardon?"

"The one shining on your bed. I've had a long day, and I don't feel much like running."

"Jesus," he whispered. He dropped his head, both hands raking down his face. "Was it Jonathan or Gabi who spoke to you?"

"What difference does it make?" she asked.

"Because Jonathan has been trying to undermine my success since we were teenagers, and Gabi has her sights set very clearly on my bed. You can't trust them to—"

"Well, they're not out to get *me*," Eden reasoned. "And did they lie?"

In that moment, finally, he had the decency to let a flicker of shame soften his stormy eyes. "Jon and I have a history."

"Yes. I know about Veronica."

Brennon's jaw twitched. "He told you about Veronica? Tell me." His voice lowered, hardened. "What did Jonathan tell you *I* did to Veronica?"

"I'm no idiot. I know better than to believe anything either of you say anymore. What I know is she was a pawn between you, and she wasn't strong enough to handle it at the time. I don't blame her for not wanting to work with both of you here. It's a shitty feeling to be used to prove some disgusting point to satisfy your egos. If I could leave this train wreck, I would, too. But I'm not Veronica. I'm 'not a leading lady yet,'" she taunted, more of his words she was happy to throw back in his face.

He closed his eyes. His chest moved on a deep inhale, the way it would before he burst into song. "You don't think very much of me, do you?"

"No worse than you think of me, apparently."

"That is *not* the way I think of you," he said, adamant.

"So you never said those things?"

"I did. I admit, I did say those things. I didn't want to make the same mistake Adam was making, getting involved with someone on a tour—someone like you, yes, who could be using me for all the reasons I warned my friend about."

"Maddox wasn't using him!"

"I believe you," Brennon replied, hushed to counter Eden's shout. "If you'll please let me explain—"

"Don't bother," she said, despondent. Numb. His explanation wouldn't help. She couldn't unhear his words, the same way she couldn't unravel his years' worth of believing "people like" Eden or Maddox weren't entitled to the same level of respect or regard he had for his own inner circle—or for himself. "You made your speech, so here's mine: You are a pompous, condescending elitist who doesn't give a shit who he hurts as long as your reputation stays golden. But don't worry, Brennon Thorne, because from way down here," she gestured to herself, "it looks like you're all set."

Something in him deflated then. Like she'd stuck a pin in the bubble of his pride. Though a small part of her registered triumph at the sight of it, her hurt spilled over. "You've put on a great show the last couple of days—it actually makes me wonder if you took Jonathan's stupid bet more seriously than it sounded like on the video Gabi showed me."

His face went slack, perhaps at the realization that none of what she knew was hearsay. She'd heard it all straight from the son of a bitch's mouth.

"You turned out to be exactly who I thought you were. Judgmental, arrogant, and entirely self-serving. You don't give a shit about anyone. I fucking hate myself for looking forward to tonight." She sidestepped him, her shoulder bumping his arm as she passed him on her way to the door. "And don't you *ever* say another word about my mother. She is honest, kind, and she has *never* stopped believing in me."

"Eden—please—"

"Shut up!" Tears threatened, but she refused to let them fall. She kept her voice firm and steady. "Stay away from my friends, stay away from me, and do not ever put your hands on me again in a way you're not expressly being paid to do, or I'll report you for harassment. Understood?" She didn't wait for an answer as she flung open the door. "Good."

It slammed behind her, and the silence of the hall rushed to fill her ringing ears.

She stood still for a beat, enough time to replay and commit to memory the words she'd used to make him understand how wrong he'd been. Had they been enough to change him as a person? To make him alter the course of his life and never speak about another woman like that again?

Somehow she doubted it. With a track record like his, it would take years of intensive therapy to undo all his narcissism. Personality traits like that tended to stick. She blew out a shaky breath and found her knees were wobbly. It had taken something out of her, too—to confront someone like that. To go off the way she had. She'd never done anything like it before, but she'd also never been so humiliated.

Almost humiliated, she reminded herself. None of this was her fault.

One foot in front of the other, she walked down the hallway to the elevator, her footsteps silent on the plush carpet.

Blooming like a rose . . . He was so full of shit.

But she'd stood up to him. For her friends. For herself. For her career. She'd come way too far, from South Bend to performing opposite one of the biggest names on Broadway, to let anyone's name tarnish hers. Reputation was everything in this business. Unfortunately for Thorne, his had come back to bite him.

Brennon shook as he reached for the arm of the sofa before collapsing onto it. His legs gave out. They'd been cut off at the knees. He dropped his head into his hands and forced air in and out of his lungs. Rage spiked his adrenaline, and frustration sharpened his focus.

He should have destroyed Jonathan March at Juilliard when he'd had the chance.

Veronica's delicate face flashed through his mind, the tears and the trembling of her chin, as she'd confessed what happened between herself and Jonathan back then. *"Brennon—I'm so sorry. I made a mistake."*

Veronica in those days had been as much of a confused and horny college kid as the rest of them, but Brennon knew she regretted cheating on him with Jonathan. When Jon told her he wasn't interested in anything more, and Brennon had shut her out, she'd taken a turn into more self-destructive habits. Partying, cocaine—she'd had to leave school because she got caught with a vial of it before a performance one night.

Veronica had struggled with her relationships in college and since, but her talent and determination ultimately won the day, and she'd made her comeback. They'd recovered at least their friendship since, and Veronica remained one of Brennon's closest friends to this day. He strongly suspected Jonathan played a part in her leaving the tour.

He was more determined than ever to see her in New York and sort out this mess.

Such a mess.

His heart thudded painfully, threatening a sudden break. He covered it with his hand, willing it to calm down. This could mostly be undone. He could clear up the misunderstanding about Veronica, and he could apologize for his drunken, thoughtless words at the bar that night. Somehow he'd skipped that part with Eden. She deserved an apology at the minimum.

What he couldn't fix, what was irreparable, was the same thing that had always been.

He'd never seal the deal. He would never get the girl. His own voice—his heart—was fundamentally flawed.

Motherless from a depressingly young age, he'd been at the mercy of his mourning father, who wasn't cruel but cold. Stoic. Hiding his pain behind his ambition and drive. Brennon was in boarding school at Sullivan before he'd even lost all his baby teeth. From there to Juilliard without so much as a fishing trip with his father in between to teach him how to connect. It was always strive, work, succeed. Love was as scarce as it was sacred.

Veronica should have been different. She'd been at Sullivan, too. They'd damn near grown up together, but *Hamlet* happened, and when Jonathan hadn't gotten the part, he took his revenge in the way he knew it'd hurt Brennon the most—by giving Veronica the type of attention she so desperately craved from Brennon. Until she'd served her purpose and broken Brennon's heart. It had taken years for her to forgive him for how he'd treated her back then once the truth was out.

Since then, as an actor, half his life had been in service to others' carefully crafted words. Outside of a theater, off script, his own words would forever be inadequate. Even offensive. They did damage he never intended, but no one had ever pointed it out so harshly at a time when it meant so much.

The effect was devastating.

What he said to Eden tonight, when he'd only meant to charm and flatter her—he'd put it all so poorly. Bringing up the infomercials, her *mother* . . .

"Fuck," he whispered.

He didn't deserve her. Likely he never would.

There was no taking any of his disgusting words back.

She'd made her case and proved her point, and in the end, she managed to get a few things right. He was insufferable, and he deserved to be alone. There was a certain calm that came with accepting the truth.

With a steadier hand, he picked up his phone, determined to fix what he could. In a year, he'd lost more of his heart than he'd been willing to spare, but he still had one of the most important pieces of it. He dialed the number and waited for his best friend to pick up.

CHAPTER SIXTEEN

Eden,

I hope this catches you at a reasonable hour and you've had a chance to sleep, and maybe (hopefully) be open to the truth.

I understand why you're angry, and my intention is only to set the record straight. You should also know Brennon Thorne is my best friend, and I have been, and remain, his biggest supporter. So I may be a little biased.

I'm afraid there's been some confusion.

First, I took a break from the tour for two reasons. Number one: I had the opportunity to audition for Bingley on Broadway. It was an opportunity that I decided I couldn't pass up. Number two: I needed some time to think about what went wrong with Mad and me.

It's only a break. I was exhausted and emotional, and Brennon was right—I needed the time. He gave me his advice, which I value, but I made the decision on my own. I have every intention of meeting up with you guys in LA, lacing up my breeches, and getting back onstage. I also have every intention of speaking with Maddox to clear the air. Please know, I care about your friend very much, and my heart is in the right place.

Next, and more importantly, Jonathan is a pathological liar. Brennon wasn't really clear about what you'd heard regarding Veronica from back in the day, and I wasn't there, but Veronica is a friend of ours. She comes to dinner parties, we see shows together, Brennon has lunch or drinks with her every month or so to catch up. They have no bad blood or ill will. If you have her number, you should give her a call and get the real scoop. I have every confidence she'll tell the story of what happened at Juilliard the way Brennon once told it to me: He was head over heels for her, and Jon seduced her when Brennon beat him out for Hamlet. Apparently things went downhill from there, but all that's Veronica's story.

Here's the one thing I know for sure: Jonathan March brings out the very worst in Brennon. That night at the bar, they were both drunk, they were both posturing, and they both chose their words specifically to shut the other down. I got him out of there as fast as I could, but the damage was done, and all I can say is, Brennon is not that man. He's one of the good ones.

In contrast, Gabi is a petty, jealous dick and no longer on my Christmas list. She's your understudy, Eden. She wins if you lose. And she's been hot for Brennon since they started sleeping under the same roof, so you can do your own math on that one. She sucks, and it's really disappointing, but there it is. Sometimes we choose the wrong people to trust.

If you're trying to find Brennon (and I think you should), he'll be staying at the Four Seasons for the rest of the week. Pretty sure you've got the room number.

He's a good man, Eden. Does he have an ego? Yes. He's been told since boarding school he's the best thing to ever step on a stage. You've probably been told the same thing. He can't help the family he was born into or the luck he's had. You can't either.

Finally, and I'm positive you don't want to hear this coming from me, but he cares about you. I know because he told me, and I know because I know what it's like to be cared about by him. I trust him with my life and my heart. He's never let me down.

Look, I know as well as anybody, sometimes we just want a little action while we're on the road. If that's all you were interested in with him, no judgment. But I think Brennon was hoping for more.

No one wins everything, not even the great Brennon Thorne. However, maybe, when you've had a chance to think about things and do a tiny bit more research . . . you could consider giving him his heart back in good condition. He'll need to use it again eventually.

Feel free to reach out to me if I can help any more. Give everyone my best, and I'll see you in LA.

Best,

Adam Eisner

P.S. Break a leg at the directors' performance today! You'll do great! Xoxo

Eden shut her laptop as a nauseating mix of nerves, regret, and disappointment rose up her esophagus. Sweat broke out on her neck and her fingertips tingled. Dizzy and off balance, she stood, making it to the toilet just in time to reject her entire lunch. Acid burned her mouth.

She coughed, cleared her throat, cursed herself, and coughed again. It only brought up more bile.

She covered her mouth to try to keep anything else from coming up. She had to get control. She had two performances today. One for the directors, and one for another sold out audience. So many feelings, and no idea how to get a handle on them.

Honey. She needed honey.

Her insides lurched again.

Calm down.

The timing of that email was the worst. The performance for the New York directors was in two hours. She'd logged on to her laptop to pay her cellphone bill, and Adam's email had popped up with the subject line: THE TRUTH ABOUT BRENNON THORNE, and hello clickbait. What else was she supposed to do but read it? It's not like she'd recognized Adam's email address. For all she'd known it could have been more dirt from an anonymous source to help her further justify the dressing down she'd given Thorne in the suite where they'd been meant to have the hottest night of her life.

Instead, it had become a crime scene. The place where she'd attempted to maim a man by crushing his ego beneath her shoe.

Her stomach flipped again, and she gripped the edge of the toilet seat, forcing a breath in through her nose and out through her mouth. Fine. So she'd gotten a few things wrong. Brennon hadn't been the only reason things didn't work out with Adam and Maddox, and Jonathan had been the jerk back at Juilliard. Shocker. He looked the part.

The hardest part to swallow about Adam's email, by far, was his theory that Brennon had real feelings for her—that he'd acted out of a true sense of desire, and not some whim to best his nemesis. Was that so hard to believe? That he could want her? After all, in her dressing room he'd shown his desire in no uncertain terms.

Could she buy into the idea that he had feelings for her? He'd infused her tea and purchased a honey dipper on a moment's notice. He'd helped her recover from a terrible performance at the expense of his own time, and he'd never once touched her without her damn near begging for it. Was it so easy to throw all that out the window because *Gabi* of all people had video evidence from last week that his intentions at some point had been less than pure?

Yes, it was too hard to believe. It had only been her fantasy. She'd love to think Adam knew what he was talking about, but it was too far of a stretch.

Shit. If she didn't find a way to start believing she was worth something—and soon—she'd never be able to hold her own with Brennon onstage again.

She stood and gargled some water. She brushed her teeth, but the acid still burned her throat. On shaky legs, she made her way down to the kitchen. She needed milk to neutralize the acid, and honey to coat her throat, and she needed to understand at what point she'd let Brennon Throne get under her skin.

It had been from the beginning. From the moment they'd met—the first joke at her expense, and then two days later when they'd taken the stage together. She'd cleared her throat, and he'd regarded her with disdain.

Or—*concern*?

Could it have been concern? No. She'd been a standby. He had no reason to notice her, befriend her, or concern himself with her. If Veronica had stuck around, he wouldn't have been forced to. Eden was not what he signed up for. He was established, and she wasn't a leading lady yet.

"Be honest with me—how bad of an idea is egg salad before this performance?"

Eden looked up from the mug of milk she'd filled as Liliana entered the kitchen. Lactose wasn't exactly ideal pre-show either.

Lili's eyes widened. "You okay? You look a little green around the gills, as my abuela would say."

If Eden didn't get some support right that second she was going to break. She pulled her phone out of her dress pocket, opened the email, and passed it over.

"Who's this from?" Liliana asked as she took a seat at the counter to read.

"Adam."

"Why's he emailing you?"

"Just read it." Eden turned her back on her friend and picked up her jar of honey. She drizzled three spoonfuls into the milk and popped it in the microwave.

Forty-five seconds passed before she removed it and turned back around to find Liliana staring at her with an expression utterly blank of emotion. "Well?" Eden asked.

"Well," she said. "I still have questions."

Eden tried to swallow, but her throat was inflamed. Or wait—no—she was crying. She wiped her eyes and took a sip of milk. It didn't go down easy, but it soothed the burn.

"Eden, I totally get why you're upset. They were both jerks, and okay—so Jonathan maybe comes out a little worse in the wash, but from what you told me and Mad yesterday, Brennon said some pretty rough shit about you, too."

Eden sniffed, nodding. Of course Adam would stick up for him. So why was this guilt weighing her down so hard? "I wasn't too hard on him, was I?"

After Eden had come back from the Four Seasons, her friends had been waiting with a box of wine, ready to hear how it had gone. There were no secrets here.

"I don't think so. Look, I know I went to Yale and everything, but these Juilliard people—they're a different breed. It's hard to blame them, but it doesn't excuse them either." Liliana gave her head a firm shake. "Forget him. How can I help *you*? We have a huge afternoon, and you look like you're about to have to call out sick."

"I can't do that." Eden had never wanted to skip a performance more, but no way in hell was she giving Gabi the satisfaction.

"Then we need to find a way to smooth things over so you can take the stage with a clear head. You have his number, right? You two should clear the air before the performance today."

Eden balked. "What?"

"I'm not saying you have to kiss and make up or anything, but acknowledge that you're two different people, you both got carried away, and it's time to get back to work. Focus."

"He won't want to see me."

"He'll have to see you, regardless. You have two shows with him today."

The milk soured in her stomach, and Eden felt whatever color that remained draining from her face. Her hand holding the mug shook.

"If you won't meet with him to talk it out, do you think you'll be able to put all this aside and do what you have to do today? They'll be watching you especially close."

Eden covered her mouth so nothing but words came out of it. "I have to, don't I? If I see him before, I'll just—" More tears spilled. She cried out in frustration. "*God*, I'm pissed. And I'm confused, and so irritated with myself for getting involved with him at all."

"Eden, please, no one could blame you for that."

"What was I thinking? Like we could work?" She shut her eyes and let the tears come. "He'll always be the star, and I'll always be a fucking joke."

"Whoa—hey. You're not a joke."

How could everyone not see by now? "A fluke, then. Right place, right time, right hair. They're gonna see right through me today."

"Eden! Stop! What is this?"

"Stop?" Eden gasped and collapsed internally, impostor syndrome practically choking her. "My biggest claim to fame is a Citaltfor commercial where I let a fifty-year-old man palm my ass in a black bikini. I took tap lessons at Fannie Henderson's Famous School of Dance in nowhere Indiana, and I made an infomercial for Shake Weights."

Liliana's lips tugged up at the edges. "Oh my god, you never told me *that*."

CHAPTER SEVENTEEN

The cast took their seats in the first two rows of the house as the four New York directors made their way onto the stage. Brennon sat between David Clarke and Carla Broderick, two of the oldest members of the cast who had the fewest fucks to give.

The performance had been a nightmare, compounding Brennon's misery with every second and every song. He was beyond grateful it was over, but the worst was yet to come for Eden.

He'd need a stiff drink after this. Good thing the minibar in his suite was stocked. Settling his arm on the armrest between himself and David, he put his forehead in his hand.

"Let's start with the opening number. Eden. We have several notes."

Brennon's heart sank. Eden had been an unmitigable disaster. There'd been nothing he could do to save the performance, and he *had* tried to save it. From the beginning she'd missed cues, she'd been slow, her voice sounded like she'd smoked a pack of cigarettes before walking onstage—at times, she'd looked absolutely lost. It had been a performance worthy of an understudy who'd gone weeks without playing the part, and nowhere near what she was capable of. It was one of the most difficult things he'd ever had to endure—because it had been his doing.

He'd undone her.

If he'd kept his mouth shut, his hands to himself, kept his feelings bottled up, she'd have been able to sparkle for the directors the way she'd always shone for the audience. But he'd gotten in her way, and for the next sixty minutes, the entire cast sat and listened while four prominent Broadway directors ripped her performance apart. The only other person who had a fraction as many notes as Eden was Maddox, and Brennon blamed himself for that, too.

Both of them were better than this.

Kip King, one of the assistant directors, looked up from his note-book and zeroed in on Eden again. "The kiss at the end—Eden, do you always cry? I didn't like it. We didn't like that. Don't."

Brennon's jaw clenched. He'd been desperately hoping he'd been the only one who'd noticed the tear slipping down Eden's face when they'd had to kiss once again onstage.

It had wrenched him, twisted every internal organ and left him man-gled. Last night she'd told him very expressly never to touch her again in a way that hadn't been specifically choreographed, and he hadn't, though his hand had ached to brush the tear from her cheek. He'd almost started crying himself, but the way she'd torn herself from him as the lights dimmed made him realize she wasn't sad, or even hurt. She was angry.

He could hardly blame her.

After the excruciating notes session finally came to an end, Bren-non rose quickly and walked directly to Shayna, who stood off to the side of the directors, about to get pulled into a private meeting with them. "A word?" he asked.

The stage manager frowned up at him, peeved. He indicated the right stage wing. She sighed and followed him there. "I'll fight to keep her," Brennon declared, once they were alone and he had her full attention.

She gave him a slow, unimpressed blink. "You're only here another month. We've got four more months after that."

"You know she's better than that."

"If she can't turn out consistent performances—if she can't take the pressure—"

"She's sick," he insisted.

"She didn't tell me that. She didn't tell *them* that."

He gestured at the seat Eden had been in as the cast filed out. "You heard her. She's obviously not feeling well."

"Look, you know I like Eden, but I don't know if either of us can save her. Let's see how she does tonight. I'll go through her notes with her in the morning. I'll see what I can do."

"She's *good*, Shay."

"Good's not good enough. You know that. I gotta go. You rest up for tonight. Maybe send up a prayer."

Brennon shoved his hands into his pockets and stared at the scuffed-up stage beneath his feet. He wasn't holding out much hope that tonight would be any better, prayers notwithstanding.

At the end of the day, the only good thing he could say about their evening performance was that he made it to the curtain without crying again.

He only wished he could say the same for Eden.

Eden sat in a chair across the desk from Shayna in a dark backstage office she'd never had the bad luck to get called into before.

"Eden, first of all—what the hell happened yesterday?"

Eden rolled her lips into her mouth and closed her eyes. Tears threatened again. She inhaled. In the hours since the show ended last night, and this meeting, she'd made several mistakes.

One: She'd watched *Jerry Maguire* with Maddox before she went to bed. It had embittered her in a way it never had before. "See?" She'd gestured at the screen. "He totally settled for her! And she's acting like she's all happy about it, but it's fake. She knows she was his last option. He never got over Avery!"

"Of course he did!" Maddox argued.

"Then why did he look like that at the wedding? Every time she watches their wedding video, for the rest of their lives, she's gonna think he could have done better."

"He literally said *You complete me.*"

"Only because he can't be alone, and he knew that was the only line that would work. This movie is awful!"

"You need to go to bed."

Two: She hadn't gone to bed. She'd called her mother.

Three: She'd told her mother how badly she bombed the directors' show and described every note they'd piled on her in detail. "I cried at the end because I knew I'd lost the part. I was so bad."

"I can't believe that's true."

"Should I go through the notes with you again?" Eden asked.

"Mm . . . maybe email them to me. I'll look through them myself later."

"They'll have to recast the role. If I'm lucky, I'll get to go back to standby, but after today, I imagine they're probably looking for someone else to do that, too."

"You have a contract," her mother reminded her.

"They have their ways."

Her mother had then taken advantage of Eden's weakened state. "You know . . . I've been emailing back and forth with Brice Phillips the last few weeks . . . he seems open to looking at your reel."

Brice was her mom's dream film agent. He was based in LA. Signing with him would mean more money, more commercials, more TV, maybe a bit part in a blockbuster—a diner waitress or something. She'd make a great movie waitress. Too bad she sucked at it in real life.

Four: Eden wrote down Brice's information, because she couldn't picture herself living in New York much longer anyway. Her failure was too humiliating. She'd ruined her entire life in twenty-four hours. *Because of a guy.*

She should quit now and save everyone the trouble of having to figure out how to fire her.

Meanwhile, Shayna continued to wait patiently for her response. "I really wasn't feeling well," Eden said to the stage manager. "I tried to pull myself together for the performance, but I'd thrown up earlier, my voice was off, my throat hurt, and I got in my head."

"Why didn't you tell me before the show? I could have warned them—they might have cut you some slack, and we all wouldn't have had to listen to them come down on you so hard. They're human, you know. They understand people are people."

"I thought I needed to suck it up." Her chin quivered. Silent tears poured. It was how her morning was going. Her forecast for the rest of the week was more of the same. God, she needed the break they had coming up. She wanted to crawl onto her mattress in her tiny downtown bedroom and sleep the entire week. It would be too hot to do anything else. The apartment she shared with two other actresses didn't have air conditioning.

She held in a sob.

Shayna pushed her notebook aside and folded her arms on the desk. "We don't need to go through your notes. You know what you did wrong. I also know you're capable of doing it right. I'm on your side, Eden. I don't want you recast, Thorne doesn't want you recast—but you've gotta step it up."

"He said that? Did you talk to him?" She hiccupped.

"Thorne? *He* talked to *me*, more like. He explained you weren't feeling well yesterday."

Eden's head jerked. She hadn't spoken to him yesterday. It was all she could do to take the stage and share it with him. She'd felt so fucking small, and his voice was too beautiful to bear. "I'm sure he noticed," she whispered.

"If you need to take the night off, I understand, but tell me now. I'll need to rearrange three of the cast and move up a swing."

"No." She cleared her throat. Cursed herself. She sat up straighter. "No, I have to do it. I have to prove I can do this. I know I'm down, but I'm not out, right?"

Shayna gave her a look that could have gone either way. "Listen." She folded her hands on her desk and leaned in. "I'm not blind, all right? And I've got eyes everywhere. Peck watches you like any second you'll have to walk over a puddle and he'll need to put down his coat, so I know there've been . . ." Her lips twisted. "Rendezvous."

"Pardon?" Did Shayna think she was messing around with Peck? Ew.

"Thorne was very passionate when we spoke yesterday."

"He was?" Eden didn't want to hear this.

"Something going on between you two that may be harming the company dynamic?"

Did she have to answer that?

Shayna waved the question away, clearing the air. "This isn't my first tour. I find these things work best when expectations are kept to the bare minimum. You feel me?"

Eden nodded.

"Helps minimize the *drama*."

Spoken like a stage manager who'd definitely been around the block. People who took on other people's personas for a living and worked seven days a week to achieve a dream that was only for the fiercest few, tended to err on the dramatic side. God knows Eden did. The whole "never touch me like that again" thing had been over the top in both conception and execution. But so had any notion that she ever had a chance with Brennon Thorne. Eden fed off dreams and drama, but they probably gave Shayna heartburn.

"You've worked with him before?" Eden worked up the nerve to ask.

Amelia Jones

"Thorne? Sure. Handful of times. Six months on *Philadelphia Story*."

He had to have been amazing in that one. It was one of Eden's favorites, but she'd only seen the tour when it came through Indianapolis years ago. Brennon would make a phenomenal Dex.

He'd make a phenomenal anything. Eden still couldn't shake the feeling she was missing some fundamental fact about him, though. A truth that lay between his sneering tone from the video and the glowing report from Adam.

Perhaps Shayna could offer Eden a less-biased perspective to help her find her footing with him again. "It's like I hear two things, from two sets of people. He's a dream—that's the word on the street, right? Or he's an ego-driven maniac who manipulates everyone around him for fun."

A laugh puffed through Shayna's lips. "Who told you that?"

"People," Eden mumbled.

"People who don't know him very well. Now, I'm not about to say the man has no ego. If he'd had to take the notes you took yesterday he would have probably had an article printed on Page Six about Kip King's extramarital affairs, but I've always found what I see is what I get with him. Aside from the fact that he only wants watermelon mints stocked in his dressing room and Waterloo Watermelon water—which isn't always easy to come by. Other than that, I've never had any issues out of him." She grinned and gave Eden a wink. "I've got a case of it in my hotel for him. Should last. Good stuff."

Watermelon mints? It hadn't been strawberry she'd tasted on his tongue. It was totally watermelon. What else had Eden gotten wrong about him? Maybe he wasn't the absolute worst. Maybe she was. She bit her lip to stop herself from crying again.

"Anyway, I've always thought he was a nice guy, easy enough to talk to, more down to earth than some of them." She waved her hand in the general direction of the dressing rooms. "If you're having differences, wouldn't hurt to talk 'em out."

202

Eden nodded, sort of on board with the idea.

"Before tonight, maybe?"

It didn't sound like a suggestion. "Gotcha."

"'Cause I really need you not to cry at the end. 'Kay?"

Then Eden would definitely have to talk to him before tonight, because otherwise she couldn't make any promises. "Right."

It wasn't like things could get worse.

The text she sent Brennon was simple: *Would you be willing to meet me for coffee before the show?*

His answer came quick.

Of course.

CHAPTER EIGHTEEN

Eden had suggested meeting at Seasons, Brennon's hotel's restaurant, insisting she wanted to cause Brennon the minimal amount of trouble necessary to meet with her. Brennon waited on the large outdoor patio, sweating in places he'd rather no one knew about. It wasn't even that warm outside, but he was a wreck. He stood as she approached, and she looked up at him from beneath the brim of her gray bucket hat.

"Thanks for meeting me."

"I ordered you a tea," he told her.

"Thank you."

Brennon gestured to the outdoor sofa, waiting for her to sit so he could give her the necessary space. Despite her eyes being shaded, he could tell she'd been crying. The realization twisted something in his chest. "I'm just gonna start talking," she said.

Sticking to his guns to stay out of her way, he gave her what he hoped was an encouraging nod.

"Adam sent me an email. I don't know if you knew that."

"He told me," Brennon said quietly.

"Did you read it?"

"He read it to me." Brennon had cringed throughout his friend's passionate recitation, but it was too late. Adam had already sent it.

"Did you ask him to do that?"

"I . . ." Brennon hadn't asked Adam to do it. He'd *hoped* Adam would do *something*. Brennon had a strong feeling anything he might try to say to Eden in his own defense would be perceived as a lie to cover up what she and others had accused him of doing. His only hope had been to call his own witness to the stand. Brennon feared, however, that what Adam had explained failed to address the core of the matter. It wasn't Eden's mind that needed changing; it was his own. But in the last few days, as they'd gotten closer and subsequently fallen apart, he'd begun to see things differently—see her for who she really was. Not a rose in bloom, or a discovery that was his to make, but a woman who moved him in ways he'd never been moved. One who was working for a life he now took for granted. A woman who needed to find her own way.

Today he had to choose his words carefully so as not to do any further damage, but all his nerves misfired. A relentless twitch between his thumb and forefinger had him even more out of sorts.

Crossing his legs, Brennon attempted to control his hand by picking at a speck of lint on his thigh. "I didn't ask him to, no."

"I'm glad he did. It was helpful." Her words were deliberate. Kind. Then she trailed off into a whisper. "And I wouldn't have believed it coming from you."

Brennon had been right about the one thing, at least. "I understand."

"I'm sorry," she said, remaining quiet and contrite.

She had no reason to apologize. It upset him deeply that she felt the need. "Eden . . ."

"Please." She held up a hand. "I didn't trust you. You were horrible to me when we met." She gave a helpless shrug. "But I get that the night you and Jonathan—that night—you barely knew me, and I'd been super shitty with you, too. I can understand why you said what you said—"

"Eden, no." That was enough. He couldn't listen to this anymore. Too many people walked on eggshells around him, excusing their own feelings in order not to irritate him or, in the case of playwrights, make him second guess his participation. Lovers had left him, citing lists of reasons gathered and curated since the day they'd first met, and yet never mentioned until it was too late for him to act. It was a pattern he refused to follow with Eden. "I was wrong. I'm sorry. Please, you don't have to forgive me now, today—I'd understand if you never did, but I beg you. Accept my apology. I had no right to say what I did, and I have no excuse. From the bottom of my heart, I apologize."

Immediately he could tell he'd fucked up again.

She stared back at him, lips parted and eyes wide like he'd begun singing at full volume in the middle of the restaurant. He opened his mouth to say more—fix it—but she spoke before he had a chance.

"Okay," she whispered.

He swallowed against all the emotion climbing his throat. "Really?"

She gave him the tiniest nod and dropped her gaze. "Thank you."

If she could give him that, then maybe . . .? "Eden—"

She spoke before he had a chance to spill any more of his guts. "I want you to know I have nothing but the highest regard and respect for you and your work. I know I got carried away with the rest of this, but I want us to be okay. Onstage, I think we have something nice— you know, whenever I'm not messing it up."

That quickly, she locked his heart in a cage and hid the key. It beat against the bars, but it was no use. She didn't want him. Not the way he wanted her. Brennon weathered the intense disappointment and found a breath to say, "Everybody has off days—"

"Do you have to tell other people that as often as you have to keep telling me?"

He didn't know what else to say. He was having a difficult enough time with the sinking feeling of being placed into the professional zone, a place he suspected was a few miles further down the road than the friend zone. She was carefully rebuilding the wall he thought he'd broken down. The wall that kept him in one category and her in the opposite. He was the duke once again, and she was the hired help.

But something about her stirred something inside him. It wasn't just her talent or her red-lipped smile or the honeyed taste of her mouth. It was the challenge to be better. Stronger. Kinder. Show his heart—not only when he was comfortable, but when it seemed like the most difficult thing in the world. Nothing about her promised to keep it safe, but he found he'd rather hand it over to her above anyone else. Somehow, it seemed she'd know exactly what to do with it. He hated where they'd wound up, but he loved her still.

He loved her.

The realization knocked the breath from his chest. A cool sweat broke on his brow, and his heart—his traitorous heart—cracked again along the same fault line a dozen other forgotten dreams for the future had left behind. He didn't merely admire her, and whatever spell his lust cast around them had ceased to be of any importance when he'd learned how deeply his careless words hurt her. Resisting the feeling was futile. He'd fallen. His heart, his hope, his happiness now lay in the palms of her hands.

How he'd let himself get to this point with another actress was a question for another day, perhaps a therapist, but she was just so fucking . . . *special*. Like the universe had drawn a heart around her to let him know beyond a doubt that she was the one. It settled deep within him, this new reality, and he would do whatever it took to stay connected with her, even if right now it meant another pep talk. "I don't mind telling you as many times as you need to hear it."

"I might need to hear it a few more times before this is all said and done," she admitted.

They sat in silence a moment as Brennon managed his disappointment. If this was where they were, then this was where he'd start. Star to standby, he said, "They used to call me a machine."

Her head tilted in question. "Who did?"

"My teachers at Juilliard. I never played sports, but they treated me like a star quarterback—put Brennon in, we can always count on him to bring the win. I was consistent. I wasn't more talented than anyone. Maybe I had a more versatile vocal range, more control of my body, but once they told me what they liked, I could always execute. It was unusual for my age and experience. I consider it my secret weapon. For most performers, consistency comes with time, experience, knowing where you fit in the industry." Jesus Christ, listen to him. He never knew when to quit.

But she *was* listening. "You also make really good choices."

Encouraged, he replied, "Yes. Consistently. Some would say I have a knack for this. But so do you."

She shook her head, doubt evident in her downcast gaze.

"Consistency will come. It's a muscle like any other," he told her.

Her posture drooped, and she leaned her shoulder heavily into the sofa. "I've never been the best about exercising."

His other hand twitched. The one nearest to her. It was a struggle to keep it from reaching out to take hold of hers.

"Your smile lights up the entire theater, Eden." And every dark corner of his heart along with it. "You're just getting started, and I want you to give yourself a break."

She shook her head. "I've been doing this my whole life."

"And now, it's finally begun."

She met his eyes for the first time since they'd sat down. Her eyelids were pink and puffy. She wore no mascara, but her dark lashes were long and damp. A few freckles he'd never noticed stood out across the bridge of her nose. A crushing ache filled his chest. What else could he have done? Was there anything left to do?

"I'm exhausted," she whispered, like she was confessing one of her deepest secrets.

The word conjured images of cuddling her close. Tucking her into his bed and keeping her warm. He closed his eyes, but the images only became more vivid when he wasn't staring her radiant beauty in the face. "Let's get through the week. Then we can all go home and get some rest." Going home to New York was cold comfort for him, but maybe she was looking forward to it.

"Don't remind me," she said, and in a slew of unguarded words told him all about her apartment: the noisy neighborhood, the mattress on the floor. She complained of the lack of air-conditioning, the roommates coming and going at all hours, and when Brennon had finally heard enough, he spoke with his heart and not his head. "I have a classic six on the Upper East Side. Air-conditioning, three bedrooms, you're welcome to stay."

"Oh."

That sound. The worst.

He'd overstepped. Again.

He hissed in his next breath. "Forgive me. Your place sounded like my worst nightmare. I should have kept my mouth shut."

She stiffened. "I mean it's not *that* bad. The neighborhood's awesome." The tone of her voice had risen. Defensive.

His worst nightmare? Had he said that? Had he lost all ability to think before he spoke?

"I didn't mean nightmare—"

"No." She let out a bitter laugh. "You did. It's okay, I get it." Moving to the edge of the couch, she took hold of the handle of her bag and prepared to stand. "Anyway, thanks for meeting with me and letting me say what I needed to say. Again, I really have enjoyed working with you, and I hope we can continue to perform together." She stood, and he stood with her. "Let's have a great show tonight for old times' sake," she said.

He held his tongue, afraid he would only dig himself deeper if he spoke.

"See you at the ball," she said, and she walked away.

The company ground out the four remaining Washington DC performances and closed Saturday night to respectable applause from a packed house. Brennon followed his own advice for once and stayed out of Eden's way. In doing so, she found her focus again, recovered her singing voice, and they finished strong. She'd never needed any of the directors' notes. She only needed to get out of her own head, and he needed to stop distracting her.

When he'd finally been able to demonstrate there were no hard feelings on his end, she'd found the space to work again. He hoped she'd forgiven herself and him, but understood from her persistent lack of eye contact offstage that doing so might take more time.

As exhausting as the demands of eight shows a week were, Brennon wasn't looking forward to the break the way so many of his fellow performers were. A break meant he wouldn't see her face every day. He wouldn't know how she was doing, wouldn't be able to wish her well or wish her luck. It meant he'd miss her.

In no rush, Brennon took a train from DC to Manhattan instead of a plane. He arrived at Penn Station at two PM on Sunday to a tourist crowd and stifling heat. His assistant Edward had arranged for a car to pick him up. Finding it, Brennon settled in for the short ride uptown, grateful for the air-conditioning, but it made him think of Eden's lack of it in her apartment.

"Welcome home, Mr. Thorne," his doorman said, immediately attempting to take his bags from him.

"Good to see you, Artie."

"I'll have these brought up to you."

"I've got them. Thanks." There were only the two.

"We're expecting rain tonight. Here's hoping it takes away some of this humidity."

Brennon made his way across the lobby to the elevator. "Here's hoping."

His apartment was sixty-eight degrees. Edward had stocked his refrigerator with fresh food and chilled beverages. No item was out of place. Brennon rolled his luggage into his bedroom and left it near the walk-in closet before stripping off the clothes he'd worn on the train and stepping into his steam shower.

The sound of rushing water chased off the oppressive silence. Chloe had lived with him for nearly a year before she left. Other than the two weeks between ending his run in the West End and joining the tour, he hadn't spent much time in his apartment alone, and he hadn't missed it. The place was too big for one person.

A long shower and an even longer nap later, Brennon made himself a plate of prosciutto and fruit and checked in with Adam.

"You're home?" Adam asked.

"For the moment," Brennon told him.

"Need company?"

"If you're up to it."

"What can I bring?"

Brennon looked around the kitchen. Everything he could possibly need to survive was present and accounted for, including an unopened bottle of his favorite gin. "Just yourself, and I mean that literally." He wasn't in the mood to entertain.

"Maybe one day this week we can all go out for dinner?"

Clearly Adam was feeling better if he wanted to gather their group of friends and make a night of it. "We'll plan something," Brennon agreed, though he doubted he'd be in the mood later, either. Since these were friends he'd shared with Chloe, he'd wondered over the last few months if they'd all gotten together without him and picked sides.

Soon enough, Adam arrived with a bag of gummy worms, a smile, and a playlist to fill the silence. Brennon was grateful for the company and the return of his friend. Adam no longer seemed maudlin and lost, almost as if he'd met someone new and moved on from the mess with Maddox.

"Catch me up," his friend said. "How did you two leave things?"

Brennon relaxed into his favorite armchair in the den and sipped an old-fashioned. "Professional."

"Sorry."

Brennon lifted a shoulder, let it drop. "Appropriate," he countered.

Adam tucked his feet beneath him on the adjacent cushion and leaned over the arm with his own drink in hand. "Do you have a plan?"

"Aside from ripping Jonathan's arms off and destroying his career, I don't."

"Bren . . ."

"You asked."

Adam patted Brennon's knee reassuringly. "Jon'll dig his own grave eventually."

"He won't be satisfied unless I'm buried with him."

Adam chuckled. "You have a point. Have you spoken to Veronica?"

"No. But I plan to."

"It always comes back to her for him, doesn't it?"

Brennon thought about the origins of their years-long feud based on the professional jealousy that began the moment Brennon first beat Jon for a lead. Veronica had served as a weapon Jonathan wielded to knock Brennon off course one time, not someone Jon had any real affection for. He doubted there was any truth to Adam's theory. Jon didn't have feelings. He only had an ego.

"I think you're reading too much into it. He wants what I have. It's why he went after Eden the way he did."

Adam's ears perked up. "Did you *have* her?"

"I might have, if not for him."

"To be fair, she is her own person."

"Who was lied to and manipulated to believe I was a pathological narcissist."

"Point." Adam nodded. "But we fixed that. Didn't we? And you apologized."

They'd certainly done all they could, and he had apologized, but Brennon still feared Gabi's video would haunt Eden—keep the wall between them impenetrable.

"I guess." She hadn't glared at him in the last few days anyway. That was progress.

"Do you plan to see her this week?"

Brennon stared into his drink. "We all need a break. She had a rough week. I'd only be a reminder of it. It's almost certain they'll recast the role."

Adam tsked, his gaze brimming with concern. "Oh no. Was it that bad?"

"For the directors? Yes. Terrible."

"Poor Eden."

"There was nothing I could do."

"It wasn't your job to save her," Adam said. "We're all out here fighting for our own survival. Her time will come if it's meant to."

"I know," Brennon said, certain of that, if nothing else.

"After all, her number one fan is very influential."

Brennon looked up at his friend who wore a teasing grin. "She wouldn't want my help."

Adam scoffed at that. "Please. This is Broadway. Who the fuck cares how we get on the Playbill as long we get there. Where we go from there is up to us—and you may not know this, but some of us have to do things the hard way."

Brennon arched a brow. "You're not suggesting the Juilliard showcase was easy, are you?"

Adam laughed. "Oh, no, of course not. Reciting a monologue in front of a room packed with the best agents in New York had to have been such a trial for someone as awkward and uncomfortable on a stage as you."

Brennon's gaze flattened. "Fine. But I do still have to audition for things. Sometimes."

Adam rolled his eyes. "When was the last time you went to a casting call?"

"Would you like another drink?" Brennon rose.

Adam followed him to the kitchen. "You should call her, offer to make *her* a drink."

"She wouldn't accept."

"How do you know?"

"Because every time I open my mouth, I insult her. It's not intentional—only a fact of who I am. Or who she thinks I am."

"I thought you said we fixed all that."

"I don't even mean Jonathan and Gabi. This is about *me*. You said it yourself—I'm terrible with people."

"She was drawn to you . . ."

Brennon's response was as bitter as he felt. "And very easily repelled, it turned out."

"Ah . . . showmance."

Brennon cut him a warning look, not eager to have his own words used against him again. Adam gave him an affable grin in return. "The heart wants what it wants," his friend said.

"Indeed it does. Speaking of which, will you be reaching out to Maddox this week?"

Adam eyed Brennon with suspicion. Brennon held up both hands in surrender. "I support whatever you decide. I was an ass."

Adam lifted his brows, clearly needing more.

"A *hypocritical* ass. I apologize."

A small smile brightened Adam's face. "In that case, I think we should throw a party."

Eden's rolling suitcases clunked up three flights of stairs in the sweltering hallway until she finally arrived sweating and panting at her apartment door. Before she could take her key out of her shoulder bag to unlock it, the door flew open, and Trista shouted, "Eden's home!"

The windows were open, and four fans were circulating the air, but it wasn't any cooler inside. Trista threw herself over the threshold and wrapped Eden up in a sweaty hug. "We missed you! We have plans. Go take a shower, we're going out!"

Despite the heat, Eden wanted to melt into the comforting familiarity of Trista's hug, but it wasn't meant to be. Her roommate pulled away much too fast. "I missed you guys, too."

Trista took one of her bags as Fallon emerged from the kitchen, skidding across the floor to get to Eden. She squealed. "If it isn't Brennon Thorne's leading lady!"

Ugh. He would be all either of them would want to talk about. Eden had forgotten to factor that in when she'd considered her rest week.

Their shared apartment in the Bowery had three bedrooms—inasmuch as one could call a cell with a window a bedroom—and, once she distributed her greetings, Eden finally disentangled herself and headed to hers. After opening the window, she took a seat on her mattress to breathe. Her longtime roommates were a lot on any day of the week, but her roommates getting ready for a reunion night on the town were another whirlwind entirely. Eden needed a minute to prepare herself.

She missed the townhouse in DC already. The calm of Liliana and Maddox. The size of the rooms. The air-conditioning. She was looking forward to seeing the condo they'd reserved in Los Angeles. It'd be smaller than the townhouse, for sure, no rentals were cheap in the summer there, but at least it wouldn't be this hot.

Still, a few days off in New York would do her good. It had been a long time since she'd had a real break.

The best part of the tour for Eden so far had been having only one job. Before she'd landed the standby role, Eden had juggled two waitressing jobs along with auditions, performances, and the occasional *Law and Order* walk-on. Every day was a whip as she rushed around the city to make it where she needed to be on time. Her roommates were excited to see her now because they so rarely did, even when she was in town. If they wanted to go out tonight, Eden would oblige. They'd been with her through thick and thin, never once leaving her lonely or unsupported in a town that could easily suck a person dry.

Of course they'd want to hear about what it was like to work with someone of Brennon's caliber. It was only that it hurt to think about him. She'd gotten through the last week of performances by keeping her head down. If she looked at him for too long, she began to doubt herself, but there was also a great deal of yearning for what might have been—and regret. She'd even caught herself lusting once when he'd passed her backstage between scenes. The confidence in his gait, the set of his jaw, the way he'd run his hand through his hair and caught her staring.

Meanwhile, she'd taken what he'd said about consistency to heart. Following his lead, she donned her character like a mask, and set her mind to repeating what she had learned through previous performances about what worked best. She managed not to embarrass herself again, but it didn't mean the damage wasn't already done. She startled every time her phone rang, certain it would be Shayna to drop the news of a recast.

Those final performances in DC might have been too little, too late. Her shine had worn off. She needed to make her peace with the possibility of it. Maybe a night on the town would help.

"It's Restaurant Week," Fallon informed her. "The Indian place down the block has a whole menu planned with craft cocktails, and I think we should do that."

Her roommates swarmed, already dressed up in short-shorts and high heels. Trista's blonde curls were a cloud around her face, both as a result of humidity and careful styling. Fallon's braids were more smartly styled, piled high on top of her head to let the air hit her neck. Eden wore her hair up, too.

She wished Maddox were there to join them, but she'd shared a cab with him from the airport, and he'd been very clear about lying low in the city for the first couple of days. Eden could tell he meant it, too. Though he rarely mentioned it, she knew he was kicking himself for what had happened with Adam. As the details of their hookup emerged over a late-night conversation following Adam's email, it became clear there had been a big misunderstanding, and even bigger overreactions, on both their parts. Eden could relate. So, while she didn't plan to let Maddox go the entire week without seeing her, she'd give him a few days to regroup.

The restaurant her roommates had chosen was far too pricey for every day, but Eden had banked some serious cash from the tour, so she offered to buy the first round of drinks.

"Tell us everything," Fallon said as they clinked glasses.

"*Everything* everything? Or are you only asking about Brennon Thorne?" Might as well get it out of the way.

"Thorne, of course."

"He's a dream to work with," Eden said.

Trista groaned. "That's what they all say. Tell us more. Like, what does he smell like? Where do you come up to on him? How big are his hands?"

Those questions were not the kind that helped a girl move on. The mention of his hands caused Eden to blush. It was a good thing the restaurant was dimly lit. "Wow."

"Is he a good kisser?" Fallon asked.

Eden's eyes bulged.

"I mean you did have to kiss him, right? He's Darcy."

"Oh . . . it's only a stage kiss. It wasn't choreographed with tongue or anything."

"And you managed to stick to that? Even with Brennon Thorne?"

"Fallon!" Trista elbowed her. "They're both professionals."

Eden wanted to die, but she knew what was required of girl talk. Trying to stay light-hearted about it, she managed a mysterious smile. "I mean, I may have slipped once or twice."

Fallon gave Trista a triumphant look. "I knew it! What does he taste like?"

"Watermelon mint." The words tasted so sour in her mouth, her eyes welled up.

Both of them immediately pressed for more. Eden steered the narrative, avoiding lamenting or gushing of any kind. She kept her delivery matter of fact. "The top of my head comes up to his Adam's apple, and he smells like something cool—whatever shaving cream he uses, I guess. And also sweat. It's a lot of clothes, and we all sweat like we're in spin class up there."

Fortunately, those tidbits were enough. Neither of them asked if Eden had gotten to know him offstage. Neither assumed anything else had happened, and why would they? They knew as well as she did that Thorne was out of their league, operating on another level entirely. If she kept telling herself it was no big deal, maybe one day soon she'd believe it. Fingers crossed, it would happen by the end of the week.

The three of them shared food, gossiped, and caught up for the better part of their two-hour meal, but Eden had to decline when they wanted to keep the night going at another neighborhood bar. "I'm exhausted. Really. Rain check?" Fallon and Trista walked her back to the apartment to make sure she got in safely. From there, Eden's roommates kept going.

Upstairs, Eden tidied up the kitchen, took stock of what was in the pantry, and made a list of the things she'd need to run out and get in the morning. All week she'd been having an intense craving for apple turnovers, go figure, so she would be sure to pick a few of those up, too.

The night had cooled the city enough to keep Eden from sweating through her sheets, but when she finally lay down for bed, her thoughts drifted uptown to that classic six. The bed in Brennon's guest room was likely a step up from her mattress and box springs on the floor. His ceilings had to be high, the air cool, the floors shiny and unscuffed.

Not that there was anything wrong with their little three bedroom in the Bowery, other than the temperature in the summer, but she'd lived in Manhattan a while now and hadn't had many glimpses of how the other half lived. In the imaginary apartment she conjured in her mind, Brennon Thorne walked from room to room, his hair loose and ruffled, his beard half-grown in, turning out the lights one by one.

She opened her eyes and stared out her window to give herself something to think about, other than the man who'd broken her heart before she'd even realized it was on the line. But his image burned the back of her mind. Haunting and beautiful.

The last onstage kiss they'd shared hovered like a ghost on her lips.

CHAPTER NINETEEN

Veronica West lived on the second floor of a brownstone in the East Village. On Tuesday afternoon, after buzzing Brennon up, the dark-haired actress gave him a side-eye through the open door. "I didn't realize you knew how to travel below 34ᵗʰ Street."

"I brought my passport and disinfectant."

She swung open the door to let him in. "I was surprised to hear from you."

"Why?" he asked.

"I figured out of sight, out of mind. Also, I abandoned you with the traveling circus."

"You certainly did, but they aren't so bad." Brennon took a look around Veronica's place. He'd only been to her old one, and this was an improvement. More windows, more light, more places to put all the Buddhist knick-knacks she collected. She preferred the Indian Buddhas. Veronica took a seat on her tufted burgundy couch and patted the spot beside her.

He sat and wished he'd been offered a drink. Forty blocks in this heat wasn't nothing, regardless of the fact he'd been driven.

"Are you checking to make sure I'm not drinking myself to death?" she asked.

"Something like that," he said. "I'm also curious why you ditched the show. A heads-up wouldn't have been uncalled for. I'd come all that way . . ."

"How was Eden? Since we're on the subject."

The question pinched. "You haven't been checking up?"

"No." Her face drew tight. "I needed a clean break."

"Something happened with you," he said, the words grim. "I'd love to know what."

She looked past him to the window, giving her temple a rub. "I'm pregnant."

On second thought, Brennon was glad she hadn't given him a drink. He would have choked on it. "Sorry?"

"I know, I'm sorry, too."

"That's not what I—"

"It wasn't what I meant, either. I left the tour thinking I'd come back here, get it taken care of—drown my sorrows for a few days, and catch back up with the show, but then . . ." She made a sweeping gesture around her living room. "I took a look around, and all I could picture was where I'd put the baby's crib, and a high chair, a swing, and then I started thinking of names, and writing lullabies, and that was that. I never even made an appointment. I quit the tour."

"I'm . . ." He had no idea what to say.

She appeared as surprised as he was, but also, there was something about the light in her eyes. Happiness? "I know, right?" She smiled.

"But why quit the tour?" She wasn't anywhere near showing, and even if she started to, Regency costumes were extremely forgiving.

Her eyes lost all the brightness they'd held as she described her future life as a mother moments ago. "Brennon. I love you, but why do you think?"

He frowned. He had no—

Jonathan.

"Please don't tell me . . ."

"Some of us never learn," she said softly.

"Does he know?"

"Oh, he knows."

Brennon took in this new knowledge with all the enjoyment of swallowing rancid milk. "*He's* why you left."

Her smile went stiff. "He has no interest in fatherhood."

Of course. Jonathan was far too selfish.

"I took the test our second morning in DC, and I spoke with him right afterward. He made it very clear it wasn't his fault, and he would have nothing to do with it. He accused me of sleeping with Donovan, even. Anyway, halfway through the tech rehearsal, I could barely breathe being in the same building with him. And I wasn't ready to tell you." Veronica placed a hand on her stomach. "I can't help thinking everything was leading to this. That maybe this baby will make all the stupid mistakes I've made worth it. Give me some wisdom and perspective."

"I hope so."

She gave him an admonishing look. "We can't all be as perfect as you, Brennon."

He scoffed. "Perfect? Please. You've been spending too much time with him. You know I'm not the person he's always said I am."

"No, but you can be impossible in your own way."

Bracing himself for another itemized list of his shortcomings, Brennon stood to get himself a glass of water.

"You're not exactly warm and fuzzy," she said.

Over his shoulder, he gave her a flat stare. "Am I cold and hard?"

She grinned like she enjoyed rankling him. "*Reserved.* I'd say reserved."

"Being reserved makes me impossible?" He opened a cabinet in the nearby kitchen and took out a tall, plastic cup.

"You can come off a little judgy, too."

Ah, there it was. The truth hurt. "I'm aware." No one had been bold enough to mention it until Eden, but why would they? Adam thought he'd hung the moon, and everyone else was afraid he'd say something terrible about them to a producer and never get hired again. He had nothing like that type of influence, but people thought what they thought. He turned on the tap and filled his cup. "It was pointed out to me recently."

"Let me guess. Eden said something? She had every right to, you know. You were a nightmare that first night."

Brennon's face went cold. He'd been a nightmare on a number of occasions, but Veronica had only witnessed his behavior in Greenville when he'd openly ridiculed Eden for the way she made her living. "I was drunk. I thought I was being funny."

"I knew that, and Adam knew that, but Eden isn't like us. It probably felt to her like you were making a point of reminding her of her place."

Brennon didn't need Veronica to tell him that anymore. "I wasn't."

"Hence the statement 'You can *come off* a little judgy.'"

Surely there were other examples she could have used from the twenty years of their acquaintance that wouldn't have had such a sucker-punch effect, but he supposed that was what he got for venturing downtown.

"I'm only saying it wouldn't hurt to soften your edges from time to time."

"People with softer edges don't stand up as well to injury. I learned that a long time ago," he said with a pointed glare.

Veronica's eyes widened. "Oh."

He lifted his brows like he'd made his point.

"I didn't realize you were still hanging on to that one," she murmured, at least having the decency to look ashamed. "You know I wasn't exactly at peak maturity back then."

"None of us were." He took a long drink of tap water. "Still, hardly an excuse."

"Ouch. Brennon, that's exactly what I'm talking about. You're judging me—still—for a mistake I made when I was twenty years old. I felt terrible about it then, and I feel terrible about it now. Slut-shaming me isn't exactly your best look."

Brennon took immediate offense. "I'm not *shaming* anyone. I'm telling you, you *hurt* me."

She sat ramrod straight on the sofa, eyes flaring with outrage. "I was *trying* to hurt you."

His hear reared back. This was a new twist. "*Why?*"

"Because I wanted your fucking attention!"

Brennon slammed the plastic tumbler on the countertop, along with his other hand. "You had *all* my attention back then."

"*No one* had your attention then." She sank back into the cushions, gracefully re-crossing her legs. "You were so focused on your lines, your songs, your next audition, your notes—I could have stripped naked in your dorm room and you wouldn't have noticed."

He would have noticed. Of that he had no doubt. But she wasn't wrong about the rest. Having Veronica as a girlfriend had taken an impossible amount of time and energy at a time when he'd already been spread too thin. Nevertheless, she made a strong point about Brennon's focus, his priorities, and his ambition back then.

Success was a difficult habit to break, even when you were in love.

"Let me assure you," he said. "Every time you took a single sock off in my dorm room, I noticed."

Her smile returned, but this time it was coy and all-too familiar. "I'm currently available, you know."

That was Brennon's cue to leave. He'd gotten what he came for: an understanding of why she'd left the tour. Reassurance of her mental stability. The teasing come-on was proof that Veronica was all right. He drained his water and put the cup in the sink. "On that note."

"Oh, stay a while. Tell me how the show survived without me. You never said how Eden was to work with."

Again, that pinch, left of the middle in his chest. He found he couldn't form the words to say exactly what Eden had been like to work with. *A dream . . .*

"You left some big shoes to fill," he managed.

"Seriously. Dish. How was she? Do I need to be worried about parts when she gets home from the tour, and I go back to work? We're friends, Bren. Tell me if I have competition."

Brennon left the kitchen. "Maybe start polishing up your dance moves."

Veronica's face fell. "I knew it. She's great, isn't she?"

"She . . ." He coughed. "Yes. She's very talented."

"Ugh. And she's like, what? Seven years younger than us? Turning into an old woman in this business sucks, just FYI."

He chucked her on the chin on his way to the door. "I think there's still life in the old girl yet."

"Ha-ha. Wait. You're not mad at me for leaving, are you?" she asked as he passed through the door.

"Actually." He held up his finger and thumb about an inch apart before heading down the stairs. "I'm just shy of being proud of you."

Edward, who'd driven Brennon to the Village, waited against the side of Brennon's black Lexus. "Home?" the younger man asked, as he stuffed his phone into his front pocket. "Remember, you have drinks with your agent at five."

Brennon hadn't forgotten, but he had someone else on his mind. "Where exactly is the Bowery?"

Edward's blond eyebrows lifted. He scratched his cheek. "How far downtown did you want to go today?"

"I'm not asking for a tour, simply a better geographical understanding."

"It runs from 4th Street down to below Canal," Edward said.

"Ah." Another world, indeed.

225

To Eden's surprise, Maddox texted early Wednesday morning with an offer to take a walk in Central Park. She accepted immediately. Sunshine, exercise, *Mad*.

Eden unpacked her walking shoes, consulted her subway app, and loaded up her MetroCard. Maddox lived up in Hell's Kitchen, so he was way closer to the park, but she managed to convince him to meet her on the east side so she wouldn't have to take two trains. The best thing she could say about him when she saw him for the first time in over twenty-four hours was he looked rested.

Showered? Maybe. Groomed? Not so much, but she hugged him anyway. She wasn't sure when he'd become her person, whether it had been the night they'd sung karaoke at a bar in downtown San Antonio and found they both knew every word to "We Didn't Start the Fire," or if it happened in Orlando on their golden day outing to Harry Potter World and tried butterbeer for the first time, but something between them had clicked into place. "What'd you do last night?" he asked.

"I partook in Restaurant Week," she said.

"How bougie of you."

"I want you to meet Trista and Fallon while we're here. Start wrapping your head around it and send me your best time and date."

He slumped dramatically. "Do I have to?"

They walked toward the park, passing a street cart selling bagels and coffee. Eden had learned the hard way that street cart bagels weren't the best, but it got her stomach growling anyway. "We should grab some breakfast and a couple of waters to go. I'm hungry."

"You didn't eat?" he asked.

"You didn't give me a lot of time."

"I guess I could eat again."

Eden scouted for a passable vendor. The neighborhood was nice, quieter than downtown, and cleaner. Even the trash on the curb didn't smell as bad. A block later, on the edge of the Upper East Side, she spotted a promising deli with plenty of fresh fruit in the window. They promised coffee *Hot Fresh and Fast!* "This looks good."

Maddox held the door open for her. Minutes later, they emerged. Eden held her extremely hot coffee in one hand and her fresh bagel in the other. She tore into it the second they hit the sidewalk.

This, she'd missed.

"Eden?"

Mouth full, she whirled in the direction of the familiar, resonant voice. Maddox came to a stop beside her, and Brennon, in running shorts and a sweaty T-shirt, jogged up to them. He plucked the AirPods from his ears and wiped sweat from his brow.

The air charged around her, spreading sparks across her skin.

He was absolutely glowing. Hands-down the most phenomenal looking jogger she'd ever seen in New York City. His nearly full beard, trimmed and kept close to his face, made the days since she'd seen him feel more like weeks. She couldn't speak, she had to chew. She couldn't use the coffee to help the bagel go down easier; it would burn the roof off her mouth.

Maddox, as if sensing her dilemma, cracked open a bottled water and shoved it in her face. She traded her bagel for his water and gulped it, trying to clear her airway.

Brennon stood by patiently as a witness to her unfolding conflict.

What the hell was he doing here? How many people lived in this city, exactly? How was this even a thing?

"Do you live here?" she finally managed to ask.

He pointed uptown. "A few blocks up."

"We were just going to the park," she said quickly to assure him she hadn't *intended* this. The park belonged to everyone. It wasn't like she often found herself on the Upper East Side, but she could certainly *act* like she came up here all the time. She was an actress.

"We can't seem to escape each other," Maddox quipped. "Every time I've done a tour this happens. I come home for a break, and I run into two or three other cast members I've never seen in real life."

"Must be a tour thing," Eden said. "Like we're in a—oh, what's it called?"

227

"Karass?" Brennon supplied.

"Exactly." Eden shared a surprised smile with him, and her heart did a flip flop in her chest.

"I've never heard that word," Maddox said flatly.

Eden was about to explain when Brennon piped up, "It's a bit of a made-up concept. Kurt Vonnegut. It refers to a group of people linked together over time."

Maddox regarded Thorne as if he'd suddenly swished a cape and taken a great bow. "'Kay."

Eden and Brennon shared another quick look. He grinned like he was thrilled to see her, his brown eyes as warm and welcoming as a hug. She had to resist a growing urge to bridge the distance to make the hug a reality.

"I always just say 'small world,' but karass is fine if that's how you two want it." Some of Mad's bitterness from learning how Brennon felt about him on the tour seeped up from the depths. Eden should get him to the park before he said anything to ruin this fragile peace, or make Brennon's beautiful smile falter. She'd mostly forgiven him for being an ass, but she understood if it took Mad more time. After all, *he'd* never gotten an apology from the man.

"It was good running into you!" Eden made her voice sound extra bright. She took hold of Maddox's arm and aimed him toward the park.

Brennon lifted a hand, causing her to pause. "I wanted to ask— I'm having a small get-together at my apartment this evening. I'd actually intended to reach out later this morning. If you two wanted to make the trip uptown again, I'd love to have you both. Adam's making some sort of cucumber-themed cocktail. I'm sure he'll have matching snacks to go along with it . . ." Brennon looked to them both, but his gaze lingered on Maddox. Eden could practically hear the apology in the invitation.

Maddox inhaled sharply, his body stiffening beside her. "We wouldn't want to intrude."

"No, nothing like that. He'd be . . ." Brennon swallowed once, dipped his head a moment, and lowered his voice. "He'd be very glad to see you. Please consider it."

"Really?" Maddox's voice and his pained expression were as raw as Eden had ever seen him.

All the sincerity in the world shone in Brennon's dark eyes, when he lifted them once again. "Really," he said with complete conviction. "I could send a car. For both of you."

Maddox turned to Eden.

Reading her friend's concern instantly, she turned back to Brennon. "Nobody wants to blindside anybody and ruin a night." God, those words. She wished she could stuff them back into her big, stupid mouth.

"I promise there won't be any surprises. I'll let him know I invited you both."

"And if he's not cool with it, you text Eden immediately," Maddox added, some of his spark making a comeback.

Brennon didn't hesitate. "Of course, or if you gave me your number, I'd be happy to let you know directly."

Brennon's Duke of the Upper East Side routine was not without its charms, and it was winning Maddox over. Eden suppressed a smile as the two men exchanged numbers.

Brennon switched his phone from his right palm to his left and stretched a hand across the distance between them.

Maddox eyed it a moment before giving it a firm shake, making their unspoken truce official. "What time?"

"Whatever works for you. I live there, and Adam hardly ever leaves . . ."

Maddox checked in with Eden again, but she was already mentally doing her hair for the event. "Eight?" she asked.

"You'll come?" Brennon looked nothing short of amazed.

How could she possibly say no? "Yes."

Brennon put a hand over his heart, his shoulders dropping in what could only be relief. "Wonderful."

"Eden, I think you just made the man's century," Maddox teased, loudly enough to make Brennon's neck turn pink.

She elbowed her friend. "Enough." He was acting just like her mother. Brennon was probably only relieved she didn't actively hate him anymore. All actors were sensitive to dislike. Surely even Brennon Thorne wasn't immune. She wasn't dumb enough to believe they could pick up where they left off after everything that had happened, or if she even wanted to, but if they could be some sort of friends after all this, so much the better.

"I'll let you both know after Adam gives me the okay," Brennon said. "But I'm confident about it."

When was he not confident? "Hope to see you later, then," Eden said.

He didn't respond as they walked away, but when she glanced back, they locked eyes. She had to catch her breath as everything in her screamed *Don't let him go*.

Maddox yanked her hand to keep her moving.

CHAPTER TWENTY

Eden's violet dress had spaghetti straps, an Empire waist, and a flared skirt that skimmed her knees. She'd worn it once on a date to see *Moulin Rouge: The Musical* with a guy she hadn't ended up liking as much as she liked the show. Showing off her bust and butt, accentuating her small waist and slim ankles, the dress gave her confidence. Enough to hold her own with Brennon Thorne in real life. Or at least make a decent show of it, fingers crossed.

As she stood with her hands in her pockets, staring at herself in the mirror, she reluctantly came to terms with the fact that she still liked him. She really didn't want to like him, but she really, *really* liked him. Of course, there was no hope for them. Miracles happened, but reality was where she lived. Down in the Bowery, on a mattress, with two roommates who were out partying in the Village on a Tuesday night. Eden was grateful for the quiet. Her mind was too busy playing scenarios over what she could expect tonight uptown. Her roommates buzzing around would only make her nerves worse.

Her phone dinged from her mattress with a message from Brennon. She clicked into it with a trembling hand.

I mentioned but didn't confirm . . . Would you mind if I sent a car for you?

Did he think she couldn't find her way herself? She'd made it all the way uptown on her own once today already—or maybe he didn't want her to have to pay for a ride? Or thought she couldn't . . .

She typed back without thinking. *I'd really rather you didn't—* then hesitated.

She didn't want to start the night off arguing. She deleted the refusal. Instead, she responded, *"Sounds great!"* She'd direct the driver to swing by Hell's Kitchen on the way, and she and Maddox could arrive together.

Address?

She typed it in.

He'll text you when he's downstairs.

Eden thanked him and texted Maddox the plan. He responded with a sunglasses emoji.

She tried not to think about what "small get-together" meant in Brennon Thorne's world. She had to concede it could mean anything from five people to fifty. Was he sending cars for all of them, or just the broke actresses downtown?

She shook off the thought, well aware she would be the only person like herself at the party.

It didn't matter. This was about Maddox and Adam. It was why she'd agreed in the first place.

Mostly.

She hadn't seen her friend interested in doing anything for weeks. She'd be there to support him, that was all, but no reason she couldn't look great doing it.

Selecting a pair of vintage, cherry red, peep-toe heels, she stepped into them, increasing her height by almost four inches thanks to the small platform built into the shoe. They were almost the exact color of her lipstick. Sweeping her hair into a high ponytail, she styled her bangs in a low swoop to the side and tucked the ends behind her ear. Without many options for earrings, she raided Fallon's jewelry chest, and found a pair of small garnets that hung from one-inch silver chains.

Ready, she stood in the kitchen, not wanting to wrinkle the dress by sitting on it in the still-humid apartment. The evening hadn't cooled off yet, and she felt sticky all over despite the shower she'd taken when she got home from her morning in the park with Mad.

Nerves kept her stomach tight, and doubts kept her mind busy. Fear of making a fool of herself, and uneasiness about one of Brennon's friends recognizing her from something embarrassing plagued her, making her question whether this was a good idea or not—whether, in the end, it would help her or harm her.

She prayed one of two things would happen—they would all spontaneously adore her and take her under their wing, or they wouldn't think twice about her. It was the middle ground she couldn't stomach—where they *would* notice her, and judge accordingly.

Her phone buzzed in her hand.

The car had arrived.

Collecting her thoughts as well as her beaded clutch, she left the apartment.

Downstairs, a twenty-something blond with a strong jawline and black-rimmed glasses stood next to the open back door of a Lexus SUV. "Miss Blake?"

"Eden. Hi."

"I'm Edward," he said. "Mr. Thorne's personal assistant."

Of course he was. "And driver?"

"When required." He smiled.

"Does he not know how to drive?"

"It's not his favorite."

Eden supposed she should get in the car, but she found herself hesitating. "Have you worked for him long?"

"Going on two years now."

"And what's that like?"

"Busy," Edward acknowledged. "But it still gives me time to do my own work."

"Which is?"

"I write science fiction."

Of course he did. No one lived in New York without a passion for something. The city itself was inspiration incarnate. It was, on its own, a dream to chase. "Oh?"

"Do you ever read sci-fi?"

Eden gave him an apologetic shake of her head.

He grinned. "Ah, well. No one's perfect." He gestured to the open door. "Shall we?"

Eden bit the bullet and got in, smoothing her dress beneath her and then across her lap. "Will we be picking up my friend?"

"I already have the address programmed into the GPS."

Eden texted Maddox to let him know they were on their way. Once he responded, she set her phone on top of her clutch and returned her attention to Edward. "If you're a writer, how'd you wind up working for an actor?"

"My boyfriend's roommate was his last assistant, but she graduated from college and got a job offer in her field in Austin. Since she was leaving, she suggested I try for it. The hours are more flexible than an eight to five."

"Do you like it?" Eden asked.

Edward turned onto Broadway and sped up to change lanes. "Most days. Like tonight. I'll get you and your friend safely inside, and then I'll hole up in my room and write until it's time to take somebody home."

"You're not invited to the party?" she asked.

He laughed. "I work for him. We're not besties."

Interesting. "Why's that?"

"Don't get me wrong," Edward added quickly. "I like the guy. But if we got too friendly, it would make my job harder."

Eden loved that Edward was a talker. She jumped at the opportunity to find out more about what it looked like to live in Brennon's world. "How do you figure?"

"I'd have to give him my opinion on, say, whether he's working too much, for example."

"Does he work too much?" she asked.

Edward shrugged. "His last vacation was two Christmases ago. He and his girlfriend were planning to go to Europe after the tour, but obviously that won't pan out."

Eden pushed her luck. "What happened with them?"

She and Edward shared a look in the rearview mirror. "It made Page Six," he said.

"I don't read the *Post*."

He didn't seem inclined to say any more. Taking advantage of the traffic and the pause in their conversation, a quick Google search gave Eden the answers she was looking for. Chloe Rhodes had left Brennon for another woman, and subsequently backed out of guest starring in *Liz and Darcy* with him on the road. Why on earth had he still come?

"Are you an actress?" Edward asked as he made the turn onto Ninth Avenue.

"I'm on the tour with him," she said.

"It's nice to meet you. You seem very down to earth."

Salt of the earth was more like it.

"I can see why he likes you," Edward added.

She froze. "Likes me?"

"He doesn't send me out to pick up just anyone."

Eden couldn't think about that. She also couldn't *stop* thinking about it. Fortunately, a few minutes later, Edward pulled up to Mad's place, and Eden texted him again. Edward opened the opposite door of the car, and Mad slid in. He looked sharp, in belted black slacks and a striped button-down casually open at the collar. He was fresh-shaven, his hair gleaming and clean, and finally for the first time in forever, a spark shone in his eyes. "You look hot," he said.

"Same," she told him.

Eden gestured toward Edward as he took the driver's seat again. "This is Edward, Mr. Thorne's personal assistant and sometimes driver."

She and Maddox shared an ironically impressed look.

"Don't let me make a fool of myself," he told her, down to business.

"What do we consider making a fool of yourself?"

"Say I were to start sobbing or something."

Eden laughed. As if.

"Or making some sort of public declaration. Begging of any kind should also be grounds for immediate removal from the premises."

"God, what do you think is gonna happen?"

"I think when I see him I might burst into tears."

"Mad—" She laughed again. She'd had a feeling there was far more inside him than he'd let on in DC. His willingness to finally open up about it gave her a much-needed boost. She was glad to know she wouldn't be the only one at the party wearing her heart on her sleeve.

"I'd rather keep all that on the inside," Maddox said.

"Maybe your need to keep it all on the inside is what got you into this mess in the first place," she told him.

His mouth tightened, lips pressing into a flat line. "Still. I want to feel the situation out before I say something I can't take back."

"Like what?"

"Like the L word."

Eden had never had any doubt love was on the line where Maddox and Adam were concerned. The other L word—*lust*—seemed to have confused the issue momentarily, but now that they'd each had a chance to process what happened between them, Eden hoped, like Maddox did, that they could see the path toward a real relationship more clearly. "I honestly don't think it would hurt anything," she said.

"Other than breaking my heart if he doesn't feel the same way?"

She gripped his hand in solidarity. "This time maybe don't leave so much left unsaid."

Maddox gave her hand a tight, anxious squeeze. "Maybe I'm not ready to know for sure yet."

She leaned her head against his arm. "I know what you mean."

"Here we are." Edward double-parked alongside one of the beautiful postwar apartment buildings overlooking Central Park. He cut the engine and put on the hazard lights.

Maddox got out of the car on his own, but Edward was at Eden's door so fast, she didn't even get a chance to try. "I'll walk you up. Whenever you're ready to leave, Mr. Thorne will let me know."

"You call him Mr. Thorne?" Maddox asked.

"I call him boss, to his face," Edward said.

Maddox huffed. "Bet he likes that."

Eden rolled her eyes as she took Maddox's hand again, and they followed Edward past the doorman, through the white marble lobby to the bank of three elevators.

One arrived quickly, and Eden half expected there to be an old man inside pulling levers or pushing buttons so the residents didn't have to lift a single finger.

In their case, Edward pushed the button for the fifteenth floor. The top floor.

"Is this a penthouse situation?" Maddox asked under his breath.

Edward replied, "No, but he has rooftop access."

"Well, obviously."

Maddox was deadpan, but Eden was already over-dazzled.

The elevator stopped, and the doors opened into another marble-tiled foyer decorated with wall-sized art and four sofas arranged in a square at the center. Edward led them to an ornate wooden door, one of four like it surrounding them. If her orientation was correct, this was the park side of the building. Rather than knock, Edward turned the latch and held the door open for them.

Eden sucked in a breath, and Maddox gave her hand one final squeeze before letting it go. Another hallway greeted them with a rush of refrigerated air. Eden shivered in her spaghetti straps. A large abstract piece of art opposite the entrance caught her eye. Paul Simon's "Graceland" played on the speaker system throughout. Edward gestured to the left. "Living area is that way. Bathroom is the first door on the right if either of you need it."

"Thank you," Eden said.

"Fancy," Maddox muttered.

They walked down the hall, gleaming wood floors underfoot, between long, plush runners. To think, if she'd taken Brennon up on the offer he'd made at Seasons that day, she'd be staying here. Trying to imagine what that would have been like, Eden failed. She could never picture herself in a place like this as anything more than a guest, and the harsh reality was a depressing weight in her chest.

A group of three women passed the opening at the end of the hall and glanced their way, squinting as if to determine whether they recognized Eden or Maddox. Coming up empty, they walked on.

Eden and Maddox continued past the bathroom, and then Brennon appeared where the women had just been.

Eden sucked in a breath as he stopped in his tracks before starting toward them with a determined gait. "You made it." His gaze bounced between the two of them, his expression inscrutable.

Eden was barely breathing anymore. It was taking her a moment to process the sight of him. Obviously she'd expected to see him; this was his place, his party. She was there at his invitation, delivered to him by his driver. But still. How beautiful could one man be?

His shirt was the softest gray, a long-sleeved V-neck revealing a few inches of his upper chest. His jeans were dark and well-fitted, rolled once at the ankle where they met the edge of brown leather boots. His longish wavy hair framed his face, softening the angles and making him look more like a rockstar than a Broadway legend. Or maybe it was both. Maybe he was everything.

Sharply, he turned to Maddox. "Good to see you." He offered his hand. "Thank you for coming."

Maddox shook it with zero hesitation this time. "Thanks for the ride. Nice place."

"Thank you. Can I get either of you a drink?" He turned to Eden again, his eyes searching what had to be every pore on her face.

Chills popped up on her bare arms as cold air from a vent whooshed past her neck. She rubbed her shoulder to warm it. "I'd love one."

"This way. Are you cold?"

"Oh. Not at all." She refused to be anything but absolutely gracious.

Eden and Maddox followed Brennon into the living area, which opened into a large kitchen. Edward disappeared through a door next to the refrigerator, and Adam turned away from the center island in time to see the three of them arrive. He looked fantastic, his charming smile back in place.

"Mad," he said, the word breathless.

Next to her, Maddox straightened, emotion puffing out his chest. "Hello, Adam."

A knuckle grazed Eden's forearm, pulling her attention. She turned to look up at Brennon, who stared down at her with a crease of concern on his face. The cool scent of him sent a shiver of anticipation through her body.

"Let's get you warmed up."

In total, there were seven other people at the party besides her, Maddox, and Adam, and not a single one of them had gone to Juilliard but Brennon. Still, Eden knew their names. Other actors, another Tony winner, one movie star, all in their thirties. Two couples and three singles. They greeted Eden kindly, asked about her work, her plans after the tour. Brennon talked her up to an unbearable degree without mentioning her commercials once, and he didn't seem to mind the way they all teased him about his obvious crush on the ingénue.

Eden refused to take any of them seriously. They'd forget her the second she left. Still, she smiled and laughed at their jokes, answered their questions, and gushed so hard her face hurt about what a dream it had been to work with Brennon.

For a full hour, she stood by his side, sneaking the occasional glance and sharing self-conscious smiles with him. He was a charming host, and a solicitous one, too. But of course he was. This was the same man who'd put out a breakfast spread complete with a brand-new hand-crafted honey dipper for her. God, she'd missed him—the man she discovered that day. She managed to refuse his offer to find something to cover her shoulders several times, but after Adam brought her a second drink, she was frozen to her core.

Brennon, it seemed, had had enough of her shivering. "Come with me."

Eden's stomach fluttered at his lowered voice that was only meant for her to hear. Dazed, she followed him to the living room couch where a throw blanket sat folded beneath a pillow. He picked it up, shook it out, and wrapped it around her. "I'm done mingling," he said. "You?"

"Should we sit, then?" she offered, full of hope and the ember of the spark they'd left behind.

He looked her deep in the eyes and nodded. "I'd like that."

God help her, so would she.

Eden took a seat in the corner of the couch, grateful for the warmth of the blanket. She snuggled into it, holding it closed with one hand and lifting her drink to her mouth with the other. Tucking her legs beneath her, she faced him as he sat beside her. Close. Not like he had in DC at Seasons. This time, his hip touched her knees and he put his arm across the back of the couch behind her.

She was dizzy with his proximity, drunk on the way he stared at her. "Better?" he asked.

She nodded. "Is this cashmere?"

"I think it's cotton." He fingered the fabric. "Chenille?"

"It's soft."

"Good."

They locked eyes for a moment so long Eden's vision wavered before he looked over his shoulder toward the kitchen where Maddox and Adam remained deep in their own private conversation. It had been going on since the initial greetings were out of the way. "Looks like they're on the mend," Brennon noted.

"Hope so."

They turned back to each other.

"I misjudged things between the two of them," he said. "I hope you know how sorry I am for that."

Over the course of the last week or so it had become clear that Brennon wasn't cruel. He'd been coming from a protective place, and if the roles had been reversed, Eden couldn't say she wouldn't have done the same thing to help Maddox. This party, and the effort he'd put forth to get them there, spoke volumes in a way words couldn't. "I do now," she said.

He let out a shaky sigh and briefly closed his eyes. "Good." Looking at her again, he asked, "How's the break been for you so far?"

His direct gaze made her heart beat too fast, but she did her best to keep her words casual. "Busy catching up with friends. You?"

He gestured to the other people in the space. "Making the rounds."

"These are your people, huh?"

He grimaced. "For now."

"Why's that?"

"Recently, I've started to question their priorities."

She frowned, lost as to what he could mean.

"My ex had an affair. They all knew, and never bothered to tell me."

"Oh." Her Google search hadn't gone into so much detail. His bluntness was flattering. Eden hadn't expected it. "I'm so sorry."

"You know, they say it could happen to anyone," he said drily, "but I find it happens to me more often than most."

"What's that?"

He turned his attention to the barely sipped cocktail she still held in her hand. "I've been told I don't make enough time for the people in my life."

Eden leaned into this moment—the one where he opened up and shared a bit more of himself. The man behind the marquee . . . She also leaned in slightly closer to him. "Who told you that?"

"More than one person." He gave her a regretful grin. "They aren't wrong."

"You have a big life. Bigger than most."

"Not bigger," he disagreed. "Just more visible."

"Do you not like that?"

Grimacing, he answered in a mumble. "Not particularly."

If they were a couple, Eden would have reached out to smooth the crease between his eyes. Soften his demeanor. But she didn't know what they were anymore. Not yet. She only knew she wanted more. More of this. More time. More him. If tonight was all they had, she'd seize every moment. "Then why do you do it?"

One of his dark brows arched. "Theater? Because I love it," he said, the question reanimating him. "The smell of the makeup, the heat of the lights, the music, the live audience . . . The rush of not knowing exactly what's going to happen every night. I can't imagine doing anything else."

Eden loved all of that too, and more. Her lips quirked, seeking to keep his eyes bright and his words flowing. "What if you got the chance to play Batman, though?"

He laughed. "In a musical?"

"No—a movie."

His nose scrunched in distaste. It was an expression she'd never seen on him, and it was adorable. "Film isn't for me. I don't like how often people recognize me now, I can't imagine if . . ." He gave a shudder for effect. "No. I'll grow old and die on Broadway, God willing."

"You must get pressure to transition though. By your agent? You have a film agent, right?"

"A very frustrated one."

"Why have one, then?"

"Just in case," he said with a grin she could stare at for the rest of her life.

"Is there a part you wouldn't turn down?" she asked.

"Maybe . . ." he said, half his mouth lifting with a mysterious grin.

Eden smiled and snuggled a little closer, willing him to share his secret. "Tell me," she whispered.

CHAPTER TWENTY-ONE

Brennon couldn't tear his gaze from Eden's mouth, six inches closer now than it had been a moment ago. Her shoulder was tucked into the bend of his elbow, and with the smallest movement, his arm could pull her closer. She could rest her head on his chest, and they could continue their conversation wrapped up in each other. He would murmur his answers into her sweet-smelling hair, rub her back, press kisses to her smooth forehead.

A laugh rang out behind him. Hillary's. He'd forgotten there were other people there.

"What's your dream role?" Eden pressed.

"Everything's been done in film."

"My mom's dream role for me in a movie is Nancy Drew." She looked down at her drink, a smirk bending her lips. "I don't think she gets me yet."

It was taking the entire force of his will not to rest his hand on her leg. But they were talking business. Keeping things professional. "Is film the goal for you?"

"At this point, I feel like I need to keep my options open," she admitted. "Staying employed is pretty much my only goal."

"If you'd like, I could make a call to my agent. Introduce you."

She blinked, her head jerking.

Shit, he'd overstepped again. "Assuming you don't have one for film, but I shouldn't assume—"

"You'd do that?" she asked, neither disgusted, nor appalled.

A few parts of him managed to relax. "Only if you were interested."

"I . . . I don't know what to say."

He ran his palm down his own thigh, his eyes following the path of it. "You don't have to say anything. Just know it was an honest offer. One you deserve, not only because . . ." *Shut up, Brennon.*

"Because what?"

I love you. I want you to have everything you want. All your dreams. Be happy.

"Because, so often, making the right connections gets you better results. I'm not above offering mine to someone with as much potential as you have."

She let out a short laugh that wilted at the edges. "That's me, a great big ball of potential."

Given their recent history he was beyond trying to guess whether he'd offended her or not, but he was beginning to sweat, and she would surely notice if he let it go unremarked upon. "Eden, you make me nervous," he confessed.

"*I* do?" Her widened eyes were both amused and surprised, likely at his tactless and abrupt subject change.

So much for keeping things professional. At the very least, he supposed, he could keep her entertained. *In for a penny . . .* "You do. I never know how my words will land. Sometimes I say the right thing and sometimes I get it so wrong, it's unbearable."

Concern—or was it pity?—drew her brows together. "Brennon—"

His chest contracted, yet he blundered on. "I hope you know it's only because I like you. I think you're extraordinary."

Her face paled, but maybe it was a trick of the light.

"If there's anything I can do, I'm here. No strings," he added.

She pressed her lips together, eyes down. "I don't know if I deserve that," she whispered.

"I disagree."

"I was horrible to you."

"I was horrible to you first." His voice threatened to break, and the rest of his words came out hushed. "Forgive me."

She lifted her gaze to meet his again, her eyes wet and shining. "Of course."

He didn't mean for it to happen, didn't plan it, but his arm made the move. His hand met the middle of her back and rubbed down her spine.

She closed the distance, her head coming to rest against his chest exactly where he'd envisioned it, and she curled into him. Afraid to upset the balance but wanting her hands free, he took her drink from her and leaned forward to put it on the coffee table. After that, the risk of moving a muscle paid off. She snuggled closer, tucking her head, and resting her cool, empty hand on his stomach.

"Warm enough?" he asked.

"Now, I am."

He closed his eyes, liking the sound of that. His fingertips stroked the end of her ponytail. He was aware other eyes were on them, thinking things, judging him, commenting about how soon this was after Chloe, how it must not mean anything, what was in it for him besides the painfully obvious—she was beautiful, sexy, young, and hungry. He knew what it looked like.

Eden hadn't wanted people to look at her like that on the road. Hadn't wanted anyone to know the two of them had briefly gotten close. The fact that she was cuddled up with him now in front of several of the more prominent eyes and ears of Broadway meant that either she no longer cared what anyone saw, or this was platonic and therefore no one's opinion mattered. Maybe she was a cuddler by nature. Maybe she did this with everyone.

He preferred to think not, at least for tonight. He was having a good day, for once, but he would squelch the desire to press kisses to her forehead.

"How long do these things usually go?" she asked.

"Depends."

"That's helpful, Brennon."

His chest moved with a short, silent laugh. "Until the drinks run out," he said.

"I'm hogging you," she said, but made no move to pull away.

He closed his eyes and counted every place where their bodies touched. He whispered, "Don't stop."

The hand resting on his stomach tightened, her fingertips flexing, applying some pressure. "I'd invite you back to my place, but it's on the other side of the world, and it's got no air-conditioning."

His eyes flew open, and his lips parted in surprise. He was glad she couldn't see his face, or how much she'd shocked him with the offer. Had it been an offer? If so, it was one he didn't have it in himself to refuse. "What about your roommates?"

"They'll be out till four. Or later. Until the men run out." She lifted her head, turning to look up at him.

Brennon schooled his expression into one of thoughtfulness. He should win a Tony for how cool he was playing this. Intense desire stirred at the sight of her face so close. Memories of her hot honeyed mouth against his, the tremble of her thighs against his cheeks, the press of her tongue. "I hate to tear Edward away from Baltica-29—"

Eden broke eye contact and waved the suggestion off. "You're right. Dumb idea."

Brennon wasn't so easily deterred. He'd see this through, dammit. He missed her too much. Whatever she'd take of him, he'd offer. "But I'm not bad at hailing a cab."

She raised her eyebrows, along with one corner of her mouth. "What about your guests?"

"Adam's here. They'll be fine. Provided the invitation stands."

Her eyes smoldered up at him. "For sure."

He was a dead man.

"You slip out first," he told her. "Wait for me in the foyer by the elevator."

"Okay."

They shared one last lingering glance before she sat up straight. He stared as she let the blanket fall from her shoulders and stood, slipping her feet back into her red heels. While she focused on the task, he adjusted himself in his pants. His erections had been much fewer and farther between since the disastrous night at the Four Seasons, but he was glad to find everything still in working order.

After she exited the room, he stood, locating Adam in the kitchen speaking animatedly with Maddox. "I'll be seeing Eden home now."

Both sets of ears perked in his direction, but Adam was the one who spoke. "*Downtown?*"

Why did no one think he ever went downtown?

"Make sure everyone leaves at a reasonable hour," Brennon said. "Edward can lock up."

"Sure." Adam grinned. "Have a lovely evening."

"You, too. See you both soon." He turned to Eden's friend, hoping the casual way Maddox was leaning on the counter meant things were going well—that he and Adam had worked things through. "Thank you so much for coming."

Maddox gave him a warm, sincere smile. "Thank you for having me."

Relief made Brennon's next breath come easy. Leaving the two of them, he retrieved his key, wallet, and a roll of condoms from his nightstand. Better to be optimistic than unprepared. Filling his pockets, he met Eden in the penthouse lobby.

"On second thought . . ." she hedged. "My place isn't the most comfortable . . ."

But he wanted to go there. Now. There was no place in the world he wanted to be more. "I'd still like to see it. I don't get downtown enough."

She gave him a rueful grin. "Don't say I didn't warn you."

He reached for her hand, and she ultimately took it. He pretended not to notice her hesitation. He was confident enough for both of them that this was an excellent idea. Brennon led her to the elevator and pushed the button.

"This place is ridiculous, by the way," she said.

"You don't like it?"

"I mean—what's not to like? You're just up here living all of our dreams."

He wasn't about to contradict her, but she couldn't have been more wrong. His dream was in the Bowery tonight. With her.

The elevator doors slid open, and he led her inside. She tightened her grip on his hand and faced him. "I've kissed you so many days in a row now, it's become a habit," she said.

Her bangs had come loose, and he reached up, re-tucking them behind her right ear. She stepped closer to make it easier, her face tilted up to his.

God, how he'd dreamed of this moment—of having her in his arms again. She'd invaded every cell of him in a way he could not have possibly prepared for. No woman he'd ever met had affected him like this, and now, with her lips so close to kissing his again, he couldn't bear another second of waiting. "We've missed three nights."

Her gaze homed in on his mouth. "I'd hate for us to get out of practice."

He smiled faintly. "Have to stay consistent."

"You don't mind the extra rehearsal?" she teased. "I know we're on a break . . ."

"I don't mind." He smoothed his thumb across the high curve of her cheekbone.

Eyes locked on her lips, he leaned in and waited, his body asking the question. She answered it with her hand, slowly moving it up his chest in that "contemporary" way she'd been warned about. His heart pounded as her hand rested against his neck, and the warm pressure of her red lips met his.

It was almost a stage kiss, lips kissing lips. No tongues, mouths barely open. It was a test of his will and a seduction all at once. Her mouth had enchanted him from day one. Exploring the outer curves of it with his own stoked a fire deep within him. Hands moving to her waist, he held her chest to chest, content for the moment with this small taste of her. Not honey tonight, but Adam's fizzy cucumber drink. He'd snuck a few sips of bourbon to calm his nerves earlier, but he liked the taste of his friend's creative cocktail, and was enjoying its refreshing bite all over again.

She ran her hands up his arms, leaving heat in their wake. The elevator came to a jolting stop on the first floor, and they separated. She put a finger to her lips and seemed to take a beat. "I guess it's time to show me how well you can hail a cab."

He took her hand. "Watch this." They walked through the lobby. Brennon nodded at the doorman. "Artie, we'd like a cab downtown please."

"Right away, Mr. Thorne."

Brennon winked at Eden as Artie stepped out into the street. "Impressed?"

She only shook her head, but he caught her smile.

Within seconds, Artie had earned his tip, and Brennon was in a cab with Eden, heading for her apartment. Bypassing Midtown, her neighborhood was a straight shot down Second Avenue. "If my roommates do happen to be home, you don't have to engage with them. You're under no obligation as a guest, okay?"

"How many roommates do you have?"

"Just the two, but they can feel like five."

"And how do you know them?" he asked.

"At one point we all worked at the same Starbucks."

"Oh, which one?"

"Wall Street. Like, the crown jewel of Manhattan Starbucks."

"Why's that?" he wondered.

"Big tips. Which was good, because the guy were such lecherous assholes."

Brennon bristled.

"I mean, that's an overgeneralization, but also my overall impression."

"So that's where you met. Are they actresses, as well?"

"Both of them," she said.

"And how are they making it?"

Eden seemed content to babble her way all the way downtown and Brennon was only too happy to let her. He loved hearing about her life and how she went about conquering her world. "Fallon's about to go on tour with *The Lion King*, so she's excited. She's an amazing dancer. She's a swing, and she's so freaking talented. And Trista's rehearsing for this new play, which is kind of a modern day, gender-flipped *King Lear*. You'd have to hear her explain it, but she's stoked. They're performing it in this old restaurant in Chinatown. Honestly, I think she has a crush on the playwright, and that's what she's most excited about because they're not paying her much at all, but anyway, it sounds sort of fun."

Brennon was still trying to wrap his mind around "gender-flipped *King Lear*." It did sound interesting, though, that sort of acting. He'd gone straight from Juilliard to ensemble/understudy roles on Broadway. From there, he'd risen to supporting characters and leads quickly, over two years and four shows. He knew his story was rare, one in a million, but he never got tired of hearing where other performers had gotten their starts.

It was no wonder, though, how a woman like Eden might find him insufferable.

He didn't want to think about that tonight. He'd prefer to think about her smooth thighs against his face and the sounds she might let herself make when no one else was around to hear.

All his unfulfilled fantasies from the Four Seasons crowded his mind, quickening his pulse, and hardening his cock. She must have noticed, because as they approached Houston Street, Eden placed her hand on the upper part of his leg, letting her finger graze the edge of his arousal.

He turned to face her.

"Is this okay?" she asked.

Heat rushed up his neck. His stomach was in knots. "I missed you."

Her lips parted as she took in his expression. He could only imagine the torture she found there. The desire, the apology—the unmitigated *hope*. Her hand wrapped around him and tugged. He nearly blacked out. He covered her hand with his own, urging a gentler touch. If she wanted him to last until they got to her room, she had to slow down.

She obliged, and he spread his legs to allow her deeper exploration. His hand moved with hers as she moved in for a kiss that went far deeper than the one they'd teased each other with in the elevator. It lasted until they arrived at her apartment. On the verge of explosion, Brennon paid the fare while Eden gathered her things. They exited the taxi through separate doors as though she hadn't just edged him in a cab.

Her building was one of the older ones in the neighborhood. Some had been through some sort of gentrification process, but not Eden's. "Don't look at it." She grabbed for his arm and aimed him at the door. She unlocked it, and they stepped inside. Mailboxes made up the rear wall, and two apartment doors were on either side of a staircase. The heat was stifling. "I'm on the third floor," she said. "Don't worry, it gets better with the windows open. Try to ignore the smell."

The smell she referred to was garam masala and fenugreek. Distinctly Indian. It wasn't unpleasant, only very strong.

Her heels clomped on the wooden stairs as they made their way up. He was outright sweating by the first landing, and he ran a hand through his hair so it wouldn't stick to his face. Nothing like a big, sweaty man coming at a woman with his hot, hard cock. He'd have to find some way to downplay the Neanderthal vibe he knew he'd be putting off the second they got inside her apartment. Maybe a shower . . .

Maybe she'd join him.

Finally, they arrived at her door. "Hello?" she called out as she stepped inside. No one answered, and she visibly relaxed. "Coast is clear. Welcome to downtown, Mr. Thorne." She moved out of the way to let him in.

The tiny living room housed a burnt orange love seat and twin navy blue armchairs. The furniture sat on a worn cream-colored shag rug and faced a decent-sized flatscreen. The kitchen was also small, done up in various shades of pink and green. It was, as promised, a more tolerable temperature thanks to the open windows, but he immediately worried for her and her roommates' security. "Is there a fire escape?" he asked.

"Outside Fallon's window."

"You always leave the windows open?"

"We're on the third floor."

"But the fire escape."

She glanced around the room, a baffled expression on her face. "What would anybody want to steal here?"

"There are worse crimes, Eden."

Realization of his meaning dawned, and she graced him with a patronizing smile. "Ah, well, we can't all have a doorman to protect us, but I assure you, you're safe with me."

He glared at her willful misunderstanding, but could forgive her easily because of the way she was looking at him. Like she wanted to devour him whole. In that, they were on the same page. "Would you like to show me *your* room?"

"You read my mind. It's right this way." She walked down a short hallway alongside the kitchen and then pointed to her left. "This is the one. I hope you're ready for this."

Brennon was nothing if not extremely ready to see Eden's bedroom.

"This is—"

"Like a jail cell? I know."

He glanced up and down the length of the tiny room. There was enough space for her mattress on the floor beneath the open window and a small dresser with a fan directed at the bed. Opposite the dresser was a full-length mirror and a rack of her clothes. Not much room to roam. She kicked off her shoes near the dresser, bent over, and pushed a plug into an outlet. All at once the room lit up with white lights, allowing her to flip off the harsher overhead. "Better?" she asked.

Brennon spun slowly to take it all in with the lighting change. The comforter on her bed was pink with yellow and white flowers. With the fairy lights, it reminded him of a secret garden at night. The exposed brick walls added to the effect. "It's very you."

"How is it like me?"

"Dreamy," he said, since it was the first word that came to mind and described her on several levels.

"Well, there's only the one place to sit, so—" She gestured to the mattress. "Shall we?"

Unlike his memory foam bed uptown, this one had a lot of spring in it, sounds included. He chuckled. "Do you know what this bed reminds me of?" he asked.

"No, but do tell me about the last time you had to slum it." She moved to stand in front of him. He looked up at her to see if she was annoyed.

She didn't appear to be, her smile as generous and indulgent as it had been all evening.

"There's a nunnery in the South of France—"

Her eyes narrowed, reading him too easily. "You were in a *nunnery* in the South of France?"

"No." He smiled. "I was going to say it reminds me of my dorm room."

She rewarded him for his joke by lifting her skirt enough to straddle his lap. "Tell me more," she said as she lowered her rear end to his thighs and draped her arms around his neck.

She glowed beneath the lights. Her skin luminous and perfect, eyes dark and sparkling. This image of her attached itself to his memory instantly. He never wanted to forget this moment, where loving her—for a few seconds—didn't hurt.

He lowered his voice. "You'd like to hear more about my dorm room?"

"On second thought . . . we've done an awful lot of talking tonight."

"We have." And every minute of it had been precious. However, he, too, was prepared to move on.

"You never said whether you liked my dress."

"Because I'm terrible at complimenting you. Haven't you noticed?"

"I have. It's sort of all or nothing with you when it comes to the compliments."

"Have I mentioned you make me nervous?"

She grinned at him. "Love that."

"I had a feeling . . ."

"Do you like my dress, Brennon?" she asked again.

"Does it have pockets?"

"It does."

He put his hands on her hips, moving them down until they were tucked into both pockets. "It's perfect," he said. Through them, he gripped her legs. She bit her lip and rocked toward him.

"I'm sweating," he said. It came out more as a blurt.

"Good. Me, too."

"I could use a shower."

She ran a hand through his hair at his temple. "You've already showered today."

"I don't want to repulse you."

"You're a lot of things, Brennon Thorne, but repulsive isn't one of them."

He managed half a smile, relief mixed with regret. "That's the nicest thing you've ever said to me."

She brushed her thumb across his jawline, her eyes searching his. "Didn't I call you a good man once?"

"I hated that day," he whispered.

"Me too," she said and kissed him.

CHAPTER TWENTY-TWO

Eden didn't want to remember that day, either. Or the night at the Four Seasons, Gabi's video, Jonathan's lies, or the first night they'd met. She wanted to remember Brennon just like this—like he'd been all evening. Nervous, charming, and alarmingly seductive.

She tangled her hands in his hair and opened her mouth against his. Warmth flooded her at the broad sweep of his tongue. Starting off at his place, and here now, in her apartment, their differences were laid bare. Not a thing in common with each other except this ever-growing desire to get naked together. It was undeniable how much she wanted him, and with his erection pressed between her pubic bone and his abs, what he wanted was clear, too. The feel of him thrilled her, and she tilted her hips in a rhythm to keep him hard.

He tasted of salt and bourbon. Their mouths slid against each other, tongues licking, teeth tugging, lips searching, hungry and a bit desperate. She kissed him like it might be her last chance. "Let's get you out of this shirt," she whispered.

With her help, they worked it up his torso, and she tossed it to the floor behind her. Her first look at him half-naked didn't disappoint. Broad across the shoulders and narrow at the hips, everything was nicely defined, golden from summer days and her fairy lights. A light smattering of black hair defined a V between his pecs. She ran her hands down his smoother-than-expected chest to his waist. He *was* sweating, and she loved it.

"You can unzip me," she said.

Reaching around her back, he found her zipper easily, like he'd already scouted its location at some earlier point in the evening. Her chest rose and fell with deepening breaths as he slipped the spaghetti straps down to reveal her upper body. His gaze followed the top edge of her dress as it drifted lower. Hurriedly, she helped herself out of her incredibly uncomfortable strapless bra. If it didn't save her ass on occasion, she'd chuck the damn thing out the window.

Free of it, she pressed into him, skin on skin. They kissed with increasingly voracious need, their hands exploring all the areas they could now touch. He groaned as she trailed her fingertips down his sides. She shivered at the sound of it.

He lifted a hip, and she thought she would fall, but he had complete control. Turning them both over, he followed her up the bed until her head was on a pillow and he hovered above her. Her shimmying had served the dual purpose of making her more comfortable *and* getting her dress completely off. On second thought, he'd probably had something to do with that, too.

He lowered himself to lie beside her, and she turned to face him. He ran a hand from her shoulder to her breast, then further to her stomach, her hip. Returning to her breast, he took hold of it and brought his open mouth to her nipple, sucking and flicking it with his tongue. A quick bite of his teeth made her yelp. With that, he took a hard hold of her ass, forcing her pelvis against his cock. "Eden."

"Sorry. I'm noisy."

"Don't be sorry." He took her mouth in one slow, drugging kiss, dragging her thigh across his body until the tip of his cock brushed her panties.

Only problem was, he still had his jeans on.

They had to deal with this.

"Stop," she said.

Immediately, he froze, lifting his hand from her butt and holding it midair. "I didn't mean—"

"We need to get your pants off."

"Of course. Yes . . ." He rolled onto his back, digging in his pockets until he pulled out a roll of what appeared to be four condoms. Nice. So he had big plans, too.

He put them on a pillow and prepared to unbuckle, but he wasn't in the kind of rush she was. No, he took his time, loosening the belt, undoing the button, and finally lowering his zipper with the haste of someone walking a plank. She propped her head on her hand and watched the show as patiently as she could manage, hoping there would be a reward for good behavior at the end.

He cast a glance her way. "You're still wearing panties."

"You have yet to show me what's behind that zipper."

Right on cue, he reached into his shorts and pulled it out.

Eden bit her lip to keep her jaw from dropping and took him in—all of him.

Thick and heavy, his cock jutted from his groin as he lifted his hips and slid his jeans all the way off, shucking his boots in the process. Immediately obsessed, Eden took hold of him, testing the size and weight, the glorious hardness. A dream to work with, indeed . . .

"Eden," he moaned as she continued to stroke him. "The condoms made it all the way downtown . . ."

"They're not going anywhere. Remember that night in my dressing room when you wouldn't have sex with me?" She moved between his legs.

"I didn't have condoms that night, and your couch was too small. We would have broken all the lights if I'd had sex with you on that table."

"So many excuses . . . I wonder what mine will be." She lowered her mouth to take him.

He grunted, slapping the mattress with his hand. "Such a vicious thing to say."

She'd said worse to him before, and she was hoping tonight would help them both forget all of it. Not that she *wasn't* planning to have sex with him—who was anyone kidding, that was totally gonna happen—but she wanted to taste him first.

Whatever the man bathed in, she'd happily drown in it. Up close, he smelled so good, all citrusy essential oils with herbaceous undertones. The fragrance both excited and mellowed her. She'd diffuse that blend all day. Stretching out to really enjoy him, she took hold of his erection, and his pulse thrummed against her palm. It was impossible to tell anymore which of them was more excited.

After another deep inhale, where she ran her nose up his entire length, she took him between her lips and sucked the head of his cock delicately, licking a circle around the ridge to see if he liked it. Her answer came with his quickening breath, a tug on her ponytail. Satisfied with his reaction, she went back to playing with his tip, giving it lingering French kisses. She kept up a steady upward squeezing motion with her hand and glanced up to find him watching her tease him, his eyes dark storms of lust.

She gave him her best fluttering doe eyes and continued to suck and taste just the tip.

He rubbed a hand across his mouth in frustration.

She gave his crown a tiny kiss. "Notes?"

He shook his head, eyes never leaving hers.

"Pick up where I left off, then?" she asked. "Or is this too Regency for downtown?"

"I am curious how the girls downtown do it."

In that case, she'd give him something he'd remember forever. "Girls like me always want it all."

She moved over him, straddling his chest to face his cock. Bending forward to take it back into her mouth, she lowered her panties to his face.

He made quick work of the silk thong, pulling it past her hips until it tore. She peeled off his socks, leaving them both completely bare. Then his mouth was on her, and she took him to her throat.

Truth was, she'd actually never done it this way before. She'd thought about it, seen it in a video a time or two, but she hadn't counted on the sensory overload—the chaos and confusion of it. At first, she tensed, clenching her thighs to resist feeling too much; this was meant to be her turn to get him off. But the way he kissed her, devoured her, held her ass in his hands and fully engaged with her pussy was the most unbearable pleasure she'd ever known.

She was useless.

All she could do on her end was hold his cock as it thrust into her hand and catch it in short, sucking draws with her gasping mouth.

She was coming in less than a minute. As a result, she pumped him so fast, he came seconds later with a growl and a sudden grunt that sounded as surprised as she felt. His warmth covered her hand, as his release came in spasming spurts. *So hot . . .* She spread it up and down his length as he cursed beneath his breath.

Still shaking from her orgasm, her dismount was less than graceful.

"Well," she said, snuggling in beside him once she'd found a way to unwind herself from their tangle without kneeing him in the face. "That was . . ."

"Efficient," he supplied.

"Yes."

They both laughed. For Eden it was one part from embarrassment and two parts amusement at Brennon's equally obvious enthusiasm.

He pushed some of her sweaty hair off her brow. "I should get us a few wet washcloths."

"Like a dozen," she agreed. They'd only *thought* it was hot in here before. "Or I could run a bath. This place might look like a dump, but wait until you see the bathtub."

"It's not a dump," he protested with some vehemence.

"Please, Brennon." Eden got out of bed and walked across the hall, still naked. Flipping on the bathroom light, she pushed the shower curtain back from the ancient freestanding tub. It wasn't fancy enough to have claw feet or anything, but it had whatever knock-off of claw feet had been available at the time the building was built. Eden ran the water, keeping it lukewarm.

He wandered in after a few minutes, and she looked up as Broadway legend Brennon Thorne darkened her very own bathroom doorway in the Bowery—naked, with his hair rumpled. Eden bit her lip as she grinned. Striking didn't even begin to describe it. For the first time ever in his presence, she was truly starstruck. Fallon would shit herself if she came home right now.

"That is nice," he said regarding the large tub.

It wasn't the Four Seasons. And it probably didn't come close to comparing to his own setup on the Upper East Side, with its gleaming floors and million-dollar views, but he clearly wasn't going anywhere tonight, and that was an epic relief. Her shoulders relaxed, but her heart continued its relentless pounding.

"Don't worry, it's safe to get in," she said. She and her roommates bleached it regularly. They all loved a nice, long bath. "We keep it very clean."

He laughed warmly. "I trust you."

Without hesitating, he got into the tub, making a space for her between his legs. She got in on the other side and let the cool running water rush over her shoulders and down her back until she was shivering. He noticed and held his hand out. "Come here."

He'd done such a good job keeping her warm at his apartment earlier, she had no doubt he would manage it again. She went into his arms, kissing his chest and his neck as she made her way back to his mouth. Body to body, she gave him a long, deep, wet kiss. His hands roamed all over her. Caressing her, pulling her more tightly to him, squeezing, massaging, stroking. He was hard again. Very. "You brought the condoms?" she asked.

"Still on your pillow."

"*God*," she groaned. She let out a dramatic sob with her forehead against his chest.

"I thought we came in here to cool off."

"But you're so hot still," she complained.

He made a low noise that turned her on so much she could barely make her brain work, and he ran his thumb across her cheek. He looked deeply into her eyes. Then, with the softest touch, he brought her mouth back to his, took a shaky breath, and kissed her again.

Oh . . .

The kiss overwhelmed her. Out of the dozens they'd shared so far, this one somehow did more work, like something inside her was being trampled—absolutely plundered—by something inside him. Her breath scattered, leaving her. She had to pull away. She pressed her hands into his shoulders and tried to make her lungs work right again.

"Eden." He tucked her bangs behind her ear, exposing so much of her disoriented face. "You are incredible."

Is this real? She met his beautiful gaze, captivated.

"I *need* to be with you," he said, a longing in his voice that cut right to the quick of her.

"I'm right here," she whispered.

"Not just tonight," he added.

She stared at him, unable to process what he was saying. She wanted to believe him, so desperately. Everything in him pulled toward everything in her. She'd never felt so drawn to someone at the core. But after what he'd said in DC . . . Was she being stupid? Was she too starstruck? Too infatuated? Those fucking words . . .

"You're not the type of woman I typically find myself drawn to. Despite my better judgment . . ."

It was enough to stop her from reading too much into the promise in his voice. Enough to make her nervous. He'd won a Tony after all.

Could this all be an act? An illusion? "I know you're excited, Brennon. So am I. But let's try not to get ahead of ourselves."

He kissed the end of her nose. "And you call *me* condescending."

She'd only meant maybe neither one of them was thinking clearly. "What I mean is we have to be realistic. Do you honestly see any way I fit into your life?"

He frowned. "Of course you fit. I'm crazy about you."

She chewed on her lower lip a moment, her heart doing its best to keep itself afloat. "Is it possible though, that you might be going through a phase?"

He regarded her warily.

She was scrambling to make sense of her feelings, and his words, and her irritatingly persistent doubts. "You said it yourself—I'm not your typical . . ." *Ugh.* Images of his other leading lady loves cycled through her mind. "Type."

He kept his arms around her, but she felt him flinch. "Eden, please, I thought we'd moved past this. You have to know I didn't mean any of—"

"But I mean onstage, too," she pressed on, becoming more convinced with each moment that this thing between them had been doomed from the start. "I'm still just a standby. I live in this shitty apartment, and I'm an unpredictable mess with a laughable résumé. I'm not like Chloe, or Gemma McClain or Skye Forester . . ."

The warm, indulgent look on Brennon's face shifted into slight disbelief. "Do you hear yourself?"

"Yes." Was he listening, though? That was the better question.

"So, you must know how ridiculous you sound."

"I've always known you thought I was ridiculous, Brennon." She kept her words soft. She was fully familiar with the truth, and how much it hurt. She'd seen it in Greenville, at their first tech rehearsal, at WRB-TV, and then faced it head on at the Four Seasons. "Because I make infomercials and peddle boner pills on TV. You knew it night one. I'm the exact opposite of your type."

His demeanor shifted, darkening. "I don't want to rehash this." He made a move to get her off him. "You heard me apologize. Accepted it. Forgave me."

"And I meant that." She used the weight of her body to pin him in place. She needed him to hear her, to really understand why it was so hard for her to believe any of this could be real. "Please, just listen to me. I like you so much. So, so much. But *this* is my life." She gestured to the bathroom and the apartment in general. "We might as well live on different planets."

"We live in a town thirteen miles long, and the distance between us is a fifteen-minute cab ride."

"I can hardly ever afford a cab."

"That's enough." He removed her from his person and stood to get out of the tub, dripping like some dark god rising from the ocean. He grabbed a towel off the rack and dried off. "All this 'I can never understand you' bullshit because you live in a walk-up and I have an elevator. You're not that hard to follow, Eden."

She sat back and put her hand on the side of the tub to get out as well. "Wait—are you leaving?"

He froze. "Isn't that what you're telling me to do?"

"No!" she nearly shouted.

He dragged his hands through his damp hair in exasperation. "Maybe I *don't* understand, then."

She stepped onto the bathmat and grabbed another towel. She was screwing this up, and badly. "I've had plenty of dreams die, okay?" she began, her voice breaking a little. "I don't need to be building another one that might not even have a chance of survival." She'd had plenty of unpleasant breakups too, but those had been like children's sandcastles on a beach, easily washed away. Brennon wouldn't be that. Winning him and losing him would *hurt*.

"Fine," he said flatly.

"You agree?"

"If you like. I guess I'll go get my things." He turned for the door.

"Wait. No. Stop." This was going sideways, and she had to salvage it. She grabbed him by the arm. Why was this so difficult? She didn't want him to leave. Ever. But she also wanted him to understand what it would mean for him to stay. "Please don't go. Not yet."

His eyes blazed, incredulous. "But you don't *want* me."

Of *course* she did. He still didn't get it. "I don't understand how to keep you, Brennon. There's a difference." She snapped her mouth shut. God, this was a lot to lay on a half-naked man who'd come here to get laid. But if he was sincere, maybe . . . Maybe? It was too much to wrap her brain around. If Eden was only a fraud who'd gotten lucky, this would give him the out he'd need. But if it was real . . .

He ran a hand down his face. "For fuck's sake."

Her heart clenched. Every rejection she'd weathered in the past would pale in comparison to this one. She bit her lip and braced herself, regretting this turn of events already. She should have kept her mouth shut. She shouldn't have let all her doubts and insecurities fly out into the open when he'd probably only come down here to have sex. No, fuck, she knew that wasn't true either. What was this man doing to her? "I want you to stay," she stated as plainly as she could while her heart was on the damn line. "Very much."

He threw the towel against the tub. "What's the point, if you've already decided it can never work?"

"I mean, I figure we have a month to try and maybe figure it out in LA . . ." They'd been in New York a few days already, and she hadn't heard a peep from the producers. Shayna and Brennon both wanted her in the role, after all. She could still be his leading lady.

"A month?" He stared at her in disbelief.

She didn't take it back; they both knew her tour contract far outlasted his. She'd stay on the road once he was done with his two months, and he'd be back here, in his circle of friends, probably opening some huge new show. If she got incredibly lucky, she'd still be singing "Detestable Man" in Des Moines, with some other handsome actor who wouldn't be half as interesting. None of that meant she wasn't falling head over heels for Brennon. None of it meant she wouldn't miss him, wouldn't forever dream of what could have been if she'd been the one at Juilliard instead of Veronica. Everything would have been so different.

"A month where we can be together. Whenever we want. What do you think?" There wasn't *no* hope. There just wasn't an overabundance of hope.

For several seconds, Brennon seemed to let the logic of her words sink in. She could tell from the way his eyes softened toward her. The way his tense mouth relaxed. "Eden . . ."

"I do want you." She took hold of his arms and pulled herself closer. "I want you. I care about you. You're wonderful. An absolute dream come true."

"But all you are is a fantasy," he said, not like a question, but like he understood, finally, where she was coming from. What the truth of the matter was.

"Not a fantasy, Brennon. Not at all. I'm just somebody who might not make it here. But I want to. And I'm working toward it with all my heart and soul. And I'm okay with just having a moment with you right now. And then we'll see?" She could dare to hope.

He hung his head in utter defeat. "All right, you win. I'll stay."

She sagged in relief. "Oh, thank God. This is amazing. Yes. Okay, come on. Let's find those condoms and put ourselves out of our misery." She put a hand on his hip, easing him toward the door, but he stood firm.

"I can't."

He might as well have slapped her. "What?"

"I didn't come here for sex. I mean, yes . . . it was on my mind, obviously, but I want *you*, Eden." His voice was urgent and low. "I'm in love with you." He put his hands on her face and made her meet his burning eyes. "Don't you see that?"

She sobered instantly.

Jesus Christ, he *did* mean it.

Her heart pounded a desperate thud in her chest. "Slow down," she whispered. To her heart. To him. To the rapidly spinning earth beneath her.

"Eden," he began softly.

"Wait. Shh . . ." She pressed her fingertips to his lips. She couldn't let him say it again; he'd already said way, way too much. She put her arms around his waist and gave him what she could—a hug. But that was more than enough to break her. His love was like another presence in the room, as real and solid as his body in her arms, and it was a revelation, too. It put words to everything she was feeling but wouldn't let herself feel, because the reality of having him was beyond even her wildest dreams. Wanting him was one thing, a showmance—a fling, two lost souls connecting through a kiss. But love? How could she guard herself against his *love*?

He hugged her back, keeping her close, although with a sigh, and some of his signature exasperation. She pulled away only enough to look into his gorgeous brown eyes. She was glad he'd already agreed to stay. As much as his declaration terrified her, she would never be able to bear letting him walk out the door now. Not after that. Not when they'd just let themselves become two, raw, frayed edges of people. She needed him. They needed each other. Those were just facts. Clear and more obvious than the heat in this place.

But she also knew what it was like to not be good enough. Acne on the wrong day. A singing voice that sometimes dazzled, but was too often overshadowed by someone with better training. She understood deep, deep down what it felt like to be overlooked or passed over—even flat-out rejected by the people she wanted to impress most in the world. She'd spent her entire life working, clawing her way up in an impossible business, only to get knocked back down time and again. If—when—the same thing happened with Brennon, she didn't know if she'd be strong enough to survive it.

His jaw ticked with so much repressed emotion. Eden prayed she hadn't smothered it completely. "Let's go back to bed," he finally said.

"But you need to understand that I one hundred percent refuse to have sex with you."

It served her right. It would probably only complicate her feelings more. "Noted." She gave him a firm, serious nod. "But promise we can try again in LA?"

His answering smile had more warmth to it, and Eden pressed a lingering kiss to his strong, bare chest.

In a month, maybe she could figure out a way to wrap her head around it—of the possibility of a life where she would never have to give him up. The directors' performance hadn't been *that* bad. She had people in her corner. Like Shayna assured her, everyone has off days. Maybe, just maybe, everything was actually fine.

If she could manage to star opposite Brennon for his entire two-month run, she might finally be able to gain some traction in her New York auditions—become a real contender. It could put her in the running for performing on Broadway itself—even as a standby, or an understudy in an ensemble. Broadway was Broadway, and if she could make it there, she could make it anywhere—including the Upper East Side with Brennon.

With her head pressed against his chest, Eden was able to detect the acceleration of his heart rate as he said, "LA with you sounds great. There's no question for me anymore, Eden. I'm not going anywhere."

It was ten o'clock when the heat woke Eden up. Their apartment was directly in the sun's rising path, and by that hour, it beat down on her mattress. She threw off the sheet and gasped when she saw Brennon sitting on the edge of the bed, fully dressed and staring down at her.

I'm not going anywhere.

Those words—and all the words from last night—came rushing back, and somehow they struck a deeper chord. He meant it. He'd meant everything. He'd weathered her excuses, her uncomfortable apartment. He'd spent the night beside her when he had no reason to believe she'd ever give him back what he so generously gave to her. He really wasn't going anywhere. Last night, hope had been a newly-hatched bird in her chest. But this morning it was growing more daring . . . *Please let me be able to teach it how to fly.*

"I have a meeting," he said. "Edward's on his way to get me."

She reached for his hand. He took it. She held on tight, grounding herself in his presence, unreal and undeserved as it was. She appreciated him, and wanted so much for him to know it.

"Expect a call from Justin Pope today."

She recognized the name, but her sleepy, warm, and fuzzy feelings made it hard for her to place immediately. "Who?"

"The film agent we discussed last night."

Now she was awake. "Oh, no, Brennon, you don't have to do that. I'm sure I—"

"You'll like him. Give him a chance to offer before someone else beats him to it. He's very good." With those quick and simple words, Brennon flipped her own internal narrative so fast she didn't know what hit her. It turned out he *was* occasionally capable of saying the right thing.

But she was speechless.

"What are your plans today?" he asked.

Eden didn't have any, and when she said as much, his mouth turned down in displeasure. "What?" She laughed. "I can't have a boring day?"

"We could keep each other company," he ventured.

She fluttered her eyelashes playfully. "Oh, so *now* you're ready to have sex with me."

He broke eye contact, a shy smile on his handsome face. "Wasn't what I meant."

Somehow, she'd already known that. "You have a meeting."

"I'll be done by noon. Lunch?"

The offer was impossible to resist. She still wanted him so much she was burning up. She just wished she didn't have so far to go before she made it uptown. Broadway was a very long street, but maybe it could lead the way. "Call me after your meeting?"

He smiled so genuinely, it nearly ruptured her heart.

If anything could give her the confidence to take on Hollywood, it was the way Brennon made her feel. Special. Gifted. Precious. *Loved.* If only she could manage to keep her own shine from wearing off.

She sat up, the tank top she'd gone to sleep in already sticking to her chest. Brennon's body blocked the air from the fan on her dresser.

Despite all that, he put his arms around her and held her close.

"Thank you for seeing me home," she said into his already perspiring neck. "And staying awhile." *Thank you for everything about you.*

"Thank you for having me," he said.

She sank into his hug. "It's too bad Trista and Fallon didn't get to meet you. They'll be pissed."

"Oh, we met."

She pulled away with a start and looked up at him. "What? When?"

"I had trouble sleeping, so I made us all nightcaps when they got home. We rehashed their night, I signed a poster. Scored four tickets to Trista's play. They're sleeping now."

She cringed more with every word. "God, Brennon, I'm sorry."

He smiled, his eyes crinkling in the corners and pushing that little bird of hope in her chest ever closer to the edge of the nest. "Don't be," he said. "They're great."

"They're obnoxious," she insisted.

"They love you."

Eden couldn't believe she was thinking it, but the words nearly spilled from her lips in that moment. *And I love you. I fucking love you. The most wonderful man. The most perfect, beautiful, totally misunderstood man.*

As much as she never would have believed she could picture Brennon at her kitchen table engaging with her over-the-top roommates, it was surprisingly easy to imagine now. Of course he had settled into the moment. He makes everything feel like home. She wished she'd been there. But, maybe next time . . .

They shared an overlong look, during which she forgot how to breathe. Adrenaline pulsed with her racing heart. She was as afraid to let him go as she was to ask him to stay.

"I'll call you after my meeting," he said.

Dizzy, she gave him a small kiss on the mouth. Their lips lingered there. Noses touching, they shared a breath. "Okay." She missed him already.

He cradled her cheek, and she leaned into his touch. Her eyes closed. "I'm sorry about last night," she said. "I didn't mean to ruin it."

He pressed his mouth against her other cheek, soft and warm. "You didn't."

God, he was always telling her that. But how many screw-ups would be too many?

She pulled away and stared into his beautiful eyes to discern whether his patience with her was wearing thin. "Thank you for giving me another chance."

His small grin was pure indulgence. "Thank me by keeping your afternoon free."

Her answering smile was as relieved as it was genuine. "I will."

After he left, Eden finally allowed herself to bask in a new possibility of her future. One filled with marble lobbies, doormen, and Brennon singing in the shower. A future where she belonged with him, as an equal, and they were unstoppable. For ten minutes, it almost stopped feeling irrational.

Then her phone rang with a Manhattan number she didn't recognize. Though it could be nothing—a robocall, a congressman asking for her vote—she suspected she wouldn't get off that easy. She let it go to voice mail. Heart in her throat, she braced for the worst as she pushed the button to listen to the message.

"Eden, honey, hi. This is Paulina Gomez, AD on *Liz and Darcy* here in New York. Listen, give me a call back when you get a chance. We're gonna go ahead and make some changes before the tour hits LA. Wanted to touch base with you about them. Hope you're enjoying your break. Talk to you soon."

Eden's grief was instantaneous, hitting her like a firm shove to the ground. She broke out in a flop sweat unrelated to the warmth of her bedroom.

She'd blown this opportunity all by herself, and there was no one else she could blame for it. Not the directors, not Gabi or Jonathan, or even Peck. She'd orchestrated her own downfall.

Her hand shook as she pressed the icon to return the call. Tears spilled from her eyes as she listened to Paulina break the news that as of next Tuesday in Los Angeles, Broadway's very own Kayla Grant would be taking the stage in the role she originated here in New York. And Eden would return to being a faithful standby, never to kiss Brennon Thorne in front of a live audience again.

Shayna called with her condolences about an hour later.

It was real.

She should have listened to her mother.

CHAPTER TWENTY-THREE

"No one else could do justice to this role."

As the director spoke, Brennon adopted his usual thoughtfully indifferent sitting-down pose. He stroked his chin and glanced at Edward beside him, who continued to scribble notes. Notes about his novel most likely.

Brennon had expressed interest in playing the title characters several months ago when he heard *Jekyll & Hyde* was returning in the fall for a limited run at the New Amsterdam. It would be demanding and grueling, and in the days after Chloe left him, immersing himself in a difficult role had seemed like a great idea. However, *Les Mis* had started sooner, and he'd wanted to get out of town. The dual roles of Dr. Jekyll and Mr. Hyde were a beast, and ones he'd never played. But rehearsals began in two and half weeks. He'd have to bow out of the tour. This was a valid reason to break his contract because it was a better offer. It paid more, it had more prestige—it was altogether a step up from what amounted to a supporting role in a traveling show.

"I'll need a few days to consider. I would have appreciated more notice."

The director gave his bald head a firm rub, as he glanced sheepishly from Edward to Brennon. "We had a funding scare. One of the producers had an accountant that went rogue, but fortunately they arrested the guy, and the authorities were able to locate all the money he'd stolen in offshore accounts."

Brennon waved the information away as though he couldn't be bothered with it, but also—*holy shit*. Did things like that really happen? He glanced at Edward, and for the first time questioned his trust in a man who used to be a complete stranger. What did he actually know about him, other than he claimed to be working on a science fiction novel and thought May 4th should be a national holiday?

They should have lunch afterward, and talk.

He returned his attention to Stu Roberson, who was offering him the part. "Who's playing Emma?"

"We have three final callbacks today, and we'll make our decision by tonight."

"Anyone I've heard of?" Brennon asked. He pictured Eden in the role. Her soprano would be a perfect fit, but she wouldn't be on the list. Her contract with *Liz and Darcy* ran through November.

Stu rambled off the names: one well-known in town, one he'd never heard of, and one B-list Hollywood actress everyone was familiar with. There was no doubt in Brennon's mind who'd be cast. Hollywood names were the biggest draws, much as it annoyed anyone who'd come up on Broadway. Regardless, as the title characters, Brennon would still have his choice of dressing room.

Often, it was the little things.

He stood to leave. "We'll be in touch then. Edward?"

Edward's head popped up, and he hurried to stand. Brennon led the way out of the offices. "I'd like to set up a meeting with Barry sometime before tomorrow evening," he informed his assistant.

"Barry? Your accountant?"

"Were you not listening in there?"

"I was—I mean, I might have drifted a few times—"

"Set something up. In the meantime, find out what people do to check up on their accountants. Does one hire another accountant to perform audits, for example?"

"I'll look into it," Edward assured him as they made their way through the lobby.

Brennon shot off a text to Eden, letting her know he was done with his meeting and asking whether she was still free for the afternoon. He waited until they were outside for a response, but then his anxiety over last night took hold. He'd said too much. Probably scared her off. He needed to change the subject.

"How is the book coming, by the way?" he asked Edward.

"I'm a little stuck on a subplot."

"Anything you want to hash out over lunch?" Brennon offered.

Edward looked surprised. "You don't have to, boss."

Brennon had to do something. Eden had yet to return his text, and he'd need some way to get his mind off her.

"Get us a table at Joe Allen, and you can catch me up."

Edward wasted no time putting in the call. By the time they were in the car, they had a reservation, and still no response from Eden.

The goings-on at Baltica-29 were not easy to follow, but Edward spoke like his life depended on getting the entire story out before their meal was served. Perhaps he thought if he took too long Brennon would lose interest the moment his appetite was satisfied.

However, his assistant described this fake place and these fake people with such knowledge and passion, Brennon couldn't help but be sucked in. While he preferred thrillers to science-fiction, he'd been a longtime fan of *Battlestar Galactica* and recently *Westworld*. "What if the cyborg—"

"Droid," Edward corrected.

Brennon waved him off. "What if the droid were somehow damaged in an engine room fire at some point? Wouldn't that cause some glitches in his programming? If it were only a glitch—" Brennon's phone rang. His heart leapt to his throat. *Eden*. He made a quick grab for it, and his heart quickly sank when he saw it was Adam.

"I should take this." He picked up his phone. "Hello?"

"Bren, hey—where are you?"

He sat back in his chair and rolled his sleeves back down. "I'm at lunch collaborating on a novel."

"You're not with Eden?"

Brennon frowned. "No . . ."

"Listen, I just talked to Mad. They recast her. Kayla's coming out to LA to play Lizzie for the month."

Brennon shut his eyes and pinched the bridge of his nose as he inhaled. "For the month," he repeated.

Adam sighed. They were both aware what a slap in the face this was to an actress in Eden's position. It wasn't even a full recast. It was a "You're not good enough to perform in one of our biggest markets, so we're bringing in the real star." It was Broadway at its absolute greediest. Tours were the bread and butter of New York theater. The producers made money hand over fist with a good-selling one.

Kayla was a bit of a hybrid, splitting her time evenly between television and the stage. She had a familiar face, with recurring roles on a number of popular shows, and she'd landed a supporting part in a limited miniseries for HBO that aired last year. People recognized her—if not by name, most everyone knew her distinctly lovely face. She was remarkably talented. Brennon had performed with her before and considered her a friend. Married to an independent film director who loved to use her in his movies, she had a bit of a cult following as well. Not to mention she was the current star of *Liz and Darcy* on Broadway. Eden would consider this a death blow.

"Did Maddox speak with her, or did he hear it from someone else?" Brennon asked, to gauge how far the news had traveled.

"She called him right after it happened, and he called me to see if we knew."

"I didn't know," Brennon said. "I had a feeling something like this was coming after the director's performance."

"I'm still having a hard time believing it was that bad. She's so good usually—"

"It was bad." He blamed himself, still.

Edward signaled for the check. Brennon stood to go outside and finish his conversation with Adam in relative privacy. "It's just bad timing," his friend rationalized. "If Kayla had wanted to do LA in the first place—which we have no way of knowing—they would have replaced Veronica, too. I think her husband's in California right now, working. That's probably half the reason she wanted to go."

While all that might have been true, there would be no way to logically convince Eden she hadn't blown her entire career with one performance. "I should call Eden."

"Or—you could give her a little space to process this," Adam suggested gently.

This was a familiar argument. He supposed the advice had worked out well for Adam. "How did things go with you and Maddox last night?"

"We talked."

"Yes?"

"For a very long time . . ."

"And?"

"That's it. That's how it went," Adam said, flatly.

Brennon managed a rueful smile his friend couldn't see. "Sorry."

"No, it's all good. Better anyway. Talking was something we'd skipped a few times, so . . ."

Enough about them. "So, I shouldn't call her?"

"Maybe give her the day, see if she reaches out to you."

The suggestion landed with a thud in Brennon's chest. "She won't." Despite how sweet she'd been this morning, he knew it as fact. His own behavior caught on tape, the condescending words he'd used, her belief about the metaphorical distance between them . . . it would all justify to her that they weren't intended to be anything more than a fling. A showmance.

"We'll all see each other at the theater on Tuesday," Adam reminded him.

Tuesday was years away.

"Oh—speaking of—how'd the meeting go?"

"I got the part," Brennon said.

Adam chuckled. "That's my boy. When do rehearsals start?"

"August first. I haven't accepted yet."

"Yeesh. This just got complicated."

"I should call her—"

"Bren, love. You were all over the poor thing last night. She knows how you feel about her. She'd have to. When she's ready, she'll come to you. If you swoop in now and try to do damage control, she might take it the wrong way."

"How do you know that?"

"I discussed this with Mad. I suggested you might call her, too, and he said in no uncertain terms to stay out of it."

The statement struck Brennon hard. Anger and jealousy flared. What business was it of Maddox's if Brennon chose to reach out to Eden? "And you agree with him?"

Adam sighed, "I do. Look, I know how much you care about her."

Did *she* though? Did Eden understand that no success or failure of hers could ever change what he felt for her? "What can I do?" Brennon asked.

"Sit tight?"

"Not helpful." Brennon had never been one for sitting back and waiting for the things he wanted to fall into his lap. He set his sights on something and went after it. His success was part luck, but the other part was sheer determination.

Edward stepped outside, and Brennon gave him a quick nod. "Fine," he told Adam. "I won't bother her today, but if there's going to be a similar rule tomorrow, you'd better bring your best arguments for it."

"I'll prepare a list."

Brennon hung up, frustration tensing every muscle in his body. The worst part was that he didn't know how Eden had taken the news. Had she cried? Raged? Taken it in stride as a part of the business? He despised helplessness, and yet that was exactly where he'd landed, in this place where he could help neither himself, nor her.

Eden was on her third beer. Maddox flipped through his phone while she stared at the people passing on the street outside the bar conveniently located on the ground floor of his building. It was five o'clock, and the sidewalk had gotten crowded since they'd started day drinking. Neither she nor Mad had said much in the last fifteen minutes, besides having an argument about her sending Justin Pope's call to voice mail.

Maddox had disapproved.

Eden couldn't be bothered today.

"I don't need his handouts," she mumbled.

"Mmhmm . . ."

"You don't think Brennon already knew, did you? And that's why he gave his agent my number? That's why he was being so nice to me last night?"

"Adam swore he didn't know."

Eden picked up her wet cardboard coaster and tore it in half. "Maybe he wasn't telling anyone who could get the news to me first."

"I don't think Brennon's diabolical. What would be in it for him?"

"Me not hating him for one more day?"

"Oh, we hate him now?"

Eden squeezed her eyes shut, attempting to shake some of the fuzz out of her head from the beer. "No. I don't hate him. But I might as well. Kayla fucking Grant. They'll be perfect together."

"You're giving me whiplash," Maddox said. "Kayla's married. And she's a doll. You're gonna love her."

"I don't want to love her. I should have listened to my mother. I'm not cut out for this. I should just go back to doing commercials. At least I'd get a second take if my first one sucked. Live work clearly isn't my strength."

"Jesus." Maddox signaled for another drink of his own. "You're all over the place. Look, if you really don't think Broadway's your thing, you should call back Pope. You're too good for commercials, but maybe you're right. Maybe live audiences don't bring out the best in you."

The words landed like a slap in the face. "Thanks a lot."

"Hey, that's not my opinion, but you're determined to believe it, so—if that's where this is headed, at least give yourself the best chance."

"I can't. Pope'll just think Brennon's screwing me and he's throwing me a bone—it's what everybody'll think. I made it this far without him. I can keep going."

"Who gives a shit what people think?"

"Everybody!" Eden said. "If one person thought I traded sex for a favor, what's to stop the next person from thinking that's how I operate? But, besides all that, if I were actually with Brennon and became an overnight sensation, I'd always wonder if it was because of him. Not me. Not *my* hard work, not *my* talent."

"Why can't it be both?"

"Are you forgetting what he said about me?" Her eyes welled up. "Because I still can't."

Maddox's lips twisted to the side, and his gaze softened. "That was before, Eden."

She nodded, trying so fucking hard to wipe the memory of his words on that recording out of her head, but since the call from Paulina, they'd only gotten louder and louder. *Shine a spotlight . . . She'll come running.* Eden knew in her heart—deep down in her freaking bones—that Brennon was sorry he'd said it, but it hadn't stopped the words from coming out of his mouth once, the laughter in the eyes of everyone else in that video with their respectable résumés and Juilliard educations. It didn't stop her from imagining the torture it would be to come back to the tour with everyone knowing she'd been replaced because she hadn't been good enough.

She was *not a leading lady yet*. And at this rate, she might never be.

Eden wiped her eyes again. She had to pick her battles today. Her feelings for Brennon were too complicated. Misogyny was easier to rail against. She was used to it. "In the world we live in, I get judged differently. I always will be. Because of where I come from, because of my résumé. Because I'm pretty, and I have a nice rack."

Letting her off the Brennon hook, Maddox gave her chest a look to confirm. "You do have a nice rack."

"Which means I don't get to have it both ways."

"I see what you're saying, okay? I just think it really sucks for the guy."

Eden shoved her hair out of her face. Her frustration with the situation had gone a lot of directions since that phone call with Paulina this morning, but right now, it turned inward. "He'll be fine. Once I'm out of his sight every day, the spell will be broken, and he'll realize I'm just another two-bit actress from Indiana with a big, stupid dream I can't manage to make come true."

"Wow."

"Am I wrong?" she asked.

Mad's brow drew together in sympathy. "Tragically."

Eden sighed. "You have to say that because we're friends."

He grabbed her by the knee, giving it a shake she could feel even through her thickening buzz. "Or because I've actually seen you perform opposite Broadway's biggest leading man and hold your own."

"Holding my own wasn't enough."

"I don't think you should give up," Maddox said.

"On what?" she asked. "Brennon?"

"I meant Broadway, but yeah. Brennon, too. He loves you, Eden. He said so, to your face."

She shivered with the memory of that overwhelming moment. "I just don't get it, Mad. What did he even see in me?"

"Besides the rack?" Maddox asked.

She gave him a flat glare.

"Adam says you light him up."

It was such a compliment, and it made Eden feel so much worse. "I honestly don't know how I could be with him. I'd always wonder if deep down I embarrassed him. If he settled."

"Jesus, Eden, for the last time: Jerry Maguire didn't settle."

Eden swallowed the rest of her beer. "Agree to disagree."

"Even if he did, which he definitely did not, that has nothing to do with you and Brennon. Maybe give the guy a call, let him know where you're at."

"Look at me—do *you* even know where I'm at?" She gestured at her face. "I don't."

"Still—to leave the guy hanging . . ."

"I'm not—I'm—fucking *processing*, okay? Worst-case scenario, I'll see him Tuesday in LA."

"I think that's a mistake," Mad murmured, signaling for the tab.

"It wouldn't be my first one."

"Maybe your mom can talk some sense into you tomorrow."

Eden squeezed her eyes shut at the reminder of her mother's visit. "You want to come with?"

He chuckled. "You're on your own, kiddo."

"Justin Pope?"

Eden refused to look at her mother after she'd accidentally dropped the name over lunch.

"*The* Justin Pope?"

"Uh-huh."

"Eden, you have to call him. If you won't do it, hand over your phone, and I will. I can sound like you if I need to."

Ripping open a pink packet of sweetener, Eden shook it into her coffee. "Give it a rest, Mom. I'm not calling him. Why in the world would he want to represent me after I just fucked up so bad?"

"Because he's not a Broadway agent. He's a TV and film agent, and he doesn't give a fig about you messing up some stupid directors' show. He'll be looking at your TV résumé—which, if I do say so myself, is quite extensive."

"Ha."

Her mother bristled. "Harrison Ford started in commercials."

"And didn't land a major role until he was practically forty."

"I don't think that's true."

"Pretty sure it is, Mom." Eden lifted her fork and wiped a smudge from one of the tines.

"I still say, no matter how an opportunity comes your way, it's up to you to grab onto it. It's no one's fault but your own if you let it slip away."

Eden picked at her omelet, for the first time in a while seeing the wisdom of Terry Blake's approach. She'd come to some unpleasant conclusions about herself in the last twenty-four hours.

One: She was a total diva. The news of being recast had hit her like a slash across the face. It had been an attack on her vanity. A scar she'd be humiliated to wear in public. The very idea of showing up to the walk-through in LA as a standby again after such an incredible month as the star made her want to crawl into a hole and never come out. More than anything else, this failure embarrassed her. Badly.

And two: The idea of watching a better, cuter actress, married or otherwise, kiss Brennon Thorne onstage every night made her so jealous she could spit. She had no faith in her ability not to attempt to scratch Kayla's eyes out on the daily, which would make her a total beast to work with, and word on her attitude would get around, making her even less desirable to directors.

Added together, she was *that* petty bitch.

She wished so much that she could blame Brennon for all this—resent him and his luck and his talent the way she had when they'd first met. But somewhere along the way, he'd gone and made himself so likable that she couldn't fault his teachers at Juilliard, the directors on Broadway, Shayna, or anyone else for wanting him to have it all. He deserved it.

It wasn't fair, but things rarely were in New York. Maybe it was time to follow her mother's advice and explore her other options. "Fine. I'll call Pope back. Might as well."

"How about an 'I'll call him back and let's see how far this takes me!'" Her mom's version of a pep talk.

"Sure," Eden mumbled. "Have it your way."

"If he finds something for you soon, you'll probably be able to quit the tour."

"I know, Mom."

Her mother actually hesitated a moment before asking in a much less domineering way, "Would you want that?"

Eden considered the question as she chewed on a cherry tomato. Her heart sank a little at the idea of leaving Maddox behind, but Maddox would have Adam locked down soon, she was sure of it. He wouldn't be hurting for company.

Eden had Trista and Fallon and a handful of other friends in the city to keep her busy—maybe set her up on some dates . . . Maybe she'd even meet someone.

But her stomach soured at the thought of sharing even a flirtatious glance with someone other than Brennon.

She'd need to check herself on those thoughts fast, though. Talk about holding herself to too high of a standard. She'd gotten way too big of a head the day of their back-to-back amazing performances. He'd bought her a honey dipper, and she'd acted like she'd won the man. Last night, when he'd told her he loved her, she'd still been his leading lady, and she'd been stupid enough to let herself hope that was enough. But it had all been a fantasy after all. The news from Paulina today was all the proof she needed that she was not enough, in any way, for Brennon Thorne. He deserved the star, and failing that, at the very minimum, he deserved to have a woman brave enough to tell him she loved him back. That she loved him so much.

Just because she'd been allowed to visit Shangri-La didn't mean she belonged there.

She'd felt the same way about New York at first, too, but thanks to Trista and Fallon, she made it her home. Eventually, she'd find some-one she could grow with, not toward. An aspiring musician, maybe. He could write the songs, and she could sing them while he played piano or guitar or something. She'd pay the rent with money she was making in TV, and by night they'd perform at coffeehouses until he made it big.

Brennon had the long, dexterous fingers of a musician. She won-dered if he could play any instruments.

She shook off the thought. She didn't actually want anyone else. Not now. Maybe not ever. But failure did not become her. Until she'd shaken the stink of that from herself, she wouldn't feel worthy of any-one's love. It was time to make a move. She needed off this tour.

"Justin Pope's office, may I help you?"

Her mother clapped excitedly across the table. Eden swallowed hard before saying, "Eden Blake, returning his call."

"One moment, Miss Blake. I'll put you right through."

CHAPTER TWENTY-FOUR

Peck was beside himself, all flushed and sort of sweaty. "It's our great pleasure to introduce you to Broadway's own Lizzie Bennet—our guest star for the entire month—Kayla Grant!"

Eden sat next to Kenneth in the Ahmanson Theatre with her arms folded moodily across her chest. Kenneth whistled through his teeth. "Didn't see that one coming."

"Save it, Kenneth."

So far LA could suck it. It was already starting—Eden's bitter resentment creeping through every pore.

Kayla Grant gave herself her own excited round of applause as she stood onstage with Peck, her bright smile lighting up her heart-shaped face. Loose, auburn locks hung all the way down her back, and the stage lights picked up all the red and mahogany tones of it. She was a stunner.

"She trained as an opera singer, you know?" Kenneth said.

"No. I didn't," Eden snapped.

"Hear she's a dream to work with."

Eden snorted. She could guarantee no one would ever say that about her.

Although Brennon had . . .

She caught Maddox glancing back at her. He was sitting two rows in front of her with Adam and the "actual" cast. Although no one had ever told her and Kenneth to separate themselves from the rest of them, the excitement of arriving at a new theater could never reach the same level for a standby as it did for the performers.

Eden felt bad when she thought about it, though. Who had Kenneth been hanging out with in DC when she'd ditched his butt for her chance to hobnob with everyone else?

One more shitty thing she'd learned about herself to add to the list.

"So happy to be here and have a chance to work with Brennon again and the rest of you! I see some familiar faces!" Kayla waved at David, Adam, and Mad, and she blew a kiss to Brennon.

All Eden could see was the back of his head, nodding toward the stage.

Though he'd attempted to reach out plenty of times in New York, she hadn't returned any of his texts or calls, afraid he'd try to cheer her up, encourage her to keep going, tell her that the recast didn't mean what she thought it did—that she *was* good enough. She didn't need to hear it from him, though. She needed to feel it. To prove it, somehow. He wouldn't mean to be patronizing, but she couldn't imagine herself hearing the words any other way. She would have snapped at him and hated herself for it. It was no fault of his own, but he couldn't relate to her, and right now, she needed to be among *her* people.

Kenneth offered her a stick of gum, and she took it.

"One final announcement. This one's sadder," Peck said as Kayla left the stage to join the rest of them. "Our Brennon will be moving on from us a little earlier than expected. Please let's all enjoy these next two weeks before Mr. Thorne returns to New York to begin rehearsals for *Jekyll & Hyde*."

What? "He's leaving?" Eden whispered, the gum halfway to her mouth.

287

Kenneth perked *way* up. "First I'm hearing about it."

Peck gestured their way. "We'll have Kenneth step in to round out Los Angeles and go from there. So how 'bout it guys, ready to see backstage?"

Kenneth sat back, all his air leaving him in a rush.

Out of the corner of her eye Eden spotted Jonathan's slow head-turn in their direction, shooting daggers at Kenneth for getting the coveted LA dates. Kenneth should hire a bodyguard for those two weeks.

"Congrats, Ken," she said as the cast stood to wander the theater.

Kenneth, short of breath, thanked her. "I wasn't expecting this."

Neither was she. She wasn't sure how she felt about it yet. Relieved? Sad? Small?

"You're gonna be amazing," Eden managed, and thought to add for emphasis, *"Kayla Grant!"*

"Oh my god." It sunk in for Kenneth all at once, and his eyes filled with tears. She knew the exact feeling.

A tap-tap on her shoulder turned Eden around. Behind her, the woman herself stood in all her auburn glory, beaming with her hand outstretched. "You must be Eden."

Eden failed to hide her grimace. Standing, she forced herself to shake the actress's hand. She was prettier in person than she was on TV. "Nice to meet you. So great to have you."

"I heard you were absolutely wonderful in DC."

"Pretty sure if you heard it in New York that's not how they phrased it." Eden couldn't help herself. Everyone knew why Kayla was here. Eden hadn't been good enough.

"I only heard raves." She smiled. "And I don't want you to think I'm here to hog LA. You had a good thing going, and I'll only be here a month. Let me know if there's a night or two you want to go on, and I'll conveniently have the sniffles. And, of course, if the directors come—that's all you." She laughed. "I get enough of their notes in New York. I'm considering this a sort of working vacay."

Eden wasn't sure how to take the other actress. On the one hand, the offer to let Eden perform in LA was generous. On the other, "working vacay" bordered on condescending. At least it cemented Eden's place in the pecking order. Sometimes it was nice in this business to know exactly where one stood.

Kayla took Eden by the hand again. "Let's go check out our dressing room."

Liliana had been the one to find the eclectic bungalow nearish to downtown LA when their condo rental had fallen through at the last minute. It wasn't exactly walking distance to the theater, but nothing in Los Angeles really was. The three of them decided they'd split an Uber to the show each night, but they were still grumbling about using the extra cash they could have saved.

The house was funky and comfortable, but it only had two bedrooms. A futon in the den served as a third spot to sleep in. Eden volunteered for it, since she wouldn't have the extra burden of actually having to perform anymore.

"Maybe we just pool our money, rent a car while we're here, and I'll be your chauffeur," Eden offered over iced tea on the patio that afternoon before the press opening.

"Have you done the math on that?" Liliana asked, skeptical.

"No, but I might as well." She slumped in her chair. "It's not like I have anything else to do."

"Okay. Eden." Liliana set her glass down on a coaster and clasped her hands, leaning towards Eden with a warning look. "I need you to stop. I can't listen to it anymore. It's having the added effect of making me feel like shit about myself for being in the show that dissed you, so it's time to bottle up all your bitterness and shut your pie hole. *Enough.*"

The reprimand stung, and while it hadn't come out of nowhere, she'd expected more of a talking to from Maddox, not Liliana.

"Sorry," Eden mumbled.

"We all have setbacks. You think I haven't had any? I didn't audition to be Lydia, here, I wanted Jane, but this is what I got—probably because people say my singing voice is too grating. It is what it is. I've been a standby before, too. It's boring. It's lame. But I didn't get to perform for a solid month, did I? No. I got to perform two times. Twice. That's it. And I probably did my share of bitching and moaning about it too, but I regret it now that I've had to listen to it for two solid days."

"I'm *very* sorry," Eden added as she mentally reviewed the conversations she'd had with Liliana since they arrived at the house. Her friend wasn't wrong.

"Just stop, all right?"

Eden raised both hands in surrender. "Okay. I'll stop. I said I'm sorry. Jeez."

"We'll still have fun while we're here, you know?" Liliana went on. "It's not like there's a shortage of things to do or people to hang out with."

"Yeah, well, I'll still look into renting a car. Nothing fancy, just . . . you know . . ." Eden trailed off. She stood, having obviously worn out her welcome, and took her glass inside.

Maddox was making dinner, humming contentedly to himself in the kitchen, and she supposed she should settle in for the long haul. They'd be in this house a full month before the tour started to move again. After this, it would be a series of week-long sit-downs in smaller markets. LA would be the last time for several weeks where they all got to stop and take a breath.

The flashing light on her phone marked a notification, and she picked it up from the coffee table to see what it was.

Justin Pope had sent her an email.

While you're in LA, here's some things I found for you. I've called the first three already because those looked to be the best fit. Let me know what you think about the rest and I can set something up.

Cheers, JP

Eden scanned the list of casting opportunities with increasingly lifted eyebrows. "Damn . . . this guy knows some people."

"What's that?" Maddox asked.

She took her phone into the kitchen and stood next to him at the cutting board to show him.

"I loved that book! They're turning it into a series? Sweet," he said in regards to number two on the list.

"I liked it, too." The thriller had kept her up all night. And it was about an actress. "But surely they'd want somebody bigger to play that part."

"You never know. If you have the look they're going for—it's worth throwing your hat in the ring."

"I'd be on a short list," Eden pondered aloud.

"Because Justin Pope's a badass who knows what he's doing."

Eden bit her thumbnail and allowed herself to get a little excited. Justin Pope was a dream agent. She hadn't earned him, obviously, he'd been more of a consolation prize, but maybe—*maybe*—if she could get a part like this, it would prove she deserved an agent like him.

"I'm gonna do it," she said in a rush as she opened up a reply to Justin.

"Go for all top three. Like you said, it's not like you're doing anything else here." The tone of his voice indicated he'd been able to hear Liliana's lecture from the patio.

"Look, I'm sorry, okay? This is one of the harder things that's happened to me since I started working, and I'm—figuring it out."

"I know, babe. So uh . . . how'd you take the news today?"

"Kayla? I feel like I knew before anybody else—"

"About Brennon."

She was not allowing herself to think about that news, and how dare Maddox bring it up? She glared at him. "I'm fine. It's fine. Who else could play Jekyll and Hyde?"

"I mean, I feel like *I* could . . ."

"Okay . . ." Eden gave him a knowing side-eye.

"Thorne probably didn't even have to audition. At his level he probably just expresses interest, and they hold a meeting to negotiate a salary and dates," Maddox mused.

"I'm sure it's more complicated than that."

Maddox studied her with suspicious eyes. "When did you become his biggest defender?"

"I'm not!"

"Sure you're not. Crumble this." He shoved a package of goat cheese into her hand.

"I'm glad he's leaving, if you want to know the truth," she said.

Maddox leaned a hip against the counter and crossed his arms. He stared down his nose at her. "That so?"

"Yep. Kayla said she'd give me a couple of chances to perform out here if I wanted, and now that I know he's not finishing out the run, I'll get to do it with Kenneth, and it won't have to be weird."

Maddox frowned and tilted his head like he wasn't sure he'd heard her properly. "Kayla said that to you."

"Uh-huh."

"Kayla offered you one or two performances of your choice in Los Angeles during *her* four-week run."

"Yeah." Why was that so hard to believe? It's not like no one ever did anyone else favors in this business. There were nice people around, too.

"So, you'll let Kayla help you, but when Brennon tries, you think there's all these strings attached."

Eden blinked, feeling a bit slapped. "I called Pope."

"And you've been sick about it."

"Not *sick . . .*"

"You're too hard on him, Eden."

Correction: *a lot* slapped.

Maddox went on. "Don't take this the wrong way, but if you weren't interested in Brennon, you shouldn't have strung him along like that. You shouldn't have kissed him the way you did onstage. You shouldn't have flirted with him that day outside the deli, and you *definitely* shouldn't have taken him home with you if all you were gonna do was kick him to the curb the second you didn't get what you were looking for. He likes you. Adam thinks he's actually in *love* with you."

Eden bristled at the accusation that she'd used Brennon, but getting angry with Mad was easier than thinking about Brennon's feelings for her. "Are you calling me a tease? A slut? What?"

Maddox's face hardened. His jaw tensed. "I'm calling you inconsiderate."

She gasped. "What are you talking about?" Of all the people in the world who should understand where she was coming from, Maddox was at the top of the list.

"Let me tell you what it looks like from the outside—from, say, Adam's perspective, who doesn't know you as well as I do. It looks like you used Brennon to get a film agent, and then you dumped him once the ink was dry on the contract. *That's* what it looks like."

Eden's stomach dropped. "Are people saying that?"

"Who gives a shit what people say? It's what Adam thinks, and he's Brennon's best friend. That's who's in Brennon's ear trying to talk him out of his hurt feelings."

"But Brennon knows that's not how it went down. He knows I didn't scam him."

Maddox put up both his hands, palms up and gave an exaggerated shrug. "I don't know. Downtown girl, down on her luck, blew her big chance, got an offer she couldn't refuse, and ghosted him? What's he supposed to think?"

"Jesus," she whispered. She needed to sit.

She pulled out a chair at the nearby kitchen table and dropped onto it with a thud. *No, no . . .*

Things hadn't ended like that. Things had ended well. With kisses and hand-holding, and a promise of another chance to see each other before they left New York.

Once she'd lost the part, though, Eden had totally shut him out. But she'd been reeling, confused . . . processing, for fuck's sake.

If it walks like a bitch . . .

She groaned. "You couldn't have mentioned any of this to me when we were still in New York?"

"I was fine with giving it a day, I even told Adam to tell Brennon to give you some space, but I never expected you to drop him like a bad habit because you didn't get your way. When we were at the bar, I told you not calling him before we left was a mistake, but you weren't ready to hear it. But when you said that thing about Kayla, I lost it a little. I'm not trying to be mean. I get what happened. He really had a few mega-dick moments, but once you were in the role, he did nothing but support you, and you've been . . ."

"What? Inconsiderate?" She desperately hoped he didn't have a worse word for it.

"A bit."

She glanced up at Maddox again to see if there was something more awful he wasn't saying. His eyes held all the warmth and affection she was used to. "I should just let him go," she whispered, afraid she might start crying again and never stop.

"You want him to walk away with all these potentially bad feelings?"

"No . . ." She didn't know what she wanted anymore. From this job, her career, but least of all from Brennon. All her feelings about him were still so mixed up in the show, the lies she'd been told, and her initial impressions. A big, confusing jumble that twisted more every time she tried to unravel it.

But whenever someone mentioned his name, she thought of him that night in his apartment, when he was so intent on keeping her warm that he held her against his chest in front of all his friends and stroked her hair.

"Just maybe let him down a little easier this time," Maddox said, his tone gentler now.

"Let him down?"

"Tell him you're not interested, but you appreciate everything he's done for you. And you're sorry you're not in the same place with your feelings."

That didn't sound right. "Why would I . . .? Because . . . I mean . . . I *do* have feelings."

"You do?"

"Well, *yeah.*"

Mad scowled, crossing his arms over his chest. "And you, what? Plan to keep him in the dark about it?"

"Mad!"

"Sorry, but dang, Eden!"

"I'm sorry!" she cried, at the end of her emotional rope.

Maddox's direct stare was uncompromising. "Don't apologize to *me.*"

"Oh my god." She collapsed into her hands.

Her friend approached and ran a comforting hand down her back. "Maybe give the guy a call sometime before he leaves for New York. Even if it's only to clear the air."

"Ughhhh," she groaned, long and loud.

Liliana entered through the sliding glass door. "Is it safe to come in? Yikes, doesn't look like it."

"It's just Eden, still trying to decide if she loves Brennon or hates him."

Liliana shrugged. "I assumed she was indifferent."

"*No* . . ." Eden's shoulders slumped.

"Well, you don't love him, otherwise you'd be nicer," Liliana said. "Right?"

"I *am* nice to him . . ."

Liliana raised an eyebrow in pure skepticism.

Maddox spoke up. "In Eden's defense, he's done some shitty things, too."

Liliana crossed to the kitchen and turned on the oven. She popped a baguette inside and took a peek at Mad's salad. "Agreed. But I feel like once you invite the guy to your apartment, you're sort of implying you've moved on from your bad first impression."

"Whose side are you on?" Eden asked.

"Honestly, I think I'm just hungry." Liliana stuffed two leftover cherry tomatoes into her mouth and spoke around them. "Sorry if I'm being harsh. I just wish you'd give yourself a chance with him. From what I can tell, he's turned into your biggest fan. I mean—have you seen the way he looks at you?"

Eden had. In public, and in private, and it was special. What they'd managed to find was special.

The first spark of hope she'd had since arriving in Los Angeles straightened Eden's spine. She'd been an idiot to believe what she'd discovered with Brennon was anything less than a connection. A real one. And she'd dismissed it like he hadn't meant anything to her because she'd been too busy trying to pretend she believed she belonged on a stage with him instead of just enjoying the fact that she was there. She'd made it. And no matter how it felt now being back in the wings, no one could take that away from her.

God, she'd been so fucking selfish.

A heavy melancholy threatened, weighing down her bones once again. She wanted to crawl into bed and not wake up for two weeks. "I suck."

Liliana sat down at the table across from Eden. "You still have us, though, which is more than Jonathan can say about his roommates."

"What are you talking about?" Maddox asked.

"Kenneth and Emily got hotel rooms once they found out about Veronica."

Maddox and Eden both stared at Liliana. "What about Veronica?"

"Oh my God, you didn't hear?"

Brennon was not a gossip, but neither was he a saint. He'd hated Jonathan March for the better part of his adulthood. The suffering he'd caused Veronica over the last fifteen years without ever facing a single consequence couldn't be tolerated. So Brennon had told one person what he'd learned in New York.

Gabi.

By the time the cast wrapped up their backstage tour at the Ahmanson, a third of them knew, and Jonathan had lost his roommates. There wouldn't be much satisfaction to be gained from the rest of this tour, but Brennon would take what he could get, especially if it came at Jon's expense. Veronica deserved better. She always had. She'd just chosen the wrong man to chase.

Brennon could relate, as he had a habit of choosing the wrong woman.

He and Adam were across-the-hall neighbors at the Sheraton Grand near the theater. Kayla had a room there as well, and she walked the mile back to the hotel with them. It was one of those mild, perfect, sunny California days people paid far too much on real estate for.

Kayla turned her attention to Brennon as they sat down for a quick meal at the hotel restaurant. "So . . . Dr. Jekyll?"

He offered a faint smile. He doubted it played. He had yet to shave for the performance, and his smile, what there had been of it, was likely obscured.

"I hear that's a tough one," Kayla said.

"I'm looking forward to the challenge. How long will you be staying on as Lizzie in New York?"

"I'm officially done. This is my farewell tour. And I couldn't miss the chance to end it with such a dashing Darcy."

"Kenneth will be pleased to hear that."

Kayla laughed and gave Brennon a light slap on the arm.

"Who's taking over your part in New York?" Brennon asked. "If you don't mind my asking."

"Veronica West."

Adam and Brennon shared a look. "No kidding?"

"The directors were impressed with what they saw on the tour, and offered. Obviously she's pregnant, though, so who knows how long she'll be able to do it, but I hear she's great."

"I'm happy for her," Brennon said.

"This is her first lead, isn't it?" Adam asked.

"On Broadway?" Brennon nodded. "I believe it is."

Adam let out a light snort. "Somebody should tell Eden."

Brennon cut his friend a harsh look.

"I meant that good things can come from going on tours. I wasn't trying to be a dick."

Adam hadn't had the nicest things to say about Eden the last few days. Scamming gold-digger was one of the kinder names he'd called her.

"If," Adam added, "one can manage not to blow the directors' visit."

Brennon, in an uncharacteristic move, thwacked Adam on the arm. Kayla jumped in surprise. "What happened at the directors' show?" she asked. "They are *all* pricks by the way. I'm not gonna lie, it was so time to go."

"Well, I wasn't actually there . . ." Adam hedged.

"No," Brennon said. "You actually weren't. Eden had an off day."

"Eek," Kayla said. "Bad timing."

"The *worst*," Adam agreed as their food arrived.

Brennon sighed, wishing he could order a drink, but they performed in three hours, and with the West Coast jet lag setting in, he didn't want to risk an unintended nap.

"I heard she was so great, too," Kayla said. "My DC friends had nothing but raves."

Of all the things to talk about, Eden's ability to light up a stage wasn't a topic Brennon was keen on. Not after the way she wouldn't even look at him today or call him back while they were still in New York. He knew she was down, knew this change had hurt her, but her continued mistrust burned. His inability to convince her to be with him had opened all his old wounds.

If he was incapable of being loved, he wished someone—Adam, Eden, anyone—would tell him already, and put him out of his misery. Then he could quit trying and save several other women over the next few decades the trouble of an uncomfortable breakup.

If Eden didn't want him, there was nothing more he could do. He'd replayed that night in her apartment dozens of times and convinced himself that if he'd had the presence of mind to bring the condoms into the bathroom, things might have all turned out differently, and they'd be in Los Angeles together.

But she still would have been recast. And in the end, that had been all that mattered to her.

"I think I'll take this to my room." Brennon rose with his plate and left the restaurant.

The principal dressing rooms in Los Angeles were nicer than those in Washington. With a long couch and two leather armchairs, Brennon had an entire seating area he could take a meeting in. Shayna had seen to it that his dish was full of watermelon mints and his mini fridge was stocked with Waterloo. He tied his breeches and checked the spot on his face where he'd cut himself shaving.

Makeup would cover it.

As he was lacing his shirt, someone knocked on his door. "Come in."

He expected Peck, or Shayna. Instead, the tall, broad figure of Jonathan March loomed in the doorway.

Brennon turned his attention to his cravat. "What do you want?"

"Did you talk to Veronica?" Jon's voice was low, near menacing.

"I did," Brennon said. "Did *you*?"

"She wouldn't see me while we were on break."

Brennon let out a short laugh. "I'm not surprised."

Jonathan took a long, controlled breath. "You can't manage to get out of my way, can you, Thorne?"

"You've always been the only one standing in your way."

"Spoken like the entitled prick you are."

"We have fifteen minutes until curtain." Brennon gestured to the hallway. "If you don't mind."

"I do mind." He shut the door behind him and stepped toward Brennon. "In school you made her feel like she was nothing. Like all of us were nothing."

Abandoning his cravat, Brennon squared off with the larger man. "So, you're saying all you did was pick up where I left off?"

"Fuck you. No. I'm saying she used me to make you jealous." Lifting a finger, he jabbed it dangerously close to Brennon's face. "You. It was always about you. And it didn't work, so she left."

"You seduced her. You used *her*, and then she had a nervous breakdown."

"Because of *you*," Jonathan snarled. "Because you couldn't forgive her."

"Because you treated her like a whore." Brennon slapped down Jonathan's hand.

"And you didn't? After she was with me, you acted like she was damaged goods."

"I couldn't trust her." Brennon wouldn't apologize for that. Veronica made her bed, and Jonathan kicked her out of it. Time and time again. Same pattern. Ad nauseam. Ad infinitum.

He was sick of this dorm room bullshit. "Both of you used each other to hurt me, and how did that work out?"

Jonathan shrugged, a small grin of satisfaction on his face. "Looks to me like you're still alone."

"We're all still alone," Brennon said, his voice cold and harsh.

"But I heard you had a little something on *standby*, back in the city."

"Watch yourself, March."

"Brennon Thorne, sneaking off to go *downtown*. How'd that go? Was it sweet? Like honey?"

Their world was still far too small. Rage clouded Brennon's vision. His hands clenched tight. "Get out."

"Also heard she landed Justin Pope. Isn't he your agent? What'd she have to do to get you to throw her that bone? Or was that her reward for a job well done?"

Brennon swung, his fist connecting with Jonathan's right eye socket.

The powerfully built man stumbled backward, but the door broke his fall. He put his hand up to his eye, checking his fingers for blood. There was some, Brennon was satisfied to note. Then, pure hatred flashed in Jon's eyes, and he rushed Brennon, knocking him over a chair and onto the rug. Instinctively, Brennon covered his face and throat with his forearms. Unable to land a punch there, Jonathan proceeded to pummel him in the sides.

"Get off me!"

It wasn't the most dignified fistfight. Not by far. Ultimately, Brennon was able to gain the upper hand by suddenly bucking his hips and knocking Jon off balance. Scrambling out from under him, he stood and landed a solid kick in Jonathan's ass. He called it a win, and went to open his door. "Peck!" he roared.

The little man came running.

Brennon pointed at Jonathan, who was rising and brushing dust off his knees. "Keep this son of a bitch away from me."

The rest of the cast crowded into the backstage hallway. Adam and Kayla both rushed over to Brennon, fussing over him, Adam with Brennon's cravat and Kayla with his hair.

Glancing past them, he noticed Eden hanging back near one of the larger dressing rooms with a baffled expression on her face.

He looked away. He hated how far the distance between them had grown.

"Open your mouth," Adam commanded.

Brennon shifted his gaze to his fussy friend. "What? Why?"

"Open your mouth, so I can see if he knocked any teeth out."

"It wasn't that kind of fight."

"Jon has a cut on his eye."

"Good." He opened his mouth for Adam anyway, just in case.

"You two . . ." Shayna said as she approached. "What's it been? Fifteen years now? You know your kids are gonna fall in love one day and accidentally kill themselves if you don't stop feuding. You all right?"

"I'm fine," Brennon growled. "He should be fired."

"He throw the first punch?" She looked dubious.

"I've already put in my notice," Brennon snapped.

"Maybe you can make it two more weeks without killing each other, then."

"No promises." He was still boiling.

Had Jonathan kissed Eden? It was all he could think about. That he'd known Eden's mouth tasted like honey. Brennon wanted to tear his dressing room apart.

Kayla gave his chest a pat. "There you go. All put back together and ready to slay LA."

Adam followed him into his dressing room. "What the fuck?"

Brennon stalked to his dressing table. "I can't get into it."

"Did he say something about Eden?"

Brennon whipped his head around to face his friend. "How did you know? What do you know? Have they been together?"

Adam stared at him in wide-eyed shock. "I *assumed*, since Jon's going to have a black eye, and you aren't really one for brawling, he'd touched a nerve."

"He did."

"Eden?" Adam attempted to clarify.

Brennon swallowed. "He insinuated they'd been . . . intimate."

"Ah."

Brennon charged him. "What do you know about it?"

Adam held him off with two firm hands on Brennon's shoulders. "I know you need to get your testosterone level checked. I also know that what Eden does is her business. And you don't own her."

Brennon fumed.

"Because you're not together," Adam continued.

"I know."

"Do you, though?"

Brennon stepped back and looked at the floor a moment to ground himself. He inhaled. Exhaled harshly. "Yes."

"If they were together, it had nothing to do with you. This isn't Juilliard."

He nodded. "You're right."

"Are you calmer?" Adam asked.

Brennon took another deep breath. Hurt, anger, and regret were at war inside him, and he hated himself for letting it take control. Adam was right. Eden's choices had nothing to do with him. Why did that make him want to find a bar and drink until he passed out? He nodded again, for Adam's sake. "I'm getting there."

"You're gonna make a dark Darcy tonight. Remember this is a musical comedy."

"I know how to do my job," Brennon grumbled.

"Yes, love. You do. Next, we'll work on how we do life."

"You can go, Adam."

"Try not to punch him during the duet."

CHAPTER TWENTY-FIVE

Something had snapped in Eden as she watched Kayla running her hands through Brennon's hair to put it back together again, triggering a jealousy that was no longer professional.

It was one thing for Kayla to take over the role she'd originated on Broadway, but it was another thing if she thought she could take Eden's place.

Without taking much time to consider the consequences, Eden knocked on Kayla's dressing room door as the hallway cleared of performers.

"Come in!" the actress called out cheerfully.

Eden stepped inside.

"Eden!" Kayla smiled. "Perfect timing! Zip me?"

"Tonight," Eden said before she lost her nerve.

Kayla's smile didn't falter, but her forehead creased in puzzlement. "Tonight what?"

"I want to go on tonight."

"Oh." Kayla's grin morphed to something more patronizing. Sympathetic. "Tonight's for the press. There's no time to make a change. The earliest we could do it is probably next Tuesday, if that works."

"That doesn't work." Eden had to act now. If she stood idly by for the next week while Kayla, who was a better actress, better singer, and more consistent performer, sang with and kissed Brennon every day, Eden would shrink into a ball of total worthlessness. She'd once again talk herself into believing she wasn't good enough to stand onstage with him, much less attempt a relationship with him.

This last-minute gesture wouldn't be much, but it would be something.

Eden had to do *something* to let him know all his support hadn't gone unnoticed or unappreciated. But more importantly, that his love had not gone unreturned. "It has to be tonight."

"Sweetie, I don't think you understand."

"Look—I don't need to do any of the other performances after this one. And it's not about the press, or the publicity. Kayla, I can't have you kissing him tonight." She raised her voice, nearing panic. "I just can't!"

Kayla's pretty head reared back, and she blinked her blue eyes. "Kissing . . . *Brennon?*"

Eden was positive she was visibly green. She swallowed hard and tried to let her pleading eyes do the work her mouth couldn't.

Kayla still appeared totally baffled. "Why can't you just talk to him after the show?"

It was a reasonable question.

Eden's answer wasn't. She couldn't let Kayla get out there and kiss him before Brennon knew Eden wanted him for real. He could do whatever he chose with the information, and he may already have written her off, but she couldn't have him spending two and a half more hours doubting what they'd had together—not when she was finally sure. It might annoy him to see her, disappoint him even, but she had to try. "This can't wait anymore."

Kayla stood back to assess Eden—not like the lovesick, desperate woman she was, but like the competition. "He won't see it that way, you know? He'll see you out there, showing off for the press. Not for him."

The words were a gut punch. "I don't care about the press."

"After speaking with Adam today, I have a hard time believing that."

She'd spoken with Adam? Great. If what Maddox had said earlier was true, Kayla probably hadn't gotten the prettiest picture painted for her.

"Eden, really I'm doing you a favor. If you and Brennon are meant to be, or whatever, a conversation later should more than suffice. You shouldn't need a spotlight to get his attention."

Okay. *Ouch.*

But Eden was prepared to tie Kayla to her chair and stick a gag in her mouth if she had to. She was running out of time to make her case. The show started in five minutes and Eden needed that costume. To punctuate the point, one of the stagehands walked through the hallway outside, announcing the time remaining.

"Please," Eden said softly, willing to beg. "If it doesn't work, then I'm the idiot, and you'll swoop in tomorrow to do the morning show rounds and open the show. You don't need tonight, but *I do.* That kiss at the end means everything to me. Before you take it away, I want it one more time. Please, Kayla."

"It's not real, Eden. It's just a role. A stage kiss."

Eden's eyes filled with tears. "It's never been a stage kiss with me and Brennon."

The emotional impact of Eden's statement didn't land the way she'd hoped. Kayla's mouth twisted grimly. "Are you planning to fall in love with every leading man you have to kiss? It's considered poor form in the industry." Though the words were shitty, Kayla unzipped her dress and slid it from her shoulders.

That tiny bird of hope still residing in Eden's chest took flight. "I'm sort of planning to lock down this one leading man while I still have a chance."

Kayla stepped out of the dress and handed it over. Eden stripped off her T-shirt and pushed down her shorts.

"He's a notoriously crap boyfriend from what I've heard," Kayla said.

Eden would deal with that later. She pulled on the costume, and Kayla zipped it up.

"Always working, never around, emotionally withdrawn."

Eden was shocked. "Brennon?" *Emotionally withdrawn?* More than once she'd wanted to put up caution tape around the heart he wore on his sleeve, although it would have only protected it from herself.

"Sit, we'll need to get your hair up quick."

Eden hurried to the dressing chair, and Kayla got to work.

"I'm warning you," she said, shaking her head, "men don't change overnight."

"Fine. Noted. Thank you."

"Meaning, you should wrap your head around the 'old' version of him, too. That's likely who you'll end up with if this works out the way you think you want it to."

"Okay . . ."

"Obviously, I can't talk you out of it," Kayla mumbled.

No. She couldn't. Eden would take her chances. It wasn't like she planned to book a wedding venue in the morning. Google searches on how to make a long-distance relationship work were the only thing in her immediate future, but to get there, she'd need to get him.

And a spotlight couldn't hurt.

With her own hands flying across her face to get some makeup on it, and Kayla making quick work of her updo, Eden was ready to take the stage within minutes.

Kayla stepped away from the dressing table. "I guess I'll go find Shayna so she can announce the change."

"Thank you so much, Kayla," Eden said. "Truly. You have no idea how much this means to me."

"You better talk me up at the afterparty." The actress disappeared through the door, and Eden took one last look at herself as Lizzie Bennet.

From her bag on the couch, she opened two honey packets and squeezed them into her mouth. As the syrup coated her throat, she ran through the opening number in her mind. Licking her lips, she stretched her jaw, and performed a few vocal warm-ups.

"Bennet family! Places!" Shayna barked from the hallway.

Eden's dressing room door flew open. The stage manager stood outside it. "Eden. Jesus tits."

"I'm sorry," she said automatically.

Shayna huffed. "Right. Well, what are you waiting for?"

Eden rushed out the door, down the backstage hallway to the stage, where she hurried into the low-lit tableau. No one even looked up to notice she was there. She took her place next to Gabi on the sofa in the Bennets' living room. When the curtains lifted and the lights went up, Iris Klein entered from offstage and announced, "Netherfield Park is let at last!" The music began as Eden and Gabi turned to each other.

The unguarded shock on Gabi's face was totally worth the cost of admission.

Had Kayla always sounded so much like Eden? Or was it Brennon's obsessive mind constantly turning the entire world into various shades of Eden Blake?

Still amped from his scuffle with Jonathan, he lingered in his dressing room until the last possible moment, not relishing the idea of taking the stage with the man whose ass he'd so recently kicked.

An impatient knock sounded at his door. "Mr. Thorne?"

He pushed himself up from the sofa, his sides sore from being pummeled. "Coming," he grumbled.

The Bennet family had already exited the stage, and Brennon had to rush to meet Jonathan at the center. He willed himself to stick to the script, the blocking. Deliver one of his trademark consistent performances. It was a duet between Bingley and Darcy, wherein Darcy tries to talk some sense into his friend and warn him of vultures trying to steal his money, and disgraceful people with country manners. It was meant to be a playful back and forth between two great friends taking a carriage ride to a ball.

Jonathan's struggle to get into character, likely due to his blackening eye—a result of the best landed punch Brennon had ever thrown—was enough to keep Brennon buoyant throughout the duet.

As the set turned, the scene shifted to the ball, and Jonathan's song fell silent as Bingley laid eyes on Jane, played by Gabi.

Next to her stood Eden, beaming, brimming with her character's inflated expectations of the ball before her, and looking every bit the vivacious and exciting woman Brennon had fallen head over heels for in DC.

His concern about what had possibly happened to Kayla to cause this last-minute change vanished with the warm look Eden threw his way. Her small smile was unscripted and fucking radiant. She'd done this on purpose. Planned it. For him? God, could he dare hope? She was so beautiful. So perfectly cast, and so promising . . .

But Kayla never would have—Shayna couldn't have agreed—Peck would have lost his—

Yet there Eden stood, singing "First Impressions" with Gabi, and sounding like the rising star she was.

His heart nearly burst in his chest. Pride. Love. Need. *Everything.* She was everything.

"Looks like your girl found a way to make an impression in LA after all," Jonathan mumbled as they left the stage. "Gotta hand it to someone manipulative enough to snag the press performance."

Jonathan's words gave Brennon pause. He hovered in the wings for a moment, watching Eden perform. She *did* look like a star tonight. Perhaps for the benefit of the Hollywood press? It was not a small opportunity to get her face and name in front of these people. Show this coast all her talent.

And yet, every note she sang sounded specifically meant for him.

Perhaps because he was the exact kind of narcissist Jon had always accused him of being.

But that didn't seem right.

As he stepped back onstage to meet Eden for the ball at Netherfield, his heart was in his throat, and it was a miracle he managed to sing a single line. But when he asked her to dance, she took his hand—brushed her thumb across the back of it, gave it a long, tight squeeze—and he knew.

He knew she'd come to claim him.

His performance took flight from there.

At the end, at the kiss, she didn't cry.

He, however, could barely manage the final note through the choked-up feeling in his throat.

She didn't say a single word that wasn't on the page, and he didn't touch her in any way that hadn't been specifically choreographed, but in the flexion of her hand against his neck, in the parting of her lips when they met his, he felt something from her he'd never felt.

Home.

After they took their bow, with her hand still in his, they lingered at center stage. She turned to him once the curtain closed and the cast began their exodus. "We should talk."

Talking was the last thing Brennon wanted to do.

It had never gotten them anywhere he'd wanted to go with Eden. But neither had ravishing her in her dressing room, so he supposed he could do things her way tonight.

"Drinks?" he asked.

She glanced up at him with fever-bright eyes, and shook her head. "I think I'd like more privacy."

"Eden . . . I . . ." He had no idea what to say. His heart still felt trampled and used up. He was excited by this turn, of course, but terrified by what she'd been able to do to him in such a short time of knowing her.

"Or I could just find you in your dressing room after I get changed?"

He shook his head. "Come with me, now," he insisted.

She nodded, maybe a bit dazed by all the commotion—or his raging pheromones. Either way, he'd take it. "Okay," she said, and let him drag her offstage.

They passed relatively few of the cast members before arriving at his door.

She went in before him, and he shut it behind her.

"Were you surprised?" She turned to face him, still wearing Lizzie Bennet's white wedding dress. He'd never taken the time to consider how well it showcased all her . . . assets.

Brennon loosened Darcy's cravat. "Is Kayla all right?"

"If you want to ask her, she's probably still right next door." Eden gestured to the wall between the dressing rooms.

He shook his head. He didn't want to speak with Kayla. The question had come out wrong, as so many things did whenever he spoke with Eden. "I was very surprised."

"And how was I?" She preened a bit, fishing for his compliments.

"I have no notes," he said, closing in on her one step at a time. She obviously knew she'd stolen every scene with her brilliance.

She eyed him from head to toe and back. "Do you know why I did it?"

"I've heard several opinions on the subject." He took another step closer to her.

She touched the back of one of the armchairs, her fingers trailing along the edge of it as her gaze focused on the path they made. "Do you want to hear the real reason?"

"If you'll tell me."

"It was the quickest way I knew to kiss you."

No feeling in the world was as good as the knowledge that he'd been right. Right about her, right about them, right about tonight. And now he finally had a future to earn.

He laid a hand on her waist. Their eyes met. Profound desire nearly swept him off his feet. "Was that all you wanted?"

Brennon's dark gaze swallowed hers. Eden was drowning. "Pretty much," she said softly.

"And so . . .?" he prompted.

She rested her hand against his chest. "Maybe I . . ."

"Go on." He brushed his knuckles along her cheekbone, the motions of their stage kiss as second nature as breathing.

"Maybe I don't need to deserve you," she said. "Maybe it would be enough just to want you the way I do. The way I have. The way I can't stop wanting you."

"That is more than enough," he whispered, as his forehead came to rest against hers.

"Is it?" she asked, because no words felt adequate. "Or is it better to tell you I care about you? That I missed you so much I couldn't go another night without showing you that I'm not going anywhere, either?"

He blinked a few times, as though processing all of Eden's haphazard thoughts. She'd wanted to make sure she covered everything—to avoid any further misunderstandings.

"No one's ever done anything like this for me," he whispered.

She lifted her hand, placing it against his neck, her eyes never leaving his. "So, I'll ask you again. How was I?"

He touched his nose to hers, a smile curving his lips. "I'd have to say you were a triumph."

She nearly sank to the floor with relief, but a thin thread of anxiety held her upright. "Tell me I'm not too late. That you can forgive me for—"

He cut her off with a kiss that was pressing and deep, burning her lips, and threatening to melt her brain.

She responded with equal ardor, gripping the edges of his coat and shoving it off his chest.

With both hands on her waist, he backed her up, maneuvering her in the direction of the sofa, going after her neck with his mouth. "Move into my hotel with me."

There were so many things to admire about the legendary Brennon Thorne, but it was no secret anymore how he'd become the reigning king of Broadway. He aimed straight for the stars.

And there was no longer any question in Eden's mind that she loved every bit of him—the man, the myth, *and* the legend. "Try to keep me away."

"Really?" He pulled away to look at her. "You don't think it's too soon? Too much? You won't try to talk some sense into me?"

"If I only have two weeks to make myself impossible to forget for the next five months, I'll move in tonight if you'll have me."

"Oh, I'll have you." He unzipped her costume. "You have no idea how many ways I'll have you." His hand rubbed down the hooks at the back of her corset, slipped straight past the waistband of her undergarments, and palmed her behind.

She let out a satisfied sigh and her hips pressed toward him.

He liked that, by the feel of things.

She went for his breeches, not trusting him to get down to business fast enough. She was still afraid that if this took too long, one of them would open their mouths and flip everything sideways again.

As she quickly unlaced him, he shrugged out of his coat. In his undershirt alone, he looked the part of a rakish duke at a brothel, and she loved it. But—oh, shit—

"Condom?" she asked, terrified she knew what he was about to say. Surely he hadn't expected this tonight.

"My new policy is to never go anywhere without one." He gave a nod to a small leather bag next to the sofa.

"Then let me go ahead and grab one in case we wind up across the room." Turning, she bent to rifle through his luggage.

Once she found them, he lifted her off her feet, only to lay her down straightaway on the sofa. He crawled over her, bunching her skirts up with his hands as he went. She shoved his loosened pants down to find him gloriously hard and ready.

Ripping the condom packet with her teeth, she extracted the precious piece of latex and wasted no time getting it on him. "I can't believe we've never done this before," she whispered.

"It's been difficult for me to come to terms with, as well."

"We can take our time later."

"No promises," he said.

She laughed, but that quickly turned into a yelp as he moved one of her legs to make room for himself. With one foot now propped on the back of the couch, and her other foot barely touching the carpet, he positioned himself with a knee on the cushion and his leg alongside hers, to leverage himself from the floor. Her skirts were everywhere, a section of hem tickling her face. As he leaned forward to kiss her, he moved the fabric away.

His other hand worked below, yanking at her underwear, twisting until they pinched her hips and the cotton finally gave way. "I'll stop wearing panties, I swear."

"You should. At least for the next two weeks if you want the ones you have left to last the tour."

Unable to wait any longer, she took him by the shirt and pulled his body down to meet hers. They were barely touching with all the clothes between them, but the warm pressure of his mouth quickly made up for the lack of skin-on-skin intimacy.

Every slick lash of his tongue against her own quickened her desire to possess him completely. "I'm sorry I freaked out in New York," she blurted as her hand slid down to grip the back of his thigh and exert some force, a desperate attempt to get him inside her.

"You weren't ready."

"I wasn't."

"But you're here, now," he said, as if to confirm the blatantly obvious.

Oh, God, he'd stopped kissing her, and they were getting danger-ously close to having a *conversation*. Her need to get things back on track verged on extreme. "Am I forgiven?"

"Eden, you've felt like mine from the moment I first heard you sing," he whispered as he lowered his mouth to hers again.

"Your Eden," she murmured, grateful to have cleared the hurdle. He'd kept his promise. He hadn't gone anywhere.

His lips curved into a grin against hers, and with the kind of per-fect timing that had made him a star, he slowly entered her.

"Oh . . ." She exhaled. "My."

They kissed. Their mouths locked on each other as she felt herself pulse around him. No longer in a rush, they found a slow rhythm together, kissing until neither of them could breathe anymore. His lips wandered to her neck. Eden ran a hand beneath his shirt, over the steadily working muscles of his back. The thickness of him lit up every pleasure center inside her as it stroked them all. She would have writhed from the feel of it, but her position beneath him didn't allow for much movement. He had her pinned in place with the length of his body and his dream of a cock.

She wasn't mad about it.

Only about him. "I like this," she whispered, her breath coming in shorter bursts.

"Mm . . ." he hummed near her ear and moved into her more forcefully.

From there, she knew she wouldn't last long. Holding his shoul-ders, she moved with him, meeting him thrust for thrust as tension coiled between her legs. Taking her hip in his hand, he deepened his angle and found where she stopped. She moaned as he filled her, even as she longed for his hands on the rest of her.

But there was something about this, too. Making love in costume spoke to the theater lover in her and turned this, their first time, into the sexiest, most romantic encounter she'd ever had. A night she'd never forget.

He managed to locate her cleavage as it had spilled out with all the thrusting. He kissed the swells of her breasts, his hand having no success getting a better grip on either of them—her corset was no quitter—but he seemed to enjoy the struggle and the bounce they gave when he began to pound her in earnest.

The desire on his face was her undoing. "Brennon—God . . ." Her thighs trembled as she tried to get a grip on herself. He kissed her, surging deep inside on a long, solid stroke, and bending her back off the sofa. Something like a confetti cannon burst inside her—all the tiny particles tingling through her body, making everything come alive at once.

She shook with the sensation—there was nothing like it—and bit her lip to keep from crying out.

He cursed, long and low, as his thick cock jerked inside her, sending a tremor through both their bodies. "Jesus, Eden. Fuck . . ."

"You're perfect. So perfect."

"Beautiful." He stared into her eyes. "I love you."

Moments passed, where they lay, still locked together, staring at the other and catching their breath. An aftershock shook him, and he finally lost some composure, landing with a grunt on top of her.

She put her arms around him, holding him close and kissing his hair. The position they were in was no longer comfortable.

Like, at all.

They worked their way through it. She wrapped her leg around his back, and he found his way to the inside of the couch. She turned to face him, tucked snugly in his arms, her skirts still making a bungle of things.

"Notes?" she asked.

"You talk too much," he grumbled, nuzzling his face against hers. "How was I?"

"Like a machine. Coming in clutch."

He laughed softly and said the words again. "I love you."

She basked in the glow of him, in the way he looked at her, so filled with awe. "You do, don't you?"

"I do."

"I wish I'd heard you say it the first time," she said, regret making a curtain call.

"I wish you'd say it at all, but I'm a patient man."

"You've been patient long enough." She pressed her lips to his. She whispered it to him. "I love you." Three words against his cheek, and again upon his eye, and before her mouth met his once more. "Don't forget," she said. "Five months don't exactly go by in a blink."

With gentle strokes of his fingertips, he brushed the hairs that had come loose off her forehead. "I'll fly you home for every break. Even if it's only for a day."

"You won't be too busy?" Eden asked, Kayla's warnings resurfacing, about the reality of the two of them making an actual go of it.

"Never for you. I'm ready for this, Eden. For us. You will always come first."

There it was again. A promise.

So much of success on Broadway was luck and timing. Reputation, looks, connections, they all mattered, but once in a blue moon, the right role came along at the right time, and the future wrote itself. Eden could wait a little longer for her big break, but being the love of Brennon Thorne's life was a part only she could play.

She was ready to take the stage.

EPILOGUE

The local weather reports had been wrong. All the risks they'd taken to continue on with the wedding paid off—there may not ever have been a better, more beautiful evening to get married on a rooftop in New York City than this April 14th.

Her mother wiped her nose with a tissue and looked at Eden, all weepy. "It was just beautiful."

Justin Pope slung an indulgent arm around Terry Blake's shoulders and gazed down at her fondly. "Softie," he murmured.

It had only been a matter of time before her mom started emailing her new TV and film agent with ideas for Eden's career, and for reasons only the man himself could explain, Justin Pope had found Terry both "charming and refreshing." A transplant from the Midwest himself, the single, silver fox had snapped her mom right up. They'd been making it work online and long distance, but any day now, Eden was awaiting (dreading) the announcement that her mother would be moving to New York. There had already been too much talk about future grandbabies.

"May I have this dance?" Justin asked her mother.

"Why, of course." Terry gave Eden an exaggerated wink, before strolling away on Justin's arm to the makeshift dance floor at the center of the rooftop reception.

Maddox swooped in, dressed in a white suit and a smile that lit up the night.

Eden beamed up at him. "Hey, you! Congratulations! I was wondering if I'd ever get a chance to talk to you alone." She gave Mad a hug, inhaling the clean linen scent of his shirt and the cool spring fragrance of his neck. "You look so handsome."

The beautiful man glowed, in fact. The white lights strung all along the rooftop didn't hurt, either, but Maddox didn't need good lighting to intervene on his behalf. Happiness was as good as Photoshop. "It turned out perfect." He took another look around at the white lights, the sprays of pink orchids, and the candles in hurricane glass.

"Have you gotten a chance to eat anything?" she asked. "The food's not too bad either."

"I will, I will," he said. "And where did your husband get off to?"

"I think he had to go grab some more tissues for *your* husband."

Maddox laughed. "He's a hot mess today, isn't he?"

"I don't know," Eden said as she took another look around the dance floor for Brennon or Adam. "I kind of like when the groom cries the entire time. Reminds me of Vegas."

"Ha! I'd almost forgotten. I was a little drunk that night."

"A little?"

Two nights before Brennon left the tour in Los Angeles, Eden and Brennon had rented a car, rounded up Maddox, Adam, and Liliana, and driven to Vegas. Eden didn't think Maddox had had so much to drink on purpose, but the drive was long, and Maddox had been nervous about the extended opportunity to spend time with Adam, so the alcohol in the back two rows of the rented Tahoe had flowed.

Brennon and Eden remained sober to take their vows in the small chapel on the strip. Her sweet fiancé of about twenty-four hours had repeatedly choked up, wiped tears from his cheeks, and proclaimed it was the happiest day of his life about thirty times before everything was all said and done.

As a rule, and as an actress, Eden typically cried easily, but that night she'd had far too much adrenaline pumping for her body to bother with tear production. However, thirty-six hours later, when she'd dropped him off at the airport, she'd been a basket case. An absolute puddle of tears, while Brennon had held her and kissed her head and promised they'd see each other soon.

He kept his promise, too. She'd learned over the last nine months of their unconventional marriage that he always did. "Ah, here he is." Eden smiled at Brennon's approach. "The most talented best man in New York. Hard to pin down, but everyone says he's a dream to work with."

"All true, all true." Maddox put an arm around the taller man's shoulders, and Brennon returned the gesture, giving Mad a squeeze and congratulating him again.

"Is Adam all right?" Mad asked.

"He's touch and go," Brennon said. "I think a few more drinks, a dance or two—should shore him up pretty well for my toast."

Eden doubted that. She'd heard the toast, and the song Brennon planned to sing, and she teared up every time he rehearsed it. "I think I might need to go grab a box of my own tissues, just in case."

Brennon winked. "Suddenly, she's my biggest fan."

"You've never had a fan like me," Eden agreed. Maddox released her husband so she could do what she did best with Brennon: cling.

She latched on right away, hands under his jacket, encircling his torso with her arms, and resting her head near his heart. He held her close and surveyed the party he'd put together. Or at least, had instructed Edward to hire an excellent event planner to put together.

Another friend of Maddox's ushered him away, and soon enough, he and his new husband were reunited and dancing their first dance to

Taylor Swift's "Lover." Eden swayed to her favorite song in Brennon's arms as their two best friends stared adoringly into each other's eyes on their absolutely beautiful wedding night.

"We should reschedule tomorrow," Brennon said. "We'll be up late."

Eden murmured her disagreement. "No, sir. It's happening. All I have to do is put my toothbrush in a baggie, and we're out of here."

"You're not rethinking it? Look at this." He swept his arms out to remind her they were indeed on a rooftop.

"The new place has rooftop access too."

"But it's not as big," Brennon complained. "And the view has a slight obstruction."

"I wouldn't call a water tank an obstruction." She gave him a reassuring squeeze. "You'll be fine in the Village. I promise. People are very nice below Midtown. I know it's scary, but I think you'll find you pick up the language and culture in no time."

"I don't know where anything is. Who makes the good coffee? The best rye . . . do they even have sushi?"

Eden smiled up at him and gave his cheek a pinch. "We'll figure it out. What an adventure."

"The first of many, I hope," he said.

It had taken a while to convince Mr. Uptown he could live in a brownstone and not a classic six. It had taken longer to convince him he didn't need a doorman. Eden would have been fine if he'd insisted on staying on the Upper East Side, but she didn't want to walk on marble floors, and she hadn't wanted the ghost of Brennon's ex hovering above everything she touched in his apartment. It had been surprisingly inhibitive, and she'd realized quickly after they married, on one of her first longer visits to her new "home," that she'd never feel fully comfortable there.

Pre-Eden Brennon had been stiff, guarded, and lonely. His apartment screamed all those things and reminded her too harshly of how she'd once perceived him. Intimidating, elitist, and condescending.

It also never failed to make her remember how foolish she'd been to dismiss him, how close she'd come to breaking his heart. No, they had to go. They needed a place of their own, a fresh start, where they could learn who they were now, both for each other and for themselves. He acted all regretful, but deep down, Eden believed he was as excited for the change as she was.

They had a month to make the new place their own before Eden had to leave again to film her television series. It had been picked up for a second season, and she'd be gone nearly twelve weeks.

Brennon's new musical also opened in May, so he'd be stuck in New York for the foreseeable future, but they'd make it work. They had before, and the separation was only temporary. She had a feeling, now that they were finally moving out of Brennon's ice palace, her short visits home would be a lot more fun.

After the series wrapped, Eden planned to stay in New York. She'd already let both her agents know she had her sights set on Broadway again. Her theater agent was on the hunt for a perfect fit.

"How much longer until the toasts, you think?" Eden asked him. She hadn't been to many weddings.

"Probably another half hour."

"I need to run downstairs and pee and change shoes. Do you need anything?"

"Just my wife, but bring her back when she's more comfortable."

"Love you," she said.

"Mm . . ." He kissed her, and the warmth of him made her heart swell. "Love you."

She couldn't wait until tomorrow night—their first night in the Village. God, the things she was going to do to him . . .

She let herself into the apartment. The ice palace was all packed up, boxes stacked in the marble-walled hallway waiting to be removed and relocated. She walked past them, relieved to close this chapter of their marriage and turn the page on the next one.

"Oh! Eden, hey. I just snuck down here for a minute."

Veronica was on the living room sofa, stuffing her boob back into her dress while juggling three-month-old Bodhi on her lap. The baby was perfection, all chubby cheeks and blond curls, with his father's dimples and his mother's brown eyes.

"Did I miss the toasts?" she asked as Eden approached, reaching for the baby. Bodhi gave the best snuggles, especially when he was sleepy, which he clearly was. Veronica handed him over.

Bodhi snuggled hard, and Eden took a big whiff of his lavender-scented hair. "Just the first dances," Eden said.

"What's Brennon got planned?" Veronica asked.

"Bring your tissues."

Once Veronica had herself all readjusted, Eden handed back the baby. She waited for them to leave before heading to the master bathroom. Before she left, she made sure her birth control pills were easily accessible in her overnight bag, alongside her toothbrush. It was lovely to see Veronica handling single motherhood so well, and Eden loved Bodhi to pieces, but she wasn't ready for her own bundle of joy just yet. Reassured, she crossed the bedroom. The closet was mostly packed, but she'd foreseen the need to change shoes after all the pictures had been taken, so she'd left out a pair of flats for herself. Kicking off her heels, she slid her feet into the far more comfortable shoes.

"You were taking too long."

Eden startled at the sound of Brennon's voice. She turned to find him approaching with a determined, and hungry, look on his face. "What's happening?" she asked.

He took hold of her by the hips and pulled her roughly against him. "I was thinking about our wedding night."

The two weeks in LA had been such a blur of hookups and quickies and long all-nighters, Eden couldn't distinguish in her memory which day had brought which orgasm. But the wedding night inside their Bellagio honeymoon suite had been different. She had distinct memories of it, too.

"You have a toast to make," she whispered.

"And I have a wife in an empty apartment."

"And an erection," she noted.

"*And* an erection."

She rose up on tiptoes to meet his lowering mouth. "Tomorrow night's gonna be epic."

His hands slid over her behind and lower down her legs in an attempt to hike up her skirt. "Will you be wearing this dress tomorrow night?"

"No, but I think you'll like what I picked out."

He kissed her until they were both breathless, his hands managing to find her bare legs and stroke them in a way that made him very hard to refuse. Very hard in general.

But he did, in fact, have a toast to make, and even if they knew exactly how to tempt each other to within an inch of their lives, they'd gotten equally good at waiting for it.

The fire they'd started all those months ago in Greenville, South Carolina continued to burn—slow and hot. If they worked hard enough, they'd keep the flame alive forever.

She took his hands and removed them from her body. He gave her his signature scowl, which read, now that she knew him better, much more like a pout.

"Maybe you should lay off the Citaltfor," she said.

Brennon gave Eden half a grin and tugged her toward the door. "Noted."

ACKNOWLEDGMENTS

So here's where I take a bow and thank every single person who made this book of my heart come to life. I want to start with Eva Scalzo, my incredibly determined and encouraging agent who found the perfect home for Brennon and Eden at last. Eva, you've been with me since idea through publication on this one, and I could not ask for a more wonderful partner in this business than you.

Jess Verdi, my impossibly amazing editor who had the exact perfect skill set and passion for this book. You are a magical unicorn, and I cannot believe how privileged I've been to get to work with you on this of all books. Thanks also to Rebecca Nelson and the entire team at Alcove for your patience with me, and for everything you've done to put my book in the hands of readers. You've been so supportive and kind, and I've absolutely loved working with you all.

To Ana Hard who took all the notes and created a dream of a cover I don't think I'll ever be able to stop staring at. Thank you, thank you, thank you!

No acknowledgment on this novel would be complete without the biggest shoutout of all time to my writing group, Rompire. Our running Marco Polo conversations kept me sane during the pandemic, one of the hardest years of my life. Your unwavering friendship and support is more valuable to me than all the book deals in the world. Alexandria Bellefleur, Lee Blair, Anna E. Collins, Lana Hrabal, Megan McGee, Julia Miller, and Em Shotwell, thank you for not thinking I was bananas when I was proud of my first draft of this book and letting me send it out for you all to beta read. And thank you for gently putting me back in my place.

A very special thank you to Julia Miller who, when I said—"I need an actual musical!" came back the next day with an actual musical for me to work with. And another very special thank you to Anna E. Collins, who wrote a whole song for me when I was like "But now I need song lyrics!" Other song lyric credits go to Julia and Em Shotwell. Y'all are amazing. There is far too much talent in our little group of eight to wrap my head around sometimes.

Thank you Peyton Crim for letting me interview you during the peak of the pandemic to find out everything there was to know about starring in a touring Broadway production. And thank you to Kathy Crim for hosting the interview at your house. Peyton, you helped inform everything about this book, from the way I developed the conflict to the plot itself. I would not have even been able to start writing this without your generous time.

Thanks to my dad Larry Janousek for helping create the Playbill, and thanks to my mom Carla for letting me steal some of his time and cheering us on.

A final, special, heartfelt thanks to my family: Robert, Carly, and Chris, who watched the 1995 *Pride and Prejudice* movie with me. I know we felt the Darcy hand flex in the bottom of all our romantic souls together, and you understood what I was trying to do with this nutty, meta idea of mine. A novel is a group project as much as it is a labor of love, and I love and appreciate you all.

Social Media:
Twitter: @ameliajowrites
Instagram: @ameliajoneswrites
TikTok: @akjoneswrites